Pronouncing Enzo

Aimee Bealer

ISBN: 1519413033
ISBN 13: 9781519413031

For Jon, Emily & Jason

Chapter I

HESTER

Friday, March 14th

HE IS RICH, famous, wildly attractive, and shamelessly flirting with me. It would be more than easy to let him slide a strong hand up my thigh, allow him to draw me closer until our lips touch in a moment of sensual bliss. But if I did that with every handsome movie star who walked into my office, I'd go out of business.

I am a Dialect Coach. I get paid to teach Hollywood actors how to speak correctly. Need a German accent to play a Nazi? I'm your girl. Want to win a plummy role as a British aristocrat but can't nail the accent? Got it covered. Want a fling with a girl who can't keep business separate from pleasure? Not on your life.

I remove Brent Logan's hand from my knee. Again.

"This would be easier if you concentrate, Brent."

"But not nearly as fun…" His grin is designed to be infectious, but it's easy to resist smiling back. There's work to be done.

Inappropriate flirtation aside, as a client Brent falls into the 'moderately difficult' range. He may have a kissable mouth suitable for onscreen romance, but his attempts at the Irish brogue are cringe-worthy.

"Get into character and try again."

Brent gives me puppy-dog eyes, but returns to the script. I can see the muscles in his jaw tense as he prepares to tackle the Irish accent. "'And after the trouble you've given me, that's all the thanks I'll be gettin'?'"

I reach out and rap him on the shoulder with my finely tapered correction stick. "It's not 'thanks', it's 't'anks'. A hard 't', if you please. Relax your jaw and try again."

He nods. "'That's all the *t'anks* I'll be gettin'? I'm the one who'll be puttin' myself at risk, goin' over the ocean to make my fortune, and for what?'"

Another tap with the stick.

He growls. "Shit!"

I lean forward in my straight-backed chair. "'For' should sound more like 'fer'." I use my Irish lilt when I speak to him. I always speak exclusively in the accent I am trying to teach when I'm with a client. Most of the time my clients entirely forget I am English.

Brent resumes reading from the script. Two sentences later he slips again. Another tap with the stick.

"Jesus!" He raises a hand protectively to his face. "Do you have to target my shoulder? I always feel like you're gonna hit me on the chin. Why do you have to use that thing anyway?"

His preening makes me frown. "Don't break dialect. If you absolutely must veer from the script, maintain the shape and tonality of the accent. And my correction stick is to create a physical memory, to help your brain reprogram a mistake to remember the right pronunciation the next time. It's very effective."

"Yeah, but it sucks." My stern expression only garners a smirk from his gorgeous but untalented mouth. "And I think you'll be gettin' a wee bit sore from that pole you've got stuck up your arse, woman." He's put his Lucky Charms accent back on, a habit I've spent weeks breaking him of.

"It's 'I *t'ink* you'll be gettin'', and the next time I hear that Leprechaun accent, you might be surprised by where I put *this* stick." I point my stick and a look that means business at him and then consult my watch. "You may go."

Brent unfolds his six-foot-two, aggressively fit frame from his chair, which means he's practically standing on top of me. He looks down and lets his eyes rove freely over my cleavage. Then he tries the proper Irish accent again. "Ya know, Miss Hastings, one day I'd like the privilege of callin' ya by yer first name." He waggles his famously expressive eyebrows at me.

I stand also and put some distance between us. "As we have discussed, I never fraternize with clients. And that accent just now wasn't half bad. Make certain you practice your r's, l's, and speaking from the front of your mouth." I give my lips a tap with one fingertip.

Brent aims a mischievous grin at me. "I never knew frosty women could be so sexy till I met you, Hastings. Though between you and me, if you would take a chance and relax a little, life might be more fun." He steps closer and lowers his voice. "Like, take a chance, baby. Let down all that gorgeous auburn hair and let a guy run his fingers through it and maybe..."

I give him my 'I could kill you with one finger if I wanted to' look, and he backs away, literally holding his hands up in mock defense. His apologetic expression is so Labrador-puppy sincere it makes me smile. "Alright, Mr. Charming. I'll see you again on Monday, and remember to *practice*."

"Okay, I'm out." He makes a show of stretching, still eying my cleavage, then gives me a small bow which he probably fancies looks dashing. "See you Monday."

After he exits my office and I hear the front door click shut, I sink down into my chair and let out a weary sigh. Brent is exhausting, yet he's right about one thing: I don't have enough fun. I can't remember when I stopped taking chances, being open to possibility. The past year flickers through my memory like a to-do list of boring chores. Work, pay bills, exercise, eat healthy salads, go on the occasional obligatory but ultimately disappointing blind date set up by my Mum. My visits with little Jessica are the only events I really look forward to. What does it say about my life that the only enjoyable time I spend is with my ex-boyfriend's seven year old daughter?

On paper it looks like I'm doing everything right. Yet even my best friend has started hinting – or perhaps I should say insisting – that I need to break out of what seems to have become a rut. But where is my excitement? Where is my adventurous side? I used to have one, didn't I?

However, a fling with Brent Logan is definitely out of the question. Heavens, no. Brent is undeniably one of the most gorgeous actors I have ever met, and I've met quite a few. Some of them are so attractive I can't help fancying them, which makes maintaining professional distance a struggle. But while

I am certainly flattered by Brent's flirtation, I have no desire for *his* attentions. The tabloids and his behavior both report his skirt-chasing ways. Plus, he reminds me a bit of my last boyfriend, Philip Brewer, and that is enough to ruin any man for me forever.

--->=◉ ◎=<---

"Goldie...Over here! Goldie!" I lean across the passenger seat of my white BMW trying to get my best friend's attention. A professional Image Consultant, Goldie spends ninety-eight percent of her time shopping. She is so dedicated to making people look better that sometimes she buys accessories for homeless women who frequent the parking lot behind the church in her neighborhood. Right now she is interfacing too intimately with her cell phone to notice me parked across the street. I wave and add some volume to my voice. "Yoo-hoo...Goldie!"

She pulls her long black hair away from her face and finally looks up from the cell phone she's been madly tapping. Goldie narrows her eyes at me and slips her phone into her leather Gucci bag. In stilettos, lacy camisole and silver leggings she's as lean and poised as a greyhound. Goldie saunters across Beverly Boulevard as though she owns it. She leans inside the passenger window and looks at me over the rims of her sunglasses.

"This is getting old, Hester." She opens the door enough to slide her slim frame into the seat. "I mean, you know I'm here for you no matter what. But it's been eighteen months since you broke up with him. If you're going to maintain a relationship with his daughter, you need to figure out how to see him without needing back-up."

I pull away from the curb to join the traffic on the road. "I know, I know. If I could just pick Jessica up straight from school or the nanny it would be so much easier. But Philip always manages to be there when I come to get her, and..."

"And he hits on you and tries to make you feel guilty that you left him even though he's a son-of-a-bitch, cheating, lying bastard and you're too nice to rip out his jugular in front of his kid."

"Exactly! So that's why I'm so, so, so, so grateful to you for coming with me. And I promise absolutely to find another solution to this, but he won't let me come get Jessica just any old time. He *orchestrates* it, I swear. He's always playing dolls with her or being 'best Dad ever' when I arrive, and I know he does it so I'll think 'Aw, look at that, he's such a sweetie.' But that's not what I'm thinking. I'm thinking, 'What an ass!' He's using Jessica to try and win me back."

"Which is exactly what you should tell him, Hester!"

"Well, I will."

"When?"

I can feel her stern look boring into the side of my head. "Soon."

Goldie lets out a sigh and removes her sunglasses. "Seriously, Hester. You're a hard-nosed dialect coach and enormously successful – the best of the best – and you can't shut down Philip Brewer? Honestly. I've seen you do your frosty British bitch thing, and you need to unleash that babe on Philip. Today, if possible."

I maneuver around a slow produce truck and merge onto the ramp for the Hollywood Freeway. "If it weren't for Jessica…but if I upset Philip too badly he might decide not to let me see her anymore."

I can feel her looking at me. "And would that really be such a bad thing?"

My heart instantly feels torn at the thought of never seeing Jessica again. "Her Mum *died*, Goldie. When she was really little. I was with Philip for three years. I know I'm not her step-mother, but the only Mummy she knows is me. I can't just drop out of her life, it would be too cruel. Plus, I love the little thing. She's sweet and loves me so completely. I don't think it's a relationship I can ever sever."

"Then you, my dear, are stuck with Philip Brewer no matter what a weaselly, cheating, lying, scum-bucket, selfish…"

"That will do, Goldie. I know exactly who Philip is, and that is why I am no longer with him."

Goldie looks out the window. "Are we picking Jessica up from the court-house again?"

"Yes. Philip's visiting clients in the jail today."

She huffs indignantly. "It is so selfish that he makes his little girl go there just so he can be with her when you pick her up. Which brings me back to my point. You need to put your foot down with him hard enough that it hurts, but not so hard that you lose visiting rights with Jessica." Goldie flicks a piece of lint from her thigh with one long silver nail. "It's sort of a shame you never married the guy, 'cause at least then you could sue for partial custody..."

"Bite your tongue, Goldie! I'm eternally grateful I didn't marry him."

"Well, then man-up and lay down the law – no more using Jessica to have contact with you. As long as he thinks he's got a shot at getting you back he'll keep trying. Men are like that. I know you're upper-crust British and therefore terminally 'proper,' but you can't be nice or even polite to him."

A sigh escapes my lips. "Men like Philip are so maddening because on the surface they seem devastatingly polite and well-bred. They come across like perfect gentlemen, and then stab you in the back. I'd rather have a man who's rough around the edges with a heart of gold, you know?"

"Yeah, that heart of gold thing?" She shakes her head. "Nearly impossible to come by. But rough around the edges you can get anywhere."

I contemplate this. It is undeniably true. "Like ninety percent of the poor sods stuck in there," I nod toward the Los Angeles Men's Jail just ahead of us. "Men who were raised rough. I'll bet if you took one of them – not a murderer or anything, one of the nicer ones who's perhaps just uneducated – and polished him up a bit, his entire life would change. Teach him a little culture, how to converse, some manners. Voila! You might have a diamond."

Goldie casts me a dubious look. "Well, if anybody could do it, it would be you."

The thought makes me sit a little taller in my seat. "I should think so. I could take a willing subject who's uneducated but reasonably intelligent, and in three months pass him off as a prince."

Goldie wrinkles her nose. "Not a prince. Too cliché. Maybe a movie star..."

"Easy-peasy!"

I can feel her looking at me sideways again. "Too easy. To be a challenge you'd have to pass him off as the latest English import...an up-and-coming Brit who'll be the next Ewan McGregor or Jude Law."

I slow to a stop at a red light in front of the jail. "He'd have to learn the accent, but also the culture, some history. Hmmm. That *would* be a challenge."

Goldie sits forward and slaps the dash. "Then let's do it!"

I laugh because I know she must be joking. But her silence makes me glance uneasily in her direction. Her face says, 'I'm serious as a heart attack.' No. She's not that crazy, is she?

"You know that's a preposterous suggestion, right? I mean completely ridiculous. It was just conjecture, harmless fantasy…"

"I'm talking about a wager, between you and me. I bet even you can't do it in three months. That's only twelve weeks!"

Alarm bells start ringing in my brain. "Hold on, we were only talking hypothetically…"

"But this is too delicious *not* to do, Hester. Plus, it's exactly what you need; a nice, juicy project that will inflame your intellectual passions and throw you out of your boring, self-centered routine."

I blanch at her frankness, blinking rapidly. "But it normally takes me three months just to teach an accent to a poor learner."

"Exactly. You will be consumed by something larger than your everyday routines. The distraction and satisfaction of changing someone's life for the better, you know?"

I am halfway between thinking she's completely mad and feeling strangely compelled by the idea of doing something so beyond my comfort zone. "Hypothetically, what would I win if I pulled it off?"

Goldie purses her lips, then shrugs. "Breaking out of your rut—which would be huge—and the satisfaction of knowing you're the best. And I'll even help you. I can be in charge of re-branding…Ooh! It could also be a publicity stunt. Like when it's done, and everyone believes he's the real deal…you could unmask him! It would be great for business."

Brent Logan's face springs unbidden into my mind. "Business is already great, Goldie. I'm coaching *People* magazine's 'Sexiest Man of the Year'. I have a waiting list."

"Well, you wouldn't have to do the publicity thing unless you wanted to. But just think what an accomplishment it would be. And you would totally change that guy forever. It would be, like, *charitable*. And if I win, you've got to deal with Philip."

"I don't know, Goldie. I couldn't fit it in with my schedule of current clients."

Goldie lifts her eyebrows, a thought bouncing into her head. "I know! He could live at your place so you can do it in your spare time…"

Now she's really lost it. "What? Let some stranger – who's just gotten out of jail – live in my house?"

"Not in the *house*, but what about the pool cabana? There's that chaise in the changing room to sleep on, a bathroom with shower, it's perfect!"

"It is not 'perfect,' Goldie. It's completely insane!"

Goldie pokes me on the shoulder, firmly. "Which is totally why it would be great for you! Think of it as a *project*. You know, like what those fix-it people do with old houses on T.V.? _Renovation..." She's staring out the window in an alarmingly determined way.

My eyes follow her gaze. As we idle at the red light the door of the jail opens, and we watch a newly released inmate share a high five with a guard before walking out. He's holding a Ziploc baggie that looks like it contains his recently returned personal effects.

Goldie claps her hands like a five-year-old. "There goes one now! I can't believe it...he's even kinda sexy. You know, in that ex-con, grungy sort of way." She eyes him up and down appraisingly. "Check out that rockin' bod...oh yes, he could work." She grabs my arm. "Hester, you could totally change his life."

I watch the man pause by a bank of payphones planted in concrete outside the jail's exit. Him? This random...convict? At the same time my logical mind is recoiling in horror, I feel a twinge of morbid curiosity. Could I do it?

My professional pride kicks in. "Well, yes I could, but..."

"Pull over! Pull over!" She's taking off her seatbelt.

Flustered, I pull into an empty handicapped spot in front of a parked police car. "Calm down, Goldie. This is a little too impulsive..."

Goldie is already out of the car.

I'm left sitting paralyzed in the driver's seat, my hands gripping the steering wheel so tightly my French manicured fingers turn entirely white.

ENZO

'Cause my last name be Diaz, people always axing me where I from. Like, 'you from Mexico?' or 'You speak Spanish?' Nah, man, I don't speak no Spanish. My Abuelo did, and my old man, he know a bit. But not me. It ain't trickled down this far. All I got from my Mexican side is lovin' Latin music and the food, man. An' I gotta let go a' my roots anyway if I'ma move forward an' all. So where am

I from? I jus' from whereva I been last. Like today, I'm from the L. A. Men's Jail. I ain't proud of it, but that's what it is. And tomorrow? Axe me again then, 'cause I got no idea where I'ma be tomorrow. Tomorrow you gonna get a whole notha answer.

Bein' let outta jail's a whole lot diff'rent from bein' put in. A few days before, you thinkin', 'Man, it's gonna be, like, a zillion times better once I'm out.' Then, you standin' there in you own threads gettin' handed the stuff they took when they put you in, an' it ain't much. An' if you's me, you thinkin' *what the hell I do now?* I got no place to go that I wanna be. Only person I wanna see I can't go to until the court say so. My old man's up in state prison, Ma's dead, my brotha Ricky be jus' 'bout brain-dead. And then I got to worry 'bout Antwon. His homies on the inside say he out to get me, but I don't know why 'cause he the one got me put away. I ain't got no money. I ain't goin' back to the 'hood, 'cause ain't nothin' there for me an' also 'cause I don't wanna fight Antwon. I'm sick a' that shit.

When them guards release me I see my man Barnaby on duty at the gate. Me and him went to school togetha before I dropt out. He musta finished, 'cause he on the right side of this establishment. Though it don't feel like a high-five moment, he give me one when I come out still holdin' the bag containin' my wallet – empty, gold chain, and my good luck charm; the lil' jade tiger Topaz picked out for me that time in Chinatown. Sonofabitch I miss that girl! I got her address, wrote to her the whole time I was in. But I gotta wait. I gotta get a job and then I'll have somethin' to stand on. They can't keep her from me foreva.

I nod my farewell to Barnaby and walk on out. It's sunny. Damn, it's bright out here. Springtime; best season in L.A. if you axe me. Then I see the line of payphones starin' at me like, do I wanna make a call? They been specific'ly put there so we can call somebody when we get out. My own phone's long gone. I look at them payphones and think about all them guys still inside who'd be jumpin' on the dial. Me, I got nobody to call.

Lookin' around I see a white BMW wit' the richest-lookin chica inside parked right up at the curb in front of a row of black and whites. She look kinda foreign, pale with reddish hair floatin' around her face all wavy. Chiquita is smokin' hot, but too classy to flaunt it. Then she turn her head. She lookin' at me kinda scared. Right at me. Then I see this otha chick clickin' down the sidewalk in my direction. She all Japanese an' rich lookin' wit long legs and – shit, yo. She comin' right at me. In 'bout five seconds she gonna be all up in my face.

Why the hell do this bitch wanna find me the minute I get out? She don't look like nobody I seen before, but that don't mean she ain't got my details from somewhere. I may've been a top seller, but I ain't signin' on for more of what got me put away. Girlfriend's smilin' at me like she want somethin'. Well, no chance baby. I ain't doin' that shit no more.

HESTER

Goldie's window is open, so of course I can hear everything she says to the fellow.

"Hi there! My name is Goldie Perkins, and it is so totally your lucky day. I've got a proposition for you..." She sticks out her hand for him to shake, but the ex-con just gives her a fierce, suspicious look.

I'm trying not to stare, but I see him glance back at the jail nervously. "Lady, I don't know who you is, but I don't do that no more."

Goldie's eyebrows furrow. "What? No...I want to offer you, well, it's kind of like a job. Or an internship. Yes, that's the right word. An internship with my associate over there." Goldie points back at me and smiles. Gives a little wave.

The ex-convict now looks me over suspiciously. Then he turns back to Goldie. "No way, baby. I told you I ain't doin' that shit no more. I jus' got out. I'ma stay clean."

Goldie grins. "Okaaay...you are *so* just the right guy."

Clearly, the man has decided she's crazy because he backs away and starts to swagger off down the street. Oh, thank heaven. Now we can just go collect Jessica.

But Goldie is undeterred. She trots after the man. Why doesn't she just get back in the car? I wave to try and get her attention, but she's facing the other way.

She's talking to him again. "Wait a minute, sir! I don't think you want to pass this up...whatever you're thinking I want from you, it couldn't be further from what I have in mind. This is legal and legitimate and can give you a real opportunity to better your life!"

The former inmate stops and looks at his wrist, which is bare. Then he sighs and looks back at Goldie. "Girl, you got two minutes."

I can see that Goldie already smells victory. Despite myself I am fascinated to know how she'll sell this scenario.

First she brushes a speck of lint off his tee shirt like they're old friends. "Okay. May I ask what you were in for?"

The man's eyes flick to the side for an instant before returning to Goldie's face. "Drug possession."

"I don't mean to pry, but did you finish high school?"

The man looks down at his scruffy sneakers. "Nah. I had otha shit to do."

Goldie practically levitates with happiness. "Perfect. So, what I'm offering you is the chance to get intensive training from a top-notch Dialect Coach who teaches movie stars how to speak well. Foreign accents, sounding more educated, the whole nine yards. Anyway, she is interested in…research, she's doing research about rehabilitating ex-convicts. She's doing a study to see if teaching previously incarcerated men how to speak more, uh, more…professionally helps them integrate back into society more successfully."

The ex-con raises his eyebrows. "So you all are doin' a study, huh? 'Bout how a poor, uneducated ex-convict like myself can get improved to, like, do better in 'society' and all?"

Goldie's eyes light up, the man's sarcasm lost on her. "Yes! And the skills you learn might help you get a really good job when you're done. What do you think?"

He looks at her warily, like she's trying to trick him. "What am I gonna have to do exacly?"

"Live in a nice neighborhood, take lessons in speaking well, learn about art, culture, history, etiquette…"

The man grunts impatiently. "Etti-who?"

"Etiquette…like putting your napkin in your lap when you go to a dinner party, or waiting until your hostess takes a bite before starting to eat. Things you do when you socialize."

The man folds his arms across his chest and just looks at Goldie. "Girl, I ain't never been to no 'dinner party.'"

"Precisely! You would learn how. Which would mean going to parties and eating good food and drinking nice wine. Learning how to walk with confidence and style. And language. How to speak like actors do."

The man's eyes narrow. "This some kinda outreach program?"

Goldie laughs. "No, just something my friend Hester and I want to do. For research, and to help you."

He cocks his head like he's considering her offer. "I got stuff to do. How much time I gotta spend on this?"

"Full time for about three months. We wouldn't be paying you a wage, but we'd provide you with nice clothes, food, training, everything you need to be comfortable. You'd be living at Hester's place. That's Hester in the car. Hester Hastings."

"What kinda name is that? Hester? Sounds like 'pester'."

"Well, she's English. It's an English name. What's your name?"

The man stands taller. "Enzo. Enzo Diaz."

"Alright, Enzo." Goldie takes a step toward the car. "Why don't you come over and meet Hester. You can ask questions, and we'll see if the arrangement sounds like it will work for you."

The man looks Goldie up and down one more time. When he chooses to allow her to lead him toward my car, he puts an extra swagger into his step. He's looking around like he's got better things to do but he's decided to go ahead and do her this one favor. "Okay, sweet thing. I'll meet your friend 'cause you hot. But you ain't takin' me no place. Got it?"

Goldie flaps a 'don't be silly!' hand at him and laughs. "Of course not, Enzo. We're just offering you an opportunity. There's no obligation on your part."

"So far it kinda sounds, like, too good to be true, ya' know? Like you got somethin' up your sleeve an' you gonna pull it out and pop me one."

Goldie unleashes her most earnest look on him. "Enzo, I promise we don't mean you any harm. This internship, which is like a job where you learn as you go, it could really change things for you. And you get a *free* place to stay and *free* food. That might be helpful until you get back on your feet, right?"

Good Lord. Trust Goldie to reel him in. They're at the car before I can move, and Goldie kind of leans into the passenger window. She gestures at me to 'come on already,' so I get out of the car and walk around to meet the convicted criminal whom I really should not invite to my home.

But I have to admit, if I was going to do pro-bono work to help someone less fortunate, he wouldn't be a bad choice. Visually he has potential. Straight black hair, caramel-colored skin that could be from Hispanic or multi-racial descent. He is unshaven, but I can see a strong jaw line under all the black stubble, and because he's wearing a fitted yellow tee-shirt it's not hard to observe that he's certainly physically fit. He must have done nothing in jail but work out. I picture him in a casually cut Armani suit with a killer haircut. As I reach out to shake his hand I am already mentally planning a regime of lessons for him that I could fit in around my paying clients. Oh my God, I can't believe Goldie nearly has *me* sold as well!

The man hesitates before shaking my hand. When he does, his grip is strong. He's tall, so I have to tilt my head up to check out his face. I need to look him directly in the eyes. He's surprised by my blatant eye contact, yet he doesn't flinch from it. There's no squirrely fidgeting in his gaze. I sigh as he lets my hand go. I can tell that he's at least moderately honest. His eyes are an unusual shade of golden hazel with flecks of green mixed in. Thick, inky black eyelashes frame them, allowing me to place them squarely in the 'dreamy' category. Physically, he is loaded with potential.

Goldie shoots me a 'come on, it'll be fun' look. "Hester, this is Enzo. Enzo, this is my friend Hester Hastings. The best dialect coach in Hollywood."

To my surprise I blush at the compliment. "Well, that's what some people say…"

Goldie nods. "It's the truth. And Hester, I think Enzo is an honest guy who's been played by circumstance. Drug possession. Guilty? Maybe, but it's obvious he's determined never to do it again. I can tell he's a hard-working guy who wants better. Let's take him on, Hester. Let's help Enzo remake his life."

Goldie's eyes are full of hope, pleading with me, like 'can we bring the puppy home? Pleeeaaase?' Clearly she's been watching too many reality-TV shows.

I think about risk versus reward. Risk: he's an ex-con and we don't know his history. Reward: the satisfaction of transforming him, making Goldie happy, helping someone in need. Plus, it is true that there's nothing short of donning a flying suit and jumping off a cliff that would be more adventurous. Could it be that Goldie is right? Could taking on this project break me out of the rut I seem to be stuck in?

Perhaps Goldie is telepathically infiltrating my brain, because a moment of madness hits me. "Well, I suppose he does seem like a good candidate." What the devil is wrong with me? Why didn't I just say, 'No, this is not a good idea'? I want to stall for time but no ideas come. "Why don't we...let's give him my details and let him think about it, shall we?" I pull one of my cards from my Kate Spade clutch and hold it out for him. "This has all my numbers and my office address. I work from my home, so it's really my only address," I laugh nervously, feeling a bit like I'm brokering an illegal deal. "So think it over, alright?"

Enzo reaches for the linen-beige card. I notice that his hands are scarred and calloused. Tough hands. He turns the card and squints at it. Oh my God, I've just given my address to a man fresh out of jail!

Goldie rubs her hands together like it's a done deal. "So...Enzo? Call Hester when you decide, okay?"

Before she can say anything else I give her a 'let's get in the car now' look and hurry back around to the driver's side of my BMW. "Bye now!" I wave at Enzo in a friendly-yet-detached way and slide behind the wheel.

Before he can walk away, Goldie taps the card in his hand. "You should totally do this. Call Hester!" She folds her long legs into the car and waves out the window as we drive off.

I can tell from her focused expression that she's not going to give up on this idea easily. She points to the road as though she can steer the car with her finger. "Now drive around the block a few times and then let me out in front of the gate. I want to check with that guard who high-fived him and make sure Enzo's clean."

"Goldie! Obviously he's not clean...the man just got out of jail!"

She makes a 'tsk' sound. "Don't be so judgmental...but all the same I don't want to shack him up with you if he's a rapist or something." She pokes me in the shoulder. "Just do it."

"This is insane, Goldie! I can't believe we're even thinking about rehabilitating that man. And he's right by the way, there are *real* outreach programs that are set up for people like him."

"You think you can't do it?" She glares at me, a challenge in her eyes.

"Of course I can do it. I told you I can. My point is…"

"Oh, then you don't want to help someone out? Give him a fresh start?" She folds her arms across her chest.

"Don't be ridiculous, Goldie, of course I like to help people. I've done pro-bono work before…"

"Yeah, for ritzy friends or those English ex-pats your mom rubs shoulders with. Never for someone who truly needs a helping hand to *totally change his life*."

I sigh, exasperated by her persistence. "Goldie…"

Her look of reproach registers on me even though I'm watching the road. "If you're sure you can do it, what's the problem? Look, you get paid by wealthy people to teach them accents. There's nothing on the line there. It's safe. This guy, Enzo Diaz, he is *real*. Teaching somebody who never finished high school and comes from the roughest background imaginable; *that* is an achievement. Changing his life is something you can really be proud of. It's something that makes a real-life difference…but then maybe you're afraid you can't pull off all your dialect tricks unless you're working with Hollywood royalty."

While it's probably ninety-five percent true that teaching an actor who is talented at transforming himself is easier than coaching an average person off the street, my hackles rise. "Goldie, there is no difference between that man and Brad Pitt except circumstance of birth and opportunity. He may not have the same talent as an actor, but he can be taught dialects."

"Then drive around the block, and I'll go check with the guard."

I roll my eyes. She's not going to give up until I do it. I check the rear-view mirror and change lanes to execute a right turn. "I can't believe I gave him my card! You had better do more than check with the guard. This was your idea… you need to get *all* the details about, what's his name again?"

"Enzo Diaz."

"Yes. Get his entire background…arrest records or whatever."

"I will, but let's start with the guard. He clearly knows our boy."

Our boy? If he was under eighteen she'd be trying to adopt him. I hesitate, thinking about how she's been racking up so many favor points by accompanying me when I have to see Philip. And I know this is her attempt at helping me reboot my life. I take a deep breath and reassure myself with the knowledge that this ex-con person will probably never call me. It is likely I will never see him again in my entire life.

I turn the car at the corner to circle the block. "Alright, but you'll have to be quick. I don't want to keep Jessica waiting."

ENZO

I stuff that English lady's card in my back pocket and get the hell outta there. Growin' up in Watts, I done met Koreans, Iranians, Pakistanis, Filipinos, Chinese, Japanese, Mexicans, and all kinds. But she the first English person I eva met. Her face put me in mind of that chica from my Mama's all-time favorite movie, *Titanic*. The girl standin' all up in the front of the boat with my man Leonardo. Her big eyes kinda blue an all. Girlfriend be pale like death, but she rockin' that corpse look like the white girl from *Twilight*. She got a bitchy vibe, though. Like she so much betta than everyone else. But she got a body. Got curves, but she also fit, like she take care a' herself. I respect that, 'cause I been liftin' since I was thirteen, man. Kept me outta some trouble when I was younger, then got me into some when I got older. Only job I eva wanted was to run my own gym. Was on track to do it for a few years, too. But then there was Topaz and all that came wit' her. Maybe I'll get back on track one day.

Right now I gotta find me a job and a place to crash tonight. Ain't no way I'm goin' back to my old 'hood. There ain't nobody I wanna run into down there. I heard 'bout a shelter ova on 5th Street. Nobody I know live out that way, so could be a okay place to start wipin' my slate clean an all.

I walk on by that courthouse where they took me to find out was I gonna get put away. I'm a hundred percent sure I ain't eva gonna be back there hearin' them words about servin' time. Thinking 'bout my choices I made an' all for a whole year done made me feel like it ain't gonna be hard to keep outta trouble if I try.

A man wearin' a suit passes me and don't even look at me. Nobody seein' me knows I been in jail. Even if they don't like the look a' me, and be scared of what I am, they can't see where I been. But them people I'm gonna have to axe for some kind of a job, they gonna wanna know. Might even run my ass through a background check. So I gotta be up front and just say so from the start. Like, 'I been in jail, but I'ma be a good employee. Show up on time, do my best an' all'. Just need somebody to give me a break.

When I think 'bout that shelter it make me feel that lady's card burnin' in my back pocket. I done slept in shelters before. They give you food an' all, but you gotta watch yo'self and yo' stuff. That make me laugh. I ain't got no stuff. I am hungry like a bitch, though.

I bet they got shitty food at the shelter, man. That Japanese girl made me hungry when she was talkin' 'bout free good food an' all. What if them rich girls wasn't foolin'? Maybe what they said was for real, ya know?

Here I am, walkin' like I know where I'm headed in life. But the sun on my skin feel good. It's true I got kinda like a plan in my head that I made before I got out. But I wasn't countin' on opportunity droppin' from the sky like that. Why do this Hester Hastings chick wanna coach me on my voice an' all? Why she wanna make me talk like them actors? I can talk pretty good when I wanna talk good. I can be all presentable an' shit.

But she do *sound* good. Her voice be like, drippin' with money. That hot girl, Goldie – what the hell kinda name is that for a Japanese chick? She said I'd get a place to stay. Hester gonna teach me better language. Would I still be Enzo Diaz if I talked diff'rent? Would I have to change myself all inside-out to be fakin' like I'm all rich? If them actors learn accents to be in movies, and then I learn to fake 'em too, is my life gonna feel like I'm actin' in some big phony movie?

Damn, yo. My life already be like some big phony movie. Only it was for real, ya know? All the shit that went down. Antwon the one turned me in. I know that. An' that's afta he fronted me bills to get threads to look the part, man. He snatched all the cash I made, too. All of it. So what if I took his lil' brotha down wit' me? Antwon got all the money. His brotha gonna be let out soon, too. Shit. Why he still afta me? I gotta watch my back.

I wish I knew what them crazy rich bitches want wit me. Wish I could trust they was for real, ya know? The only time I been around rich women was before Antwon turned my ass in. An' that was like some kinda movie too; me actin' like somethin' I'm not. I don't trust 'em. The shelter be skanky and feel like some kind of charity bullshit, but no one want nothin' from me there. 'Cept maybe my gold chain.

HESTER

By the time I find a parking place at the courthouse and drag Goldie to the lobby, it is almost lunchtime.

In her ridiculous heels, Goldie has to trot to keep up with me. I am charging ahead, scanning the crowded lobby for Philip and Jessica.

"Hester, slow down! I'm starving and you're making me burn my few remaining calories. You're getting me lunch after this, right?"

"Yes, of course. Jessica wants to go to the PBJ place, you know, the one where everything on the menu has peanut butter?"

Goldie wrinkles her cute nose. "Fab. Do they have peanut butter salads?"

Before I have a chance to answer, a small missile with long blonde hair dives past three surprised people to attach itself to my waist. "Jessica!" I bend down to hug her. "I can't believe it's been a whole week since I've seen you! Stand up straight and let me see if you've grown." I align her in front of me and make a show of measuring where the top of her head comes to. "You have! You are definitely at least a millimeter taller than last week."

Jessica's earnest face tips up toward me, a huge grin revealing the gap where her two front teeth used to be. "I've been eating lots of healthy food, so that's why I'm bigger!" Her big brown eyes gaze up at me in adoration. Honestly, how could anyone ever let a seven-year-old down?

Goldie distracts Jessica with a double high-five greeting and then leans down to whisper something in the child's ear that elicits giggles. My smile dies when I hear the voice of my ex.

"Hester! So good to see you." Philip the cad appears out of nowhere and reaches out to take my hand, holding it between his own. "Jessica and I have been looking forward to seeing you again." He smiles warmly at me, as though he never lied and cheated on me. I gently extract my hand from his grip.

From behind him Goldie rolls her eyes at me and then makes a funny face when she notices Jessica is looking also.

"Hello, Philip." I half-smile and reach for the pink, fluffy overnight bag he's holding. "I guess we'll see you on Sunday. I'll drop her off at your place on my way to see Mother."

"Sounds perfect." Philip leans in close to my ear. It's all I can do not to pull away. "Though I was thinking that when you drop her off I might have a word with you in private. She's been kind of down lately, and I'm wondering if it might have something to do with our break-up. I mean, one minute you were there all the time, and then the next you were gone and she only sees you every other weekend."

I put on my sternest expression, imagining lasers of liquid ice blasting him. "Philip, she's had nearly a year and a half to adjust, and young children are resilient. I've promised Mother I'll be on time, so I won't be able to stop in. I'm sorry…"

"Maybe you could come by a little earlier…" He draws even closer to my ear.

Goldie's silver bag whacks Philip in the shoulder so suddenly it throws him off balance. "Oh my God! I'm so sorry, Philip." Goldie's eyes are filled with contrition when he rounds on her. "I was just trying to hit a nasty fly and…" she shrugs.

Philip eyes her with suspicion as he brushes the sleeve of his well-tailored suit.

I jump at the opportunity for escape. "Alright Jessica, come along. Let's go get you some lunch, yes? Bye, Philip!" I wave over my shoulder as I lead a happy Jessica away by the hand. Goldie trails behind me, a satisfied smirk on her face.

Chapter 2

ENZO

AFTER EATIN' THE mushy scrambled eggs they give us at the shelter for breakfast I get the hell outta there. Three nights is already too much. I been around to all the places that look like I could do some kinda work there and ain't nobody hirin' within five miles a' this shelter. Not hirin' an ex-con anyway.

Shitty food and roommates that stink make me start on Plan B. I done took a shower last night and washed my shirt in the sink. Put it on wet and slept in it so nobody can take it from me. It's dry, but look like it got put through a wrinklin' machine. They got maps at the shelter and I looked at 'em to see how to get over to north Los Feliz where that English lady's card say her studio at. I ain't gonna call like she said. She mighta changed her mind 'bout lettin' me stay there. Showin' up right in her face gonna make it hard for her to turn me away. I thought about what she said an' if she for real I can do that shit. Learn a new way a' sayin' shit. Accents an' all. Ain't never learnt no foreign language, 'cept my Abuelo speakin' in Spanglish to me when I was a kid. But how hard can it be?

Ain't no chance Antwon gonna find me over there. That Japanese chica said I'd get food and a free bed. I ain't sure they don't want somethin' else from me that they ain't sayin', but I got legs and can walk away if they want somethin' I ain't gonna give. They don't seem nothin' like the rich women I seen before. But all rich women

20

who be in'trested in somebody like me got something specific on they minds. I don't know what these two chicas have on they minds, but I might as well find out.

An' the main thing on *my* mind is Topaz. Sooner I get a job and a place to sleep, sooner I'ma get to see Topaz. I got to get my girl back. If them ladies can help me get a betta job by teachin' me stuff, I gonna be all ova that. I jus' hope they for real, man.

I know how to study and learn. People first meet me, they think I ain't smart. But I just quiet. I did good in school. Coulda made it through high school if things had been diff'rent wit Mama. But like the chaplain said to me when I was in; it ain't eva too late to learn somethin' new.

HESTER

I'm on my way to the kitchen to make lunch when the doorbell rings. My ten o-clock just left, for God's sake. And it was a bear of a session. Brent Logan at his worst, managing to sound more Scottish than Irish. I had to abandon the correction stick technique for a more intensive approach; holding his jaw in my hands as he spoke and making manual adjustments as he attempted to read from his script. Unfortunately, Brent seemed to enjoy having my hands on him more than he should have. But all the same, he finished the session sounding almost properly Irish. I think he's ready to start working with the mirror.

Excellent; the doorbell has gone silent. If it doesn't ring again I'll assume it was UPS with a package. Have I ordered anything lately?

I'm almost through the yellow door when the bell chimes again. There's no help for it, I'll have to answer the door. No one but clients and UPS ring the doorbell. It must be some actor who's gotten their scheduled appointment time wrong. Well, they'll just have to come back at the slot scheduled on *my* calendar. I sigh, thinking hungrily of the Caesar salad I will make when I get rid of who-ever's at the door, and head back down the hallway past my office and studio. No matter how insistent they are that they've got the appointment time right, I'll set them straight and send them packing.

The front of the house is where I run my studio. The yellow door at the end of the hallway – which I was just about to open before the doorbell sounded – leads to my sanctuary. My living space is sacred. No client has ever been through the yellow door, even the most scrumptious actors for whom I was tempted to break my 'no fraternization' rule. It's a simple arrangement; front of the house, clients. The rest belongs to me.

I catch a glimpse of my visitor through the small stained-glass window in the front door before he sees me coming. Bloody hell! Definitely NOT a client. I duck back into the hallway for cover, flattening against the wall like an intruder in my own home. My heart rate has just blasted off for outer space.

It's *him*. The ex-convict I'd more or less forgotten about since Friday when I handed him my card. Oh, Dear God! Why did I hand him my card?

Okay. Breathe deep. It's no big deal. It's just an ex-felon knocking at your door expecting you to take him in like a stray and let him live with you. Oh. My. God.

Goldie. This is all Goldie's fault! Silently, I pull my phone from my back pocket and bring it to my ear. "Goldie," I whisper the voice dial command. Please let her pick up…please…

Goldie answers on the second ring, "What's shakin' Hess?"

"He's here! He wasn't supposed to actually show up…and he's ringing the doorbell!"

"Philip?"

"No, not Philip. The *convict*! There's a convicted felon at my door…wait, is drug possession a felony? Oh God, he's knocking now. What do I do, Goldie?"

"Answer the door, you nutjob! He's our project. Mold him, shape him into a fabulous, sexy, British masterpiece."

I hesitate. "I could…I can. But Goldie, he's a man, a big one, and he's fresh out of jail. Isn't this a little too risky?" My memory of our exchange on Friday sharpens. "Wait, it was your job to find out all his details…what did you turn up?"

"Hester, not all guys who go to jail are really *bad* guys, okay? Welcome to the real world. I checked with that guard who knows him, remember? This guy is totally not going to rape you. Put on your big girl pants and let him in. Do an evaluation. Show him where he can hang his hat. This is just another client. A less fortunate client whose life you are going to completely change. Think of how much better off he'll be when he can go to a job interview and sound like someone who can do more than stock shelves. Man-up, Hester, and open the door! Oh, and definitely turn on your security alarm when he's not in the house…maybe hide your best jewelry, too. I'll drop by later with a few shirts, boxer briefs, swim suit, and some jeans to keep him dressed for now. Let's see, I think he probably wears a thirty by thirty-six…oh, and let me know when you're sure he's staying…I can hardly wait to take him shopping!"

I shake my head in annoyance and end the call. Of course Goldie would think this was all a good laugh. She isn't the one who has to live with him and 'shape him.' But back to the matter at hand. There's a convicted criminal knocking on my door!

Alright, Hester Regina Hastings, you can do this. He's totally safe, like a big puppy or a horse. Yes, think of him as an untrained horse who needs to learn manners and how to be ridden. Oh no, that's too sexual, isn't it? It's too…

He's knocking harder. I take a breath and compose myself, adjust my pearls and smooth back the few stray hairs that have come loose from my chignon.

"Just coming!" I trill as I creep toward the door. Putting on my most professional smile, I open the door to the convict.

My boarding school 'charming hostess' training wars with my instinct to hold the door between us like a shield. I wind up hanging onto the doorknob for dear life, leaning sideways like a soused Martha Stewart. "What a delightful surprise!" Oh, hell's bells, I've completely forgotten his name…What is it? My mind dives for Friday's memory of our introduction. Ah! "Enzo, is it? Won't you please come in…"

I back away from the door to make way for him to enter, one hand clutching my cell phone in case I need to dial 9-1-1 in a hurry. Too late I realize my feet are still bare. I kicked off my ballet flats after Brent left. Well, at least my toenails are a freshly polished shade of teal. Being presentable at all times was drilled into me by my mother, a quality further developed at the posh boarding school she sent me to. No one ever catches me out on that count.

Enzo enters the foyer tentatively, as though easing into a cold bath. I can see that he's nearly as terrified as I am, though in a manly 'I'm too tough to care' sort of street way. Oddly, this relaxes me a touch. His yellow tee shirt, the same one he was wearing on Friday, is so rumpled it appears to have been twisted when wet and dried that way on purpose to attain maximum unpresentability. For some reason I find this strangely endearing.

He nods vaguely in greeting, and I watch his dreamy eyes wander around the foyer, taking in the crystal chandelier, the Persian rug he's standing on, and the antique ebony hat rack in the corner. Though my home is not palatial, I presume to think it is quite tastefully decorated.

Oh! Now his eyes are on me. They are freely roving over and perhaps even *through* my shell-pink silk blazer and matching trousers, instinctively sizing me up. Though it is certainly not the first time I've been visually undressed, his gaze is unsettling. Is it because I know he's been incarcerated? I flinch inwardly at my own bigotry. I draw myself to my full height and pretend I am in a foreign country where the rules of etiquette dictate a visual undressing upon initial acquaintance.

Interesting, he's making no attempt at all to hide his ogling of my body. Yet I can sense that there is no malice of intent in his roving gaze. Now his expression changes suddenly to one of appreciation, as though his visual inspection has not found me wanting. Hmm.

I clear my throat in an attempt to bring his attention back to my face. "Enzo, I must take you to task straight away. If you are going to place yourself in my hands for instruction on how to behave in a manner that will make you socially acceptable in, shall we say, more genteel society, you will have to learn more than just how to pronounce words. You must learn how to behave as people expect you to. I understand that in your experience it is perfectly acceptable to 'check people out' with your eyes upon acquaintance, but in wider society, you must look at someone's face, not examine and rate their entire body when you first meet them. A full body appraisal must be reserved for when it is invited. The appropriate place to lock your eyes is on my *face*." I point to my own eyes and smile in what I hope is a kindly, yet school-teacherish way.

Enzo looks at me sideways. "Say what?"

I sigh. "Don't undress a woman with your eyes when you first meet her."

He cocks an eyebrow. "Why not?"

"It isn't polite. It puts people off."

Enzo looks doubtful. "Fancy people don't be checkin' each otha out?"

"Well, they do, but not so other people see them doing it. You have to learn to be discreet with your eyes."

"Dis-what?"

"Discreet. Subtle." His eyes still don't register understanding. "You mustn't let people see you doing it. If you simply *must* do it, you make it sneaky, so no one else notices."

Enzo shakes his head. "Girl, it's like you and me is from diff'rent planets. We don't even speak the same language. I don't know what I was thinkin', comin' here." He starts to back out the still-open door.

To my surprise, I reach out and place a hand on his arm. "Forgive me. I began too soon. Please stay, Enzo." He lets me guide him into the hallway, and I close the front door. "I have a studio in there." I point to a green door on the right side of the hallway. "And through the other door is my office." I point to the eggshell-white door to his left. "Let's sit down together, and I'll do an evaluation."

"What, like a test?" He looks so nervous I almost reach out to pat his shoulder reassuringly.

Instead I infuse my voice with extra kindness. "We'll talk, and I'll ask you questions and perhaps have you read to me a bit to see what kind of work we'll need to start with."

He doesn't move, so I walk into the office. Enzo follows me warily, full of swagger. When I gesture to one of the two armchairs in front of my desk he sits heavily, letting his legs fall open in complete relaxation, elbows planted on knees. He sniffs loudly and wipes his nose with the back of his hand as his eyes search his surroundings.

I press my lips together, forcing myself not to correct his posture or his manners. I make a mental note to demonstrate elegant seated posture at a later date. "Alright." I lower myself into the other armchair gracefully, crossing my legs and placing my clasped hands in my lap. But he is oblivious to the example I am trying to set for him. So I put on my most soothing voice and move on. "Let me explain how this process works. I am a Dialect Coach. I spend time helping people, mostly actors, learn to master accents that are not natural to them. Sometimes, that involves helping them learn about the history of the country whose accent they are copying, or the manners of that country's people."

Enzo nods. "I unnerstand, I seen movies with people talkin' in accents they wasn't born with."

This is the first time we seem to find common understanding. I feel a surge of hope. "Yes, precisely. Most of my clients come in for a few sessions a week. What Goldie proposes is for you to live here, in the cabana house out by the pool, and study intensively, every day. Sometimes, I will be working directly with you, but you will work on your own as well. It will require dining with me at times so I can teach you manners, and going on outings, both social and recreational. Goldie will take you shopping for a new wardrobe, and we will provide you with food. The proposed length of your stay is three months. That means you'll be here halfway through June. I will not allow any drugs, heavy drinking, women, or friends I do not approve in advance here on my property. These are very strict rules, and if you break them, the arrangement will be severed and you will leave. Do you agree to my terms?"

Enzo looks away from me, an odd expression that I can only read as embarrassment on his face. "There ain't nothin'...like, sexual involved?"

My eyebrows pop up so high I'm instantly sure they've created a new wrinkle on my forehead. "What?! No. Absolutely not. Never. No!" I think my face has invented a new shade of red.

Enzo nods. Wait, is that relief I see on his face?

He's moving on. "If I stay, can I use your phone?"

I shake myself from my momentary shock and nod. "You may use my landline for local calls. No long distance unless you ask in advance." I lean forward, completely recovered. "Enzo, I will be instructing you on your behavior as well as your language. You must not argue with me. You must agree to do as I say or I will not be able to teach you properly. There will almost certainly be times when you get annoyed or frustrated with me. Can you agree to do as I say even if it seems ridiculous to you?"

Enzo shrugs. "I don't see why not. I done plenty a' things in my life that was stupid because otha people made me do 'em."

His eyes shift suddenly to mine. He's looking straight into me, no holds barred. In them I can see repressed anger. I see raw frustration. But more than anything, I see determination. In this man there is a will to succeed. I see it in the set of his jaw, in the way he holds his shoulders. This man has seen depravity and perhaps done a lot he isn't proud of. But I can see a glimmer of pride still in him. If I can harness that, build it into something that makes him feel like he is master of his fate…well, maybe Goldie is right. Maybe I *can* change his life. Give him something of value to walk away with that he would never have gotten anywhere else.

Enzo chooses this moment to make a dreadful sound in the back of his throat. Then he sniffs loudly, and I can see that he's coughed phlegm up into his mouth and then loudly swallowed it back down again along with the mucosal contents of his nasal cavity. Ugghh.

"*Enzo!*"

He gazes at me warily.

"Do not *ever* make that sound or do that…swallowing thing again in front of anyone."

He's looking at me with eyes like question marks. I sigh. There is a mountain ahead of us. In addition to breaking him of unsavory habits, I shall have to teach him proper American English before I even attempt the British accent Goldie has challenged me with. I look at him appraisingly. Does he have any natural ability?

I rise from my chair and select an old script from the bookshelf. It's from a play I helped Pierce Brosnan prepare for two years ago. I flip to a well-worn page containing a lengthy monologue. The language is fairly simple; I don't want to throw anything difficult at him yet. I just need to hear him read, so I can assess the amount of potential he has for improvement. Believe it or not, I've heard reading voices in the past that have far outstripped the expectations I'd formed based on the actor's speaking voice. If I'm lucky, Enzo will be one of those; a sleeper.

"Alright, Enzo." I hand him the script open to the selected page. "I want you to start here and read both pages without stopping unless I tell you to."

I drag my antique wooden chair over next to his armchair. Sitting in it allows me to stay close to clients while they speak without being an imposing figure hovering over them. Being able to reach out and change a client's posture or the shape of their mouth as they speak is essential. Some dialect coaches believe that all speech work should be done standing. I disagree. Standing makes a person feel self-conscious and unnatural. For the initial stages of instruction, I like for clients to remain comfortably seated. I am convinced it produces a more natural tonality and ability to slip in and out of accent without having to assume a standing posture to do so. After situating my chair as close to Enzo as it can possibly get, I lower myself onto it.

A perplexed look flashes across Enzo's face as I perch within intimate proximity. He sits up straight to get some distance, which is actually what I want him to do. Then he leans back further. "Lady, you the expert an' all, but I ain't sure it's polite to sit all up in my face."

I can't keep a small smile from curling my lips momentarily. For a man who was undressing me with his eyes not ten minutes ago, he is surprisingly bashful. "I'm not being *polite* now, I'm being your teacher. I need to see your mouth when you are talking, and I might reach out to make corrections as you go. You may start reading whenever you're ready."

Enzo backs up another few inches in his chair and looks down at the script. "Okay, you want I should start here?"

"Yes." I can sense his nervousness. "Just pretend I'm not here."

"If you say so. 'I was a...'"

He's stopped. "Go on," I urge.

"'a young man then...and in those days...there were lots of...distrac... distractions'." Enzo looks up at me. "More?"

"Yes, just keep going until I stop you."

"'Women...liq...liquor,'" Enzo moves the page closer to his face. "'Liquor, fight...fighting, trying to find...some work that paid decent wages.'"

As Enzo struggles on with the monologue, I purse my lips. His reading is pathetic. Not only is he far from reading fluently, his accent is not any better when reading than when he speaks. Oh Lord, what have I gotten myself into? Am I going to have to teach him to read also?

I let Enzo fight on for a few more sentences, watching him move the script around in an attempt to get a better lock on the typed words. After a few tortured minutes, I hold up a hand. "Alright, Enzo. Thank you, that's enough of that." I take the script from him. "I think what we'll do next is have you imitate my accent. I'll say a few words, and then you say them back to me, trying to copy the way I sound. Repeat after me: 'Hello, I've come all the way from Brighton'."

Enzo looks around the room as though checking to see if anyone is watching. Then he sighs, screws up his mouth, and talks from his lips in a high-pitched voice. "Hello, I've come all the way from Bright...Brighton?"

I suppress a smile. "Yes, Brighton, but you don't have to try and sound like a woman. Just use your normal voice, but copy my accent. Let's try again: 'My home is my castle, and my castle is my home.'"

I pause to give him an encouraging look. His face is only eleven inches from my own. I noticed how he was instinctively watching my mouth while I was talking in my native accent to try and imitate the shapes it was making. A good sign. When he speaks this time it is with a voice slightly different in timbre and pitch from his own. "My home is my castle, and my castle is my home," he repeats.

I shake my head. "You're changing your voice when you copy me. I call it 'putting on the ritz'; it's a false voice people use when they try an accent for the first time." Many of my clients come to me using it when they put on an English accent. Part of my protocol is to break them of the habit immediately. I know they need to use their natural voice for the accent to sound authentic.

"Try to use your own voice; I want the words to sound like they're coming from your mouth without trying to sound like someone else. Let's try one more time: 'The queen has invited me to tea next Tuesday.'"

"The queen," Enzo catches himself in the 'ritz' voice and tries again. "The queen has invited me to tea next Tuesday." He looks around the room again, embarrassed.

I clap my hands. "Enzo, that was very good! I confess your reading will take some work, but you can imitate my accent fairly well, and you've only just begun trying. Well done."

Enzo smiles at me, and it's my turn to sit back. It's the first time I've seen him smile, and it takes me by surprise. It grows slowly, from the corners inward, and completely transforms his face. He goes from looking like a vaguely handsome thug to a movie poster 'hottie'; his features lit up from within. I'm sure my surprise must show on my face because now Enzo seems confused. The smile disappears, and his defenses are back up.

He looks at his hands. "What now?"

It's do or die time. I either send him packing now or commit. Though my inner uptight, in-a-rut, fearful self is screaming 'nooooooo!', I ignore her and smile at my newest client. "Now, I show you where you'll be staying, because I have a one-o'clock appointment, and I haven't eaten lunch yet. You can settle in until I'm free this afternoon to work with you again."

Standing, I gesture for him to follow me. I lead him down the hallway to the yellow door that separates my professional life from my personal one. Without meaning to, I pause before pushing it open. Enzo Diaz will be the first client to have passed through this door. It feels as though once he enters my kitchen I will be committed to seeing this 'project' Goldie dreamed up through to the end. I know he's not a real 'client', per se. For one thing, he won't be paying me for instruction. But is allowing this man into my personal space a huge mistake I will regret forever?

I don't give myself more time to think. I just push through the door and voila, we're standing in my kitchen.

Deep breath, Hester! I turn to Enzo, whose eyes are wide. "Right, so obviously this is the kitchen. You may help yourself to anything in the refrigerator, but make a note on the pad here," I point to a magnetic pad on the front of the fridge, "if you use the last of something so I can buy more. I think we should plan on eating most of our meals together to maximize the time we have to work on your manners and voice. There will be a strict rule in effect that you must use your best speaking voice...Enzo?"

I can see I've completely lost his attention.

ENZO

Hester's goin' on about the fridge and somethin', but I ain't listenin'. I been in some nice-ass hotel rooms, but I ain't never been in somebody's home as nice as this place. I knew it's in a ritzy neighborhood an' all when I came up here. Shit, I ain't neva even been up in this part of L.A. before. Mama used to clean houses ova here before she got doped up, but she neva brung me.

This kitchen is like somethin' off one a them cookin' shows on T.V. It's like, all snowy white counters and cabinets and lots of stainless shit, man. It even smells good; like cinnamon churros. I bet the appliances all together cost more than we got paid for my Abuelo's house when we sold it to cover Mama's drug debt. There ain't even one speck of dust on the white tile in here. Who has a white kitchen floor, man? Damn. I shoulda taken off my shoes before I stept in here.

All the kitchens I eva lived wit' was cockroach motels. Them sons 'a bitches went runnin' soon as you turned the lights on. Bathrooms, too. They'd crawl on your toothbrush if you din't wrap it up. This here kitchen is like some kind a' church.

Through a door that's all glass, I see a pool out the back with lots of plants and shit all 'round it. Then there's this, like, porch with all this wood furniture with cushions an' stuff. It's all outside with just a roof over it, all there so Hester and her homies can chill out by the pool. The wood porch is connected to a mini house. I'm thinkin' this must be the 'cabana' house she tole me 'bout back at the jail. Damn! Why I ain't come here sooner? I wasted three nights in that nasty-ass shelter when I coulda' been here in my own 'cabana', man.

Then I turn 'round an' see her livin' room and it's all leather sofas the color of my Abuela's café con leche and she got them things you prop your feet up on when you hangin' out watchin' T.V. She got two wall-to-ceiling bookshelves either side a' this sweet flat screen that mus' be four feet across hangin' on the wall. Only people I know wit' a box that big be sellin' shit they shouldn't.

Now she stops talkin' and she's lookin' at me like she want me to listen. I nod, like, 'I'm wit' cha.'

She showin' me the 'laundry room'. This lady got a room bigger than the one me and my brotha shared when we was kids jus' for getting all her threads clean. Ya know, I'd be okay sleepin' in *here* if that's what was bein' offered. Hell, I'd sleep on the leather sofa no problem.

She rich. An' I don't mean like, 'she got a good job' kinda rich. I mean like, she come from rich way back. Daddy rich, Mama rich, Granddaddy rich. Hester

Hastings prob'ly got some expensive shit lyin' around in this place. I know people who'd wait till she go to sleep and take it all. Be in San Diego by morning wit' all that shit.

I think about Topaz. I think about all I done for that girl to try and make it better. Where I ended up. I think about how much all Hester's shit would bring in.

HESTER

I wait for him at the sliding glass door adjacent to the kitchen. His eyes are lingering on the living room television. God, I hope he's not a serial T.V. watcher. No matter, he'll be too busy watching my instructional DVDs while I'm working to tune into Jerry Springer.

The noise of the sliding door when I open it catches his attention. "Let's go out back, and I'll show you the cabana, where you'll be staying."

I lead him along the stone pathway that's surrounded by white gravel and native plants. My back yard is compact, but I did pay for some beautiful landscaping to enclose the pool, cabana, and parking pad, creating privacy from the neighboring yards. The pool is oval, the length of a tennis court. I admit I don't use it as much as I thought I would when I had it installed. But it is lovely on hot days to go out and have a paddle to cool off. It's also great for parties. I had the cabana built next to it to provide a shaded area for sitting, an open-air dining space, plus, of course, a changing room, lounge, and bathroom.

Enzo whistles appreciatively. "So how much this place set you back...Hester?"

He's said so little that the sound of his voice surprises me. It is the first time Enzo has called me by my name, and it makes me hesitate. Do I want him calling me by my first name? I've always maintained a distance with clients, and having them call me 'Miss Hastings' has worked well to remind them of the professional relationship. Wasn't there good reason to apply the same strict standard to this unconventional arrangement? Yes, I should maintain professionalism at all costs. "Please call me Miss Hastings, all my clients do." I smile to soften the correction. "And asking how much I paid for my house isn't a polite question."

Enzo looks shocked. "Why the hell not? If this was my crib, I'd be braggin', yo. This here some prime real estate, Miz Hastings. I ain't neva even took a bus through this neighborhood before. An' I might as well say that if people see *me* up in here, they gonna think the wrong thing."

He's concerned about my reputation? "It's 'I've never *taken*, or *ridden* a bus through this neighborhood,' not 'I ain't never *took*.' And it's no one's business who you are or what you're doing here."

Enzo shrugs. "Okay, jus' don't be surprised if someone call the cops at the sight a' me on your property."

I nod; he's got a point. Though it's concerning that his own perception of himself is that of a threatening thug. Perhaps his self-esteem needs a make-over also. "Consider me warned. Though I suspect you'll be surprised by how at home you'll look here once Goldie begins dressing you." Hmm. I shouldn't get ahead of myself. "Of course," I add hastily, "You'll have to prove you'll be able to do the hard work to make progress before she can take you shopping." This isn't a free ride.

I stop halfway along the path that skirts the pool and look back at him. "Do you swim?"

He nods. "Learned at the Y when I was a kid."

"Well, if you're a competent swimmer, you are more than welcome to help yourself. The pool is heated, so it's lovely and warm, even first thing in the morning. The cabana will be your temporary home. There are plenty of clean towels in there." I continue along the path until it slopes up to the cabana porch. It still thrills me a little bit to see my pool and cabana house. Growing up in the cool climate of rainy England I'd never have guessed that one day I would own both. I love my outdoor furnishings. Curling up on a cushy sofa in the shade of the porch on a hot day with a good book and a glass of lemonade makes me feel as though there's not a thing wrong with the world. It is my escape.

Now we are past the dining area, and I open the cabana house door to reveal a spacious lounge with tall cubbies for up to six guests to hang towels, swim bags, and personal belongings. I designed it myself. A large upholstered chaise in a deep purple and chartreuse paisley print is the focal point of the room.

Two comfortable chairs done in white and green gingham, a vanity table, and a maplewood bench complete the furnishings. Two large windows let in the bright California sunshine.

"The changing room, bathroom, and shower are through there," I point to a white door, "and we can move anything else out here that you might need." I glance at Enzo, hoping he won't be disappointed with his accommodation. He is looking around, his face unreadable.

"So, I'm s'posed to sleep on that?" He points to the chaise.

"Yes. It's obviously not a proper bed, but it's long enough even for you." I laugh, feeling awkward instructing a grown man to sleep on an oversized chair-bench.

Enzo stands in the middle of the room, taking in the soft furnishings, the lilac walls, and the floral curtains framing the windows. "This is some girlie shit, man." He shakes his head, amused by the idea of living in it. "But you got everything I need in here."

Watching his 'tough-guy' posturing and careful movements, it suddenly strikes me that Enzo wears his 'street' persona like armor. I know people, many people, who over-do their make-up and hair to achieve the same objective. In L.A., you'll find people of every color and ethnic background all over the city. And you'll also find lots of people pretending to be something they aren't. Perfecting one's outer persona is something of an art form here.

I am confident that Enzo is not what at first glance he appears to be. What makes him look like a thug is how he stands with his wide shoulders held defensively, as though he might need to fight at any moment. It's his swaggering walk and how he crosses his arms in an impenetrable pose when he feels insecure. I can practically feel his rough history emanating from him, and I have no idea what's happened to him in his life. It makes me feel small and over-privileged.

I break the silence. "Are there any belongings you need to pick up from somewhere?"

"Nah." He smiles ruefully and holds his arms out. "This all I got."

I wonder what it would be like to have nothing. No home, no change of clothing, no money, no car, nothing but the clothes on my back and the contents of my pockets, whatever they may be. Imagining that as my reality elicits a panicky feeling. I've always been surrounded by comfort, had a warm bed and shelter over my head. But then again, I've also always had freedom. A luxury this man has recently been denied.

"How long were you in jail?" I voice this despite knowing it is not polite to ask.

The question doesn't faze him. "'Bout a year." He shrugs as though it doesn't mean anything to him anymore. As though it does not define him.

"Well, you have freedom here. But remember my rules, Enzo. I don't make rules lightly. I expect them to be followed without fail."

"Yes, ma'am." Enzo makes a cocky salute, then looks away as though he's gone too far. "I mean, yeah, I get it. I follow 'em."

I nod, satisfied. "Alright then." Not knowing what else to do, I head for the door. "I'm just going to get my lunch and head back to the office. If you have any questions, my one o'clock appointment will be finished at three. While I'm gone you can eat and then go to the living room. I'll leave a DVD on the coffee table that I want you to watch. Start repeating the words and try to imitate the accent as best you can. It's just Standard American English, but sounds a little, um, different than yours."

Enzo nods, and I leave. And that's how I wind up with an ex-convict living in my cabana house.

Chapter 3

ENZO

Thursday, March 20th

I BEEN HERE three days and can tell you two things: This crazy bitch like to work a man to death. That, and she ain't got nothin' but rabbit food in the fridge. Lettuce, cabbage, carrots, spinach. Some shit I don't even recognize. The best thing she got is these smoothies in plastic bottles. Fruit an' yogurt an' shit all blended up togetha and ready to drink. They good. So far I ain't put nothin' on the list she got stuck to the fridge. But my jeans is gettin' loose, so today I find a tiny pink pencil in a drawer and start writin'. Beef. Pork. Hot dogs. Sausages. Bread. I even write down soda, but then put a question mark next to it 'cause I don't know how she feel about soda. Seems to me she ain't got nothin' but bottles of plain fizzy water to drink. I've been up in all the cabinets lookin', too.

She crazy. First, she got me callin' her 'Miz Hastings' even though she ain't no older than me. Second, she make me watch myself in a big-ass mirror makin' faces and sayin' stupid shit. She say it's workin' on vowels, but it feels like some kinda freak show. I try to wait until she leave the room before I start, 'cause doin' it make me look like a dummy. But then I find out she's makin' videos of it. Yeah, they's a camera hidden in that mirror, man. I found out 'cause she made me watch myself on that big-ass T.V. screen makin' all those stupid vowel sounds so I can do it betta. Bett*er*. She say I got to pronounce my 'er' sounds, 'th' sounds, and what else? Oh yeah, finish my words endin' in 'g'. End*ing*. I got to memorize whole speeches from watchin' DVDs an' then tell 'em back to her. An' I have

36

to be thinkin' all the time when she listenin' – listen*ing* – 'cause she catch me out and be whackin' me with this stick she got. She also be changin' her voice all the time. One minute she's American, the next she's English again. Make me feel like I'm livin' with two crazy bitches. It's confusin', if you axe me. Oh yeah, I can't 'axe' nothin' no more; she say I gotta 'ask' it.

I don't say nothin' to her unless we workin' or she axe me – <u>ask</u> me – a question. Here's what she call my 'regime of learning':

8-9am - Standard American English vowels – that's an hour of makin' stupid sounds in a mirror.

9-10am - Standard American English consonants – that's another hour of makin' stupid sounds.

10am-3pm - Video time – this when she in her studio teachin' somebody an' I get to chillax on the leather sofa watchin' DVDs. An' guess what? She's the star of the show on all of 'em. She on them DVDs talkin' 'bout mouth shapes, melodic patterns, articulation, pronunciation, an' all that. From the screen she make me repeat words like she sayin' 'em. It's like she cloned herself so she can be always workin' me.

Then when she done teachin' clients she comes back in all cheery like Mary fuckin' Poppins and takes me out to the pool and makes me walk up and down wit' toy plastic buckets full of water perched up on my shoulders. If I spill I got 'too much swagger' and got to fill up and start over. First two days I was soaked. Today I'm gonna do better. Then I volunteer to watch more DVDs so I don't have to eat wit' her. I'm not ready to eat in front of the Manners Nazi.

I get a few minutes before I sleep at night when I can think 'bout Topaz. I know what I got to do to get her back. I just gotta find time to do it, man. Hester-Pester be such a slave-drivin' crazy bitch I feel like I ain't ever gonna get outta here.

Right now I got to start my DVD watchin' 'cause she in the studio workin' on some other dude. I can't believe he pay her for this. She bossy. She say I got to watch her mouth when she talk an' 'Observe, Analyze, and Imitate.' I watch her mouth talkin' so much in front of me and on screen I still see it when my eyes is closed. But I do it. I do everything she tell me to. But I got news for the sista; when a man's half-starved on rabbit food, he ain't in no mood to Observe, Analyze or Imitate nothin'.

HESTER

Friday, March 21ˢᵗ

I've decided it's time to begin teaching Enzo some basic table manners. For the past four days he's managed to avoid sitting down to eat with me. He claims he's not hungry and then eats when I'm with clients. In fact, I've never actually seen him eat anything; food just disappears from the fridge.

Tonight, I'm making dinner for us so I can see him in action with a fork and knife. Enzo is practicing vowels in front of the mirror in the studio. I've prepared the Caesar salad and have just started in on the salmon en croute when I see my mother's black Lexus glide in and park beside my BMW.

As I watch her sashay up to the sliding glass door my knife stops halfway through the first salmon fillet. After cringing deeply at the thought of Mum's reaction to Enzo, I decide the best thing to do is get her out of here as quickly as possible.

"Hello, darling!" my mother calls as she lets herself in. She wears one of her own creations, no doubt freshly sewn up by her tireless couturier. It consists of a chiffon, Greek-inspired knee-length tunic and an aqua cowl encircling her shoulders. It is not a look many older women could pull off, but accented by her halo of blonde silky hair and sparkling accessories, the outfit looks like it was made for her. Which, of course, it was.

"Hello, Mum!" Barefoot, I cross the cool tile floor to greet my mother, European-style, mwa-mwa, one air-kiss on each cheek. "You didn't tell me you were coming today…do you remember our talk about calling or texting or tweeting, or something before you come?"

My mother waves her jeweled fingers in the air vaguely. "Oh yes, all that bother about the time I caught you and Philip…"

"Yes, Mum. Yes, that was what precipitated the talk about calling first. Besides, aren't we having lunch tomorrow?"

My mother claps her hands together delightedly, rings jingling. "Yes! We are, and I have the most gorgeous luncheon partners arranged for us. Sort of like a double date…how quaint and American, don't you think? I've come to brief you on the situation. Give you a leg up, so to speak…"

"Yes, but couldn't we do that over the phone, Mother?" I'm trying to shepherd her back toward the door she came in.

She side-steps me without missing a beat. "Ah, but I have pictures! Surely you want to get a look at him in advance. I'm quite sure you've never met him because, my dear, he's *English*! Fresh off the boat, as they say. I thought perhaps since you've had just the very worst luck with these American blokes, a fellow Brit will be just the trick…" My mother's keen eyes take in the table in the breakfast nook that I've already set for two. "O-ho…now I understand. Expecting someone?"

"Well, yes. But not in the sense you are clearly imagining. It's a client."

"Male?"

I roll my eyes. "Yes."

"Since when are you in the habit of dining at home, in your personal space, with male clients?" My mother raises her flawlessly penciled eyebrows insinuatingly.

"It's rather an unusual situation…" I take a deep breath as my mother lowers herself regally onto the dining chair meant for Enzo. "I think it might be better if we talk later, Mum. How about we meet for coffee tomorrow before lunch and you can brief me then. Pictures and everything."

"Coffee before lunch?" Mum manages to look entirely scandalized. "I couldn't possibly. Besides, now that you're trying to be rid of me I'm determined to know whom you are entertaining this evening. Anyone I know?"

"Definitely not. Mum, he's a client. I have to teach him table manners, so…"

Her eyebrows fly upward again. "What kind of a man doesn't know table manners? Do you mean the table manners of the Czech Republic or the Holy Roman Empire? Are we coaching?"

"Yes, *I* am coaching. *You* are leaving...please, Mother, before you scare him with your flamboyance."

"Me? Flamboyant?" My mother spreads her arms innocently, revealing floating fabric wings stretching from her tunic to her sleeves.

I sigh. "I mean that in the very best, most tasteful, winged-fashion kind of way, Mum."

"Oh please, darling...Please let me stay? I *adore* coaching. I think about taking it up professionally all the time, giving you a run for your money. You're not the only one who learned a few linguistic tricks from your father." She shakes a finger at me. "You've referred clients to me before for specialized coaching, and I do so love having a pet project. You know I do...since your poor father died..."

I roll my eyes again. She must be desperate to invoke Dad twice in one monologue. Father died four years ago, leaving Mum with an enormous fortune and too much time on her hands. Since then she's been involving herself in my life a bit more actively than is strictly healthy. I had half hoped that Mum would meet another man and remarry by now, after completing a pre-nup of course.

"Mum, there are times when I know a client can benefit from your expertise. But this is not one of them..."

She points at me, bracelets jangling. "Oh, there's where you are absolutely wrong, Hester my love. *All* of your clients can benefit from my expertise. Whom do I not know who is worth knowing? Where have I not been that is worth being? I am a wealth of knowledge and culture, and if you ask me, your clients could benefit greatly from the treasure in my trove."

I just stare at my mother. Is she perhaps going a bit senile? No, she's just lonely. Despite regular shoulder-rubbing with British celebrities and throwing big Hollywood parties, the life of a widow is making her a bit desperate.

"Mother," I sit down opposite her, prepared to dismiss her gently with promises of riotous fun on the morrow.

Enzo chooses this moment to come swaggering in from the studio through the yellow door. He is shirtless, and his casual manner makes it crystal clear that he feels absolutely at home in my kitchen. I've never seen him without his habitual tee shirt on before, and the visual effect of tan skin stretched over muscles worthy of a heavyweight boxer leaves me temporarily dazzled. I note that he sports a tattoo of a skull on his left shoulder. He is halfway to the refrigerator before he realizes he has an audience.

Standing half-naked in front of me and my mother, at first he appears unfazed. Then self-consciousness creeps over him, and he tries out a little smile. He points at the fridge and then turns to open it, his pectoral and back muscles flexing in the process. Oh! Two more tattoos on his back; a leaping tiger top left, and lower, the word TOPAZ, written in elaborate lettering with the 'O' stylized as a sparkling gem. He's wearing the gold chain he's worn every day since he moved in. Either it has sentimental value or he's attached to his only possession of value or both. His washboard abs ripple as he finds what he came for and straightens up, smoothie in hand.

"Hey, Miz Hastings. I just come in for this. Don't mean to interrupt or nothing. I didn't realize you was having company." Though the grammar isn't perfect and his street accent is still there, I can tell that the accent reduction program I have him on is working. Even in his unguarded moments I can hear the difference. I smile proudly before I realize that Mum is staring at Enzo like he's fallen into the kitchen straight from an episode of *The Wire*.

But my unflappable Mum isn't at a loss for long. She rises elegantly and offers her braceleted arm to Enzo for a handshake, looking back at me for an introduction.

"Enzo, this is my mother, Miriam Hastings." I turn to my mother. "Mum, this is Enzo Diaz, my newest client."

Enzo accepts my mother's hand as though it's a leash attached to a pit bull. He dutifully shakes it and pulls away at the first opportunity.

"Hello, Mr. Diaz. I'm so pleased to meet you." Mum dials her smile up to full wattage.

"Um, me too." He bows slightly and then realizes that wasn't quite the right thing to do. He chuckles to break the awkwardness. "My bad; you ain't the queen or nothing. But I'm pleased to meet you, too. Just like you said."

Well, I think, at least he's using his best Standard American English. I'm actually less horrified by this exchange than I thought I would be. He's come a long way in a short time. When Goldie introduced herself to him a few days ago he ignored her hand and glared. Now he's smiling at Mum, which makes him look intelligent and handsome. The thick stubble he sported when I met him is more of a beard now – I suppose perhaps he doesn't even own a razor. If he was wearing a hoodie and an attitude, the facial hair would make him look like a thug, but here in my kitchen it makes him look a bit cozy, rather like a friendly bear. The fact that his naked torso is hot like habanero salsa doesn't hurt either. My mother is charmed.

She smiles up at him. "So, Mr. Diaz, I hope my daughter is treating you well…she hasn't stolen your shirt, has she?" Her laughter is like tinkling bells.

Enzo looks down at his bare chest. When he chuckles at his own nakedness his biceps flex. "Nah. I didn't know we was havin' no one come over." He looks at me.

I smile tightly and resist the urge to go get my correction stick. He's still dropping the ends of his words. My mother is also staring at me, one eyebrow raised. Clearly, she didn't miss the 'we' in his last sentence. He's made it sound like he lives here. Oh, wait.

I address mother's raised eyebrow. "Mum, Enzo is sort of a…project rather than a proper client. Goldie and I have begun research into rehabilitating under-privileged individuals. Enzo is our first case study."

The eyebrow is still up. "Oh, how lovely. Which part of him are you studying?"

Enzo actually stifles a laugh with the back of his hand.

"Mum, Enzo is living in my cabana house while we conduct our study. He's working hard to master Standard American English, and he's rapidly making his way through my accent reduction DVD program. We thought it would be best if he lives on-site because of the intensive nature of this experiment. And anyway, it's none of your business where he's living or what he's doing here half-naked in my kitchen. I'm thirty-one years old, and I won't be made to feel like a horny teenager in my own home."

Mum walks over and drapes an arm around my shoulders. "There's no need to be defensive, darling. I never accused you of anything. I'm sure Enzo is a fine student, and you will make great strides in his education. May I ask how you came to be engaged with this…research project?"

I do not want to tell her, or Enzo, that Goldie challenged me to a bet. "Actually, it was Goldie's idea. And now that I think of it, I realize that Enzo really could benefit from your help after all." I hadn't planned what Enzo's final dialect test would be because it seems ages away, if we ever get there. But one of Mum's big parties would be ideal. She's known in certain circles of Hollywood as the patron saint of British ex-patriot actors. Everyone comes to her elegant fetes, and a party at her expansive home would be the perfect venue to throw him together with the right people to see if he can pull it off.

Mum is looking at me eagerly, hands clasped together in hope as I deliver more information. "Once he's ready, we'll need to bring him out into society to try his wings. I'm thinking one of your parties would be ideal..."

Mum claps her hands, taking the bait with bracelets jangling merrily. "Oh Hester, you know I adore throwing parties! We'll have canapés and escargot and..."

"You know best what we'll need, Mum. I leave it entirely in your hands." I'm not even going to try and explain about my plans to teach him Standard British English. Even Enzo doesn't know about that yet. One thing at a time...he might not even last long enough for me to get to it.

My mother is clearly delighted with her newly assigned role in my 'project'. She can't suppress her toothy grin. "Well, simply let me know when it's time, and I'll get everything sorted for you. Oh, what fun!"

What fun indeed.

I've no sooner gotten my Mum out the door when my cell phone rings. Caller ID tells me it's Philip Brewer. I frown at the lighted display. "Excuse me, Enzo. Dinner might be a little later than I'd hoped." I head to my office, hoping the person calling is actually Jessica and not her father.

"Hello?"

"Hethter?" At the sound of Jessica's lisp I can picture her little face and the two missing front teeth.

"Yes, sweetie, it's me. What is it darling?"

The sound of tears makes my heart break a little bit. "I miss you, Hethter!"

ENZO

Hester-Pester is AWOL, and my stomach's growlin'. Grow*ling*. I see them salmon pieces she left on the counter. I don't know what she was gonna do wit' em – with them – but I got an idea. I look in the fridge and find those sausages she bought me off the list. Then I dig out some potatoes from the drawer where she keep 'em. I grab one 'a her fancy chopping mats and a nice, sharp knife and start dicing the potatoes. The pots are in the cabinet next to the stove, and I grab one out. Throw the potato pieces in and fill the pot with water. Some salt, too. I take the plastic wrapping off the sausages and start fryin' 'em up in a big old pan. The salmon won't take but a minute so I leave it for last.

By the time she come back in, I'm just puttin' the last touch on the plates. Slices of lemon and some fresh cilantro she had hid way back in the fridge. She's staring at me pretty hard, which makes me remember how I never put my shirt back on. When I try and slide past her to the studio ta get it, she say, "You pre-pared dinner?"

Duh. "Yeah. Seemed like you was gonna be a while on the phone, and I got hungry. I'ma just go get my shirt. S'cuse me." I know she a fan of proper manners and all, so I use my polite voice.

When I get back from the studio with my shirt on, she sittin' at the table waiting with her hands all in her lap. I sit down across from her an' put my nap-kin in my lap. I bet she didn't think I knew to do that.

She look across the table at me all nice. Her face is diff'rent from when she drivin' at me with the vowels and rules and shit. "Thank you for making dinner, Enzo. That was very thoughtful. I didn't know you could cook."

I shrug. "Had a job once in a restaurant. No place fancy. But they had a surf n' turf on the menu and I learned about cookin' fish and meat."

"Mmmm…the potatoes are lovely, too. I like the garlic in there." She takes another bite.

I don't know what to say to that so I just nod and eat.

"Enzo, when someone gives you a compliment, it's good manners to say, 'Thank you.'"

"Thank you…I'm glad you like it."

That gets me the smile she give when I do right. Make me feel like an obedi-ent dog.

Next she slides a silver key across the table. "I've decided you should have a key to the house, Enzo. It's starting to feel a bit odd to make you knock to be let in every morning."

I give her a look like, 'You sure you wanna do that?'

She laughs at me. "If you were going to steal from me you would have done it by now, Enzo. Don't sell yourself short; you've earned this key by showing me you are trustworthy." She lifts a finger. "But I expect I will only see you in the house between seven a.m. and eight p.m. Try not to slink around and scare me half to death, will you?"

I put the key in my pocket. "Thanks, Miz Hastings."

Then I'm happy to be eatin' meat and enjoyin' some silence when she start up again. "I guess we should go over table manners." She just like a girl. Can't eat in silence. Not like in the joint, where some meals all you hear is forks clinkin'. "So, when you're eating with friends or family, you can be casual. But when you are out with people you've just met, or in a fancy restaurant, you use your best manners. I set the table with two forks at each place because I was planning to serve a salad to start…"

Shit. I skipped the salad.

"So technically, since you began eating with the salad fork, you are using the wrong fork for the entrée."

I lift my fork and look at it. Then I pick up the other one I didn't notice before. "They be – they're different sizes."

"Yes, the salad fork usually has shorter tines, but not always. When you finish your salad, if you had one, you would lay your salad fork across the plate and let the waiter take the plate and fork away when they clear the table. Then for your entrée, you use the next fork, the longer one."

I nod 'cause I understand. She's bein' nice compared to usual, and I listen to everything she says for the whole rest of the meal.

Chapter 4

HESTER

I WAKE UP at six-thirty, already dreading the 'double date' Mum has arranged. I enjoy spending time with Mum on her own, but this is not the first time she's tried to set me up. There was the architect who ate like a bulldozer, the horticulturist who held on for three dates before I'd had enough of his incessant nose-blowing, and then the politician, a man who'd run for political office an impressive thirteen times and never won. All three had been well-groomed, moneyed, and connected – Mum doesn't know anyone who isn't – but much to her disappointment they were definitely not enticing enough to be worth the effort of dating.

Usually, I'm a 'jump out of bed and get started' kind of gal. However, this morning I burrow all the way under my silk quilt and Think.

Mum is worried I'll end up alone. No husband, no kids. She married my father at twenty-three. Frankly, she was lucky it worked out. If I had married the man I'd fancied myself in love with at twenty-three, I'd surely be divorced by now. I understand why she's throwing eligible men at my head; and I suppose I wouldn't go along with it if deep down inside I didn't have the hope of meeting Mr. Right. But does such a man even exist? I'd thought Philip Brewer was The One, steadily worked at building that relationship for three years. Everything was pretty much great until he proposed, and I refused, and it all went to hell. Though Goldie thinks I refused him because I wasn't that interested, the truth is that when I refused his offer of marriage it had been a kind of test. I'd wanted to see if he would persist, double his efforts to win my eternal devotion. After all, I hadn't broken things off with him when I said 'no'. We'd carried on with our comfortable routine; two evenings a week and weekends at his place with Jessica. I had my time at home alone three nights a week and enjoyed it. A woman can't play mother and 'wife' without some downtime to recharge. The subsequent discovery of his blatant infidelity – Jessica's nanny spilled the beans by accident; he hadn't bothered hiding the other woman from her – so astonished me it took a few days for the anger to set in. Ultimately, it was the careless deceit more than the physical fact of infidelity that kept me from forgiving him. If I'm brutally honest, it's not fair to paint Philip as a villain. But the disappointment, the betrayal of trust, the bald-faced lies he'd told to try and win me back – all of it broke something in me. I don't expect perfection in a man, but I do expect honesty. I expect a level of trust and loyalty that Philip does not possess. My little test revealed a side of him I needed to see even though it broke my heart. It allows me to say with no trace of doubt that if not for Jessica, Philip Brewer would be erased from my life like an errant pencil stroke.

And though Mum might be determined to throw single men my way, it's my job to dodge any or all that don't fit the bill. Truth is, because I don't need a man for traditional reasons like financial security or protection, I have the luxury of choosing to be with one, of holding out for someone who meets my standards for companionship and intimacy.

I emerge from the bedcovers, pleased to confirm that Mum's romantic concerns and efforts on my behalf – though well intentioned – do not define me. There's nothing wrong with being single. If I wanted a man, I'd have one. I turn on the shower and wait for the right temperature before stepping in. While lathering in a dollop of fragrant lavender shampoo I inventory the number of implicit offers I could rack up if I made myself more available. I could have any number of men with practically a snap of my fingers. Judging by the way he flirts, I could have Brent Logan for God's sake! Well, for a time anyway. In-demand actors are hardly material for monogamous, long-term relationships. If I were interested in flings, several former clients whom I truly did fancy spring to mind.

By the time I towel myself dry, I am certain that I am not interested in flings of any kind with anyone from the Hollywood set, that I could get a date with a high class of man with one phone call, and that I do not wish to do so at this time. My mind moves on to more pertinent matters.

Normally, I work a full schedule on the Saturdays Jessica's not with me. But because of Mum's luncheon date, I have a light day planned in the studio. The ten o'clock who's working toward an English accent that will prep her for a turn playing Lady Macbeth; and my three o' clock, who needs a Polish accent in short order to secure an audition for Spielberg's latest project.

Which brings me to the rather special date I have planned for this evening. Jessica's teary call prompted an emergency scheduling of some visitation time. Though technically it's an off weekend, Philip is being obliging to let her come over for a few hours, and I'm looking forward to it. I think about what we'll do with our time together as I throw on my Donna Karan silk wrap dress and apply some mascara.

Oh, and of course, there's Enzo. But he'll be fine on auto-pilot today, doing the regular exercises. Tedious but necessary, the vocal repetitions will work wonders over time. I glance at the clock remembering I told him seven-thirty sharp for breakfast. It's seven-sixteen; I'm right on time. It's remarkable how quickly he has become part of my routine. Quiet and studious, he's become a fixture of sorts. He is making steady progress, but there's more than his language that needs polishing; his manners, conversation – or lack thereof – and even how he carries himself, the swagger and rough indifference he wears like a shield; everything needs more work.

By the time I open my bedroom door, the smell of cooked sausages is wafting up the staircase. Strange…Enzo's never come in to cook his breakfast before I'm up and about. When I reach the kitchen, he has two plates on the table; vegetable omelets, still steaming, and sausages, one for me, three for him. Strawberries for garnish.

"Enzo! That looks gorgeous…but you didn't have to cook all this for me."

He shrugs, and because he's wearing a tank top it's hard not to notice his shoulder muscles flexing. The skull tattoo stares at me with its hollow sockets. "I was hungry. An' even I know it's rude to cook all that jus' for me and not you, when we're eatin' together an all."

I sigh. The man does like to eat. Judging by the items he's been adding to the grocery list, he's a believer in meat at every meal.

"Yes, but if I keep eating like this I won't fit into my clothes anymore!"

He looks at the floor like I've reprimanded him. "I done gave you a smaller helping."

"It's lovely, Enzo. And I do appreciate it…"

"Seems like with you teachin' me and letting me live here and stuff, I can at least do something for my part of the deal."

Regarding his earnest expression, I allow that he's right. "I'm being ungracious, Enzo. Please accept my apology. It's just that I'm not used to this." I sit down at the table and lay my napkin in my lap. After last night's conversation about properly setting the table to fit the meal, he's remembered to put everything on the table that should be there for breakfast, even juice glasses even though we're out of orange juice. "Let's make a deal, shall we? You can cook breakfast, I'll prepare lunch, and we can make dinner together. It will give you an opportunity to practice conversation, which is a very important skill you must master. But we'll start tomorrow because I have lunch and dinner plans for today."

He nods and tucks into his omelet. I suppose we've reached an agreement. As I watch him lean over his plate and section off bites of sausage with his fork, my mind switches over to critique mode.

"Sit up a bit straighter, please. You need to maintain good posture while you eat."

He straightens up.

"And please use your knife to cut your sausage, remember? Like I showed you yesterday."

Enzo moves his fork to his left hand and picks up his knife.

"Right. That's better. Now let's practice conversational eating. Remember you must wait until you've swallowed to speak, just like we talked about at dinner…"

--≒◎ ◎≒--

Goldie calls at just past nine, when I'm getting Enzo set up with a pair of headphones at the mirror in the studio. I don't usually take calls when I'm working with someone, but since I'm always with Enzo when I'm not with a paying client I make exceptions with him.

"Hester!" Goldie's voice is ebullient. "Today is the day. You have to let me take our man shopping today. I've been waiting forever…"

"I know. And not patiently either. How many messages did you leave for me yesterday?"

"You promised I could do his rebranding. I won't wait any longer. I've got an opening in my schedule today, and I want to take him to The Grove. I can pick him up if you need me to."

I think about it. Enzo's been working hard with no complaints. "Alright. I think he's made enough progress to go on a field trip. Come get him at eleven, and take him to lunch first. Somewhere fancy. He needs to practice his table manners. Engage him in small talk, he's not great at that, and remind him about the silverware." I realize too late that I'm talking about him as though he's not sitting right in front of me. I press the 'play' button on the old diction machine I still use for repetitions. Enzo will listen to a sentence and then repeat it back into a microphone that records his voice and matches it against the dictated sentence. At the end it will give him a score. I've told him to aim for ninety percent. Once he's begun the exercise I leave the room.

Goldie is talking. "So I'm going to get him a few things to start and let him wear those to see what he likes. He needs a suit, some decent pants, shirts, accessories, shoes. Then in a few weeks we'll go to the salon for personal grooming and do another round of shopping."

"Fine. As long as he ends up looking clean cut and stylish without appearing too 'made-over' and prissy."

"Hester, we're talking about Enzo Diaz. I defy you to try and make that man look 'prissy'. Have you forgotten where we found him?"

"You know what I mean. He shouldn't look too fussed over."

"Give me some credit, Hess. There's no need to worry. In three weeks, I'll have it all done. With a new haircut, a shave, and some decent clothing, he'll look like a God. Trust me."

ENZO

Hester-Pester left me a note telling me Goldie's coming at eleven to take me shopping. No shit. I heard when she said it on the phone. I got the ninety percent score she wanted after an hour and forty minutes on that machine. I'm so tired of seeing myself talk in that mirror I might put my fist through the thing next time she sit me down in front of it.

Goldie's right on time. I'm already in the driveway, leanin' on Hester's car soakin' up some sun when she pulls up in a powder blue Lexus convertible. Talk about custom. The hubcaps alone is worth more than all the money I made in the year before I got lifted.

Girlfriend's got her long black hair pulled back and big sunglasses on. I ain't never sat beside anyone who made me feel more classy by association. 'Cept maybe Hester-Pester. But she don't count 'cause she also make me feel like a dog wit' fleas. Only so much a man can be pushed, pulled, and corrected before he start to feel like less than he is. Like my Uncle Dwayne with that wife who was always swearin' and hittin' at him and always tell him he a pile a' shit. I think we was all glad when she took off wit' that pansy-ass plumber.

I like Goldie. She got class and looks all snooty, but I can tell she decent on the inside. It also don't hurt that the girl is totally slammin'.

We drive down to The Grove, where I only been once before when Antwon told me go get new threads. She takes me to lunch at this place that has two gold lions out in front. The writing on the menu is in gold also, but I don't get to choose my own food. Goldie orders and the waiter – no joke, he's wearin' white gloves – brings us this fizzy drink with orange juice in it.

I've had champagne before. Room service in hotels. Usually with some raspberries or pomegranate seeds all in. This is jus' champagne and the juice with maybe a twist of lime or something. It's in a tall, skinny glass, and Goldie don't say nothing to make me feel dumb, she jus' shows me how to hold the glass and lift it up for a sip without looking stupid.

The whole meal goes that way. The waiter keeps bringing plates out with just little dabs of food on 'em and instead of talkin' at me about what to do, Goldie just shows me by doing it, and I copy. Hester-Pester could learn a lot from Goldie about teaching manners. I got eyes. I can see when Goldie takes butter and puts it on her own bread plate before spreading it on her roll. She don't need to explain every step like I'm from Saturn or somethin'.

She talks while we eat, the 'small talk' Hester told her to make me do. It's okay.

"My Dad worked on Wall Street when I was little," she tells me. "Then we moved out here when he got into real estate. What does your father do?"

"Steal shit. He been locked away 'bout sixteen years now. Armed robbery."

Goldie doesn't blink. "Your Mom?"

"Dead. Cardiac arrest from smokin' too much crack."

Her face goes all sad. "Oh, I'm very sorry to hear that, Enzo."

I shrug, and she waits a minute to see if I'm gonna say more. I take another sip of my drink.

Goldie does the same, and then she starts again. "Okay, how about brothers or sisters?"

"I got a little brother. Ricky. He got shot in the head when we was teenagers, and he ain't right in his brain. He still stayin' with my Aunt Latrice – I stayed there too, way back – and she park him nearly every day at a center for broken down people. But I couldn't live at Aunt Latrice's no more after she let her boyfriend take Ricky's disability money. I kinda messed him up, and she said I gotta go. But that was a long time ago."

Goldie is quiet, so I ask, "You got brothers?"

This makes her happier. "A sister. She got married last year."

"How 'bout you? Married?"

She lifts up her left hand and shows it to me. "No ring. I've got a boyfriend…we've been together a while but I don't think he'll last. He wears pleated chinos." She wrinkles her nose.

I look at her like, 'don't be no dumb-ass.' "A man's more than whatever chinos he got on, homegirl!"

"He also works too much."

"Maybe he workin' so much so he can buy you a nice ring."

She shrugs. I can tell she don't love him. Then the next plate comes with something covered in sauce on it, and I'm copying her with fork and knife again.

→━◉ ◉━◄

After lunch we get down to the shoppin'. Goldie leads me up into the Barney's New York store. Man, if I walked in here without her, both them security guards who standin' around would be clocking me the whole time, just knowin' I was gonna try and lift somethin'. Some*thing*.

Goldie don't even ask me what I want. She load me up with stuff in a dressin' room. She say, "Enzo, come out and show me every outfit once you have it on."

First time I come out she tells me, "Turn around. I need to see how your ass looks in those jeans."

I've had a lot of weird shit said to me, but I ain't never had a girl say that to me before. She thinking 'bout me like I'm some Ken doll to dress up. She wanna get me lookin' all dope and make me shine like money. All the same, I like the way she look at me better than the way Hester do. Does. Yeah, Goldie be looking at my ass and sizing me up 'cause she wants to make me over. But at least she neva look at me like I'm less than she is.

I'm carrying two bags when we leave the store. She's already into a new shop when I see the gold links they got in the jewelry place next door. I hope she gonna hook me up with some a' that. All I got left is my one chain I never take off. The one 'Topaz' Mama gave me.

Goldie come back to find me starin' in that window. "Enzo? What are you doing? We need to get you fitted for a suit." She follow my eyes to see what I'm lookin' at. "Oh no. No flashy stuff, Enzo. Your look is 'updated classic chic', not 'downtown gangsta.'"

I give her a hopeful look. She frownin' at me. "Which one do you like?"

I point in the window at the heavy gold one with the chain links.

Goldie makes a face like she just poured sour milk on her fruity pebbles. "Absolutely not, Enzo. Too flashy!"

I point at the other one that caught my eye. It has a badass fist hangin' down.

"Ew! No. If you're going to wear bling, it has to be classy. Like…that one." She points to a chain that looks to me like something my Mama woulda worn.

"That's some girlie shit, Goldie."

"No, it's very tasteful."

"Yeah, well 'tasteful' don't make a statement."

Goldie looks at me like, 'Exactly.'

"I like the one you have on, Enzo. It suits you." She reaches up and touches my neck as she fingers the chain around it. I don't expect her touch to hit me like a brick but it does. I gotta back up.

"What's wrong?" She's got that concerned look on her face.

I don't even know. "Nothin'. Where we going next?" I look around like I'm interested in more shoppin'.

⤙═◎ ◎═⤚

Goldie bought me so much the bags fill up the trunk of her hot custom Lexus. When she starts drivin' I ask her a favor.

"Can you drop me down in Westmont?"

"Sure. You going to visit someone?"

I nod.

She lifts her eyebrows. "Is it a woman?"

I nod again.

She smiles like she knows something, and it about makes me laugh. If she knew Lola, she wouldn't be smiling.

"You want me to come back and get you?"

"Nah."

"Okay. I'll just drop your new clothes off at Hester's."

"Yeah...Thanks."

"No problem, Enzo. Today was fun, right? And in a couple weeks, I'll take you to see Giovanni at my salon for a new hairstyle."

I nod, but I'm thinking 'bout Lola. I hope she's still living in the same place.

I called her from Hester's, but the line's been disconnected. I have Goldie drop me on a quiet street in Westmont, and I'm just happy Lola don't live in Watts, 'cause last thing I need is for Antwon to hear word I'm around. I know Lola won't tell him on account of her love for Topaz.

Lola's the last person I know was looking after my girl. She was helping me out while I tried to make that wad of cash Antwon ended up with. Lola's just as likely to be drunk as sober any time of day. But she's Topaz' grandmamma, she don't do drugs, and she don't work. If she didn't have a record, Topaz would prob'ly still be with her right now.

I can hear the wordless humming of a small child at play on the other side of the door as I stand on the stoop. It takes me back to when Topaz was a baby, and she was livin' here with her Mama. Now I bang on the door.

"Lola! You there?" I pause with my ear to the door. The child goes silent and then I hear it start to wail.

"Hey, baby. Shush now…Shhh!" Says Lola. Then to me through the door, "Who there?"

"S'me, Enzo."

"You know they done took her out a' here after you went in." Lola opens the door, and I can see the past year ain't been kind. She looks ten years older than the last time I seen her. From her eyes I can see she been drinkin'. She's holding a snotty-nosed toddler on her hip. The baby looks at me with fear in his eyes.

"Whose is that?"

Lola looks at me sideways, and I know that baby was made by her son before she says anything. "Antwon's. Baby's Momma done took off." She hushes her own voice. "You know he be lookin' for you. Heard you got out."

"Yeah, ain't no problem. But I wanna know how Topaz was last time you seen her…you seen her since the police came and took her?"

Lola shakes her head slowly. "I went once to see where they took her. You know, make sure she was okay."

"You ain't gone but once?"

Lola's look tells me Antwon didn't want her to go more than that once.

"When you went, was she okay? Did she look happy?"

"She screamed like they was killin' her when they took her outta here, but yeah, she seemed real happy with them other people. They looked like good people, Enzo. Clean. Got a nice apartment. When I saw her they'd got her a new Barbie an' all. An' they only had two other girls livin' there. It wasn't like that place you told me they put you in once, the one where they had kids crawlin' out the windows."

I sigh and nod. I got to call that caseworker. Got her number, but I ain't done nothin' with it yet. I don't know what kinda paperwork I need to fill out or what rights I got, but I'ma do anything I need to. She's my daughter, and I want her back.

"Okay. Be good, Lola. Be good for that baby boy." I tickle the soft fat beneath the baby's chin gently with a finger, and he give me a shy smile. Topaz' cousin.

Lola waves me away with her skinny hand. "Go on now. I ain't tell him you was here."

She shuts the door on me.

HESTER

"Darling!" Mum greets me outside the restaurant with kisses meant to avoid leaving lipstick stains. Then she raises an uncertain hand to her heavily sprayed up-do, smoothing back imaginary errant hairs.

"Hello, Mum." I take in her ensemble; it's a deep shade of plum and of a surprisingly conservative cut for her – all sleek lines and defined edges. She's trying to impress. "You look lovely…"

She waves her hand at me. "I'm an old woman, there's no hope for me. But you…" she holds me at arms' length admiringly, "you are a vision!"

My eyebrows raise. I've hardly made an effort to look any better than I would for a client. If she's trying to build my confidence she's gone wrong. Her overdone demeanor is just making me feel a bit suspicious. "Tell me again whom we're meeting?"

"Your fellow is Nigel Hemsworth. He's a solicitor from Surrey and has been cited by Prince Charles for his work on behalf of immigrant children, though his money comes from corporate litigation. But don't mention that. There's been some sort of little scandal or other having to do with it. He's come to L.A. to start over…I think he has aspirations of writing a movie script."

Mum opens the door to the restaurant, and we go in. The dim interior is all deep red upholstered chairs and gilt-edged tables. It takes a moment for my eyes to adjust.

Mum waves at a silver-haired gentleman sitting in the far corner. "That's Christopher Davies, my friend. And I should perhaps mention he's become quite a close friend." I give her a look that says, 'exactly how close?' She ignores it. "He used to photograph wildlife in the Serengeti, but now he has his own rig-boat contraption and dives for sunken treasure. Can you imagine?"

I can't reply because Christopher has met us halfway to the table and extends his hand to me. "You must be Hester." His handshake is warm and firm. "I'm Christopher. It's such a pleasure to meet you after all Miriam has told me about you."

I raise an eyebrow at my mother, then smile at the man I presume is her boyfriend. "It's my pleasure to make your acquaintance, Christopher."

He extends his arm to Mum and escorts her to the table, where he pulls out a chair for her, makes sure she is comfortable. Once we are all seated he looks at his watch, frowning. "Please excuse my friend's lateness. I suspect Nigel is still on London time. I'm sure he'll be here any moment."

Indeed, as soon as we've been handed menus he shows up, all apologies for being five minutes late. Nigel appears to be in his mid-thirties. Short dark hair, clean shaven, pale. He's a bit taller than me, which means he's of average height for a man. Attractive, but not in a showy way. Dignified. His subtle cologne smells of bergamot with a hint of citrus. So far, so good.

We are introduced, and he seats himself next to me, across from Mum and Christopher. The usual chitchat about the weather is exchanged, and we discuss how Nigel likes Los Angeles so far. Our willowy waitress, who is so clearly the 'trying to make it in Hollywood' type, gives a dramatic reading of the specials and takes our order. Then Mum asks Christopher about his next treasure hunting adventure.

He smiles and rubs his hands together. "Yes, I'm quite excited about this one. I'll be teaming together with an old friend to search for the lost Flor del la Mar, a sixteenth-century Portuguese vessel that sank off the northern coast of Sumatra. According to lore, at the time it sank it contained priceless archaeological treasures and sixty tons of gold. We aim to find out if anything's still down there."

Mum's eyes are wide. "How exciting! And what's the last treasure you actually found?"

"We dove on a wreck east of Norfolk last April. Terrible visibility and dreadfully cold. There was nothing much left of the wreck, but fifty-five meters to the southeast, we stumbled across an unknown wreck buried so deep we nearly missed it. Turned up some fourth-century Roman coins on that one. Gold."

Mum reaches across the table and grips my wrist in excitement. "Isn't that the most incredible thing? I'll bet those coins are simply priceless. Hester, can you imagine finding something so valuable?"

"No, it must be absolutely thrilling..." The waitress arrives with drinks and a terra cotta dish filled with bread sticks. Nigel is the first to snag a breadstick as he watches the waitress' backside depart. Sensing my mother's impatience to discuss her new beau, I refocus on the conversation at hand. "Christopher, if I might ask...where is your home base when you're not diving for treasure?"

"I keep a flat in London, which I almost never see, and a place in Santa Barbara. I sometimes manage entire months at a time there, though it can be a bit lonely on my own. I prefer being out on the sea, having a project."

Mum is gazing at him rapturously. Then she suddenly comes to herself and swivels her gaze to me. She pats my hand, and I know instantly she's about say something embarrassing. "You're not the only one with a nearly impossible project, Christopher. My daughter has taken on quite an assignment. You know she's a dialect coach, yes? Have I told you that?"

Christopher and Nigel nod in unison, which makes me wonder with dread what else she's told them about me.

"Well, Hester has made quite a name for herself in Hollywood. Works miracles with actors.

And lately she's taken a more charitable bent. In fact, what she has on the go now will be an absolute coup if she can pull it off."

Nigel looks at me as though I've invented a dime-sized battery than can power an entire nation for a year. "Really? Tell us, Hester...what are you up to?"

"It's not that interesting actually. I'm just giving intensive lessons for one particular client..."

"Don't be modest, darling." Mum turns to the men. "She's completely transforming a less fortunate individual who never received a proper education. He needs help on all fronts: manners, language, fashion, personal grooming. It's quite a massive undertaking..."

"Mum, it's not that big a deal." At the edges of my memory I recall there's something I need to tell her about that. What was it? "Oh! Though I forgot to tell you I'm going to teach him an English accent also. Right now it's just the American one and sort of an image make-over. And Goldie's helping me."

Mum turns to Christopher. "And so am I! Hester says when he's ready, I get to throw a huge party and invite him as..." She looks to me questioningly. "Perhaps as our dear cousin from London?...Or perhaps he can be from Manchester, don't you think, Hester? And he can try out his new skills in real life."

Christopher nods in approval of such a noble undertaking. "Where's the fellow from?"

Mum leans forward excitedly. "He's from the slums right here in L.A. Hester's going to teach him proper American English and now a British accent on top of that. So you can see it's quite a lot of work."

I shift in my seat. "He's doing the hardest bits on his own, Mum. Please don't make me sound like a hero."

"Nonsense, darling." She points at me. "What you're doing *is* absolutely heroic. You're giving that young man a future he wouldn't otherwise have."

"Mum, he's at least as old as I am, not a 'young man.' Please don't make it out to be more than it is." My mind searches for a new topic. "So Nigel, what do you think of Los Angeles so far?"

Nigel laughs. "Well, it's entirely different from any place I've lived before, that's for certain." And we're off and running, blessedly saved from any more mention of my charitable, selfless project.

ENZO

Takes me three busses to get back over to Los Feliz. It's past five o'clock, and the roads is jammed with crazy traffic. I got five blocks to walk once I get off that last bus, too. Gives me time to think about shit. Hester-Pester prob'ly be wondering where I am. She wants me to start eatin' breakfast, lunch, and dinner with her now. Always telling me how to eat and what's 'proper.' I know I signed on for this shit, but sometimes it gets on my last nerve. Thing is, maybe she'd be okay to hang out with if she wasn't always correctin' me and making me feel like a kid who don't know nothin'.

It feels phony to try and talk like someone else. Like puttin' someone else's skin on over my own. She's got me watching DVDs about history and shit now after I finish saying all the sentences into that machine that scores me. I also get to watch real shows, which she says will give me 'cultural expansion' and all. The actors all talk like she does when she's not speaking her American at me. It's weird how she can just turn them accents on and off. I guess that's what she's training me to do. Soon I'll be switchin' from Ghetto Enzo to Standard American Enzo and back again.

When I get close to the house I hear what sounds like kids playing outside. Then I come 'round the back and see what's going on. There's a kid in the pool. Little girl in a blue suit with that frog princess on it that Topaz used to love. Kid don't look much older than Topaz. Makes my heart squeeze tight to think about my girl. I wonder does she still love that frog princess.

There's a woman there with the girl. Hair all wet. She got her back to me, standing on the edge of the pool ready to leap in and chase the kid, who be laughing like crazy. Girlfriend got on a bright green suit with pieces cut out all over. Little gold hooks is all that's holding the top to the bottom. I can't see the front, but she got a tight round ass that looks good for grabbin'. She jumps into the pool all wild and…son-of-a-bitch; it's Hester-Pester.

HESTER

Jessica splashes me, and the water shoots right into my eyes. When I turn away from the splashing to clear them I see Enzo standing by my car looking shifty. Goldie dropped off his clothes hours ago. I wonder where he's been?

I wave and gesture for him to come closer. Soon he's standing above me, blocking the sun and looking larger than life.

"Goldie left your new things in the cabana." Jessica wriggles her way past me and looks up at Enzo. "This is my friend, Jessica. She usually comes to visit every other weekend, but we have a special play date this evening, don't we, sweetie? Jessica, this is Enzo. He's one of my clients."

Jessica reaches up with her wet right hand, and Enzo bends to shake it, bemused.

"It's a pleasure to meet you, Jessica." I taught him that.

Jessica smiles, the sun in her eyes now that he's squatting down to talk to her.

"You got a bathing suit, Mr. Enzo?"

His expression turns hesitant as he mentally inventories his new wardrobe. "I think so."

"Put it on and come play with us! Daddy couldn't stay, and if you swim with us, I bet you can throw me really far." She grins and then dolphin dives away.

Enzo's head is almost level with my own now, and he's smiling. Even though he looks the same as he did the first day Goldie recruited him, and I've seen him every day since he showed up at my door, that smile is still a surprise. It's delicious.

I shade my eyes with my hand. "You don't have to. You're finished studying for today unless you want to watch one of the DVDs."

He nods and stands up, heads for the cabana.

A jet of water hits the back of my head, and I turn to see Jessica wielding the mega water gun I bought her for Christmas. Screaming in mock outrage, I go after her. I'm sure her squeals of joy can be heard two streets over.

My eyes are closed for a game of Marco Polo when I hear the most enormous splash. A mini-tsunami hits me right in the face. Jessica laughs hysterically as I wipe water from my eyes and open them in surprise to see Enzo, post-cannon-ball soaking wet, ten feet away. Jessica climbs out of the pool and doesn't even wait to make sure he's ready before launching herself at him from the edge.

"Whoa!" He catches her, dunks her under, and then tosses her easily into the deep end.

She comes up laughing. "Do it again, Mr. Enzo!"

As soon as she gets within reach, Enzo grabs her and throws her again. Her smile is huge as she flies through the air. Enzo is smiling too, and when Jessica surfaces he dives down to grab her legs and haul her back under.

I push through the water to reach the mega squirt gun floating by the steps, and when they both come up I take aim and fire.

The jet of water elicits shrieks of joy from Jessica and a rumbling laugh from deep in Enzo's chest. I realize I've never heard him really laugh before. Though we've been spending lots of time together, it's been all business. No playful banter or light chit-chat. Every interaction has been weighted by the fact that I'm the teacher and he's the student.

Well, isn't that right and proper considering the situation? He's a diligent pupil, if quiet. No complaints, no attitude. He does what I tell him to with no comment. I've never had a more compliant client. I wonder what goes through his mind when he's quietly listening and saying nothing.

Looking at him now, black hair and thickening beard shining with droplets of water, broad chest and shoulders showing above the waterline, it's hard to imagine him behind bars. The tattoos are the only reminder of his personal history, and since there are plenty of mega-stars sporting ink these days, no one meeting him for the first time would jump to conclusions based on the tattoos alone. He's wearing the gold chain he never seems to take off. I wonder if it has some sort of special significance.

Jessica jumps on his back, and they retreat to what they think is a safe distance in the deep end while my gun remains trained on them. When I squeeze the trigger, the spray just barely reaches, but hits them squarely on the head and shoulders.

Enzo whispers some secret war plans to Jessica. She nods and tightens her grip on his shoulders. He dives and comes straight at me, Jessica along for the ride. I have no time to reload. When he tackles my knees, I have to let go of the gun as I get taken under. Jessica sees me release it and separates from Enzo to claim the prize. Which leaves me and Enzo underwater, eyes wide open, his arm still around my legs.

When I come up for air, he stays under. I feel his head and shoulders pass underneath me, and then he's scooping me up as he stands. Somehow, he's managed to plant me squarely on his shoulders. I've got a hand on his head to steady myself as he storms toward Jessica. She's spraying us mercilessly with the gun as we advance, but we don't stop. We're almost on her when she stops shooting us to wave happily at someone whose shadow approaches from the parking pad.

Enzo and I turn as one, my hands on the top of his head for balance. Standing by the pool steps is Philip, dressed in a suit and scowling.

He waves distractedly at Jessica and turns his attention back to the tower that is Enzo and myself.

"Hi, Hester. I didn't realize you would have company while Jessica was here." Philip's voice is on the verge of hostile.

"It was unexpected. But I was under the impression that I'd be dropping Jessica off at your house after our evening together. I remember agreeing months ago that it would be better if you don't come here."

"I thought maybe it would be a fun surprise to take you girls out for dinner."

I frown. "You need to communicate about these things, Philip. You can't just show up without warning..." I dismount from Enzo's shoulders, but stay close. It feels safe to have him near me when Philip looks so upset. Jessica swims over and nestles between us, her arms around my waist.

"Because you might have your new boyfriend here? Didn't you think I might want to know what strange men are hanging around my daughter? I find it odd that you didn't *communicate* that little detail to me."

I don't want Philip becoming any more worked up. Enzo is tall and silent beside me. Thank heaven he's not getting into this.

"For your information, Philip, Enzo is not my boyfriend. I didn't know he would be here, and Jessica invited him to swim with us."

"So who the hell is he? The cabana boy?"

I can't help it, I laugh out loud. "Actually..." No, it's not a good idea to tell him Enzo lives in the cabana house. "Enzo is a client and just happened to stop by..."

"In his bathing suit?" Philip's hands are on his hips. "Really, Hester. I should think you would realize how inappropriate it is to have a man playing with Jessica who hasn't been vetted by me first. After all, it's not like you're her mother..."

"Hold on a minute! I would have let you know if I had planned for him to be involved in my time with Jessica, but I've already told you I didn't. It was a fluke, and we were all having a great time. So cool down, Philip. There's been no harm done."

Philip's lips are pressed together so tightly they've gone white. "Jessica, it's time to go, sweetheart. Get out of the pool and get dressed."

"But Daddy, we haven't even had dinner yet! We were going to make our own pizzas!"

"*Now*, Jessica."

We can all see that Philip means business. Because she's attached to my waist, it's easy to bring Jessica along with me when I head for the steps to get out of the pool. "Come on, sweetie, let's get you a towel."

As though he can sense I could use some back-up, Enzo follows us. Philip steps back as we all climb out of the pool and grab towels from a lounge chair. Enzo is a few inches taller than Philip and much wider through the chest. I can see the men sizing each other up like gorillas.

It's funny; although I am aware that Enzo is at least my age and very masculine, I'd sort of considered him to be younger than me and, because he's my student, somehow not a man in the traditional sense. Now that I realize this, it feels as though I've been indirectly insulting him the whole time he's been living here. I've been treating him as less than the grown-up man he really is. Fleetingly, I wonder if it's really because he's my student or maybe has something to do with the fact that his background is so opposite of my own. Ruefully, I admit to myself that the fact that he's been in jail factors in also. I've been bigoted and judgmental, and haven't allowed myself to see Enzo as a whole person.

Once Jessica seems dry enough, I hand her the bag that contains her clothes and point to the house. "You can run into my room to change. I'll be right here."

Once she's gone, Philip really rips into me. "Hester, this is her last visit with you. I trusted you to keep her safe," he glares at Enzo, "but now I realize that was a mistake on my part. For all I know, this hooligan has been hanging around the scene when Jessica's been here before." He looks me in the eyes. "I can't have that, Hester."

It's like he's punched me in the gut. I can't believe he'd do this to Jessica or to me. "Philip, honestly. I think you know me well enough to understand that I'd never put Jessica in any danger." As I say this, alarm bells are ringing in my mind. Enzo's an ex-con. If Philip knew that he'd really have my head. "Please don't do this. It'll damage her, Philip. She won't understand. She'll think she's done something wrong...please."

Philip is unmoved. "Goodbye, Hester." He walks to the house and calls to his daughter. *His* daughter. Despite four and a half years of standing in as her mother, I have no claim on her.

I feel tears forming and pressure building up in the back of my throat. But I won't cry until they've gone. It would frighten Jessica. And be too satisfying for Philip. He's hit me below the belt and knows it.

I go to Jessica when she comes out and hug her to me even though I'm still damp. I bend down and kiss her on both cheeks and then her forehead, like we always do when we say goodbye. I can't speak without letting out my tears, so I press my hand to her heart and then take her hand and press it to mine. I smile and wave as Philip grabs her hand and leads her away.

"Bye, Hethter," she calls softly as he picks her up and deposits her into the booster seat in the back of his vintage Camaro convertible.

ENZO

When the Camaro pulls away and Hester starts crying, I'm not sure what to do. We still wearin' suits and towels. She's just standing outside the house, tears coming like crazy. It ain't a pretty kinda cry, either. It's a red-faced, snotty kinda cry. The type Topaz used to throw in the weeks after her Mama died. She was so little she didn't even know what death was. Jus' that her Mama wasn't never there anymore.

Hester don't move, she so lost in them tears. Finally, I jus' pick her up and carry her over to the porch where she got all that furniture. I sit out some nights on that sofa, and a few times I've slept out there. Now, I put her down on it and kinda look at her, like, 'you want me to stay?'

She nods, and I sit down next to her. Hester leans on me, her tears wet on my arm. She wipes her nose on her towel, a thing I wouldn't imagine an uptight person like her would do. I guess she really upset.

It don't make sense to say nothin', so I stay quiet. After a while the crying lets up, and she sits up off my arm a little.

"I'm sorry." Her voice is soft.

"Ain't a problem."

"I was with Philip for three years. Jessica was a big part of my life then, and I don't see her much now. Just every other weekend. She called me last night, when you made the sausage 'surf and turf,' remember?"

I nod and she keeps going. "She said she missed me too much, so we scheduled tonight to get together. And now, Philip's ruined everything."

Me. Me being here ruined everything. "I never shoulda come out to the pool. I shoulda gone in and watched some a' them DVDs you started me on yesterday. Then this never woulda happened."

When she don't correct a single thing I said wrong, I know she's in trouble. This thing's hit her hard.

"Jessica's not my child, but I love her like she is." She starts crying again, and it seems like she might never stop.

I sit and listen to it for a few minutes. But then my own girl pops into my head so fast I say it before I can think. "I got a kid." I didn't mean to ever say nothing 'bout Topaz to Hester, but at least it'll distract her. She gettin' all snotty again.

It works. She blinks at me in surprise. "What?"

"I got a girl. Six years old."

Hester be staring at me like I got two heads. "Where is she?"

"Foster home."

"What? Isn't she with her Mum…"

"Her Mama dead."

"Oh, Enzo! I'm so sorry…that's the most awful thing. But how come your daughter's in foster care?"

"When I got 'rested, them social services people done took her. I ain't… don't have any family that would take care 'a her."

Hester gettin' all righteous now. "Enzo! You've got to get her back! You're going to get her back, right?"

"That's the plan. But I ain't got much time with all this learnin' to talk stuff, and I'm thinkin' them social services people won't give her back to me yet when I ain't…don't have a job or no place to call my own."

"No, they can't do that, can they? Keep you from her now that you're free? You paid your dues…they can't keep your daughter. I'm sure of it."

"I'ma find out. I got the number of her foster care case worker."

"Enzo, you can have all the time you need to figure this out. Your daughter is more important than learning to speak Standard American English."

She's sat up off me and shifted over so she's looking right in my face. I look back at her and see more than Hester-Pester. She got more to her than just workin' people to death. I ain't seen that in her till now. The lady barely knows me, and she's all worried 'bout my little girl. "Yeah. I'ma call on Monday. But I can still do my study time, too."

She nods like 'that's more like it.' "What's your daughter's name, Enzo?"

"Her name's Topaz."

"Ah, that explains the tattoo…it's a pretty name. Unique."

"She was born in November, an' her Mama say the birthstone is topaz. So that give her the idea for the name."

Hester leans back on the sofa again, and we sit in silence for a good long while. When she talk again, she sound all soft, like she tired. "Was it hard when her Mum died?"

"We wasn't together when she passed, but yeah it was hard. I still cared about her, but it was worst for Topaz. My baby girl was three years old. She cryin' all the time for weeks. And I'm all of a sudden a full-time Daddy. I ain't got no one can take care of her 'cept her Grandma when I was workin'. And that woman be drunk most of the time. Made me worry when I left Topaz over there. But I had a plan to make it better." I'm saying more than I meant to. "I was gonna earn me some good money, then start up my own gym, you know? Jus' a small, torn down place I was gonna build back up. I been a trainer before, worked a long time down at a place in Westmont. It was a dump, but had a good rep."

"So that's how you ended up in jail, isn't it? Trying to make money so you could build a better life for you and Topaz."

I hate rememberin' it. Regret is not a big enough word for how I feel about what I did. "Seemed like a no-fail kinda idea at the time." I shake my head.

She puts her pale hand on my shoulder. "Enzo, you mustn't be ashamed. You were doing the best you could at the moment. We all make mistakes; you just had the misfortune of being caught making an illegal one."

But I am ashamed. And I'm ashamed of lying to Hester about it, too. If it was just drugs, it wouldn't be so bad. Before I started, it seemed like it was gonna be free money, like fun even. But now I look back and can't think how I let Antwon talk me into it.

I stand up. I need to stop running my mouth and take a shower. Hester need to get inside her rich house and do whatever rich chicks do when they alone. I said too much to her already.

Chapter 5

HESTER

Sunday, March 23rd

"ENZO, ENZO, ENZO! Focus on the written words. Think of them as old friends, and let them float up into your brain and flow out your mouth like water from the faucet. Try again." I give him my most encouraging look.

Enzo lets out a frustrated sigh and lifts the script to his field of vision. It's the fifth script I've given him within half an hour. He's trying, he really is. "The dragon ro...roars at the sight of all the b...bl...blood. It is a kee...keen...keening wail," he moves the script closer to his eyes, willing himself to comprehend the words. "Keening wail that comes for...forth from scaly lips like a si...sire...no, siren of an...ang...anguish."

Enzo lowers the script and gives me a miserable look. I can't help but frown. Can he really be this bad at reading?

I stay calm in the face of his frustration. "Why don't you take another drink of water..."

"I'm not thirsty. I just can't read this shit." He throws down the script in a display of pique the likes of which I've never seen from him before.

"Did you ever have trouble reading in school?" The thought of dyslexia looms in my mind.

"Nah. Was easy." Enzo leans back in his chair and rubs his eyes.

Curiouser and curiouser. I am sitting in my wooden chair, parked ridiculously close to him. "When was the last time you did any real reading?"

"What, like read books?"

"Yes. Did you read to pass the time in jail?"

"Nah. Spent most my time working out. Thinking."

My eyes narrow, studying him. He regards me warily. "What?"

"Hang on." I go to my desk for a blank piece of paper and my black Sharpie. On it I write the first bit of Shakespeare that pops into my brain. I go to the wall opposite where Enzo sits and hold up the paper. "What does this say?"

"'A fool thinks himself to be wise, but a wise man knows himself to be a fool.'" He looks at me and shrugs. "It's deep and all, but what the hell has it got to do wit' reading?"

"Wait." I grab the script he threw on the floor, flip it open, and hold it two feet in front of him. "Read."

"'The dragon lim...limped.'" He squints at the words. I step back another two feet. "'Limped along in a...agony. A sorry f...fel...'" I step back another two feet. "'A sorry fellow with an open wound at his scaly throat. He was a conquered beast whom sword and stealth had vanquished...'" Enzo straightens up in his chair. "'I, the warrior who dealt the lethal blow, feel pity at the writhing of the great beast and regret that something so majestic has come to such a lowly end.'" I am grinning over the top of the script at him as he finishes, and his eyes meet mine, relief written in them. His slow smile spreads as frustration shifts to revelation.

"See? It's not you, Enzo. It's your eyesight. You, my friend, need glasses."

Enzo's smile fades. "Glasses? Aw no, man. I ain't wearing no glasses."

I'm taken aback. "Whyever not? Glasses are perfectly respectable. Many of my own friends wear them. I use them for reading sometimes myself."

"Yeah, well, where I come from, glasses is no good. Glasses mean you weak, make you like a target. My lil' brother Ricky wore glasses, and they popped his ass for the fun of it."

I am aghast. "Enzo, are you saying your brother got shot for wearing glasses?"

"Not 'cause of the glasses, but 'cause of what they made him look like. Like a target."

I simply stare at him, trying to imagine a culture in which wearing glasses can get a person shot. "Enzo, that's appalling! Is he okay? Did the police catch who did it?"

"His brain ain't right 'cause the bullet went through. Ricky in a wheelchair 'cause he can't walk or nothin' either. Police didn't never even look real good for who did it." A hard edge comes into his voice. "They too busy putting people like me away."

"Well, that's just…I never…I'm so sorry, Enzo." I don't know what else to say. What I'm learning of Enzo's life is one tragedy after another.

He doesn't appear eager to discuss his loss, so I return the script to the shelf and turn around. Standing in front of him, I feel self-consciously privileged. The most hardship I've had to face is my father's death and the heartbreak of broken relationships. This man has weathered a disturbing childhood, his brother's in-jury, the loss of his child's mother, jail time, and his daughter being taken from him. Suddenly, I understand better the studied distance he wears like armor. He's not quiet because he has nothing to say. Enzo keeps to himself because it's become a method of survival.

I take a breath and push on. "Well, perhaps we can go with contact lenses then. Would that be acceptable?"

Enzo gives a begrudging nod. "It lunchtime yet?"

"Yes, let's get something to eat. Then I'll see three clients this afternoon while you work on pronunciation. Tomorrow, after you call Topaz' foster care worker, you can go visit the optometrist."

"Who?"

"The eye doctor."

-->==◎ ◎==<--

Before bed I call Goldie. She answers on the sixth ring and doesn't sound happy. I look at the clock; it's only nine. "Hey, it's me. Did I wake you?"

"No. Andrew's been arguing at me again."

Ah, the boyfriend who, in my opinion, isn't a keeper. "I'm sorry, Goldie. Was it bad?"

I hear a sigh of frustration. "He's so hell-bent on his career, spends next to no time with me…remember when I bought those salsa dance lessons for us to take together and he wouldn't even go once? I had to dance with the instructor!

And then he's surprised when I don't get excited about the idea of marrying him and having his kids…"

I make a sympathetic noise. "Go ahead, vent."

She sighs again. "Thanks, Hess. But there's really nothing more to say. You know the deal, and you'll only tactfully suggest that I break up with him and move on. So let's skip it."

"Well, I have a few things to tell you that will take your mind off it. Ready?"

"Go."

"First, I found out Enzo has a daughter…"

"What? Get out…"

"No, really. Her name is Topaz and she's in foster care and he wants to get her back. Her mother's dead. Can you imagine?"

"Oh my God, Hester. It's like a sub-plot in *Days of Our Lives* or something."

"Also, I went on that double date with my Mum and that Brit, Nigel, asked me to go out with him. I told him I would."

"Wow, that's huge, Hester! It's been months since you had a second date with anyone. Is he fabulously sexy?"

"Don't be silly, he's English. And I'm mostly doing it for Enzo."

There's a moment's pause. "Wait, no comprendo…what the hell does your date have to do with Enzo?"

"Well, Nigel's well spoken, has great manners, and can be an excellent role model for Enzo to imitate. He's never met a real, live Englishman, so it'll give him an image to strive for when we get to teaching him the British accent."

"Hester, I think you might be into this rehabilitation thing a little too much. I don't think it's healthy to go on dates so your student can have a good role model. Can you hear yourself?"

"Alright, I admit it's an unconventional approach to dating. But who knows, maybe Nigel will grow on me in the process. He's not bad, really."

"Okay, what else have you got for me?"

"I found out today that Enzo has bad vision. He needs glasses. That's why he can't read well!"

"Oh, he'd look fab in glasses…maybe something horn-rimmed but super rectangular…"

"Whoa…stop the fashion horse from running away with this. He won't wear glasses. Apparently, in his culture they can make you a target for violence."

"Okay, so…contacts?"

"Yes. Tomorrow. When he can see to read better, I'll start him on books about elocution and the classics as well…"

She's laughing. "Poor Enzo! Maybe he was better off blind."

"Don't be ignorant. He needs more than just the ability to speak properly. We've got to give him an abbreviated education as well."

"Whatever you say, professor…oh, have you decided what color dress you're wearing to Jimmy's wedding? I don't want us to clash."

"Honestly, I haven't even thought about it. I'll have to get back to you on that."

"Okay, but don't forget. Jimmy always notices what we wear. I want us to look fabulous for him." She sighs yet again, and then I hear a partially stifled yawn.

"I promise to get on it. But now I've got some work to finish and then I'm off to bed. Good night, Goldie."

"Yeah, same here. Talk to you tomorrow."

"Hey, I'm sorry about Andrew. Maybe he'll change."

"He won't change. But thanks."

ENZO

Monday, March 24th

I shouldn't have never told Hester about Topaz. After I get back from that eye doc she sent me to, she waitin' for me with lunch all ready – salads – and she's lookin' all hopeful at me, like I'ma pick up the phone and call right now before we eat.

"So, did you have any trouble with Doctor Mayer?"

"Nah. He gave me an exam and ordered the contacts. Said they'll mail 'em to me right here. He say…said he couldn't believe I've been walking around without being able to see."

Hester shakes her head, like 'no kidding.' "But he's got you fitted and soon it won't be a problem anymore. And you're going to call the case worker after lunch?"

What is she, my Mama? I nod and start eatin'. At least she put some grilled chicken in all this green stuff.

"Alright. I have appointments back to back after lunch, and then we'll have a session on speech rhythm and intonation. You still remember the speech you memorized last week?"

I nod again.

"Enzo, if I were a blind person, I'd never know if you were replying to what I've asked or not. Please use your words."

"Yes, I remember the speech."

"Good, we'll use that, and I can correct you as you go. I'll come get you after my four o' clock leaves."

I nod. Then, when she's still staring at me, I say, "Okay…I'll be working on that DVD you gave me about pronunciation."

"Excellent. Make sure you balance a penny on your nose when you do the verbal response section. It seems silly, but it makes you really think about what you're doing with your lower jaw. You still have the one you used last week?"

I have to 'use my words' again. "Yes, I got the penny."

I guess she's run outta things to say, because she's quiet while we finish lunch. Salad tastes better when you ain't got no one talkin' at you non-stop.

-→-▬-◉ ◉-▬-←-

Four o' clock rolls round, and two minutes later, she's calling me into the studio. I tuck the penny into my pocket, grab a smoothie, and go in.

She's waitin' for me, whacking stick in hand. After I sit down she pulls her narrow hover-chair right up to my knees and looks at me like, 'let's hear it.' I pull the stupid-ass speech up on the screen of my mind and start talkin'.

"I was going to the post office to buy a little stamp for the envelope I'm sending." This shit is so dumb it's hard to say without feeling like a first-rate loser. "I'm sending the envelope to an acquaintance I know in Argentina, a region of South America not known for fine wine." Did she write this shit herself? "I prefer fine wine from France, Italy, or Spain. I'll be goin'...."

She taps my shoulder with her stupid whacking stick. I fix it. "I'll be go*ing* to Italy next Autumn and will visit another dear friend of mine named Arthur Atholson."

She reaches out and taps my chin with her finger. "Make sure your tongue makes it all the way between your teeth on the 'th' sound. It's sounding rather like an 'f'. Not 'A*f*olson', but 'A*th*olson'." Her tongue is between her teeth demonstratin' it like I don't understand.

"A*th*olson." I say it so hard drops of spit nearly spray out. "Ar*th*ur A*th*olson." She nods so I keep going. "He hasn't lived in Italy for long, and I've been wantin'..." I see her stick comin', and I can't help what I do next.

HESTER

His hand reaches out and grabs the end of my stick before it makes contact with his shoulder. Twists it out of my grasp.

He is looking at me like he wants to get up and hit something with it, maybe me. "Don't do that no more."

His tone is quiet, but the nearly palpable tension emanating from his body says what it doesn't. A vision of the harm he could do to me if he decided to flashes through my mind. But he isn't threatening me. He lays the stick on the floor beyond my reach and unexpectedly takes up where he left off in the speech.

"I've been wan*ting* to visit Arthur for some time..."

"Enzo, why have you taken my stick?"

"I don't like being whacked."

"It's just a tap, to remind you of your mistake without interrupting you."

"Find another way to 'remind' me of my mistake. You ain't...aren't using that stick on me anymore. And I hate this speech. It's stupid. Makes me feel like a stupid mothafucka."

I am speechless. He is calm, but the look he's giving me is deadly serious. Gathering my wits, I stare straight back at him. "I'll clap my hands instead of using the stick. If you hate the speech, we won't use it again. And it's 'Mot*her* Fuck*er*.'"

We stare at each other in silence for a moment, the tension that's built up looming between us. Then his veneer of deadly seriousness cracks, and he lets out a snort of laughter. The snort busts into a true guffaw. "Girl, I can't believe you just said motherfucker!"

I feel my face turn red, but I can't help laughing at myself. He's right, that was the first time those words ever crossed my lips in that order. "Well, if you're going to say it, you might as well pronounce it correctly."

Enzo allows himself another amused shake of the head, and then his mirth dies.

"What's wrong, Enzo?"

"Noth*ing*." He won't look at me.

"Enzo did you...did you call the case worker?"

"No."

"Why not?"

"Shit, I don't know." He exhales heavily, leans his elbows on his knees.

Something in me cautions to keep my mouth shut. So, I sit quietly, inches from the man, silently willing him to say more.

The minutes pass. Enzo rubs his face with his hands and stares at the floor. When he sits up and looks at me, his eyes are watery. "Maybe Topaz is better off with that family they put her in."

"Oh, Enzo..."

"Maybe she'll have a happier life, you know? With two parents and lotsa toys and shit." He spreads out his arms in a gesture of emptiness. "I got nothing to give her."

I can't keep silent now. "You have *everything* to give her. You are her *father*. No one can love her like you can." He shakes his head and averts his eyes. "You've got to give yourself time. You've just gotten out of jail...you need time to get back on your feet again. You've provided for Topaz in the past, and you'll do it again in the future. In the meantime, you've got to get the ball rolling. You've got to file whatever forms are needed to start the process of getting her back. Jump through whatever hoops are necessary to show them you can be a good father to her again."

Enzo leans back in his chair and presses the heels of his hands to his eyes. A small tear squeezes out and rolls a few inches before he wipes it away. Then he sits up straighter, nods.

"Why don't we call it a day, Enzo."

He shakes his head. "No. Let's keep going, but not with that stupid speech. You write that shit yourself?"

I laugh. "As a matter of fact, I did. It features all the words that contain the sounds and cadences you need to practice."

"Well, it's worse than bad. So, here's what we gonna…we're going to do. You give me a list of them words that have all the right sounds, and I'll write a speech that don't make me feel like the dumbest jackass on earth…okay?"

I smile. "Sounds good to me…and Enzo?"

His voice goes quiet. "I know. I'll call in the morning. You got my word on it."

ENZO

Tuesday, March 25th

Hester's gone off to 'work on-set' wit' some actor today, so I got the place to myself. I been sitting on the sofa with the phone in one hand and the number of Topaz' case worker in the other for 'bout fifteen minutes. I'm thinkin' about how hard it's gonna be to get a job with that conviction on my record. How am I s'posed to support my girl when I get her back? Hester says all this studyin' to talk better's gonna pay off and win me a good job. I sure hope she's right.

I dial the number. When it starts ringin' I get them butterflies in my stomach and have to stand up and walk around to shake it off.

After about a million rings, some lady answers, and she puts me on hold right away. I'm waitin' and thinking about Topaz and how she looked at me last time I seen her. She can give a look that says 'trust' and throw her skinny little arms around my neck like I'ma be able to protect her forever. I wonder when I see her again will she ever give me that look like she used to. Now I been gone from her life over a year. I hope them people she livin' with read her all them letters I sent. I drew pictures in there too, even on the envelope. Me and her together, holdin' hands. Girlie stuff I know she likes. Princesses an' unicorns an' shit like that.

I wonder does she know what I done that got me put away? Even if somebody told her, would she understand? I wish there was some way I could make sure she'd never find out, man.

Then the lady come back off hold and ask if she can help me. I put on my best Standard American English voice and ask about what I can do to get Topaz back. That lady look me up on her computer and tell me I got a long road. I got to fill out a form, which she say is online. She say I got a right to a free lawyer, and that lawyer has got to set up a review hearing. I got to find a safe place to live and a job to prove I can be a fit parent. Then she tell me the best part; she can set up a visitation schedule so I can see Topaz, do I want her to do that? YES!!

I ask the lady if Topaz is in a good home. If she happy. Does she have good foster parents. Lady tells me she can't say anything about all that but when I visit I'll see the foster home and meet them people who been takin' care of her. I ask how soon we can start the visiting, and she say she'll get on it and let me know. Do I have a phone number where I can be contacted? I give her Hester's digits.

When I get off the phone, I got hope and excitement all in my chest. I can't even do the mirror exercises Hester told me to do. I gotta lift something. I been doing push-ups and swimming some, but I ain't lifted since I got out. Hester ain't got no barbells or nothing, but there's got to be something around that's heavy enough to do the job. I go out by the pool and start some push-ups while I think. It's middle of the day hot so I pull off my shirt and go over under the porch shade. I'm looking around when my eyes settle on the chair I like to sit in after swimmin'. It's got a wood frame, solid. Looks to be about fifty pounds. I throw the cushions off and slide under it. Feels a little strange to be liftin' a chair at first, but then I fall into a rhythm, and fifty pounds makes a decent warm-up weight.

HESTER

When I pull into my driveway after three hours of on-set coaching with Brent, the first thing I see is that Enzo has re-arranged my patio furniture. I also see a teak chair being raised and lowered as though on a pulley. It is balanced on top of a second teak chair, cushions removed, which is rising and lowering in conjunction with the top chair. My matching teak sofa with its overstuffed, all-weather-upholstered cushions conceals the source of the lifting. What is Enzo up to?

When I walk past the pool and peer around the sofa I see two ridiculously fit tan legs in shorts, a naked torso of bulging muscles, and the very red face of Enzo as he's bench-lifting my teak lounge chairs with powerful but controlled upward thrusts.

"Enzo, have you thought about how much it's going to hurt if that upper chair comes unbalanced and falls on your legs?"

With a grunt of effort Enzo finishes a repetition and lowers the chairs all the way to the ground. "I got it balanced just right." He slides out from under the two chairs and grins at me. "You worried about me?"

"Well, if you get crippled by a blow from my chair, it makes me liable doesn't it?"

"If you had some decent weights instead of them sad, pink, ten-pound dumbbell things you got hidden in the laundry room, I wouldn't be liftin' no chairs."

"This is not a gym, Enzo. It's my home. And where else besides the laundry room have you been poking your nose?"

"I was just looking for some more soap when I found them little girlie weights day before yesterday. You ever use them things?"

"'*Those* things'…and yes, I do use them sometimes. When I'm watching television."

"Well, they ain't…they're not going to do you any good. You need heavier weights. Shoot, if this was my house I'd turn this porch here into a workout zone. Get a rack of decent weights, a bench, chin-up bar, punching bag…"

I laugh at the thought of all that macho equipment on my cabana porch. "Is that all?"

"And a jump rope. It'd be a kickin' home gym. Man; that would be all I'd ever need."

The excitement of his vision shows on his face; his inner kid shining through.

"Really? A home gym is all you need to be happy?"

"In a perfect world it wouldn't be no home gym. It'd be my own gym where I'd train people, make 'em stronger. I done a lot of it when I was in jail, man. I helped lots of guys bulk up good and learn how to do it without getting hurt. Some guys, they lift too fast, too soon. End up busting something and havin' to stop. You got to do it smart, gradual."

"Sounds like you have some experience."

He manages to swagger without taking a single step. "I been liftin' since I was a kid. Learned how to do it right and how to do it wrong. I worked at a gym once."

Our conversation from the swimming disaster pops into my mind. "Yes, I remember you mentioning that. Before or after the restaurant job?"

"After. I used to think maybe one day I'd start up my own gym."

"Why not? That sounds like an excellent goal to me. You certainly look like a walking advertisement for a gym."

He looks down and waves his hand at me. "Nah. Anyway, I got too much to think on to dream about some gym that'll prob'ly never happen."

I remember the phone call he promised to make. "Did you call the case worker?"

He nods. I'm not sure from his expression whether it was a good phone call or a bad one. Then he kind of ducks his head and rubs his scruffy chin, and when he looks up again he's trying not to smile and failing miserably.

"I don't know when, but soon I'm gonna...going to get to see my Topaz."

ENZO

Hester's happy look is all careful, and I know she can see that there's more than just the good news about the visits. "I got to fill out a form, get a lawyer to arrange a hearing, and I need a job and a home to prove I'm fit to parent before they'll return custody to me."

"Seriously? She's your daughter!"

"I know it."

I see her brain start workin'. She gets that look like when she thinks up something new for me to work on. "Enzo...I think I know how we can make it look like you have a job. And I'm pretty sure you can claim the cabana as your rented apartment."

She know I can't pay her nothing, so I stay quiet.

"It would be an arrangement on top of the arrangement we already have. You can work as a personal trainer. I know at least a dozen lawyers, and one of them can draw up a lease for the cabana so it looks perfectly legal. Are you on parole?"

"No, I done served my time. Just need to prove I can support my baby girl."

"Well, to get a legal document drawn up you'll need proof of who you are. Do you have a valid photo ID? Driver's license, passport, something like that?"

"I got a social security number…and a mug shot."

Her face goes all horrified. "Oh no, you'll need something else. I think a passport will be easiest at this point. You can apply for it at the post office. Make sure you get the 'express' option; I'll pay. Everyone should have a passport for heaven's sake."

I wanna let out a big fat laugh at that, but I keep it together. "Who am I gonna personally train?"

"Me, for a start. We'll put up an advertisement at the bagel shop, they have a bulletin board where people can post their details. Maybe register you on Craig's List in the personal services column…and we can purchase some of that equipment you were talking about."

"Miz Hastings, you can't do all that. You already pay for my food and my contacts, everything. I ain't got no way to pay you back."

"Yes, you do. You can work your hardest and make your social rehabilitation a success. And when you get some real fitness clients, you can start paying rent. The gym equipment will be mine, and when you get enough saved up and move on with your life, you can buy it and take it with you. That gym you dream about might just become a reality, Enzo. You'd have to start small and perhaps take a class on managing your own business, but if you're good at it…"

I look at Hester sideways, and I can't believe her face is serious. "You really do all that for me?"

"Well, it would be for me, too. Do you think I'm going to pay for my personal training sessions?"

She's got her hands all on her hips like she drives a hard bargain. But I got to think on all this. It's like I'm in a whole 'nother universe from where I was when Goldie jumped me outside the jail. So, I smile at her, but not like I just won the lottery or nothing. Her eyes have gone all narrow, and I can see she's studying me like I'm some kind of wildlife.

HESTER

It all makes sense, so I'm not sure why Enzo's giving me that guarded look. It's true that it seems like he's getting the better part of the deal or maybe even all of the deal. But none of it will cause me any extra grief at all. And I can get fit into the bargain.

Enzo's enthusiasm about bench pressing my furniture appears to have run its course, and I'm sure the difficulty about getting his daughter back is weighing on his mind. Which reminds me of my problem with Jessica.

"Well, just think about it as an option, and we can talk about it more later, alright?"

Enzo nods and turns to unstack the chairs. He shoves the furniture back into place as I make my way toward to house. As usual, I'm proving myself to be better at fixing other people's problems than my own. Easy enough to buy exercise equipment and have some legal papers drawn up. But how do I win my time with Jessica back?

->==() ()==<-

I'm chopping onions to start the chili I have planned for dinner when Enzo shows up to help. I know he hasn't finished all the elocution exercises I gave him to complete, but I've decided to cut him some slack on that count for today. He can make it up tomorrow.

I point to the recipes I have set out side-by-side on the counter. "Chili and cornbread. Can you grab the chilies from the fridge and start on those?"

Enzo retrieves a cutting board from the cabinet beside the sink and fetches the chilies. We are quiet as I pour oil into the pot to heat and he scrapes seeds from the chilies and dices them. It's the second evening we've prepared dinner together, and so far I've yet to get him really talking, which is sort of the whole point. He can't learn as much if I'm just talking at him. Perhaps I should invite Goldie or Mum around for tomorrow night so he'll have a harder time avoiding conversation.

He showed such enthusiasm earlier when we talked about exercise that I decide to try a similar topic. "Do you follow any sports?"

Enzo shrugs as he throws the chilies in on top of the onions I've just added. I stir the pot and the savory aroma wafts upwards.

"Football?" This elicits a shake of the head. "Ever play soccer perhaps?"

"In school at gym. But we never had money for me and Ricky to play the rec leagues."

"I bet you'd have been good at it."

Enzo is opening a package of ground beef. It is clear that he's not going to respond.

"You know, I'm not making conversation to torture you, Enzo. And I'm not doing it to try and turn us into best buddies. It's part of your training to learn how to make small talk. It's something you'll need to know how to do when you go to parties and meet people you don't know. People who might be interesting or be able to offer you job opportunities. So can you please make an effort to meet me halfway?"

Enzo dumps the brick of ground meat into the pot, and I start to break it up with my wooden spoon.

He clears his throat. "I used to shoot hoops on the court down the street from my Grandparents' house when I lived with them."

"There we are…not so hard to hold up your side of the conversation is it?"

"But people I meet at these parties you keep talking 'bout aren't going to want to talk on playing basketball. They gonna want to talk 'bout stuff like the stock market and politics and fine wines and shit. I don't know nothing 'bout any of that."

I hand him a can opener so he can add the crushed tomatoes when the meat gets brown. "Fair enough. You're worried people will talk about things you don't know. But here's the beauty of mastering small talk…when you get good at it, you become adept at controlling the conversational subject. When I started the conversation we just had about sports I could have chosen any topic. I could have asked what you thought about the Governor's decision to limit export of produce because of the drought we've been having. I could have commented on the latest fashions in canine couture. Because I wanted to draw you out and get you talking, I tried to choose a subject I thought you might be interested in."

I throw the garlic I've chopped into the pot and give it a stir. "Conversation can be powerful. You can use it to make people feel included or stupid. You can use it to one-up an enemy or make your best friend look better in front of a potential employer. I realize that where you grew up intelligent conversation might not have been valued highly. I realize that perhaps saying nothing was a lot safer than expressing your opinion. But in my world, expressing your opinion, hopes, frustration, worry, or affection is second nature. Words are not weakness, Enzo. They can be liberating. Certainly, there are times when it's better to keep one's mouth shut, but I've talked my way into and out of some tricky situations, and I suggest you learn the art of knowing how and when to say the right thing."

"You make it sound like it's so easy, but for me, it's like, I don't know, like an out-of-control feeling when somebody say something that don't make sense to me, and I have to figure out what to say back. Like when the teacher call on you in school, and you don't got the answer."

"Don't *have* the answer." I nod to him to add the cans of tomatoes.

Tomato juice splashes out of the pan when he dumps them in carelessly. "Whateva."

"Enzo. You are not a teenager. You are a grown man. An intelligent, talented, capable man. If you keep hiding what you've got to offer, one thing is certain; no one will ever see it. If you put yourself out there and try, like you've been doing here with me, things you've never dreamed of might be possible. Now please go see if you can find a big can of kidney beans from the pantry. I forgot to get it out earlier."

Chapter 6

ENZO

Saturday, March 29th

FOUR DAYS SINCE I filled out that form and requested a lawyer for the hearing to start getting Topaz back, and I ain't heard nothing from that case worker. Good news is there's a gym outside my front door. Hester had me move the dining table out the way and rearrange the furniture on the porch yesterday before it got delivered. Today, she showed up for breakfast in her workout threads. Tightest clothes I ever seen her in aside from that hot green swimsuit. She look all cute like one a them girls that go jogging around the neighborhood all the time.

Now I got her flat out on the bench with twenty-five pounds on a barbell over her head. She's worked up a good sweat, and now we got to cool her down and stretch.

Her face is all pink. "You weren't joking about those heavier weights. After lifting the big ones this twenty-five pounds feels like nothing...well, almost nothing." She parks the barbell and breathes like she means it.

I don't say nothing, but toss her a towel from the cabana.

"Is it going to be like this every day, Enzo?"

"Nah. No. Some days we'll do cardio, kickboxing, maybe some yoga..." She's staring at me like I got three heads. "Yeah, that's right. I'm from the ghetto, and I know what yoga is. A man can learn all kindsa stuff when he gets put behind bars. There was a Buddhist doin' time for growing weed, and he taught me some power yoga, man."

"I wouldn't have pegged you as a yogi, Enzo."

"I'm not saying I like to do all those pretzel twisties or nothing. But them… those power moves and the stretching do good things for a body."

She wipes off with the towel and sits up slowly. "Oh my God. My biceps are already sore!"

"You was working hard, girl! Now you need to stretch out and cool off." I offer a hand to help pull her up to standing. She takes a wrist grip on me so I wrap my hand around her skinny wrist and raise her up.

"Thank you," she says. Then she puts some distance between us and starts doing a good biceps stretch. I can tell someone's taught her how to do it right.

When I'm putting away the weights she starts talking again. It's like she can't stand being quiet. "We need to get you some more clients…I was thinking about asking Nigel if he'd like to buy some sessions."

"Nigel?"

"Didn't I tell you about him?"

"I don't remember anything about a 'Nigel'."

"Mum set me up with him…we went out for lunch last weekend. Actually, I'm going out with him again tonight."

"What, like on a *date*?"

"Yes…and don't look so shocked. I do like men, you know. Oh, and lucky you – no need to suffer through making dinner with me tonight. Anyhow, Nigel seems nice, and honestly, I was hoping you can spend some time with him also. He has excellent manners and would be someone you could learn from. So I'd like to get…"

"Isn't he gonna think you're a little freaky if you start askin' him to spend time with your human experiment?"

"You are not an 'experiment,' Enzo. And I can explain what a good role model he'll be for you. Anyway, I'll ask him if he's interested in the personal training sessions."

"Only thing he'll want to be training is you, homegirl."

She gives a big sigh. "Why is it that men's minds always go directly there?"

I shrug. Seems pretty clear to me. And that Nigel guy best not be thinkin' all that about this girl unless she wants it.

Her cell phone rings, and she stops stretching to answer. When she looks at the screen her face goes all tight.

HESTER

I take a breath before answering. "Hello?"

"Hey, Hester. Don't be all pissy…I'm calling to apologize."

"Philip, I am never 'pissy', and if you want to apologize, I'm listening. But I hope you've apologized to your daughter, whose fun evening was interrupted by your jealous fit."

"Okay, I admit I was a little bit jealous. But *you* have to admit that it's not acceptable for you to have a man playing in the pool with Jessica without running it by me first."

I point to the house and wave goodbye to Enzo. "I promise you I had no idea it was going to happen until he showed up and Jessica invited him to swim with us. It was a spontaneous thing!"

"And that's when you pick up your phone and call Jessica's Dad to ask if he has a problem with a strange man hanging around with her while she's practically naked."

I take a deep breath and let myself into the cool house. "Philip, you and I both know that Jessica is like a daughter to me. I would never, ever leave her alone with someone else without your permission. I was there the entire time, which, by the way, was only about fifteen minutes. I'm sorry I didn't think to call you when Enzo joined us, but I never had any intention of leaving Jessica unattended for even a second."

"Okay, well, anyway, I'm willing to forgive and forget if you promise, and I mean swear on your mother's life, that it will never happen again. I realize you're like a Mom to Jessica, and I don't want her to lose you completely because I had an overprotective moment. I'll also admit that I was shocked to see you with your uber-ripped new boyfriend. Where the hell did you find him?"

If he only knew! "Honest to God, Philip, he is *not* my boyfriend. He's a client. It's rather a special situation, and I do spend a lot more time with him than

I do with my regular clients, but trust me, there is absolutely nothing going on between me and Enzo."

"If you say so." His voice is dripping with doubt. "Anyway, I've decided I can let you visit with Jessica again, but my stipulation is that you visit her at my house. I'm not ready to go back to every-other-weekend sleepovers for her at your place."

Is he serious? "I think that's a bit unreasonable, Philip. I don't feel comfortable spending long periods of time at your house. And I don't think it's necessary for you to penalize me so drastically for one small transgression."

"It wasn't small to me, Hester. If you want to see Jessica, those are the terms."

"You realize you're holding me hostage here, don't you?"

"Don't be so dramatic! I just feel the need to supervise your visits until I'm certain your lapse of judgment was a one-time thing and Jessica will be safe in your care."

I am so angry I don't trust myself to say anything before mentally counting to ten. "Philip, I think it's despicable of you to use your daughter as an excuse to hold me hostage. If you think you can win me back this way…"

"Win you back?" He laughs. "This isn't a ploy to win you back, Hester. In fact, I'm seriously dating someone now. I can't believe your ego."

Now, I'm really ready to explode. What other reason would he have to force me to spend time at his house in order to see Jessica? "I have to go, Philip. I will consider your terms, but for the record, you are hurting your daughter more than you're hurting me. Good bye."

I press the 'end call' button so hard the phone drops out of my hand. It lands on the rug, unharmed. I wish I could say the same for my heart.

ENZO

When her date comes to pick her up, she plays a trick on him. 'Oh,' she says like she's all surprised. Then she tells him she's got to go make one more phone call, so important that it can't wait…only she forgot about it 'till now. Then she makes him sit down on the leather sofa in the living room, with me. I've got orders to 'make conversation.'

I don't know who Hester done told him I am and why is it I'm here in her house. If it was up to me I'd be liftin' pounds on the porch out back with them new weights. But this here's an 'assignment' she gave me, and I'm stuck. This guy, Nigel, he's some kind of British lawyer or something like that. He got an accent even stronger than Hester's. I'm supposed to be 'controlling the subject of conversation,' but he's already taken over.

"Have you been in the military services at all Enzo?"

"No." I want to add, 'But I spent some time in uniform', but I don't. "Have you?"

"Territorial Army. Not full time. Sort of like weekend warriors, you know. I think your American equivalent is called the National Guard."

I nod, 'cause I know what they do. But I think he expects it's my turn to talk, so I try and change the subject. "Do you live in L.A., or are you just visiting?" I think Hester would like that one.

"I've moved here recently from London. I'm going to try my hand at screen-play writing."

That's actually kinda interesting. "What kind of movies you want to write? Action? Sci-fi?"

"My particular interest right now is a political thriller based on the time right before the Cold War ended. I'm fascinated by the relationship between Gorbachev and Reagan. I'm told there's a real nostalgia for that era now, so I'd like to take my shot at capitalizing on that."

I got nothing to say to that, but Hester says I have to reply to people no matter what they say, so I nod like I agree. "That sounds pretty interesting. I wish you luck, man."

"Thank you." His eyes wander, searching past the kitchen for any sign of his date. Hester ain't back yet, so he's got to keep talking. "And what line of work are you in?"

Hester done prepped me for this. "I'm in personal fitness."

"Ah, yes. I can see you're in quite good shape. I've heard the Californians are very into their exercise fads. What's your thing: kickboxing? Power-yoga?" He smiles like it's funny.

"I ain't into no fad, man. I mean, I've been studying about lifting weights and body building over fifteen years now. In fact, Hester's one of my clients." Hester's my only client, but he don't know that.

"Really? Oh, well, then you spend quite a bit of time together. Tell me, what's your take on Hester? She seems very…efficient."

Efficient? What the hell does he mean by that? "Miz Hast…Hester's a hard working woman. She's really good at her job, and she wants her clients to succeed. You like her, huh?"

I've caught him off guard. It's kinda satisfying to see him fish for an answer. "Well, she's quite attractive. I suppose I've always had a thing for women with ginger hair. And she's very successful in her field."

I nod. "Yeah. And you're right, she's hot. She doesn't wear clothes like she's hot though. She likes that classy cover-up look. I know men would be looking at her more if she wore, like, tighter shirts and maybe some of them leggings like her friend Goldie wears."

Nigel don't like that. "Well, now, I don't think she wants us men to see her every asset, if you know what I mean. She dresses to accentuate her beauty without inviting men to view her as a woman of loose virtue. I like for a woman to leave a little something to the imagination." He winks at me like we understand each other.

Nigel don't even know how some women want men to look at 'em. If he saw half of what I've seen women want he'd get a real education. But I smile and wink back.

Hester told me to study how he sits and his manners and all. Now that I got the conversation under control I pay more attention. Nigel's sitting on the sofa like it's not too comfortable. His hands are folded in his lap. Looks like he's waiting for the nurse to come call his name to see the doctor. I been leaning my elbows on my knees out of habit, I guess. But I sit up and relax back in my chair like I'm waitin' on the doc, too.

He crosses his arms over his chest. "I hope you don't mind my saying, but you're not as young as I thought you would be."

What the hell does that mean? What did Hester tell him about me? "I been around a while. I'm younger than you, though, right?" I smile again, like 'uh-huh.'

Nigel straightens his tie. "Um, I think you've got me there…so are you married? Have a girlfriend?"

"Nah. No. I'm not married. Don't have a girlfriend either. Don't have the time, you know?"

Nigel smiles and nods. "Oh yes. Women do have a way of taking up a man's time. Believe me, I've been married and divorced. Here's some advice; marry a career woman. My first wife was a socialite, no job. Too much time on her hands. Wanted me to be her best friend and go shopping together." He shakes his head to say what a hot mess that was. "Career women don't have the time for that nonsense. They fit you into their schedule, and that's just fine with me."

"So that's what you like best about Hester, huh?"

"Well, she has many fine qualities, but it's up there on the list."

I can hear Hester coming down the hall about to push through the door to the kitchen. So I nod at Nigel like I agree. Then I look square at him and fire one last shot. "She can be a real bitch, though."

Nigel's eyes pop open wide like a freight train's comin' at him. "What?"

Hester arrives in the kitchen, all smiles. "Yeah." I shrug. "Just sayin'."

Nigel stands when Hester clickety clacks into the living room on her high heels, and so do I. Nigel's still got a funny look on his face, but Hester don't notice. She makes a fuss about how she's sorry to keep him waiting and then they tell me 'goodbye!' and leave me to the pronunciation DVD I'm supposed to finish watching. The one that makes me repeat after clone-Hester the most. Where did I leave that son-of-a-bitch penny?

HESTER

Monday, March 31ˢᵗ

I'm exhausted. Coaching Enzo means I have virtually no down-time. The weekend came and went in a flurry of phone calls with Jessica, lessons with Enzo, needy clients, and meals spent trying to drag decent conversation out of a reluctant participant. There were also two harsh sessions with my new personal trainer during which he seemed to be attempting to exact revenge on me for all the times I've corrected him with my stick or made him balance a penny on his nose. My body feels as though it's been tackled repeatedly by the 49ers defensive line.

But today is a blessed relief because Enzo has declared that my muscles need a 'resting day.' Hallelujah.

I am busy with back-to-back clients all day, and when I finish at five o'clock, Nigel stops by for his first training session with Enzo.

He's come to the front door again, for which I am grateful because it maintains a level of formality in our relationship. Thank heaven he isn't one of those men who expect instant intimacy.

"Hello, Hester! So lovely to see you again." He gives me a dry peck on each cheek. Nigel is wearing tennis whites, and I wonder what kind of exercise he is anticipating.

"Lovely to see you as well, Nigel. I hope you've had a restful weekend?"

"Indeed. In fact," he leans forward conspiratorially, "I had a fantastic date Saturday night."

"Oh, well…" I know I should be playful and flirt back, but the words don't come. "It was a nice restaurant, wasn't it?" Which is perfectly true, if not playful. The meal was quite tasty.

"I hope we can do it again soon?" His eyebrows are raised, and he looks as though he wants to slide an arm around my shoulder.

I nod and lead him through the yellow door into the kitchen. "Enzo's just out the back. The cabana porch is his gym. He's, um, renting the space from me for now."

Nigel glances out into the yard and takes a step closer to me. "You really are quite an idealist, helping this fellow out." A look of concern wrinkles his brow. "I only hope you're not too trusting with him. It seems to me that Enzo has a bit of an edge to him."

"Well, he is still rough around the edges if that's what you mean." I lower my voice. "As you might imagine, he's endured quite a few personal tragedies. But I've spent enough time with him to be convinced that, at heart, he's an honest person."

Nigel peers at me questioningly, then pats me awkwardly on the shoulder. "I truly hope you're right, Hester."

I look at my watch, it is five minutes past five. "I don't want to waste your workout time, Nigel. Let's get you over to Enzo so you can begin your training."

I open the glass slider and click across the pavement in my low heels. Nigel follows me like a fuzzy duckling. On the porch, Enzo is standing with his back to us, the house phone in his right hand. When he turns he's wearing an enormous grin.

"Miz Hastings; that lady just called with a date for The Visit. Next week, Thursday."

"Oh, Enzo!" I can't help it, I give him a celebratory hug. "That's wonderful!"

Nigel stands seven paces away, watching us like a startled deer trying to decide if it's better to run or hold its ground.

"Enzo has just received some fabulous news," I explain breathlessly. Nigel now appears to be taking measure of my muscle-shirt clad pupil carefully.

"How delightful. Congratulations, Enzo." Then he gestures to the weight bench. "Shall we begin here?"

⋆⟞⊚ ⊚⟝⋆

From the kitchen table, I can keep tabs on Nigel and Enzo while I organize my calendar for the coming week. Each time I look up, they have moved on to another exercise. Right now, Enzo is leading Nigel in some sort of boxing exercise with the punching bag. Though the Englishman looks a trifle awkward wearing boxing gloves, he's not holding back.

He's a good sport, Nigel. Didn't even blink when I suggested he buy a set of training sessions with Enzo. I hope he understood that I wasn't suggesting he needs to get more fit, though he is slightly soft in the stomach, although in a very dignified sort of way. He has fair skin like me, and I can see that his face is already quite pink from the exertion of lifting weights and the light cardio workout Enzo is leading him through.

I suppose he will ask me out again. And I'll go. He is quite a decent fellow, and it will be helpful for Enzo to have a role model when we begin the British accent phase of training. I tap my chin absently with the end of my pencil. Which means I'll need to keep dating him for at least another month or so. Perhaps longer. Well, he's a good conversationalist, Mum likes him, and he seems to get on well with Enzo. I just hope he's prepared to move slowly; I confess I don't have any keen attraction to him physically. He's handsome enough though, so I'm sure that part will develop as I get to know him. I haven't uncovered any objectionable qualities as yet, so there's no reason not to accept another date when he asks.

Hmmm. A thought I've been pushing from my mind since Enzo arrived suddenly jumps front and center. I've never exactly outlined the fact that I'm planning to teach him an English accent. Well, not to him anyway. We didn't draw up a contract, and I'm not entirely certain what his expectations are.

I suppose I've assumed that because he's an unemployed ex-convict he'll just stick around and absorb all the teaching I see fit to administer. Is that terribly presumptuous of me? But then I am supplying free room and board. Plus now the exercise equipment. Does doing charitable work for someone mean you have a de-facto right to expect them to complete an undefined set of requirements in return?

Oh dear. I don't think it does.

Chapter 7

ENZO

Thursday, April 3rd

TOPAZ' JADE TIGER is sitting on the sink countertop watching me while I change my shirt in front of the long mirror in the shower room of the cabana. I tried on three shirts so far. I'm not sure if I should, like, dress to impress the foster parents so they give a good report to the case worker, or dress to make Topaz happy. When I usta let her choose what I wear, she always picked out the same color: red. Goldie done hooked me up with some dope threads, but she only got me one red shirt. And it ain't got no sleeves. I've got it on, and I'm looking for something with buttons to wear overtop. I don't want to wear no black, 'cause it seems kinda angry. Green's not gonna work; it ain't Christmas. I put on white, but somehow that seems like I'm tryin' too hard.

In the end I go with gray. Short sleeves with a collar and enough buttons left undone so the red tank is still there for Topaz. And the jeans Goldie told me to wear when I want to make a 'good casual first impression.'

Next, I try and tame all this hair. It's longer than I ever worn it before. Comes down over the collar. I slick the sides and front back best I can with water, but I know when it dries it won't stay there. If I had a razor, I'd shave. But Goldie ain't bought me one. So I just smooth down the beard with water and stand in front of the mirror to see what kind of Daddy my baby girl is gonna see.

I look real different from last time I seen her. Different clothes, a beard I ain't had before, hair all shaggy now when before I always kept it short or shaved.

Damn. Is she even gonna know it's me? What if she cries 'cause I don't look like Daddy? What if she don't wanna talk with me?

Shit.

I slip the little jade tiger into my pocket and leave the cabana. It's bright outside. I look at the watch Goldie bought me. Four thirty-six. I got to leave here by five if I wanna make it on time.

In Hester's kitchen I drink a smoothie. I don't think I'll be home in time for dinner, so I take out a pack of turkey sandwich meat and start eating straight out of the box. Hester walks in right when I'm chewin'.

"Hey," she says, all surprised to see me stuffing my face with turkey meat straight out of the box. The fridge is still open behind me. I reach back with my heel and push it closed.

She's looking at her watch. "Isn't it time for you to be going?"

I nod, 'cause my mouth is full and she's told me not to talk when there's food in my mouth. Like seventeen times.

I see her eyes rating how I'm dressed. "You look nice."

I finish chewing and swallow. "You sure it's okay? 'Cause I still got a few minutes to change. I wore this red shirt here 'cause Topaz loves red. But I don't think it looks too great 'cause normally I'd just wear it for liftin'…"

"It's fine, Enzo. You look very presentable." She's smiling like I said something funny.

"What? Do I got meat in my beard?" I brush at it with my fingers, just in case.

"No, no. You're fine. I just think it's sweet that you want to put your best foot forward for your little girl."

I put the lid on the turkey box. "Yeah, well…what if she don't recognize it's me?"

"Do you look that different?"

"Pretty different, yeah." I think about the me I was over a year ago. I don't just look different.

"Well, I don't know Topaz…but it seems to me she'll know it's you. And even though it might take her a moment to adjust to how you look now, she's going to be too happy about seeing her Daddy to care what you look like."

HESTER

It's still weird to think of Enzo as a father. I'm just now starting to get over my habit of viewing him as a teenager. Even though secretly I wish I could be a fly on the wall when he is reunited with Topaz, his next words catch me completely off guard.

"Miz Hastings…you don't wanna…would you have time to come with me?" He's looking at the box of turkey cold cuts he's still holding like it's the most interesting thing he's ever seen.

My hesitation surprises me. I'm burning with curiosity about his daughter, with whom she's living, and what kind of relationship they have. Is it wise to allow myself to be drawn in this deep? I'm already invested in his new job, providing the equipment and recruiting clients for him. Forget 'wise', is it *healthy* to get pulled in to this degree?

"Never mind…forget I asked." Enzo is putting what's left of the turkey back in the fridge.

I sigh. "Oh Enzo, I wasn't not answering because I don't want to go. I just didn't expect you to ask." I suppose I even feel a bit honored that he's asked. "I'd be happy to come with you. I was planning to offer you a ride anyway."

His eyebrows go up as if to say, 'really?' He's always so surprised when people do nice things for him. Seems instinctively distrustful of kind offers. It makes me feel rather sad.

He's looking anxious, waiting to see if I'm serious about coming along. "Just let me throw on a fresh shirt and run a comb through my hair. I'll meet you by the car in a few minutes."

→━◉ ◉━←

The address Enzo hands me is in Bellflower. At first glance I think it will take less time to get there by car than what Enzo has allotted via public transportation. But then I look at the clock on my dashboard and realize we'll be crawling in rush-hour traffic a good portion of the way.

When we pull up on Vista Street in Bellflower, I find a parking spot right beside the apartment complex listed as the address. Villa La Pueblo is lush with foliage; shrubs, flowers, palm trees, and magnolias abound. A crystal blue pool surrounded by aluminum-frame lounge chairs is located in the central courtyard onto which all the rental units open. Three teenagers are splashing around in it noisily. A lone adult, perhaps the teens' father, reclines in a lounger, soaking up sun.

The complex is two stories high, and we walk up a set of stairs by the pool to get to the second level. The place reminds me of a well-maintained motel. By the way Enzo's head is swiveling to take in every detail with appreciative eyes, I'm guessing he's never lived anywhere this pleasant.

Topaz' foster family resides in apartment 12-B. We move along the covered walkway overlooking the pool, counting up as we pass doors. At number nine Enzo stops cold.

I turn to see him observing the teenagers in the pool. "Enzo? She's in number *twelve*...it's just ahead."

When he looks at me, I see the uncertainty in his eyes even before he speaks. "Maybe she's better off here."

"Enzo." I backtrack to where he stands, keeping my voice low. "She's better off with her father."

"You don't know that. I can't give her none a' this." He spreads his hands, looking around as though we're standing amidst Beverly Hills mansions. "I'm gonna drag her down. I don't want to be the one who does that."

I take a step closer and look straight up into his downturned face. "Listen to me. You are going to be able to provide everything your girl needs. You think if you leave her here this family will adopt her and she'll be so happy for the rest of her life?" I shake my head. "Not likely. Even if you relinquished your rights to her, and this family did adopt Topaz, she'd have the pain of knowing you abandoned her for the whole rest of her life. Imagine your daughter as a grown woman wondering why you never came back for her. Is that the life you want for her?"

Enzo shakes his head. "I want her to have opportunity, like I never did. I want her to finish school, go to college, have a chance to be somebody."

I place my finger in the middle of his chest, on the shirt he wore because his daughter likes red. "You are the only one who can make sure she gets those things." I search his eyes with mine, summoning that inner strength I know he has.

He nods. Takes another look at the shimmering pool in the courtyard. Then he straightens up, puts on his street attitude, and brushes past me as though I'm the one with second thoughts. "Hell, this place ain't so nice...I got a private pool right outside *my* front door."

That's the Enzo who's going to get his daughter back and make a good life for her. I watch him move on past doors ten and eleven to his target. He's ratcheted his natural swagger up about five notches.

A woman in her late forties opens the door to Enzo's confident knock. She is white, which I can see takes Enzo by surprise. Instead of inviting us in, she slips out of the apartment and holds the door closed behind her as though we might try to bust past.

She extends her right hand to Enzo. "You must be Mr. Diaz...thank you for coming." They shake hands while Enzo tries to peer past her. "My name is Martha. I didn't tell Topaz you were coming because, unfortunately, sometimes parents don't show up for their scheduled visits, and it breaks my heart to see the children so disappointed. My husband has taken our two other foster girls to the playground, and Topaz was a little miffed to be left behind with me. She's calmed down, but I wanted to tell you all this before you see her."

We nod. I extend my hand to her. "I'm Hester. I'm a friend of Enzo's."

Martha looks me over and shakes my hand, a curious expression on her face. "Nice to meet you." She turns back to Enzo. "Are you ready to go in?"

Enzo takes a breath and smiles his slow smile. His eagerness to get through that door is palpable.

Martha lets us in. The apartment smells like alphabet soup — the canned kind Jessica likes. Topaz is sitting at a round dinner table next to the kitchenette. She holds a doll in her lap and is busily brushing its dark hair. The room is large, doubling as living room and dining area. It is comfortable and well-maintained. This is a home with order to it.

Martha goes to Topaz and kneels next to her. The child doesn't stop her energetic brushing. Martha places a hand on her shoulder. "Topaz, there's someone here to see you."

Topaz looks up at Martha, who turns to look at us. The child's gaze follows, and I see Enzo's eyes peering out from a small, caramel-colored face. Her hair is wavier than her father's, but is black and long, plaited neatly into two braids.

There is a moment of stillness in which we are all frozen. I am holding my breath as Topaz looks first at me, and then at her father.

Eyes locked on her Daddy's face, Topaz carefully places the doll on the table. Pink plastic doll brush still in hand, Topaz slides from her seat and moves slowly past Martha. Her gaze shifts to me as the distance closes, examining me head to toe. Then she stops three feet in front of Enzo and swivels her eyes back to his face.

He slowly lowers himself into a kneeling position in front of her as her eyes bore into him like lasers. In his expression is an emotion I've never seen there before. Pure love. When he speaks, his voice is soft. "Hi, baby."

Topaz regards him for a few long seconds with a maturity beyond her years. Then she plants her fists on her tiny hips and cocks her head suspiciously. "Where you been, Daddy?"

Though her attitude leaves me far from certain she's ready for hugs, Enzo offers her no excuses, makes no apologies. He simply opens his arms to her in reply.

In a split second a grin sprouts on her face and she jumps to throw her skinny arms around his neck, pressing her cheek to his. As Enzo embraces his daughter, both sets of eyes are squeezed closed in joy.

ENZO

I been dreamin' about this moment for three hundred and seventy-two days. I got my girl in my arms, and now I know everything is gonna work out somehow. I'm gonna make it work out. Wish I could pick her up and walk straight outta here with her. That ain't how it works, but I don't ever want to have her living anywhere but with me again.

Topaz lets me hold her for about five minutes, and I'd go longer 'cept she pulls away and runs to get her doll. Martha hands it to her, and she runs back.

"Daddy, this is Cocoa. She has two outfits I can put her in, and look." She holds the doll up next to herself. "She looks just like me!"

I reach out, and she hands me the doll. Its hair is wild from all the brushing. "She's beautiful, just like you." That makes Topaz smile. I can't believe I haven't seen that smile, that face in over a year. Not even a picture. Next time I get a picture of her I'm keeping it in my pocket all the time. She looks older, and she's got her hair done different. Before she had all them braids Lola used to make her sit for while she weaved 'em in. It doesn't look like she's lost no teeth yet, which makes me think I got a shot at playin' tooth fairy.

"Daddy, that lady over there is Martha. She got two other girls here 'sides me. They're littler than me so I have to help get 'em dressed an' all." She turns to Martha. "How come you didn't tell me my Daddy was comin'?"

"I wanted it to be a special surprise, Topaz."

My girl throws her arms around me again. Fine with me. Then she runs over to Martha. "I know you tole me he can't take me back first thing. But when can he, Martha?" She looks back at me, her eyes all big. "Daddy, when can you take me back?"

"Baby girl, I'm gonna take you back as soon as I can. I'm workin' on it hard as I can, okay?"

She trails back over to me, staring at Hester on the way. "Who's that lady?"

"That's Miz Hastings. She's helpin' me learn stuff so I can get you back faster."

Hester bends down and offers a hand to my daughter. "Hi, Topaz. It's a pleasure to finally meet you."

I have to lift Topaz' hand up to shake Hester's. "Daddy, how come she sounds funny?"

"She comes from another country, baby girl. But she's nice."

"I like her even if she does talk funny. Miz Hastings?"

Hester leans forward like she's about to hear the secrets of the universe. "Yes, Topaz?"

"You help my Daddy real good so he can take me back fast, okay?"

Chapter 8

HESTER

Wednesday, April 9th

"HESTER, HE'S READY." Goldie has just returned from the salon with Enzo and is standing next to the fridge with one hand on her hip and the other holding a bottle of sparkling water.

I look through the glass slider out toward the cabana. They're so late getting back the darkness of night is falling. "Where is he?"

"In the shower. He said his neck was itchy and he needed to wash the hairs off."

"Oh. You left the beard, right?"

"Of course. He needs to remain unfinished until the big reveal. But Giovanni shaped it and tamed all that shaggy black hair. Now he looks like an ad for some kind of aftershave."

I try to imagine an aftershave advertisement and come up empty. "Is that a good thing?"

Goldie attempts to finish a swig of water while nodding violently. The result is a trail of water down her shirtfront. "Hell yes. If I was single and saw him in a club, I'd want to dance with him."

"And you really think he's ready?"

"Yeah, why not? He's got the American English down, and his manners are all polished up. We can't wait forever to unleash him on a high class event."

I hesitate, knowing that as soon as the next words are out of my mouth Goldie will jump all over them, and there'll be no going back. "I was tentatively thinking of taking him to Jimmy's wedding."

Goldie's eyes widen in excitement. "That's perfect, Hess! We'll both be there, it's up north, no one from L.A. will be there...except us, of course. Low key, small, yet high class." Goldie gives a nod of approval. "He'll be your 'date'?"

"I can't think of any other guise under which to bring him. Besides, I have no one else to bring anyway."

"What about that Brit, what's his name?"

"Nigel."

"Yeah, that's the one. How's that going?"

"I'm not ready to bring him as my date to an out-of-town wedding, but he's nice enough. He's been a help in role modeling good manners for Enzo. Impeccable grooming. And he's a paying client for Enzo's personal training enterprise."

"Well, I'm just glad you're dating again. It's healthy, you know?"

"I suppose." A sigh escapes my lips. "But I'm not getting into anything serious, I can promise you that."

Goldie looks past me and sets her water down on the counter. "Okay, here he comes. Get ready." She takes a deep breath, and her face takes on the expression of an artist pleased with her latest effort. "But don't make a big deal over him. I think he feels self-conscious..."

I hear the glass slider open and turn in time to see the back of Enzo's head as he closes the door behind him. From behind his hair looks sleek and shiny, still wet from his shower. It's been buzzed neatly along his natural hairline. Then he turns to find us staring at him.

"Oh my." I don't mean to say it but Goldie was right. He does look like an ad for aftershave. His beard has been trimmed close, shaped to accentuate his chiseled jawline. The moustache part has been clipped neatly to outline his lips, which now vie with his unusual eyes as the focal point of his face. His hair is cut short on the sides and left longer on top, and he's slicked it back. Though when it's dry it will likely fall forward to give him a clean-cut yet fresh-from-the-bedroom look. Overall the effect is dramatically altered from the rugged hobo look he was sporting just hours ago. He looks like he could be cast opposite Katherine Heigle in a sexy rom-com.

We are still staring at him, and he looks everywhere but back at us. When he ducks his head and puts his hands in his pockets I notice that he's wearing a new shirt. A tailored emerald green button down in a seersucker fabric. Very trendy, and very Goldie. I nod approvingly; she knows what colors to put him in. The green catches the highlights in his eyes and compliments his deeply tan skin tone.

"Nicely done, Goldie." She beams with pride like a new parent. "Enzo, you clean up quite well."

Enzo looks embarrassed, and fingers the buttons on his shirt.

Goldie walks around the island countertop and adjusts his collar. "And I discovered something interesting about our man here at the salon. Giovanni couldn't cut the hair any shorter because of the ink he's got under there."

"Tattoos? On his scalp?"

Goldie nods. "If you look closely at the back of his head, where the hair's been buzzed short, you can see a bit of it. But Enzo won't tell me what they look like."

I'm sure my surprise shows on my face. "You used to shave your head?"

He nods and shrugs. "It's no big deal. Lots of guys do it. But I got some ink laid down a long time ago that I'm not so proud of now."

Goldie puts a hand to the side of her mouth and whispers in my direction. "Gang stuff."

Now I'm shocked. I hadn't pegged him as gang oriented. "You were in a *gang?*"

He waves the question away. "Nah. Not really. They had me on track when I was thirteen, fourteen. They ruled the 'hood, you know, and joining made sense to me at the time. What else was I going to do? But then when Ricky got shot I gave it up." His face shows regret. "But by then I'd already got the tats."

"'By then I'd already *gotten*.'" My correction is automatic. His flinch is almost invisible, but makes me realize that now is not the time for honing his grammar. "So, we have good news! Goldie and I think it's time you attended a social event. We think you're ready to put all this work we've been doing to the test."

Goldie can't wait, she has to give him the news herself. "We're taking you to a wedding up north, in Mendocino. You'll be Hester's date – in name only of course. I'll be there with Andrew, and so you'll have both of us with you for support. The objective will be for you to blend in, converse, and practice your best American English."

Enzo takes all this in stride. "What happens after?"

There is an awkward moment of silence. I know what he means, but since we don't have a contract of any sort, and I never got around to broaching plans beyond achieving competency in Standard American English, I can't quite look him in the eye. "Well, the next step would be to begin working on the Standard British accent. Mastering that will make your American English even sharper…"

"Why do you want me to learn to sound like you?" Enzo is still standing by the glass slider, and when he shoots me his questioning look, a strange sort of guilty feeling creeps over me.

Goldie jumps in. "It can be very useful. If you decide to use this training Hester's giving you to go into voice-over work, you know, radio, television commercials and stuff, having an English accent in your bag of tricks can help win jobs. Even if you're a waiter in a swanky restaurant, you make better tips when you sound all posh like Hester."

Enzo takes a step forward. "But all I want to do is run my own gym…"

I decide near-honesty is the best policy. "In reality you'll be doing me a favor, Enzo. I'm hoping that when you've mastered the two accents you'll agree to appear in my next set of dialect coaching DVDs." A thought occurs to me. "In fact, I'm hoping you'll help me create a DVD geared toward actors who want to learn your natural accent, the one you learned growing up in your…'hood."

"Like the DVDs I've been watching to learn the American English?"

"Exactly like those. Only you'll be in them with me so it's not just my voice people will study. It will be yours also. I'd pay you a fee for appearing in them."

"How come you want to pay me when you've been buying my food, my clothes, and letting me live out by the pool for no rent? I can't never pay you back for that stuff – can't ever pay you back, I mean."

"Enzo, if you agreed to be in the DVDs, it would only be fair to pay you. I told you at the beginning that I didn't expect anything in return for this arrangement but your best effort at learning what I teach you. You've been an excellent student so far. You're keeping your part of the bargain."

I can feel Goldie looking at me as I hold Enzo's gaze. I've never discussed the DVD idea with her, and I feel more than a shred of dishonesty in not divulging to Enzo that this whole scheme is based on a wager. But truthfully, the idea to include him in my next set of DVDs occurred to me about a week after he'd been living in the cabana. None of my paying clients would be willing to appear in them; most of them are too famous, and I couldn't afford their exorbitant fees anyway. But it would be excellent marketing to have a student of mine demonstrate dialect. Frankly, I think the idea about him doing a DVD on the 'ghetto' dialect is a stroke of genius. I don't know of any dialect coaches who teach that. But judging by the plethora of movies and HBO series being made about gangs and life on the street, it could be useful to actors for whom that dialect is a challenge. Because of all the work Enzo has already put in watching my DVDs to learn American English, he understands about breaking down consonants, vowel sounds, linguistic rhythm, dialect tonality, and pronunciation patterns. If he pulls off the American and British dialects, he'll be my biggest success story. And I will admit that Goldie's original idea about using his turn on the proverbial red carpet as publicity is tempting; I could sell a lot more DVDs with that kind of promo. However, I'm not sure yet that I want to go there, and Enzo's success in our venture is still far from guaranteed.

Enzo looks from me to Goldie, and back again. "So, we go to this wedding, and I play like I'm all rich and educated and speak like this all the time. Like a test." He raises his eyebrows at us, and Goldie and I basically answer 'yes' by saying nothing to contradict his words. "Then we come back here and start learning British, and I can keep doing my personal training, and then when I have that accent down we have another test?"

Goldie and I exchange a 'sounds good to me' look. I nod. "That's the general idea, yes."

Enzo stands for a moment, his eyes on the ceiling. Then he brushes past Goldie and opens the fridge. He gets out a smoothie and tears the foil top off.

It takes him about ten long seconds to drink the entire thing in one go. Then he leans against the countertop, wipes the back of his hand across his mouth, and looks straight at me. "When do we leave for this wedding?"

ENZO

Friday, April 18th

Since they told me about the wedding 'test,' Hester's been examining every last thing about how I speak, move, eat, walk, sit, and think. I'm surprised she ain't asked to come with me to see what I do in the bathroom.

Goldie came over for dinner last night, and those two girls turned the evening into the 'Fix Enzo' show. They made me do simple stuff like walk and sit down. Then they told me to do everything over again better, sayin' like, 'Enzo, walk down the hallway again, but this time, don't do that swagger even a little,' 'Enzo, make sure you hold doors open for ladies and let them do things before you,' and 'Enzo, maintain eye contact with whom you are speaking.'

I've been trained in hand shaking, drink ordering, drink holding, chair-pulling out, expressions of greeting, conversational openers, what Hester calls 'general gallantry,' how to sit without ruining the crease in my suit pants, what Goldie calls 'escaping deadly conversations,' and how to politely deflect 'unwelcome advances.'

Goldie came out to the cabana and helped me pack my new suitcase. Hester gave me last-minute lectures about safe conversational topics: the weather, sports, anything about the other person. And warnings about unsafe ones: politics, technology, business, anything about me.

The way they've been flapping around me for the last week, it's like being with crazy chickens in a hen house. I've begun to look forward to when Nigel comes for his workout training time. The dude might be more boring than cheerios without milk, but at least he's another guy.

I don't know what all to expect at this wedding. Hester said there's gonna be cocktails and dinner tonight when we get there. Then tomorrow's the wedding and a big party after with dancing. That's one thing at least they didn't force me to do in front of them. Neither of those women took a break from freakin' out about my manners to make me dance for them to be sure I won't screw up when the DJ cranks up the music.

I'm supposed to be Hester's pretend 'date,' though I'd rather be Goldie's. She's more fun. But Goldie's bringin' that boyfriend she don't love, Andrew. Don't know the guy, but it'll be good to have a dude around to break up all the girlie shit I got to put up with and keep them from harping at me all the time. Hester's got rooms booked for all of us to stay in. She told me real specific that I'll have my own room, wantin' to be sure I know the whole 'date' thing is just an act.

If Miz Hastings thinks for one minute I don't understand that, she's stupider than dirt. I'm real grateful for everything she's done for me an' all, but I can see she still looks at me like I'm some stray dog she's just puttin' out kibble for.

I hope she's happy with how I do at this wedding. If I do like she wants me to, I can stay here longer. Topaz' case worker says the longer I stay at the address, the better it looks on the court documents. I've been to see Topaz four times since that first visit, and next, I get a whole day to take her out on my own. Staying on with Hester and learning that English accent she wants gives me more time to find people who want to pay me to get 'em fit. Money and a permanent address is what I need to win me what I really want.

HESTER

The four of us fly into Oakland, already dressed in our just-a-notch-more-casual-than-cocktail-attire, and rent a black Lexus SUV for the drive to Mendocino. Enzo and Andrew have been so silent for the whole trip I keep forgetting they're with us. But I'm busy thinking about my soon-to-be-married friend anyway. I can't believe it's been nearly ten years since we spent study breaks sharing pints of Ben and Jerry's with Jimmy Foster at UCLA. Since our partner in crime moved north, we've made it a point to keep in touch with him. But even so, I haven't seen him in probably three years. In tandem with Goldie's tough love approach, his humorous emails kept me sane during my break-up with Philip. When he spots us in the lobby of the classically elegant mansion-turned-hotel wedding venue, he throws up his hands in delight.

"Darlings!" He grabs us both to him in an enormous hug. "It's been ages! Can you believe I'm getting hitched?! I never thought I'd settle down, but I am so, so happy...and I'm so delighted you're both here to share the big event with me!" He steps back to admire our frocks.

"You are both visions of loveliness...Hester, you always look radiant in cobalt, and Goldie, that racy red number is flaming hot! Raaaaaowr," he growls at her. The three of us laugh at his over-the-top fashion commentary.

He spots Enzo and Andrew lurking behind us. "And are these handsome fellows with you?" Jimmy's hand is already extended toward Enzo.

Enzo accepts Jimmy's gregarious hand-shake. "It's a pleasure to meet you, Jimmy."

Well executed, but he forgot to introduce himself. I lay a hand on his arm. "Enzo is with me, Jimmy. He's a personal trainer from L.A."

Goldie introduces Andrew, and Jimmy looks the two men over with delight. "Charmed, gentlemen. I'd hoped these vixens would bring truly worthy partners, and here you are. Welcome!" He looks at Enzo admiringly. "Tell me, how did you score my gorgeous friend here?" Jimmy throws an arm around me and squeezes as he waits for Enzo's reply.

Enzo looks to me, but I'm determined not to help. He needs to learn to think on his feet. "I met Miss Hastings through Goldie. She introduced us."

Jimmy snickers and squeezes my arm. "He's quite a formal fellow, isn't he, *Miss Hastings*?" Then he winks at me, mouths 'so cute!', and then sweeps to the concierge desk and takes up a tray of champagne flutes. Handing them round, he motions for us to knock it back quick. "Let's get the celebration started with some bubbly lubrication...there are a bunch of boring old stiffs out back." He motions to the terrace doors that open onto beautifully colorful, windblown gardens. "My relatives, of course. Quite a yawn, but I had to invite them, didn't I?"

We sip at our champagne as Jimmy ambles with us toward the doors. "The concierge will take care of your luggage, my dears. Go, drink, and be merry in the heart of Shangri La!" Jimmy throws open the glass doors with a flourish, and we wander into the impressive gardens where a handful of older couples are already milling about.

"My fiancé will be here shortly...we'll join you when the rest of the traveling guests arrive," Jimmy calls to us before turning back to his task of greeting friends and family.

Enzo leans close to me as we head down the lawn to the shade of some ancient-looking sequoia trees. "What kind of crack is that guy on?"

I laugh. "Jimmy's one of a kind, Enzo. You'll get used to him. Oh, and remember to call me Hester now. Goldie's the only one here who knows we're not really a couple, and Miss Hastings sounds decidedly odd if you're supposed to be my date."

ENZO

The champagne is pretty good, so I stick to that even when a lady wearing a suit that looks like a tux comes over to axe – ask – if we want anything else to drink. Once the party's got going, it's not nearly as hoity-toity and boring as I thought it was going to be. People are laughing, eating little snacks that Hester calls 'orderves', and drinking like crazy, man. There's four guys playing violins parked under a round hut kinda thing, and more guests keep coming out into this garden. It's real pretty out here, smells like some kind of mixed-up perfume. The weather's cooler up here than down in L.A., and we get a breeze blowin' past that helps keep me from getting too sweaty in this dress shirt, tie, and dinner jacket. Whoever invented ties is a son-of-a-bitch. But Hester's doing most of the talking so far, so all I got to do is hang out and work at emptying my glass.

When the sun starts to go down, some candles get lit all around the garden. They smell kinda lemony. I'm standing with Hester and a couple who look like they come from China when the violins quit playing the soft music and start up real loud like they want us all to pay attention.

Then out of the house come Jimmy and some guy wearing a purple suit – and they're holding hands. They stand up on the patio, and everyone turns and looks at them like, 'wow.'

Then they wave like they're royalty and look at each other all dreamy and start to kiss.

Hold the fuck up! "God-*damn*; you seein' that, Hester?"

She puts her finger to her lips like she's embarrassed. "Shh. That's Victor, Jimmy's fiancé."

Say what? I make my voice whisper. "You mean Jimmy and Victor the ones getting married tomorrow?"

"Yes. Didn't I tell you that?"

"No! Damn, girl…they getting married, like, to each other?"

"Yes! Watch your grammar, it's slipping."

"Shoot, chica. I ain't never…I've never seen anything like that before."

"You must be joking…" Then she sees my face ain't laughing. "There are no gay couples where you come from?"

"I seen 'em around before. But I never known any, like, up close. Or any who was married to each other an' all."

"Didn't you notice the other gay couples?" She points to a group of guests not far away. One guy has his arm around another dude's waist. Oh. How'd I miss all that? "Have you got a problem with homosexuality, Enzo?"

My hands go up in surrender before she gets on her high horse. "Hey, I got nothing against it…I just never seen it all up close and personal."

"But you were in jail…I thought a lot of that kind of thing went on behind bars."

This chica never even been near the joint. "Maybe in them long-stay prisons, and maybe even in L.A. Men's Jail, but I kept to myself and didn't see nothing too funny."

Hester shoots me her deadly x-ray glare. "Well, grow up. Being gay is perfectly normal."

A server passes by me, and while everybody's clapping for Jimmy and Victor, I help myself to a fresh glass of champagne.

HESTER

Goldie comes looking for me when I'm talking to a couple from Sacramento. They are both architects and are wearing beautifully tailored matching navy suits.

"Excuse me, I need to borrow my friend for a few moments." Goldie grabs me by the elbow and strong arms me to a path between beds of fragrant blooming lilac.

Goldie's brow is wrinkled with worry.

I look around, suddenly paranoid. "What is it?"

Her eyes are searching the clusters of guests. "Where's Enzo?"

"I sent him off to schmooze on his own."

She raises her eyebrows at me. "You think that was wise?"

"You're the one who said he was ready. And I've been keeping my eye on him...at least until a moment ago." I scan the gardens for his tall, well-built frame. It's getting dark and hence difficult to discern people's silhouettes.

Goldie shakes her head. "I've made the rounds and haven't seen him anywhere. Do you think he's hiding? Maybe this was too much for him to start with. Maybe we should have begun with a little soirée or..."

"Hang on, look up there at the house. Isn't that him? Just through that window to the right of the veranda doors?" The lights are on inside, and when the man we're staring at turns his head, his profile becomes clear. It is Enzo, and he is chatting with a statuesque blonde woman.

Goldie squints and then grabs my hand. "Yes! I didn't think to look in the house. Oh, thank God. I was so worried, I thought..."

"Who's that blonde he's talking to?" I start walking toward the house, being careful to balance on the balls of my feet so my stiletto heels don't puncture the lawn.

Goldie follows me, peering at the window. "I don't know her."

We enter the house through the terrace doors and take a right to locate the room where Enzo is chatting with an attractive older woman. I'm not sure why my hackles are raised, except that the body language I observed through the window seemed to be overly familiar on her part.

We turn a corner in time to see her smoothing the lapel on his Versace dinner jacket flirtatiously. A diamond and emerald ring sparkles on her left ring finger. She leans in close and laughs at whatever he's just said.

"Enzo!" My voice has gone an octave higher than usual. "There you are. I believe dinner will be served in just a few moments." I float over to stand by his side, lay a hand on his shoulder as though he is really my date. Goldie hangs back and watches from just inside the neighboring room. I don't know where Andrew has gone to. I haven't seen him since he went to fetch a gin and tonic over an hour ago.

"I don't believe we've met," I address Enzo's companion while keeping one proprietorial hand on his sleeve. "I'm Hester Hastings."

"So pleased to meet you." The hand extended for me to shake is glittering with more gems. Too many rings on one hand to be in good taste, in my opinion. "I'm Liz Nicholson. Editor of *Urban Style* magazine. I was just telling Enzo that he's extremely photogenic. But he claims to have done no modeling, which, if you ask me, is simply shameful. A man with his facial structure should be on the cover of a magazine, don't you think?" She regards Enzo admiringly.

Liz is taller than I am by a good three inches, though I notice that she's wearing five-inch heels. I smile graciously. "Enzo is in physical fitness. He's a personal trainer, not a model."

"So he's told me." Her eyes don't leave Enzo's face. "Enzo, my dear. Do contact me if you decide to try your hand at modeling. I know a lot of people in the industry, and the agencies are always looking for fresh faces." Liz actually winks at him as she waggles a flighty goodbye to us with long fingers. She bumps against Goldie on her way out, offering no apology.

I look at Enzo, who is slightly flushed. I wonder if he's a little drunk. "Well, you're welcome."

He appears to be truly surprised. "What for?"

"Getting rid of Liz, of course."

"She was really nice. I was making conversation, like you said to."

"Yes, but you're aware that she wants to make more than conversation, right?"

"She pretty much offered me a job, sounded like."

"She pretty much wants to add you to her stable of toy boys, more like."

Enzo says nothing, but his expression makes me think he's not sure that would be such a bad thing.

"Believe me, Enzo. Liz is trouble. Let's find the dining room; you'll be happy to know it's time to eat."

ENZO

Dinner means we all sit down at a big, round table with people Hester and Goldie went to college with, including Jimmy and Victor. I try and follow the conversation for a while, but with everybody talking at once it's loud and I can't keep track. Plus they talk about stuff that's not exac'ly up my alley.

The food is good, though. First we get a salad filled with olives and cheese and gourmet shit. Then we get a plate full of steak, some kind of garlic potatoes, and grilled zucchini stuffed with what tastes like mushrooms and them sun-dried tomatoes Hester likes all mashed up together.

When cheesecake with cherries on top gets served people start making toasts with freshly served champagne. Hester explained toasts to me, even made me practice a few. But in real life they seem just kinda like drunk people making fun of Jimmy and Victor or saying stuff about how they was made for each other. Jimmy and Victor laugh until they get red in the face, and they kiss a bunch of times. I still ain't used to that. There's lots of clapping and lifting of glasses, and I clink mine with Hester and Goldie every time someone finishes a toast.

I figured out all the forks, knives, and spoons without any help from Hester. There's even three different wine glasses, but I didn't have to figure those out because the waiters just cleared the old one and filled the next glass when a new plate came. No problem.

By the time coffee gets served, everybody's drunk, except maybe Hester. Even Goldie's all giggling and pink in the face. Her boyfriend's not laughing. He just watches her like he's pissed off and doesn't talk to anybody. Though nobody notices because the old college friends are all talking and laughing about old times. Makes it easy to just sit and sip coffee and stay out of trouble.

I'm thinkin' about how different this whole dinner would be if it was my old homies gettin' together. We'd be at the Hacienda over in South Gate in the party room. There'd be beer instead of wine, and tacos. Burritos, queso, fried beans and rice, maybe enchiladas and then we'd go after to the club and get loose on the dance floor. Plus that would have been the wedding meal. There wouldn't have been no dinner the night before the wedding, no open bar, no wearing fancy suits. But up here in Richville, this here meal is just the beginning; we still got the wedding and more eating tomorrow.

I've met some decent people here though. Liz was cool, even though I've met enough women like her to know what she be wantin' from guys like me. Made me laugh when Hester came to rescue me. She don't even know.

I'm sipping my coffee all nice like Goldie showed me when Jimmy comes by. He stops, unsteady from the wine, and leans down to my ear. "Hester is a special lady, my friend. You two look good together. I like it. Makes me feel better about her after she's been alone so long." He squeezes my shoulder, his breath smells like the grilled zucchini. "Victor noticed you'd both been crammed into twin rooms, so he got you upgraded. He's thoughtful like that." Jimmy gazes across the table at his fiancé all lovey-like. Then he winks at me, and mouths, 'you're welcome.'

Why do people think they're doing me favors all over the place tonight? Hester thinks I can't handle my own self with Liz, and Jimmy's throwin' me curve balls. An upgrade. Sounds like I been put in a room with Hester and one bed? That girl is gonna freak out. I wish all of a sudden I hadn't let the waiter clear my last wine glass before I'd drunk the last drop.

HESTER

I lose track of Enzo briefly after dinner, but then spot him on the periphery of an animated discussion with a trio of older men. They sit out on the patio in wrought iron chairs, smoking cigars. If I didn't know him, I'd assume from his relaxed demeanor that he was accustomed to smoking cigars with the well-to-do. His long legs are crossed casually like I taught him.

Goldie and I are making small talk with a gay couple from Ottowa while I listen with one ear to the conversation through the open terrace doors. Between amusing anecdotes from the Ottowans, I snatch glimpses of orange embers flaring at the tip of each cigar as the men inhale smoke in the late night air.

I detect the cadence of Enzo's voice, but I can't hear clearly. Claude from Ottowa is too loud. I edge innocuously toward the door, away from Claude, and begin to make out words.

"It's like a social experiment...all those inner city kids being raised by one parent around drugs and violence..." I don't recognize the voice, but I'm already on high alert. "It's a recipe for disaster."

"What I don't understand is," this is a deeper voice, and I think it belongs to Jimmy's father, "why do they direct the violence at each other? If I was a young black man raised in the slums and left to be parented by drug dealers and gangs, I think I'd want to take a bus on out to the suburbs and do drive by shootings on wealthy white folks. Why is the rage directed toward a neighbor rather than the people who have so much more?"

The first man chuckles, takes a pull on his cigar. "They bring plenty of crime out to the suburbs. Look at all the theft, vandalism, car break-ins. Hell, I had to get a window replaced on my Jag last week. They took my golf bag. Golf! What on earth are they going to do with my four iron? What police need to do is develop some kind of test to measure a kid's likelihood to join a gang or commit a crime in the first place. Did the kid get abused? Does he drop out of school? Does he do time in juvenile detention? Does he have a violent mindset? The deck is stacked against these kids, and it's no wonder they're shooting each other in the streets."

"You all can stop right there." Enzo's voice is so quiet I have to strain to hear him. "The gangs do violence to each other because they got to prove how tough they are so they don't become targets themselves. They do it because they were raised on hate and fear, and they can't be sure of anything in this world except life and death and pain. They do it because they been told by the only role models they know that this is the way to go about your business. They're raised on it, see it every day, get brought up thinking about which gang to join, or about how when they're old enough they're gonna take down so-and-so because he shot their uncle Reggie. They do it because it's a rite of passage. It's belonging, it's brotherhood, it's becoming a man like the men they see walkin' down the street and lookin' cool hangin' together on corners. They do it because belonging and holding a gun is powerful, man. But they don't hold nothing sacred, you know? Not even life. They've seen too much shit, been smacked too many times, been given up on by teachers too often to hold back from pullin' that trigger." Enzo stands, stubs out his cigar on the iron chair arm. "You might wanna walk a mile in another man's shoes before you start judgin' on what they do or don't do."

I refocus on what loud Claude is saying as Enzo comes into the house, passes through to the concierge desk and asks where his room is. As I smile and nod at whatever Claude has just said, I feel a swell of pride run through me. On tough conversational ground, Enzo held his own. His English slipped a bit, but he spoke carefully and made himself understood perfectly well without making a scene.

Once I've excused myself from my conversation and said goodnight to Goldie, I go to the concierge as well. He looks up my name and hands me a key for room fourteen. Upstairs, he says, in the east wing. I head up the stairs, thinking about how easy it would have been for Enzo to go off on those men, and how no one who knows his background would have blamed him. He showed restraint and maturity, while at the same time speaking his peace. I smile to myself as I head east at the top of the stairs, traveling down a long corridor. Gold numbers on beige doors: ten, twelve, fourteen. I insert the key in the lock and turn the bolt.

The bed is massive. California king, I would imagine. Red rose petals are scattered across the white coverlet. Two flutes of champagne and a silver bowl of chocolate-dipped strawberries have been left on the bedside table. It's so clearly the wrong room that I start to close the door, half afraid I've interrupted something.

"You in the right place."

"Enzo?" I poke my head back inside the door. He's sitting in an overstuffed armchair situated in front of an unlit fireplace. In the dim light, I see his eyes examining my face. Is he watching for my reaction? Did he arrange all this? I don't know what to say. It's so clearly inappropriate, yet he's never shown the slightest sign of seeking anything more than the teaching I've offered him.

"Victor upgraded the two rooms you booked to this one. Guess he thought we'd like to be in the same room seeing as how I'm your 'date' and all."

Ah. I suppose, in retrospect, I should have divulged the real reason for Enzo's presence to Jimmy. At the time, it had seemed wise to keep quiet, giving Enzo the best chance not to be outed accidentally. "He probably thought the two rooms were the last on offer when I booked. Oh dear, I wonder who he bumped to the twin rooms?"

"I don't know, but I hope it was Charles and Margot. Did you meet them? They is without a doubt the most boring people I ever met. And I knew a couple a guys in the joint who never said a single word the whole time I was there, man."

I shut the door behind me and drop my key on the dresser beside it. "Well, the place is cozy at least. It was really nice of him to arrange the rose petals and champagne. If we were together we'd be thrilled, right?"

"Yeah. Real romantic." Enzo's voice sounds distant, like he's not convinced.

"I'll have to remember to thank him tomorrow. Might as well play along. He'd feel bad if I told him the truth."

Enzo rises from the chair and grabs the bowl of chocolate strawberries. "These look good." He pops one into his mouth. "Might as well eat 'em." He holds out the bowl to me, and I walk over and select one. It is rich and sweet and makes me thirsty. I pick up a champagne flute and take a sip.

"You have the rest. Too sweet for me after that rich dessert."

Enzo shrugs and bites into another one, dropping the uneaten leafy stem back in the bowl. He's still wearing his dinner jacket, but he sits down on the bed, propping the pillows up behind him and biting into another strawberry.

I'm so tired, I don't even think about it. I lie down on the other side of the bed and put my head on the pillow. The bed is so huge that we could sleep the whole night here together and never touch even by accident.

I push my strappy stilettos off my feet and let them drop to the ground, one at a time. "Did you have a good time tonight?"

"It was okay. I was in a half dozen conversations I didn't understand. But I smiled and followed along best I could, you know? Just kept my mouth shut most of the time."

"You seemed to fit in just fine." I yawn, adjust my pillow.

"It's kinda like hangin' out with my homies, only we're all dressed up here and talk fancy. Money makes us look pretty, and education makes people say shit with conviction."

"That's a good word, Enzo." It's only after I say it that I realize the dual meaning of the word. I hope he doesn't think of it. "Did you learn anything useful?"

This makes him thoughtful. "How to smoke a cigar. I had cigarettes before, but a cigar you got to handle differently. And I learned how these fancy shoes hurt like a bitch." He kicks the offending footwear off and puts his feet up on the bed.

"Enzo?"

"Yeah?"

"I think you're a really classy dude."

He chuckles. "Glad I got you fooled too, Miz Hastings."

->==o o==<-

In the morning I wake slowly, my dress wrinkled, a mascara stain on the white pillowcase. Enzo is still asleep on his side of the bed. He's removed his dinner jacket and his shirt, I suppose he got hot, and because I'm staring at his back I can't help examining his tattoos. Done in black ink, they are indelibly stark. Across his left shoulder blade is a leaping tiger. TOPAZ is written in gothic letters across his lower back, the 'O' stylized as a multi-faceted gem.

I don't know why I let myself reach out and trace the outline of the tiger with my fingertip. It's entirely inappropriate. But in the uninhibited hold of residual sleepiness, that's what I do. Enzo's skin is warm.

ENZO

I wake up feeling her finger stroking my back. It's not the same touch as when a fly lands on you, or when some kinda something's poking at you. Her touch glides real smooth, light and sure of itself. Why's she doin' it? I ain't mad, it just don't compute. Maybe she likes tattoos. Plenty of women do. I open my eyes and focus on the feeling her fingertip is sending through me. I ain't been touched ever like this. Shoot, I ain't been touched in any good way in over a year.

I don't even feel the bed move when she lifts her head off her pillow, but her finger stops moving at the same time my eyes find the mirror over the dresser straight ahead of me. Her face is reflected above mine, and she sees me find her eyes watching me.

She don't say nothing, but her head disappears behind mine in the mirror. When I roll over, she ain't looking at me no more.

HESTER

I'm not ready to meet his gaze after he's caught me in the mirror. When I reached out and touched his back, I thought he was asleep. Why didn't he move? Why did he let me think he was unaware of my finger tracing the tiger on his back? I feel like I've been caught doing something I shouldn't. In fact, I have been.

I can feel his eyes on me, but I can't look up. When he talks, his voice is deeper than usual. A morningtime waking-together voice. Enzo's voice in a way I was never meant to hear it.

ENZO

"I can't figure out what you're getting out of giving me so much."

I leave it there for a minute, but she don't say nothing. "You're teachin' me to talk better and act more educated. Why? I don't get why a woman like you would want to do that for nobody like me. You know where I slept the three nights between when you handed me your card and I worked up the nerve to ring your doorbell? A homeless shelter. I might still be there if you wasn't letting me stay in your pool house." It's easier to say stuff when she's not looking at me. "Nobody ever helped me without wanting something in return. Usually, I come out worse in the bargain. Is that what's gonna happen with you? You gonna ask me for something I can't give?"

Her eyes fly up to meet mine.

HESTER

"It's your choice to learn from me, to study what I teach you. That first day you knocked on my door, I was so frightened by the idea of you. I thought maybe you might take something from me, that you were dangerous." *Like the tiger on your back*. I think about how I anxiously armed the security system that first night, about how now your presence in the cabana makes me feel more safe than the security system ever did. "When you went to get that tattoo, you could have asked for an eagle, a dragon, a cobra. But for some reason you got the tiger, and it fits. You have something quiet and stealthy in you, Enzo. You've crept up on me with your cooking and your weight lifting and your companionship. I'm not used to that. I thought I'd teach you, and it would be one-sided. You'd learn, gain competency, and move on. I didn't count on getting to know you. I didn't count on caring what happens to you. You're not like anyone I've ever met…and I do care what happens to you. I want you to get your daughter back. And I want to see you succeed with the accents I'm teaching you."

ENZO

"You sure don't cut me no slack, girl." I can't help laughing at the memory of some of those crazy-ass things she made me do. "From the start you were like, bam…do this and do that, and I thought like maybe you were kind of a bitch, you know?" I watch her face go all outraged, but then she smiles all soft and prim. "You're the strictest teacher I ever had. But my teachers in school, they always acted like they expected I'd fail anyway. You always act like you think I'm gonna make it. Sometimes, you make me feel kinda stupid, like I'm a kid and don't know anything. But you don't know me. You don't know what I know already and what I don't. So, it's mostly okay. And girl, I'm sorry, but you are so tight-assed," her face goes all shocked again, and I nod. "Uh-huh, I said 'tight-assed'…and all 'proper' with your hoity-toity accent and your upper crustiness." I make my voice all like hers, "No, no, Enzo. Pronounce the entire vowel and put the ending on the word. You can't drop the 'ing' in every word; it's not proper English!"

Then I think, man, there ain't no going back from telling her this shit.

HESTER

"Well, what about you? You didn't say a word about anything to me for weeks unless I forced you to talk with me at meals. I felt like a prison guard…" Oops! Bad analogy; his eyes go wide like, 'Oh no you didn't!' and I laugh. "Alright, maybe you know a thing or two already about prison guards. So, perhaps it was more like a mum with a sullen teenager. You are one tough nut to crack. That night you confided in me about Topaz, I was so shocked that you told me something personal, I almost forgot about losing my visits with Jessica."

We are smiling at each other. There are walls that have come down. It feels good to make him laugh, to see him happy. His smile is so infectious; it's a crime he doesn't unleash it more often.

Then there is the strained moment when the smiles die out. I see uncertainty in his eyes. He's still a full arm's length away from me, a safe distance on the king-sized bed. In the silence, I feel him retreating already from the candid words we've spoken. I'm not surprised when he rolls over and sits up, reaches for his shirt. The tiger tattoo disappears beneath the fabric, and I'm not sure when I'll encounter it again.

HESTER

Saturday, April 19th

By the time we are seated on the white chairs lined up in the garden, I am more ready for a glass of chardonnay than I have ever been. After Enzo left our room this morning, I put on my exercise clothes and went for a long, head-clearing walk. A casual buffet luncheon was served in the dining room between twelve and two. I dropped in for a bite, but saw no one from my party. After, in our room, I saw signs that Enzo had been back to shower and shave. When it became clear he wasn't coming back soon, I took advantage of the luxurious Jacuzzi tub to take a long, hot bath. Enzo managed to return and dress for the wedding in the room so quietly I never realized he was on the other side of the bathroom door.

I spent the time after my bath preparing for the wedding and fretting about where Enzo was. Once I'd checked where his wedding clothes should have been hanging and realized he'd already donned his James Bond-style tuxedo Goldie had chosen for him, I wondered if he was avoiding me due to feelings of awkwardness or as a courtesy to allow me my privacy. After shimmying into my gold strapless Chanel and managing to do up the zip on my own, it was time to join the gathering throng of guests in the garden.

I find Enzo lurking near a cluster of blooming camellias by himself, drinking a pre-wedding gin and tonic. As I join him, he offers only a nod to acknowledge me and remains distant. When we catch up with Goldie and Andrew to find seats, it's obvious they are in the silent aftermath of another argument. The hostile tension between them is palpable.

But when it is five o' clock, the string quartet from the night before begins to play Tchaikovsky's Dance of the Sugar Plum Fairies. Laughter ripples through the audience. Then Jimmy comes down the grassy aisle first, looking dashing in a charcoal cutaway tuxedo, a red rosebud pinned to his lapel. Victor makes the journey next, and they are both grinning as the distance between them shrinks, their eyes glued to each other.

The vows are short and sweet, and we all throw birdseed at them as they promenade back down the aisle hand-in-hand. Flushed and joyful, the newlywed couple leads the procession to the white tent that has been erected at the bottom of the garden.

One half of the tent is a dance floor, and the other is filled with tables set for dinner. Fresh flower arrangements of striking purple iris and creamy magnolia blossoms are on every table. Borne by a gentle breeze, the fragrance of magnolia infuses the tent. Everyone flocks to the three tables set up to serve drinks. Enzo and I wait in the queue with Goldie and Andrew. For some reason, we are all avoiding making eye contact with each other. Goldie's eyes are a little red, and I wonder if she's been crying.

Once we have our wine in hand, Andrew wanders off without a word to any of us. Enzo surprises me by leaning close to my ear and whispering, "She doesn't love him anyway."

I nod sadly, observing Goldie's melancholy look as she sips her sauvignon blanc.

Enzo gives her a gentle nudge with his shoulder. "So, what do we do now?"

Goldie musters a smile. "We mingle. Come on, I'll introduce you to Dave. He's funny and easy to talk to."

Enzo permits Goldie to lead him through the crowd of wineglass-laden guests, and I breathe a sigh of relief. He's back to normal and better at this social stuff than he lets on.

ENZO

When they put the plates down in front of us, Hester tells me dinner is lobster stuffed with crab. I ain't never eaten lobster before. But it's moist and rich, and they didn't skimp on the serving. The sauce is buttery and something I wouldn't mind eating on pretty much anything. I scrape my asparagus and then a dinner roll in what's left of that sauce even though I see Hester's dirty look sayin' 'that ain't classy'.

Wine again through dinner, white, and they keep pouring it every time my glass gets low. I could get used to drinking wine with every meal, man. By the time our plates get cleared, I'm chilled out and enjoying the show that's goin' on around me. Everyone's jabberin' at each other, laughing too loud, and there are a few couples you can tell only just met each other but are gonna totally hook up tonight. On my left, Hester is busy talkin' and talkin' with her old college homies.

When the music starts, Jimmy and Victor get up and do disco moves to "Macho, Macho Man." They ain't bad, but they dance like, well, you know, a little like girls. Then they get all kissy, which I'm still getting used to, and people up and flood the dance floor when the DJ puts on "Celebrate." It's that kind of crowd. Arms are waving in the air, and hips get swingin'. Me, I'm just chillin' and enjoying the view – it ain't every day I'm front and center watchin' uptight, rich white people get down – when Goldie rolls over, without her man, and grabs Hester up from her seat. As Goldie pulls on her, my dialect coach reaches out to me like she's falling overboard and wants me to save her. She gets hold of my sleeve, and though she can't pull me hard enough to get me to 'come on already,' I ease up outta my chair and follow her onto the dance floor.

At first I just copy what everybody else is doin'. After all, I'm here to soak up the 'culture' as Hester would say. To observe, analyze, and imitate and try to fit in and all that. Champagne is being passed around again, and everybody's got a real buzz on. DJ's playing the stuff they must be used to dancing to at weddings. He hits us with "La Bamba," "I Gotta Feeling," and "We Are Family" right in a row. I down more champagne because I need it to dance to this music. Hester can shake it better than I woulda guessed, but she needs some work. Goldie's moves are hotter and don't play it so safe. She's actually hittin' me some with hip grinds and a little salsa slide. I play along, and I kinda like it, too. Girlfriend is *fine*. Even though I'm holdin' back, it feels good to move. I ain't been out to dance since... shit, since I can't remember when.

When DJ throws on "Macarena," I got to go pay him a visit. I know he just tryin' to keep his audience happy, but bro gotsta step it up. He smiles when he hears what I want and says he can play some of it in between the songs Jimmy and Victor asked for.

After I give him my play list, and I didn't go all gangsta rap or nothin', DJ puts on "Los Manos Arriba," and I can't help it, I start to move.

HESTER

Goldie must be drunk, because when Enzo comes back from the DJ's table and starts his Latin hip hop or salsa or whatever style of dance it is, she is all over him. In her chili-pepper red lace and tulle confection of a dress, Goldie wouldn't look out of place in a ballroom competition. Together, they are turning so many heads that people around them are experiencing accidental dance collisions. I begin to leave the dance floor, but it's so packed I almost have to push my way to the perimeter. From where I end up, I catch sight of Andrew. He is on the opposite side of the tent and is definitely watching Goldie gyrating on the dance floor with Enzo. His naturally stern face shows a combination of anger and disgust. I need to get over there, to alert him that Goldie is drunk and upset and not aware of how her behavior looks to him. Most importantly, I need to assure him there is nothing going on between his girlfriend and Enzo.

I start to work my way around the guests crowding the dance floor. People have stopped dancing and stepped back as spectators, a circle widening around Enzo and Goldie. Though I'm not watching them, I can tell from the noises the crowd makes that those two are putting on quite a show. I guess the salsa lessons Andrew refused to go to are paying off for Goldie.

I'm halfway to Andrew when the song ends, and a slow one begins. As couples drift onto the dance floor, Andrew breaks his way through to Goldie. Oblivious to the drama, Enzo has exited the scene, and I catch sight of him grabbing a flute of champagne from a waiter with a tray. But the main action is still on the dance floor. Andrew has confronted Goldie, and they are shouting at each other. Though I can't hear what they are saying, their voices are audible over the incredibly loud rendition of "Endless Love." The couples who are trying to have a romantic dance begin to take notice, and soon almost everyone is watching the argument. Goldie is crying, but she's also pushing at Andrew's chest and jabbing her finger at his shoulder. This will not end well.

But then Andrew just turns and leaves. Stalks off the dance floor, away from Goldie and Jimmy and Victor and their wedding. He continues up the lawn through the gardens and into the house. When I look back to see how Goldie is faring at being abandoned mid-scene, she has already left the dance floor. I know she doesn't love Andrew enough to follow him, to fight for what they have together. A flash-forward pops into my head of Goldie clearing all of Andrew's belongings from her house. I have just witnessed the death of their relationship.

My best friend gathers her purse and sequined pashmina from our table and then stands at the edge of the tent. She is too drunk or stunned or both to decide where to go. I hurry over and wrap my arm around her. She allows me to lead her to a chair far from the dance floor, and we sit down. It's too soon to talk. That will happen later, after the DJ has packed up and gone home. For now, we sit. She cries a little, and I hold her hand. Then we watch the dancers for a while.

I keep my eye on Enzo, but he seems to be managing fine without me. He sips champagne quietly, transitioning to the dance floor when he likes a song. Each time he deigns to dance, he is quickly surrounded by women and men who want to bask in his shadow and copy his dance moves. Some of them are my old college friends; even Jimmy and Victor join Enzo's impromptu fan club. I frown when that cougar Liz manages to lose her husband and shimmy up against Enzo like he's catnip.

Finally, the dancing peters out, and the round table displaying the wedding cake is carefully rolled onto the dance floor. It is a towering confection of chartreuse with purple orchids cascading down in a spiral pattern. On top are two little smiley-face stick figures in top hats. Jimmy and Victor cut the cake amid cheers and fist pumps. If there's a sober person left in the room aside from me, there's no sign of them.

Enzo is standing among guests who surround the cake-eating ritual, watching everything. He has dropped the cautious detachment I've become so accustomed to. I know he's had too much to drink like everyone else; I wasn't keeping count of the glasses of champagne he's imbibed, but I know he's had more than his share.

When Jimmy and Victor have smashed pieces of cake into each other's mouths and kissed messily, a microphone begins to circulate. Friends and family are being encouraged to say a few words about Jimmy and Victor's union. Lubricated by alcohol and emotion, most of the speech-givers are highly flattering in their expressions of delight for the happy couple.

Goldie grips my arm, and when I see her staring at the mansion where we're all staying, my eyes follow suit. There, outside the back door, illuminated by the floodlights, is Andrew. He's holding his suitcase, and as though to make a point, he stares down at the party tent. I don't know if he can see Goldie from where he stands, but he certainly isn't looking too friendly. His face hard, he turns, walks around the house, and is gone.

I'm searching the table in front of us for a clean napkin for Goldie's fresh tears when I hear Enzo's voice magnified for the listening pleasure of all who are present. I freeze. Though my instincts tell me to duck and cover, I slowly turn to locate Enzo in the throng surrounding Jimmy and Victor.

"I just wanna say that I'm glad to be here celebratin' Jimmy and Victor's wedding." His pronunciation and grammar have slipped, but I'm about to discover that's the least of my worries. "I ain't never known any gays before, and it feels real weird to see two dudes get married and all. I don't know how they figure out, like, who's the guy or if they take turns or whatever, but I respect them and hope they have a real good life together." Everyone has gone silent; people look away in discomfort as though they can avert the train wreck by not watching it happen. I pray to the God of Bad Speeches to let Enzo pull something that will fix this out of his hat.

Drunk and oblivious, he forges on. "My folks was straight and wasn't never happy together. And now one of 'em's dead, and the other might as well be. Maybe if they'd been gay it woulda worked out better. But then I wouldn't even be here, right?" He's the only one who laughs. "So I guess Jimmy and Victor, I wish for you guys to have a long and happy life. Don't die or get put in prison, and you should be okay." Enzo lifts his champagne glass, which only has a swallow left in the bottom, and drains it.

127

There is some nervous laughter, and mercifully, Enzo hands the microphone to the person next to him. Mentally, I scribble furiously on the notepad of my mind; give Enzo a lesson on *tactful* speechmaking!

With both Enzo and Goldie too drunk to function properly on their own, as soon as speeches end, I gather them up and tow them to the mansion's lounge. I leave Enzo looking like he's about to pass out on the overstuffed sofa and take Goldie upstairs to my room. She's started crying again, accelerating the downward momentum of the mascara splotches under both eyes. I tell her to wash her face and that I'll be right back. Then I fish in her purse for her room key and, without the option of pockets, tuck it into the center of my strapless bra.

When I get back to Enzo, Liz has found him – is he wearing some kind of homing beacon? – and is massaging his shoulders while he slumps forward drowsily.

I bend down to encourage Enzo into a standing position and smile sweetly at Liz. "Thanks ever so much for looking after him for me." I lower my voice as though sharing a secret. "He's had a little too much, I'm afraid. But he'll be right as rain in the morning; never gets a hangover, lucky thing!" I have no idea if Enzo gets hangovers or not, but Liz doesn't need to know that.

Liz waves at us, looking a little blurry herself. Despite myself I experience a moment of pity for her. But then she lurches forward and plants a kiss of red lipstick on Enzo's cheek, too close to his mouth for comfort. "Night night…" She waggles her fingers at him as we depart.

I drag Enzo upstairs, which isn't easy considering he's rapidly transforming into a pre-pubescent female. He giggles and pulls at me playfully as I try to drag him up the stairs. Then he runs ahead, and I'm chasing after him. I lose track of him altogether for a few heart-stopping moments. Then he jumps, or more like slides, out from behind a corner at the top of the stairs and shouts, "Boo!"

"Shhhh…Enzo be quiet! It's the middle of the night."

He puts a finger to his lips and then smirks at me. "Baby, this night ain't even started yet…"

Ugh. "Just don't say anything. Come on."

I manhandle him over to the next set of stairs and fish Goldie's key out of my bra.

"Oooh, girl! What else you got in there?" Before I can stop him, Enzo hooks a finger into my cleavage and takes a peek.

I smack his hand away. "Stop it! You're being positively adolescent, Enzo."

He waggles his eyebrows at me suggestively and displays the slow smile I like so much. Only this time it contains an undertone of salaciousness. Is he trying to make a pass at me?

"You're drunk, Enzo. When you sober up, remind me to lecture you about the social pitfalls of intoxication; you've fallen into several of them tonight." In the dimness of the corridor I peer at Goldie's key. Number twenty-six. I think that's one more floor up.

His face takes on the look of a scolded schoolboy, but he follows me up the stairs. When we find twenty-six and I unlock the door, Enzo pulls me in and launches both of us full-throttle onto the king-size canopy bed in the middle of the room. We land, sinking several inches into the puffy down duvet. The only light comes from the hallway, and as I orient myself in the darkness, my eyes find Enzo's face above mine. He suddenly looks sober, almost hungry. The way his eyes are taking me in makes me think of the tiger tattoo on his back. If he decided to, he could do whatever he wanted with me, and I'd have no chance of fighting him off.

But he touches my cheek lightly with his fingers and lifts a strand of hair that's fallen across my mouth out of the way before gently leaning in to kiss me. It's such a tender moment that I surprise myself by stopping his lips short of mine with my index finger.

"Enzo, you're drunk," I whisper. "You're not in your right mind. I'm sure you've missed…female companionship while you were in jail, but I can't…"

I don't have to say more because he's rolled away. He lays still, flat on his back for so long I worry that he's crushed by my rejection to the point of being unable to speak to me. But when I finally lean up on one elbow to see better, I find he's passed out cold.

Well.

I clamber off the high bed and smooth down my rumpled dress. Goldie's suitcase is open on the ottoman by the fake fireplace. A slinky negligee lies on top – she won't be needing that. I toss it onto the armchair and search for suitable sleeping clothes. Ah, leggings and a tee-shirt, that's more like it. As an afterthought I grab a peasant-style tunic that can be worn over the leggings to go to breakfast in. I gather them in my arms and close the door quietly behind me, leaving Enzo to sleep it off.

ENZO

The throbbing of my head and dryness in my mouth wake me. Sweet Jesus, I'm thirsty like a bitch. And it's really bright in here. I sit up slowly and look around, my eyes adjusting to the daylight.

What the fuck?

This ain't the room I'm s'posed to be in. I look down and see I ain't got no clothes on. Oh no, no, no. This ain't right.

My clothes is thrown all around the bed like I flung 'em off in a hurry. I rub my eyes, trying to think what happened. I remember the dancing, Goldie's big fight with her stuck-up boyfriend, the cake, the champagne. What the hell happened after all that?

I find my boxer shorts and pull 'em on. There's a pink suitcase lying there open, and I look at it like it's gonna give me some answers. A sick kind of feeling hits my gut. Goldie's suitcase is bright pink just like that one there. A lacy nightie's been thrown on the chair next to the bed.

I look at the bed. The covers are all whacked out of place like somebody's been wrestling on 'em. Oh shit. Oh shit oh shit.

I sit down on the chair. It couldn't have…there wasn't… we didn't …did we?

Son of a bitch. I look over at the bathroom door. It's closed, but I don't hear no water running or anything. I get up and go knock on it. No answer. I open it. Whew. Okay.

Then I catch sight of my face in the mirror above the sink. Is that lipstick? I wipe at the red smudge by my mouth and look at my fingertips. Double fuck.

But at least she ain't here. That thought brings my pulse down a couple digits.

Hold up. Where the hell is she? Did she just get up and run off when she figured out what we done? Auto-correction: what we *did*.

Oh, shit. I bet she went off to Hester to tell on me. But we were drunk, and she was all crazy out of her mind because of Andrew...wait a minute. She was *using me* because of Andrew.

Now, that's fucked up.

I remember it. She was dancing all up on me and flirtin' like we was at a club. Then she had that ugly fight with the boyfriend, and he went off and left. What happened next? Somebody was rubbing my shoulders. Did she give me a massage? Yeah. And then we was in here on the bed, and I kissed her.

Damn. *I* did it. She might have brought me here, but *I* kissed *her*. I remember. I wanted it. It's my fault.

Shit! What's Hester gonna think of me now? She's gonna chuck me out of the cabana, and I'll never see her again. I bet she won't even talk to me no more.

Triple fuck.

I start searchin' around the room. There's gotta be something heavy enough. I need to lift some pounds and get my head straight.

HESTER

Goldie's still asleep when I tiptoe from the room to find some coffee and breakfast. In the dining room, people are eating and chatting and pretending not to be hung-over. I pour myself black coffee from the silver urn on the sideboard and sit by myself in an alcove overlooking the garden.

There was surprisingly little post-breakup analysis to do with Goldie last night. In fact, she seemed rather relieved that it's finally over. The one who threw me a curveball was Enzo. I know he was drunk, but there was something, well, worrying about it. I replay the moment when he leaned in to kiss me. What would have happened if I hadn't stopped him?

Nonsense. He was drunk. The only thing to do was stop him.

And then I see Enzo sidle into the dining room looking shifty. He pours coffee from the same urn I used a moment ago. He's dressed in his tuxedo trousers and the white short-sleeved undershirt he must have worn under his dress shirt last night. The sleeves are tight, showing off his muscles and contrasting with the caramel shade of his skin. When he brings the porcelain coffee cup to his lips to take a sip, his bicep flexes.

Then he catches sight of me and freezes. There's a sheepish, uncertain look on his face. He must remember trying to kiss me last night. I smile reassuringly and wave him over. He approaches even more cautiously than usual, without a trace of the habitual swagger that marks his natural movements.

He puts down his coffee and takes a long drink from the pre-set glass of ice water. Then he eases into his chair like I've taught him to and surveys me with an odd expression that I can't quite read.

I'll have to set a tone that puts him at ease. "You feel alright this morning?"

"Yeah. Thirsty."

"Well, you had quite a night."

Fear. That's what's in his face. "Hester, Miz Hastings…"

"I think we can stick with Hester now, don't you?"

"I'm so sorry, Hester. It was the last thing on my mind. I shoulda never drunk all that champagne…"

"Don't worry so much, Enzo! It can happen to anyone. You haven't had much alcohol in a long time, and it went straight to your head." I pat his hand. "These things happen."

His eyes are wide. "Really? You're cool with it?"

I wave my hand as though it was nothing. Essentially, it was nothing. Nothing happened. "Yes. Let's just forget it. But I will insist on your best English today. You're not drunk now, after all."

Enzo breathes a visible sigh of relief and takes another sip of water. "Man, I just can't believe you're so chilled about it. I thought for sure you'd take a chunk out of me. I said to myself, 'You got to go down there and apologize even though she's probably going to call the whole teaching arrangement off and throw you out on your ass.'" He takes another breath, then looks at me with serious eyes. "And I *am* sorry, Hester. I never meant to…it was the last thing on my mind. I wish it had never happened, and I'd take it back if I could. I swear it. I'm never gonna…going to get drunk again."

For some reason, his vehemence annoys me. It was just a misjudged attempt at affection. Is he that horrified that he tried to kiss me? "It's fine, Enzo. Let's move on."

ENZO

Move on? Hell yes, let's move on. But how come she's letting me off so easy? Is this some kind of trick? I can't believe Hester's being so cool about me and Goldie gettin' it on, man. Seemed to me she's the type that would really freak out and rip me a new one. But then, maybe she's not as prim and proper as I think she is. She does hang with all them Hollywood clients. I look at her, wondering what she's really like when I'm not around. You'd think spending all the time together like we do she'd be lettin' it all hang out by now. But maybe she's being a kind of role model for me or something like that. Maybe when I'm not there she's thowin' wild, nasty pool parties with hot Hollywood actors and shit.

I try and look at her with new eyes. She's sipping her coffee just as proper and posh as the queen.

Nah. The combo of Hester Hastings and wild, nasty parties don't play.

Then why isn't she fussin' all up in my face?

When I see Goldie come through the doors, I get ready for fireworks. But she just piles a plate with enough pastries for all of us and sits down next to Hester, more cheerful than I'da thought after the breakup last night and what we done. But she's actin' all normal and don't even seem hung-over.

Damn, yo. Guess I'm the luckiest son-of-a-bitch there ever was.

Then we all just eat croissants and fruit. I got my best manners on and don't say a single thing, and somehow everything's cool.

Chapter 9

Wednesday, April 23rd

I HAVE A plan to get Jessica back. Since we returned from Mendocino, I've been considering my options: a) Only visit Jessica at Philip's like he's mandated. b) Refuse to cave in to his demands, and thus forego visits with Jessica. c) Invite Philip and Jessica to a gathering at my place so that he can gradually become accustomed to the idea of Enzo – which will absolutely work better if Topaz is here as well. If Philip sees that Enzo is also the father of a young girl, they might find common ground. And if Philip can relax and trust me that Jessica is safe here despite Enzo's presence, my battle is won.

Of course, this will also involve admitting that Enzo actually lives here. Even after I've explained why he's residing in my cabana, Philip will need another nudge to be convinced that my relationship with Enzo is platonic.

Therefore, Nigel is also invited.

A risky move, I know. But Nigel is less threatening than Enzo in almost every way, more palatable as my new beau to Philip's ego. With benign Nigel on the scene, Philip is more likely to accept that Enzo lives in the cabana because I am simply helping him rehab his life.

It's complicated, but worth a shot anyway.

I've already invited Nigel, Mum, Christopher, and Goldie. Tomorrow at six. We'll swim, barbeque some lovely prosciutto-wrapped scallops, marinated chicken, corn on the cob, have a few cocktails – it will be the perfect soirée to encourage relaxation, trust, and family values. All I need to do is convince Philip to come with Jessica and ask Enzo to bring Topaz along for a swim to cap off their first full-day visit together.

Enzo is so excited to have his daughter for a whole day. He's been planning where to take her and what he'll wear. Now that he's earning a little something from Nigel's personal training sessions, he's bought himself a fire-engine red tee shirt for the outing. He was a little worried that Goldie wouldn't approve, but when he showed it to me I assured him it would be fine.

Today is a 'resting day' from my fitness regime, so I've slept in a bit. Before even opening my bedroom door to go down for breakfast, I smell the most heavenly, chocolaty scent wafting up from the kitchen. The greedy child in me is already imagining what scrumptious concoction Enzo has whipped up for us that smells this wonderful.

He is shirtless and busy at the oven when I creep in through the living room. Because his back is facing me and I can get away with it, I slink behind the wall that separates the kitchen from the living room and peek around the edge.

I can hear Latin music playing softly and look for its source. Enzo must have purchased a radio when he bought his tee shirt because there is a small, army-green radio sitting on the edge of the island counter near where he has started building a pyramid of cookies on a platter.

My mouth, which was already salivating nicely, is now sending messages to my brain about getting to the stack of cookies as quickly as possible. They look and smell like chocolate chip, an American delicacy of which I am particularly fond.

Enzo does a few dance steps in time with the music while he pulls on one of my flowery oven mitts. The sight of him in nothing but shorts and an oven mitt is one that might stay with me for a while.

He opens the oven, and eight seconds later I get a fresh blast of chocolate-sugar-butter fragrance in my nostrils. I feel a tad voyeuristic watching him re-move the sheet of cookies from the oven and place them on a rack to cool. Spatula in hand, he executes a spin and a rock-step that looks mambo-esque.

My conscience prods me to make my presence known, but this is the best entertainment I've enjoyed in a long time. I allow myself a few more minutes of watching him dance along to the music while he happily scoops the last of the cookie dough onto a fresh cookie sheet and pops it in the oven.

Then I force myself to retreat back into the living room and make a noisy approach to alert him. When I round the wall I've just been using as cover, Enzo is moving to turn off his radio.

"You can leave that on, Enzo. It's rather cheery and goes well with the chocolate smell you've created. Are we having cookies for breakfast? Not that I'm complaining…it's just a change from the norm."

Enzo grins, his eyes practically sparkling with delight. "I'm making cookies for my picnic with Topaz tomorrow. Chocolate chip are her favorite. But there's enough to let you have some. I made you a fruit plate for breakfast."

My eyes find the kitchen table, already set with small glasses of grapefruit juice, plates of fruit as advertised, and a few tubs of Greek yogurt in case I want some with my berries and melon.

"I will admit to a weakness for chocolate chip biscuits…we call all types of cookies 'biscuits' in England. May I?"

He nods permission to approach the tower of cookies he's built. I take two – ooh, still warm – and bring them to the table with me. Enzo sets the timer and joins me.

"I got my last batch in. Later, I'm making tamales…another of her favorites. Everything has to be ready by tonight because I'm picking her up early tomorrow. I want to have the whole day with her…Have you got a backpack or something I can borrow to carry the food in?"

I nod while finishing a sip of grapefruit juice. "Certainly. I even have one that's made for picnics; forks, napkins, plastic glasses. It'll be just the thing. Where are you taking her?"

Enzo swallows the strawberry he was chewing and smiles. "Griffith Park. That's why we need to bring plenty of food. They got the gardens, hiking, the observatory, a merry go round, and everything. I used to take her there on her birthday, but I missed the last one. We can spend the whole day there."

"That sounds fantastic…do you think she'd like to come back here for a swim when you finish at the park? I'm having my Mum and Goldie over for a little cook-out, and it would be lovely to introduce them to Topaz. Does she like to swim?"

He's grinning again. "Yeah…yes, she loves swimming. I started teaching her when she was little at the same Y where I learned." He nods, deciding. "We can come for swimming. A cook-out sounds real nice, Hester."

I can tell he still feels strange saying my name after all that time he called me Miss Hastings. Admittedly, it feels odd to me as well. But he's said he'll come to my pool party, which is perfect.

"I'm hoping I can convince Philip to bring Jessica…it would be fun for the girls to play together. I do hope he'll come to his senses and let Jessica sleep over at weekends again."

Enzo looks at me sideways, eyebrows raised. "If you want him to come to this party you better not tell him I'm going to be there…"

"I'm hoping to convince him to come in part because I want him to spend time with you and Topaz, see what a great father you are. If he sees you as just another Dad and realizes we're not a couple, maybe he'll relax a little. Do you mind if I tell him about all the learning you've been doing? Why you're living in the cabana?"

"I don't think you want to tell him I'm fresh outta jail…"

"No, no. Not that part. Just that you're really trying to make something of yourself, and I'm simply teaching you skills to help you along."

He shrugs, a gesture that makes his shoulder muscles and biceps bulge. "Sure. No problem."

I start to tell him he should wear a shirt at meals, but then stop myself. There's no reason not to enjoy a little eye candy with my breakfast. After the last bite of cantaloupe, all that remains on my plate are the two cookies. I bite into one and actually speak with my mouth full. "Oh my God, Enzo. These are so good!"

He smiles. "I put a little cinnamon in. And extra chips." The timer goes off and he jumps up to fetch the last batch of cookies from the oven.

I savor the rest of the cookie and brush the crumbs from my lips with my napkin. "All I can say is, Topaz is one lucky little girl."

ENZO

Thursday, April 24th

I wake up early. It's already a good day. Last night, while I was makin' tamales after dinner, I got a call from a lady who saw my ad up at the bagel shop. She's looking for a new trainer and lives close. She's gonna come by with a friend and try a workout with me, so if she likes it I might get another paying client.

In the kitchen, I'm real quiet so I don't wake Hester. We're gonna skip liftin' today 'cause I got to get out so early. But after packing up the picnic backpack she loaned me I leave a plate of cookies and tamales on the table for her breakfast. She kept tellin' me how good them tamales smelled last night when I was making 'em.

Takes me two busses and a short walk to get to Topaz' door. I knock soft 'cause them other girls might be sleeping. Martha answers, and I ask her to please get Topaz' swim suit so I can bring it with us for later. Then Topaz comes out of the bathroom and leaps at me for a big hug. When we get out to the sidewalk, I lift her on my shoulders so she don't get tired out from walking to the bus stop.

The day at the park goes by in a blur of smiles and laughin'. Topaz and me are so happy bein' together; I swing her around and around until we have to lie down all dizzy on the grass. We ride the old merry-go-round and sit on horses right next to each other. She's going up while I'm coming down, and she laughs at how much taller she gets than me. We have our picnic and eat all the tamales. She likes the smoothies I brought; strawberry for her, blackberry for me. The cookies we get out and eat all through the day whenever we feel hungry again. I brought about a hundred, so we never run out.

We hike the easiest trails, the ones I used to take her Mama on before Topaz was even born. I show my baby girl that I still got the little jade tiger we bought together, and her eyes go big 'cause she thought it was lost. Then, because I didn't give her anything except a letter on her last birthday, I unhook the gold chain from around my neck and put it on my daughter. I tell her it was from her Mama, and she needs to keep it real safe. She looks at me like I just gave her the moon and keeps touching it.

Admission for the Observatory is free, which is good because it means there's enough money for us to see the Planetarium show and still have bus fare to get us to Los Feliz for the pool party.

At five o' clock I ask Topaz how would she like to go swimming next? Baby girl freaks out, jumping and hollering about what a great idea that is. So, we catch the bus and eat more cookies.

When we get to Hester's place, there's three extra cars in the driveway. Topaz is ridin' up on my shoulders again, but I know her eyes are all big because she's never been to a house this fancy before, and her grip on my hair tightens. I hold onto her legs more secure so she knows I got her covered on all fronts. But when we walk around the back of the house she starts to wiggle on my shoulders in excitement. At the sight of the pool she squeals so loud, there's no chance of making a quiet entrance.

Everybody turns to check us out. Even Jessica, who's already in the pool splashing around, spins her head to get a look. I stop to unload Topaz, who's squirming so much I can barely walk straight.

"Daddy, get my suit! I wanna change now and get in…"

"Just a minute, baby girl. I gotta introduce you to all these people who've never met you before."

"I done met Miz Hastings…Hi, Miz Hastings!" She waves her arm real big, and Hester waves back. I lead Topaz through the gate and wave hello to all the faces. Everybody's smiling but Philip. He looks like he just got served barbequed lizard on a stick for dinner.

Hester comes over, and Topaz gives her a hug. "Hey, lucky girl…" She touches the gold chain my girl's wearing. "Did your Daddy give you this beautiful necklace?"

"Yeah! It used to b'long to my Mama, and Daddy says it's mine now. But I'm not gonna wear it to school, 'cause I don't wanna lose it."

"You know, Topaz, I have a little velvet box just the right size for you to keep your necklace in when you're not wearing it. Would you like to have it?"

My girl's eyes are bright and happy like sparklers. So excited she can't even say nothing, just nods real hard.

"I'll make sure you have it before your Daddy takes you home tonight, alright?"

Topaz nods again and looks at me with such a happy smile it makes my heart hurt a little.

Then Hester's Mom gets up and comes to give me a hug. This is what rich English people do: a hug that doesn't go all the way around and a kiss on each cheek that don't actually make lip contact. I've seen her do it with Hester so I copy and say, "It's such a pleasure to see you again."

Hester's smiling, so I know I did it right. Then she introduces me to somebody named Christopher, who must be the Mom's home skillet. He gets a sincere smile and firm handshake with, "It's a true pleasure to make your acquaintance."

I'm proud when Topaz holds out her hand to shake with Hester's Mom and the home skillet just like I taught her on the bus. She don't say nothin' out of shyness, but smiles real cute so it's okay. Kids can get away with just about anything if they cute.

Goldie's next, and she introduces herself to Topaz, who kinda hides behind me with a shy smile. I understand 'cause that's how I woulda done when Goldie first stuck her hand out at me if I could have. Then Goldie hugs me, which doesn't feel too crazy considering what happened at the wedding.

Nigel's face is all red, but that's how I'm used to seein' him. We did some training just yesterday so we acknowledge each other all cool with nothing but a nod. I know he's here mainly to make sure Philip knows me and Hester ain't knockin' boots.

Now we're down to Jessica and Philip. I can see Philip don't wanna shake my hand even when Hester makes introductions as though we haven't met before. But I stick out my hand anyway, and he gives me a tough-ass grip of steel to show I can't compete. "It's good to get a proper introduction this time around," I say and then give my most sincere smile without overdoin' things. I don't wanna know what all Hester done told him about me to ease his hate, but for her sake, I hope it works.

Jessica is out of the pool and leaving a trail of wet that ends up on me when she hugs me sideways and then takes Topaz' hand all friendly and tows her along to the cabana.

"Hold on, baby," I call after my girl. Then I got to fish her suit out of the backpack and chase her down to give it to her because, of course, those girls didn't slow down one bit.

Hester's Mom laughs, and Hester offers me a drink, which I take. Some kinda something with lemon floating in it. But it's got ice, and I'm hot, so I don't care what it is.

Then Christopher, who's grill-master, hands around scallops wrapped up in some kind of bacon, and everyone stops staring and smiling at me and eats.

HESTER

Saturday, April 26th

Before I'm dressed for my pre-breakfast workout I hear voices outside my window. Pushing the curtain aside for a quick peek reveals two bleach blond supermodels lifting dumb bells on my cabana porch. At least they look like supermodels; perfect bodies, uber tans, fake body parts.

By the time I have my exercise kit on and exit the glass slider downstairs they are waving goodbye to Enzo and leaving through the gate. They don't even notice me. Enzo is tidying up his workout space and looks so happy I have to make the first words that pop into my head different when they come out my mouth.

"So, were those girls new training clients?"

Enzo smiles. "They came to try a session and see if they like it. I hope they decide to be clients, 'cause I could use the business."

I nod and begin stretching for my workout.

"Hey," Enzo looks worried, "is it okay to have people you don't know coming and going for workouts here?"

I shrug. "It's the only way for you to get enough clients to make any money, so it's not very fair if I don't allow it. I guess maybe just let me know when they're coming."

"Okay…and thanks again for setting me up with all this." His gaze lovingly turns to his outdoor gym. "I still can't believe it's really real, you know?"

I wave my hand as though it's nothing. "I think of it as a business invest-ment. You're a good bet, Enzo." I flex a toned bicep. "You're really good at whip-ping people into shape."

He cracks a smile. "Likewise, Miz Hastings." His expression turns serious again, and he looks at his hands. When he speaks his voice is so soft I have to lean forward to hear. "I can't think of a time in my life when things have been this good for me. When I get Topaz back, I'll have everything…back behind those bars I never dreamed all this could happen."

I think about the character he has displayed during his time here. How he has risen to every challenge. "Well, you're hard-working and you're talented. That combination can take you places…all you were missing was the opportu-nity to get started."

"Yeah, well. Anyway, thanks."

ENZO

For a second, it seems like maybe we should hug or somethin', but it doesn't happen. I'm kinda glad 'cause she's in her spandex, and it mighta been intense to feel her all up close. Plus I'm pretty sweaty already from the workout with the Barbies. They were some strong-ass girls.

Hester starts bicep curls with the weights I set out for her, and as soon as I get on the bench to do my reps, she starts talking.

"Thanks for bringing Topaz to my barbeque party the other evening. It was a risk to invite Philip because of our history and because Goldie and Mum don't care for him much, but I think it paid off. Did I tell you he called yesterday?"

I hold the barbell up longer than necessary so I can talk clearly. "No. What did he say?"

"He asked about Nigel, which is so funny because Philip claims he's dating someone seriously. Why would he care what my relationship is with Nigel if he's not hoping there's a chance he and I might get back together?"

Easy question. "I can feel the brother on this one…when things didn't work out for me with Topaz' Mama, it was like, okay, I didn't want to be with her, but

I still cared about who she was with. I mean, it was different because we had Topaz together and all, but I got jealous about the parts of her I still liked going to somebody else, you know? I still felt like she was kind of mine in a way. You never felt that way about somebody?"

She thinks for a minute. "Not really, no. I prefer a clean break, which won't happen with Philip if I'm going to stay in Jessica's life. I honestly don't care who he dates or what he does. But he needs to stop feeling like he gets a say in what's happening in my life. He's trying to control me with his rules about when I can get together with Jessica."

I lower my barbell on an inhale before I speak. "What did he say about all that when he called?"

"He said he still isn't comfortable with Jessica being here, but I can take her out on my own to other places. Rather like your day out with Topaz. But neither you nor Nigel can be with me when I'm spending time with Jessica."

"He's just protecting his baby girl. I know 'cause I worried my ass off about Topaz livin' with foster parents the whole time I was in. Like, what if they hurt her or made her live all up in a dirty bedroom with six other kids, or didn't feed her enough, or what if one of the other kids was older and hurt her somehow. Or maybe the Dad was no good. You know, stuff like that. Seeing her in there where they live made me feel better. But I still worry. I told her she's got to tell me if anybody does anything she don't like. *Doesn't* like."

Seems like I just got to the point where I was perfect with my words around Hester all the time. And now I'm gettin' more comfortable around her and keep slippin' up. What the hell's that all about?

Hester finishes a set of squats and lowers her weights. "I suppose Jessica and Topaz are lucky their Dads care enough to be protective. Even though I don't like Philip much, I have to admit that he is a pretty good father most of the time. And I have to focus on the fact that I'm making progress. I'll schedule a few days out with Jessica and then push for time here again. There's no reason it can't go back to being like it was before, right?"

"It'll help when I move out." I slide from under the weight I been liftin' and start to take fifty pounds off each end to get it ready for her.

Hester don't say nothing. Just picks up her weights and starts lunges.

She ain't doing it quite right. I come over and put one hand on her back and the other on her knee to adjust her lunge posture. "Here, you got to make sure your knee doesn't go past your toes. Remember?"

She nods. "Right, thanks." Her leg comes back, and she steps out with the other one, looking like it's a real effort. But the knee stays in the right place.

"There you go."

She finishes a set and puts the weights down. "You've never told me what your plan was for when you got out of jail before Goldie roped you into working with me."

Not much to tell. "Get some kind of job, find a place to live, get Topaz back. I didn't have a plan as much as thoughts about gettin' out there and see who was willing to hire me."

She doesn't correct me. Just starts another set of lunges. "So you were just going to walk around and look for 'help wanted' signs?"

"Something like that. But I wasn't going back to the 'hood."

"Why not?"

"Nothing left there for me. And I don't want Topaz growing up there."

"Where is the 'hood?"

"Watts, mostly."

She gives me a look like, 'are you serious?' "I hear Watts can be pretty rough."

"Yeah, but it's not so bad as people think. You ever been there?"

"You know, I don't think I've ever even driven through it."

"You should go, man. It's a real education. And it's got a good side too. Some cool sights, and they got awesome food if you know where to find it. There's some museums and the Towers."

"That's right, the famous Watts Towers. Someone told me about them when I first moved to L.A. I always meant to go, but haven't gotten there yet."

"Aw, man. You got to go. The Towers is powerful. I used to go and just look at 'em when things got rough. Always made me feel better." Imagining them Towers makes me think of Ricky. I wonder if he's still spending days at the Center.

When I check her form again, Hester has this look on her face that I don't know what it means. The she nods like she's decided something. "Let's go see them then."

Just like that? Spur-of-the-moment don't seem like her thing.

Hester puts down her weights and takes a deep breath. "Today, let's go. Brent cancelled his on-set appointment, so my first client isn't until two o' clock. I was going to spend the time organizing my closet, but going to see the Watts Towers sounds like a lot more fun. Besides, you've been stuck in my world for six weeks. Don't you think it's about time you showed me where you come from?"

HESTER

Enzo says that to get a real feel for his old life we have to take the bus. He also instructed me to dress down, so I've got on capri jeans and the aqua tank top I usually wear when I'm organizing my closet. My hair is up in a ponytail, and the only jewelry I put on is a pair of emerald stud earrings.

We run into the bagel shop for a to-go breakfast and are standing at the bus stop by ten past nine.

We work on our bagels for a while and watch three busses that Enzo says are the wrong ones pass by. "You know, I probably shouldn't confess this…but I've never been on an American bus."

Enzo looks at me like I've just told him I was raised by dragons. Then he rubs his hands together in mock excitement. "Girl, you are in for a treat. Riding the bus means you get to wait on the curb no matter whether it's rainin' or what. You get to enjoy that fresh smell of whatever rotten stuff be rolling around on the floor, and you get to lean all up against other people and listen to whatever crazy-talkin' hobo had enough money to pay to ride without going nowhere." He pauses to pretend like he's just thought of something amazing. "You know what, after you experience all that, you might just never go back to your sweet little BMW."

I laugh, but the truth is that it's fun to be doing something outside of the normal routine. The last time I rode a bus was in London with my paternal Grandmother. I was eleven. And it really was a wonderful adventure. She'd let me sit upstairs on the double-decker, and I still remember how exciting it was to peer out at all the shops we passed on Oxford Street.

By the time Enzo flags down the bus we want we've finished our bagels. I follow him up the short flight of steps. He pays for both of us and leads me to yellow plastic seats toward the back.

"Don't get too cozy, we're going to change to another one in about fifteen minutes."

Sitting next to Enzo on the bus, I try to imagine what it would be like not to have a car. How would my life be different if I had to depend on public transportation? What would it be like to have such a meager paycheck that owning a car was completely out of reach?

It's not long before Enzo signals for the next stop and we get off. We wait a while with an old man wearing an army jacket, winter scarf, and gloves even though it's already at least seventy five degrees. He doesn't get on our bus, the next one to stop.

I look out the window as we roll along, watching the streets, buildings, and the pedestrians rushing along like they're so busy. It's a little overwhelming to think how every one of them has a complicated life, people they love and who love them, jobs, hobbies, personal tragedies. As we get closer to Watts, the people I observe become more casually dressed. Men begin to display a street swagger. I see a stony-faced young woman towing her little boy behind her as though he was freight. There is a visible shift in attitude; people seem to be rushing less, are more aware of their surroundings, defensive in an offhand way.

When Enzo signals it's time to exit the bus I follow, holding my purse a little closer to my body. I don't mean to be guarded, but people who are waiting for the next bus stare at me when I step off. I feel their eyes slide over me and Enzo, taking us in.

ENZO

We walk like we're in no hurry down 107th. I see her lookin' at the little box homes, the small plots of land people have laid claim to. The sun is bright, and she's got her sunglasses on, reddish hair pulled back into a ponytail. Nigel called her hair 'ginger'. I think it's more like paprika or chili powder. With it pulled back like that she looks young like maybe she's just out of college. Lookin' at her, you know she's been to college. Even in jeans and a tank she looks like money. It's in her skin, the way she moves. She's sure of herself in a way I've never known anybody else to be. Seems like all the people I ever known are scared most of the time. Me, too. I guess I'm hoping some of whatever Hester's got rubs off on me.

You can see the Towers from a long way off. But until you get right up on the triangular slice of land they sit on, your eyes don't catch the color, the design built into them. When Hester sees the walls with the colorful pops of ceramic mosaic she can't get enough. Ignoring the stalls set up to sell stuff to tourists, she walks along the whole decorated wall before ducking into one of the arched doorways.

We look up and around, taking in the scaffold-like circles that go up and up. It's quiet because it's early and not many tourists have gotten here yet.

I don't know why, but when I lean over to talk, I whisper. "This old Italian dude spent thirty years building this all by himself outta pipe and wire and cement and all these bits of broken stuff."

"It's like an eclectic, open-air cathedral." Her voice is a whisper also.

"Whenever I come and look at these things, it makes me think about what that old guy gave the rest of us by building all this. Makes me think about what I want to build and leave behind for whoever wants it after I go."

Hester takes hold of my arm and points to a weather-worn cement face that's been molded into one of the tower rails along with bits of shiny and colorful mosaic. "It's incredible how one person can take ordinary, everyday materials and turn them into something so completely extraordinary. It must have been a labor of love."

I think about how many times I came here over the years and wondered if I'd ever be able to build something of my own. Not towers, but something to be proud of. Something only I could make happen. I used to think about how the guy who built all this must have had days when he wondered whether he'd get it all finished. Or thought maybe it was a waste of time after all. And then the days when he felt inspired, or happy because he'd found a broken blue plate he could smash and knew just where he wanted to mount the pieces. How he must have enjoyed the thrill of climbing up so high to attach the next length of pipe.

Hester is quiet for almost an entire half hour while we walk around looking at the structures from all angles. Then she buys us cold bottles of water from one of the street vendors, and we sit down against the mosaic walls and drink.

Since she said we should come here, the idea of visiting Ricky's been rolling around in my head. It's pulling at me like both a good idea 'cause we're so close to the Center and a really bad one 'cause Hester's with me. I should have let her drive us so she could just leave while I go up to the Center. Makes me feel guilty that I haven't been to see him since I got out. What kind of brother am I?

It kicks around in my head, and the guilt wins. "Hester...I wonder if you would mind?" Nah.

"Mind what?"

Maybe today's not right. "Nothing. Forget it."

Hester lowers her sunglasses and hits me with them blue eyes. "Enzo, what were you wondering if I would mind?"

"There's a place not too far from here...it's a Day Center for people with disabilities, you know?"

"You want to go there?"

"Well, I don't know if he'll be there on a Saturday. Or even if he goes there at all anymore. But my brother, Ricky, he used to go there, so I thought..."

She pops her sunglasses back in place. "Of course! Yes, we must go and find out if your brother is there. Heavens, Enzo...I had no idea. When was the last time you saw him?"

"Maybe year and a half."

Hester stands and holds out a hand to help me up. I take a wrist hold on her and pretend like she's helping. I point north, and we start walking.

HESTER

I look back every now and again to view the Towers as they recede in the distance. Their whimsy and eclectic beauty spoke to a part of me that understands the need to do something meaningful. While Enzo is hardly a tower and I'm certainly not a builder, the time I've spent working with him and watching him push to achieve something concrete has filled that space within me. I suppose having a child or creating art of some kind might achieve the same end. Being a part of Jessica's life has absolutely felt that way.

Helping Enzo get a leg up on life has been satisfying in ways I wouldn't have dreamed when we first met him that day he was released from jail. He's literally blooming, and while I like to think my instruction has been the cause, it's probably more true that the support and opportunity Goldie and I have provided in the last six weeks has been more important than what I've been teaching him. Is he a different person now from the one who first knocked on my door? Yes and no. It's a paradox I may never unravel. His essence, his Enzo-ness, has not changed. His attitude, his expectations, his understanding, his perspective on life – all those have shifted.

It would be inappropriate to pat myself on the back for a job well done. The person who has achieved this transformation in Enzo is Enzo himself. But I confess that I take pleasure in believing it might not have been possible without my intervention.

The neighborhood we're walking through seems to be just waking up. I hear the sound of a screen door banging shut as a resident departs for wherever they have to be on this sunny Saturday morning. Cars roll past. The bright sound of children playing outdoors can be heard.

Enzo's voice startles me from my reverie. "Hester…I should warn you that some of the people at this place are a little tough to take."

"Thank you for the warning." I picture damaged people in varying stages of mental and physical despair. Scars. Drool.

"Ricky's not so bad. He always was a good kid, and you can still see that in him."

"Is he anything like you?"

He considers for a moment. "Yes and no. We both look like a cross between Mama and my Dad. Dad was pure Latino, both parents from over the border. Mama was more mixed up. Had Italian and Portuguese in her. Mama named me Enzo after her mother's Italian grandfather. She had browner skin and could pass for black or Latino. So we got a love for Mexican foods and music from Dad, but because Mama was the one who spent more time with us, we were raised on typical American-ness. I know that's not a word, but that's the best way I can put it.

"Ricky was better than me. Smart in school, good to Mama all the time. Made friends with kids who didn't get into trouble. The way Mama died just about crushed him."

Uneven pavement makes us drift too close as we walk and my arm brushes his. He moves left to give me more sidewalk space. I look over at him, notice his swagger is back. "How old were you when your mother died?"

"Thirteen. But she was kinda dead for a while before that. When she moved from booze to crack it was just about all over. At least she didn't have to see what happened to Ricky. She was gone before that."

"Enzo, I don't mean to sound dramatic, but your early life sounds so brutal. How did you deal with all the trauma?"

He shrugs like it was no big deal. "I spent a lot of time with my Dad's parents up until I was twelve. Lived with them sometimes when Dad was in jail and Mama was on the street. When she tried to get clean they even sold their house to pay off her debts, give her a fresh start. But of course she couldn't stay offa crack, and my grandparents had moved into a tiny apartment. First Abuelo died. Then my grandmother, mostly from the loss of him I think. And that was that."

"Where did you live after your Mum died?"

"Foster homes for a few years. Then Ricky got shot, and Mama's sister, my Aunt Latrice, took us in. She was so sad about the way things turned out for Mama. But then I moved out 'cause of the misunderstanding with her boyfriend. For all I know that guy's still takin' Ricky's money. But at least they got him in the Day Center so he doesn't have to be in that fallin' down house with them all the time."

"I hope he's there today so you can see him."

Enzo nods, takes a deep breath. We walk one more block in silence and then he stops in front of a brick house with a wooden walkway built over the original steps to admit wheelchairs. There's a sign out front that says, Watts Support Center for Disabled Adults.

Enzo turns to me, concern on his face. "You sure you don't mind going in?"

"Why would I mind, Enzo? I'm delighted to have the opportunity to meet your brother."

Enzo gives me a look like, 'okay, you asked for it.' He leads me up the wheelchair ramp and we go in.

The smell of urine is unmistakable. There's no front desk like you might find at a clinic. All the walls that must have originally segmented the house into separate living spaces have been torn out. It is a large room with a few tables covered in arts and crafts supplies. Five people slumped in wheelchairs are parked in front of a television in the far left corner of the room. A lady with nut brown skin and white curly hair is sitting at one of the craft tables, aimlessly playing with a basket of colorful pom poms. They dot the floor around her chair.

A heavyset nurse in pink scrubs approaches from the kitchenette that's been left intact. "Can I help...Enzo? Is that you?"

Enzo grins at her, and she smiles, revealing two gold-capped teeth. She hugs him. "I ain't seen you for the longest time...where you been?"

"Nowhere. How you been, Tonya?"

"Aw, you know. Jus' puttin' one foot in front of the otha." Her eyes finally take me in. "Who this you got wit' cha?"

I decide I'd rather speak for myself. "Hester Hastings. I'm pleased to meet you." I extend my hand.

Tonya throws a reproachful glare at Enzo that perhaps would have been better timed if I hadn't actually been looking. But then she shakes my hand and gives me a grudging half-smile.

Enzo looks around. "Is Ricky here today?"

"Mmmhmmm. Sure is. You know how much he love the sunshine. You can find him out back. But you gotta sign in. Hang on, I'll get the sheet."

Tonya shuffles through a pile of papers on a small desk in the corner opposite the television. She brings us a yellow sheet of paper and a green pen that reads, 'have an awesome day' down the side. We sign, and then she bustles off to see to a young man sitting by a window who's started to moan.

I follow Enzo through the room to a door that takes us down another wheelchair ramp. There's a different nurse outside supervising seven individuals, all in wheelchairs. This nurse doesn't know Enzo. But there's no need to ask her where his brother is. Sitting in a blue and silver wheelchair near the bottom of the ramp is Ricky. Aside from the slackness of mouth, glasses, and a nasty scar on the left side of his forehead, he looks almost exactly like Enzo.

"Hey, homefry!" Enzo leans down and hugs his unresponsive brother. Mouth open, Ricky rolls his eyes to focus on his brother's face. It takes about twenty seconds before recognition sets in, and Enzo is rewarded with a grunt of joy. Enzo pats Ricky's shoulder and then travels a few yards to retrieve two plastic lawn chairs from a stack next to a long-unpruned azalea bush. He sets them down right in front of his brother's wheelchair, and we sit, keen to begin our visit.

Ricky reaches out a slim hand, and Enzo takes it in his own. "How they treatin' you?"

A roll of the head and an open-mouthed smile is the reply. I realize that, among other functions, Ricky has lost the ability to speak.

Enzo continues his one-sided conversation. "That good, huh? I'm sorry I ain't been over to see you for so long. Truth is, I thought about you a lot over the past year. And look at you, not changed one bit. Still the handsome dude all them ladies fall for, huh?"

Ricky grins, and his head swivels a bit unsteadily. His long body is skinny from lack of exercise. It is folded into a wheelchair that is at least one size too small for him. His knees come up to his elbows. His eyes are locked onto his brother's face.

"This here is Hester." Enzo points at me, and Ricky's eyes flicker over to me and then return to Enzo's face. "She's a pretty awesome kinda lady. I think you'd really like her. She's got a house with a pool, and she's lettin' me live there, yo. And guess what? She's set me up wit' some dope trainin' equipment, and I'm startin' my own business. Seriously. I got a few clients already. What do you think about that?"

Ricky nods in a wobbly sort of way, and his gaze swivels to me for a more serious appraisal. I have no idea how much he understands, how strong his cognitive abilities are. If I had to go on visuals alone, I'd say he's pretty much out to lunch. But there's something in the way he responds to Enzo that makes me feel as though some key synapses are firing up there in his bullet-damaged brain.

"Hello, Ricky. It's a pleasure to meet you. Is Ricky short for Ricardo or Richard?"

He stares at me, an open-mouthed smile on his face. Enzo leans over. "He likes you. Ricky's short for Ricardo. We called him Rico when he was real little, then it kinda morphed into Ricky." He waits for me to resume my conversation with his brother. "Go on, you can talk to him. I don't know how much sticks in there, but that's kind of the beauty, I guess. You can tell this guy anything."

I shift in my chair and address Ricky. "I've met your niece, Topaz. She's such a sweetie." I turn to Enzo. "Does he know who she is?"

"I've brought her here, but she was born way after he got like this, so I don't know if he realizes she's my kid."

Turning back to Ricky, I lean forward and place a hand on his bare knee. "I'm one of Enzo's fitness clients, and I'll tell you, Ricky...that brother of yours knows how to crack the whip. My muscles are sore all the time now."

"Hey! I'm not that bad...it's not like I'm torturing you." He turns to Ricky. "She makes me balance a penny on my nose while I practice pronunciation, and she makes me do weird sounds in a mirror. And for a while she was whacking me all the time with this stick she had..."

"All right now. Ricky, don't listen to him. He signed on for all of that willingly. I promise I've done nothing to take advantage of him." Oh, that didn't sound right.

Enzo raises his eyebrows at me and leans toward Ricky. "She keeps me in her pool house and makes me sleep on a giant purple sofa, man. I've been like, chained to her Standard American English DVD set for over a month. And now she wants me to start in on the Standard British English set." He leans further in with a loud whisper. "Homefry, you got to break me outta there..."

I laugh, and Ricky does also. It's a kind of seal-like bark, but it's surprisingly infectious. Enzo joins in the laughter, and then we all quiet down until awkward silence reigns.

After a minute Enzo pretends like he hears Ricky talking. "What's that? You wanna know how a lady like Miz Hastings got all the way from England to L.A.?" He turns to me. "You heard him. He wants to know more about you."

I give Enzo a Look and turn to Ricky. "Well, I was born and raised in Kent, which is a little bit south of London. My family had a manor home there, passed down through the generations to my father. He was a linguist, a professor. But the ancestral home became too much of a burden financially, so my father sold it to the highest bidder and left rainy England for a job here in sunny California. I was still at boarding school when they moved, but when I graduated I applied to UCLA for college to rejoin my Mum and Dad, and that's how I ended up in L.A."

"Ricky wants to know why a fox like you wants to date a guy like Nigel. I mean, no offense, but the dude's kind of boring." Enzo crosses his arms, watching me.

"I think that Ricky needs to mind his own business...Oh wait, what's that, Ricky?" I hold my hand up to my ear as though to hear better. "You think your brother should tell me how he came to be arrested for drug possession?"

The unhappy look that passes over Enzo's features makes me cringe. I might have crossed a line.

ENZO

I was hoping we'd never have to go there. It takes me a minute to think what to tell her. This would be a great moment for Ricky to up and say, 'You know I'm just foolin' with this disabled act, right? How 'bout them Dodgers?'

But he just sits there with his mouth all open and stares at us like he's waitin' to see what happens next. Me too, Ricky.

I want to give her the truth, but there's parts I just can't tell. Not to her. So I aim to get as close as possible.

"When Monique, that's Topaz' Mama, when she died, things got real hard for me and Topaz. I had to find a job where I could take care of my girl and still have time to work. Something real flexible. So my buddy Antwon hooked me up with some people who set me up with a job I could do at night. I'd leave Topaz to sleep the night at her Grandmama's and go do what I needed to do. It was good money, and I could take care of my baby girl, too."

"So you weren't actually doing drugs yourself?"

I shake my head hard like, 'Hell, no.' "My Mama died from crack. Monique OD'd on heroin. You think I'm ever gonna touch any of that stuff?"

"But it's okay with you if other people do?"

This is why I wish I could tell her the truth, even though the truth would freak her out more and maybe make her throw me offa her property. I hate the idea of anybody thinkin' I was feeding drugs to people. But it's a hell of a lot less embarrassing than the truth.

I guess she can see that I don't want to talk about it anymore, because her eyes get a look too close to pity in 'em for comfort.

"I'm sorry, Enzo. I don't mean to judge your actions. It's just...I find it difficult to imagine you involved in all that."

"You just ain't never been so desperate that you had to consider making a choice like that." I hate letting her go on believing it, but the other option is worse.

I hand Ricky some serious credit for great timing when he starts his 'take me for a walk' routine. He throws himself side to side in his chair until you think he's just about gonna topple over.

"Okay, Ricky." I let go of his hand and go around the back of his chair. "He wants me to push him. I'm only allowed to take him around the block over and over, but he likes it."

I wave at the skinny nurse who's out there, and she yells at me the rule about only around the block. Hester replaces the chairs on the stack, then catches up with us. Ricky lets his arms hang over the sides of the wheelchair and leans his head way back so he can look at me. His goofy upside-down grin makes me laugh.

Hester walks next to me all quiet for a few minutes and then asks another question. "Do you ever feel lucky it wasn't you who got shot instead of your brother?"

"All the damn time. And then sometimes I wish it had been me instead of him. Seein' him like this and knowing there isn't any way to get his future back hurts. It's like this pain that doesn't ever go away but you get used to walking around with it always there. This is gonna sound bad, but it's easier not to visit him. Then it's not in my face, like, 'look at Ricky who's never gonna have a woman, or have kids, or do all that science shit he was always so excited about.' Sometimes I wonder if God picked the right brother to get fucked up."

She don't fuss at me about the bad words. She don't say nothin' at all. In fact, it makes me realize that she hasn't even really been workin' me that hard since we got back from the wedding.

"How come you haven't started in on my ass with all the hard core British accent stuff, man?"

She tilts her head like she's not sure herself. "I suppose it's been nice to have a little break."

I look down at Ricky, and his eyes are closed. Either enjoying the sunshine or fallin' asleep.

But then all the peace and harmony is over, 'cause way down the block I see somebody comin' this way. And even without seeing his face clear, I know who it is.

Antwon.

HESTER

Enzo tenses up, his grip tightening on the wheelchair handles until we slow to a stop. He doesn't turn his head, but when he speaks his voice is low and deadly.

"You gotta go back to the Day Center."

I understand the seriousness in his tone, but I don't comprehend the reason behind it. "Why? What's happened?"

"We're gonna have company, and I can't promise that some bad shit ain't about to go down."

I look all around, down the street in every direction. Except for a few kids playing outside, there's only one other person on the sidewalk. He's not as tall as Enzo, but his shoulders are massive. He has lots of braids all over his head, tattoos down both arms, and his swagger is bold enough for two men. Even though his pace is reasonably relaxed, from the way his gaze fixates on Enzo, I know this man is headed straight to my student and that he means business.

I look down at Enzo's brother, who appears to be asleep. "Should I take him back?"

Enzo nods slowly.

"Should I call the police?"

A quick shake of the head. "No."

"Enzo…"

"Go on. Now. Take him back."

Enzo turns the wheelchair around in one fluid movement. I take the handles when he lets go and push as fast as I can without jostling Ricky too much. He wakes up anyway and looks up at me.

I go about a hundred yards, back to the safety of the Day Center porch. From there I'm out of the way, but I can see what's happening. The braided man walks straight up to Enzo and shoves him hard in the most hostile greeting I've ever witnessed. Enzo holds his ground, hands up like he's ready to fight but he doesn't want to. As the man circles him, Enzo turns so that he's always facing his opponent.

Then the man stops and says something. I can hear sound, but not meaning. His manner is aggressive, pushing up against Enzo with his barrel chest like they're having a test of who's stronger on their feet.

Ricky makes a noise that sounds like a laugh. His mouth is open, but for the first time since I met him, he's not smiling.

When the braided man puts a hand to his waistband, I can see a gun handle protruding from the top of his oversized athletic shorts.

"Oh my God…bloody hell." I reach in my purse for my phone and dial 9-1-1.

ENZO

"You son-of-a-bitch piece of shit…I should bust a cap in your ass. You broke wit me, man. You took Shawn down wit' you."

Antwon's all up in my face, and I have to push him out to arm's length. "*You* broke with me, man. As soon as they came lookin' for names, you gave 'em mine. I did a year, man. A year of my life I can't get back 'cause of you. I can't believe you've got the balls to try and tell me *I'm* the one who done *you* wrong…"

"It was me or you, bro. And they came to me first. But you s'posed to take it like a man. You ain't s'posed to go and tattle like a baby on nobody else, man."

"Actually, the way I see it, we're even. Except for the fact that you stole my roll of bills. So maybe that puts me ahead and you owe me."

"Listen to you, all 'actually, the way I see it' pompous full of shit. A wad of cash ain't worth the same as my brotha. Maybe I should put a bullet in you, make you match up with lil' Ricky, and we'll see who's ahead. How you like that?"

He makes a show of pulling out the Glock, but he isn't pointing it at me yet.

If he thinks his pissy little Glock scares me he's dead wrong. I hold up a hand, change the subject. "How'd you know I was here, man?"

Antwon laughs. "Tonya'll do anything for some bills, yo. I told her call me when you show up. You and Ricky so tight I knew you'd be down in here."

I shake my head. I can't believe I let that bitch hug me. "Let's call it even then. You got my money, and Shawn's almost done his time."

"I don't know." Antwon scratches the side of his head with his gun. "Tonya said you had some fancy-ass lady wit' cha. Seems to me I see her right ova there at the Day Center wit' Ricky. Mmmm...that girl be white like sugar...you got you a sugar-momma?"

"She ain't nobody. Just showin' her around."

"You don't take a 'nobody' to meet Ricky." He smiles. "Where'd you find her? 'Cause maybe I want one, too."

"Look, you and me was friends, remember? We got history. Time to let by-gones be the hell gone, yo."

He looks at me like he knows everything I ever done. Which is almost true. "You told her yet?"

"Shut the fuck up."

He laughs at me. "You ain't told her, man! And girlfriend looks like some good money." Antwon sniffs at me, checks out my new clothes. "That girl's got you smellin' and lookin' like greenbacks, bro. You sure that sweet piece of ass is ready to hear all about Homeboy Gangsta? I don't think it's fair to have secrets from such a fine lady, you know? I think I'll just take myself on over there and give her some knowledge...who knows, maybe once she's done wit' you she'll take me on."

He moves like he's headed toward the Day Center. I grab his arm 'cause I'm not about to let him anywhere near Hester.

"Whoa, man! Looks like you don't like that idea, huh?" He yanks his arm out of my grip. "I unnerstan...a lady like that's worth too much to lose, right? So how about you slide me some bills, and we can forget all 'bout it."

"I ain't got nothin', Antwon. They only let me out six weeks ago, man."

His look is hard and mean. "I don't care when you got out. If you hangin' with a lady fine as that one you got access to somethin' you can turn into green-backs. And I want 'em."

"I ain't got nothing! I'm trying to…"

There ain't even any sirens but we both look back past the Day Center at the same time. Two black and whites are way up at the top of the street, lights flashin'.

Antwon's got the gun. He's the one who's gotta get out of here.

"I'ma find where you stayin', yo. I'm gonna come get them greenbacks, or I'ma tell your sugar-momma what you is. Hear me?"

He points the gun at me while he's backing down the street away from the squad cars. Then he has to turn and run.

One squad car follows him, the other stops next to me. Big Latino police-man gets out. Eyes me up and down. "What's goin' on, man?"

Time to see what my new skills can do. I hold out my hands like I'm as sur-prised as he is. "Nothing. We came to see my brother at the Day Center," I point to where Hester and Ricky are holed up on the porch, "and some guy tried to take my wallet. Thank God you came, because he pulled a gun on me."

When the policeman hears my Standard American English, he's all polite and reasonable. "He didn't get the wallet?"

I shake my head.

"You and your girlfriend okay then?"

It feels pretty damn good that his first guess is she's my girlfriend. "Yes, we're fine. I hope you catch him because he scared the hell out of her."

He nods. "We'll do what we can, sir. You wanna take a card with the number for counseling? Sometimes these things can shake you up, man." He offers me a business card that says, 'Victim Counseling Resource Center'.

"No, thank you. We'll be alright. You sure showed up at the right time and I appreciate the help."

"No problem. Well, keep safe. We'll be patrolling the neighborhood for a while, so don't worry about that guy coming back, okay?"

I nod, like 'that's great, thanks so much.' Then he gets in his car and takes off around the corner. That's it. I'm like, shocked. Police ain't never treated me like that before.

Hester's staring at me like I got three heads, but I'm staring back for a whole 'nother reason. I can't believe that Standard American English and some uptown threads just bought me Respect.

→═◉ ◉═←

It's not until we're on the bus that I'm ready to talk about it. She started in on me with questions back at the Day Center, but I told her let's focus on Ricky. I've been feeling her waiting for me to explain for the entire walk to the bus stop.

We sit down on the hard plastic seats at the back of the bus, and I take a second to breathe.

"That back there, what happened...that was Antwon. We went to school together, shot hoops at the courts near my Abuelo's house. He joined a gang, I didn't. His gang treated him worse than a dog, so he dropped out and started freelancing. He works the edges. Nothing hard core. Mostly, he finds people who need money and hooks 'em up with people who need bodies to sell or do stuff that isn't strictly legal. Keeps himself out of trouble, runs other people smack into it."

"Did he help get you the flexible job involving the drugs?"

I need to tell her. But this ain't the place. Not now. "Yeah."

Her eyes narrow like she's all furious. "I can't believe the nerve of him! How did he even find you?"

"Remember that nice lady who signed us in at the Day Center?"

Her face is horrified. "No! She hugged you!!"

"Yeah, well. Some people will do anything for money. Place was booby-trapped. He had her revved to call him the second I stepped in the door. Wanna know something even more messed up?"

Her eyes go wide like 'there's more?'

"Antwon is Topaz' uncle. Monique was his baby sister."

This is shocking for her. Clearly, her family don't go around waving guns at each other. "Oh my God, Enzo." She puts a hand to her chest. "I thought he was going to shoot you."

"Nah. Antwon don't want to get in trouble. Likes to make a show and demand stuff. Thing probably wasn't even loaded."

"Well, it looked pretty convincing…"

Thinking I can play it off, I fake like I'm all emotional. "I'm touched you were so worried about me."

I thought she'd roll her eyes at me, shake her head at my stupidity. But instead her eyes get watery, and she tries to stop the tears but a couple roll out anyway.

I turn, put my arm around her. "Hey now…everything's okay. I'm sorry it shook you up…but I promise it wasn't that big a deal, Hester. I mean, it turned out to be pretty good that you called the police and all, but he wasn't gonna really hurt me. Just needed to throw his weight around."

"Well, I'm not used to that, Enzo. I really thought he might kill you."

"Nah. You're not getting rid of me that easy."

She starts riflin' through her purse. When she finds a tissue she dabs at her eyes impatiently. Then she lets her head relax back against my shoulder. "I had no idea that teaching you was going to be such a roller-coaster ride, Enzo."

Girl, you don't even know.

HESTER

By the time we walk back into the driveway it's just past one-thirty. I'm sweaty and have just now managed to stop getting upset every time I think about Antwon pointing a gun at Enzo. I have twenty-two minutes to shower, compose myself, eat a little something, and meet my two o' clock appointment. Thankfully, Enzo heads straight for his workout zone. No doubt he needs to 'lift some pounds' to process the harrowing experience of having his life threatened.

Oh, bloody hell. I just remembered that Nigel asked me to go to dinner with him tonight. How bad would it be to cancel? If I did, does having recently watched someone get threatened at gun-point make an acceptable excuse?

Get a grip, Hester. Calm down and breathe. One thing at a time: shower.

-->=◉ ◉=<--

Six o' clock finds me refreshed and nicely turned out in a white sundress and navy knit bolero with cap sleeves. I wanted to situate Enzo in the kitchen and draw Nigel in for some conversation before we headed out, but Enzo is nowhere to be found, and Nigel seems to have a bee in his bonnet about whisking me away as quickly as possible.

Indeed, he's a bit different tonight. Quite touchy-feely in fact. He strokes my arm in the process of helping me into his Lexus convertible. Then places his hand proprietorially on my knee while driving.

We have to park a block and a half from the restaurant he's chosen; Cinnamon Persimmon. Greek fare, I believe. While we're walking he slips an arm around my shoulder, leaning in close like he's trying to smell my hair. Trying to walk while he's holding me close feels bumpy and awkward; I have to lengthen my stride in order to synchronize our tandem movement.

At the restaurant, he repeats the arm stroking when he pulls out my chair, and reaches across the table for my hand while we're viewing the menu. Once we've ordered, I try subtly to ascertain what has inspired this change of behavior.

"It was lovely of you to come to the little barbecue dinner party at my place on Thursday. I hope you didn't find it too boring."

His smile is cagey. "On the contrary, I was delighted. I had a little chat with Philip. He's quite interesting, and of course, it's not every day one gets to converse with the ex-partner of a lady one is dating. Actually, he offered me some food for thought."

This gets my back up. Philip offering Nigel advice…what about? What to expect from me? Favorite sexual techniques? I blush at the thought. "May I ask what exactly he suggested?"

"You may, but I'm not telling. Let's just say I'm holding out on making a final analysis for now."

I have no idea what to make of that so I change the subject.

"How is the screenplay coming along?"

He sighs. "Slow yet steady. It's lonely work, but the process is enormously entertaining. I'm pleased with the results so far." He raises one dark eyebrow. "And how is your human project coming along?"

I frown. "I'm not sure I would call Enzo a project...but the answer is things are becoming more complicated than I expected."

His other eyebrow goes up. "Oh? How so?"

"It's become rather more involved than it seemed at first it would be. He has a daughter, as you know..."

"Yes, a delightful little thing. Seemed to have an absolute blast playing in the pool with Jessica."

I smile. "Yes, they did hit it off. But you see, he's trying to regain custody of her, and then of course, I've been helping him get his personal training business off the ground, and he has a brother with traumatic brain injury from a gunshot wound, and..."

"You feel you're being drawn into the tangled web of his life a bit further than you expected perhaps?" He drives his index finger at the table like a torpedo, striking the glossy surface. "You have to set boundaries, you know. He's a bit like a stray dog...you start by putting out a dish of food, and before you know it, he'll be sleeping on your bed."

"Nigel, what exactly are you insinuating?"

His casual shrug implies innocence. "I'm insinuating nothing. I just think it would be wise for you to remain mindful of the fact that this bloke has nothing to lose and everything to gain from getting as close to you as possible in every way. You've already fronted him a place to stay, a new wardrobe..."

"Goldie paid for that. She's in charge of rebranding."

"Well, you bought him all that exercise equipment."

"It's an investment. He's going to pay me back as his business ramps up."

"Of course he is." Nigel takes a breath and looks me straight in the eyes. "Hester, I have to tell you something you're not going to like hearing. Are you ready?"

Now, how can I be ready when he puts it that way? "I don't know..."

"I'm going to tell you anyway. About Enzo. From the outside, from the perspective of someone who doesn't understand the scope of your 'project,' it rather looks like he's a kept man."

"A what?!"

"You know, a man without means being supported by a wealthy woman with a need for...companionship."

I can't believe we're having this conversation. "Nigel, that's ludicrous. Enzo lives in the cabana house! There's nothing untoward going on between us…" I've just realized who must be behind this. "Hold on. Just back up a second. Does all this have anything to do with the 'food for thought' Philip shared with you?"

He gives me a look that says, 'maybe it does, and maybe it doesn't.'

The waitress chooses this moment to bring our appetizers, and I'm so flustered by the portrait Nigel has painted of my life that I wave her away. "Now look here, Nigel. I'm sure this is all coming from a place of concern for my wellbeing, but you are completely out of order in being so forthcoming about your opinions on this subject. Enzo is my *student*. He's doing brilliantly with his education, and he is not…not some 'stray dog' who's going to wind up sleeping on my bed, thank you very much. Enzo and I have a very professional relationship based on his desire to better his prospects in life and my desire to help him do so. And for heaven's sake it wasn't even my idea! It was Goldie who roped me into this whole experiment…her idea from the beginning. So don't come to me with your suspicions and insinuations, telling me to watch out before Enzo plays on my oh-so-lonely heart and cons me out of my home and personal fortune."

Nigel raises both eyebrows. "Methinks the lady doth protest too much."

He waves the waitress back over with our appetizers and tucks into the tzaziki and pita triangles he's ordered, ignoring my glare of indignation.

Because I am well-bred, the idea of making a scene or leaving in a huff is abhorrent to me. Instead, I pick at my mini lamb kebabs, pointedly saying nothing at all. Nigel sips his wine and makes the odd murmur of gastric joy over his food. I can't help letting what he's said play over again in my mind. What would I presume about my arrangement with Enzo if I were viewing it from an outsider's perspective?

By the time our appetizers have been cleared and the entrees arrive, I can sense that my silence is making Nigel nervous. He tries twice to get us started on a new topic, but quickly finds that without a partner there is no conversation.

The food is absolutely delicious. I'm enjoying fragrant grilled eggplant with halloumi and roasted red pepper sauce. It is accompanied by a delicately spiced rice pilaf that puts me in mind of a trip to southern Cyprus I made with my mother as a teen.

When I look up from my plate, Nigel is staring at me. Do I have sauce on my face?

"What?"

His gaze deepens to sincere affection. "Hester, I like you. I'm…I'm attracted to you, and I can't help but notice that you don't appear to feel the same way about me." He scans the room self-consciously and lowers his voice. "I'm not stupid, I know you invited me to your barbeque to deflect Philip's romance radar away from Enzo. So I came along, playing the part of the sexless, bland, unthreatening love interest for you. What concerns me is that you cast me in that role for a reason; is that really how you view me?"

His directness catches me without a satisfying reply. "I…I'm not sure what you mean…"

"You know precisely what I mean, Hester. You think I'm a 'nice guy,' I have potential because I'm reasonably good-looking and prosperous. But what about fire? What about a little electricity when we touch? Do you feel any? Because I do, and if it's not there for you as well, then frankly, it's better to give up now and move on."

"Nigel…are you breaking things off with me?"

"No. I'm asking if you want me as more than a platonic boyfriend who's willing to spend money for fitness sessions with the man you're really hot for?"

Now it's my turn to look around and lower my voice. "Nigel…I hardly think you have an accurate view of the situation."

"Really? Are you certain? Because I think my vision is 20/20, and you're the one who needs glasses."

I sit up a little taller, draw self-assuredness around me like a cloak. "I don't think you're qualified to make that judgment. How long have you known me, five weeks?"

"I know you well enough to understand that the way you blushed a moment ago when I mentioned our personal trainer gives me the answer I need."

"Nigel, that's not fair, and you know it." Do I want to fight this or let it happen?

We fall into an uneasy silence that ends when our plates are cleared from the table.

Nigel takes a final sip of wine and regards me sadly. "It would be a shame to end what's been an enjoyable friendship thus far..." He casts a regretful glance at me and regroups. "So I propose that we remain friends into the foreseeable future. Does this plan meet with your approval?"

I suppose my pride should be hurt that he's dumping me, but he is correct on one count; there is no fire between us. I can't conjure passion where there is none, and though I like him very well, that's not enough reason to backpedal and claim there's a romantic future for us.

So I raise my glass of pinot noir and incline my head in acceptance of his proposal. I see fleeting disappointment in his expression before he raises his wineglass and we toast.

"I am sorry this couldn't go further, Hester. You are a very desirable woman, and it would have been my pleasure and privilege to be your inamorato."

-->==O O==<--

It's not late when Nigel drops me off at home. I can hear music from what must be a neighbor's party as I say 'goodbye' to him. There's no chaste kiss, no final attempt at intimacy on his part. We understand each other, and with any luck, we will remain friends. I wave as he backs out of the driveway and walk around the corner of my house to discover that the 'neighbor' throwing a little party is my tenant. Though it appears that only one guest is in attendance, and the 'party' on the cabana porch is some sort of macho, male-bonding ritual.

From cover of darkness, I can see Enzo and another man who looks oddly familiar from the back. They are both lifting weights, and Latin music is blaring from Enzo's radio. Several empty plastic Power-Ade bottles have been tossed poolside. I watch for a moment as Enzo says something that amuses the other man so much he has to put down his weights before he loses control of them from laughing so hard. Who...?

When I see his profile, I'm dumbstruck. What the hell is he doing here with Enzo?

ENZO

I catch sight of her standing by the side of the house and feel right away like I've been caught doin' something against her rules. She's got her X-ray death glare on, and it's aimed right at me. When she sees me see her, she starts walking over.

"Oh shit..."

"What?" He stops laughing and turns to see Hester comin'. But he smiles at her all friendly and gives her a 'come join the party' wave.

"She don't look happy..."

"Don't worry about old Miss Hastings. That whole frosty bitch thing is a total act. I can handle her."

She marches past the pool and right up onto the porch. The death glare eases into a cold smile, I guess 'cause she has to be nice to this guy at least.

"Brent Logan...what on earth are you doing here at," she looks at her watch, "at nearly nine o' clock at night? With Enzo Diaz?"

Brent puts on the accent she must be teaching him. "Why hello there, Miss Hastings! It's lovely to see ya, to be sure. *Tanks* fer stoppin' by."

"I'm delighted you've mastered the accent, Brent, but there's no need to show off. And please don't dodge my question: why, precisely, are you here this late at night working out with Enzo?"

"Relaxify, darlin'...here's how it went: I had to cancel our session this morning because the shoot got replaced by pre-publicity...that part you know. But I was hoping you'd have time to go through that big scene I can't quite get a handle on. I called and got no answer, so I thought I'd swing by and see if I could catch you." He gestures at the home gym set-up with admiration. "I had no idea you have a live-in trainer...now that's dedication. This dude is awesome. He was here working out and seemed like he didn't mind if I hit the weights, too..."

"So you're poaching free training from him?"

Brent spreads his hands, like, 'what's a guy to do?' Then he slips an arm around her, which is totally a mistake because he's all sweaty and she's all dressed up from her date. "Hey, you need to *relaxify*. Enzo's cool with it, and he's been showing me some amazing moves. Have you tried that power yoga lats builder he does with weights? It's killer!"

"Brent, you can't just 'swing by' any time you want help from me...since Enzo rents the cabana from me, I can't reasonably prevent your being here if he's invited you to work out. But personal training is his livelihood. If you want to work out with him again, you need to pay..."

"You've got to chill, darlin'! We already worked it out. I'm gonna stop out here with him for an hour every time you and I have a session. First time on..." he turns to me. "When did we say?"

"Tuesday."

"Yeah. Tuesday. So no worries, okay? You don't need to go all Mama Bear on me."

Hester still don't look happy, but her face is less tense. That girl could use a workout to help loosen her up. It don't look like her date went all that well.

"You wanna change and come lift some pounds with us?"

"Thanks, Enzo, but I'm beat. I think I'm just going to go to bed."

Brent still has his arm around her and makes like he's gonna go off with her. "Bye, dude, thanks for the workout...I gotta get this little lady ready for bed."

Hester pushes his arm off, but laughs at the same time. "Brent, you're incorrigible."

Then she lets out this deep sigh, like she's had a rough day. Brent ducks his head a little to see her face better. "Hey, frosty little sweetheart...what's wrong? Did your date get fresh with you?"

"No." She laughs real small. "In fact, he dumped me."

"What?" Brent rubs his hands together. "Then this is my big chance to catch you on the rebound." He turns to me. "Be my wingman?"

I ignore Brent. "What happened? I thought you were all into him?"

"Actually, that's the problem. I wasn't so much into him. I *wanted* to be. On paper, he's pretty perfect for me. But he's all suspicious with these crazy ideas about..." She looks at me and then away again. "Never mind. It's for the best. I would have had to let him go at some point down the line anyway. He just got to it first."

Brent steps in front of me, puffing out his chest like a rooster. "Look here, Miss Hastings...or may I call you Hester now that we're sharing deep, heartfelt moments?"

Hester shoots him with the X-ray death stare.

He deflects it with a shield made from rich-and-famousness. "S'okay; 'Miss Hastings' is kinda more sexy in a wrong sort of way. Anyhow, I fail to see how your getting dumped is a problem. You weren't that into the guy, he's called it off, you're here with me in that little dress that screams 'I'm a modest but sexy vixen,' and it's clear to me that you're in need of a little TLC…am I right?"

Hester smiles, then gives him a 'get real' look. "Brent, perhaps if you were not the man-whore who makes front-page headlines in the tabloids practically every day for your sexual escapades, perhaps then I would allow you to come into my house, brew me a comforting cup of tea and rub my feet. But as things stand, I will thank you for your offer of companionship and tell you that it's Never. Going. To. Happen."

Brent leans closer to her. "You gonna believe everything you read in the tabloids?"

"In this case? Yes. And if you're in dire need of coaching, I can fit you in tomorrow evening. I have a date to go to the zoo with a young friend of mine tomorrow, but I have to drop her off at home by five o'clock." She turns to me. "Enzo, do you mind if we skip dinner together tomorrow evening so I can help Brent?"

I shrug. No skin off my back. "No…I've got some legal papers to fill out I can work on."

For some reason, what I say makes her snap her fingers. "That reminds me, I've got a stack of books to give you. We need to get cracking on the literary side of things…I want you to start with *Gulliver's Travels*, then *Robinson Crusoe*, by Daniel Defoe, some Dickens, and we'll fit in George Bernard Shaw as well. Your contact lenses are working, yes?"

I nod. Sounds like phase two of working me to death is kicking in.

"Good. Then you can spend tomorrow evening reading." She turns back to Brent, who's giving her an adoring yet broken-hearted look in a final try at getting into her pants. She laughs him off. "Tomorrow at five?"

He dials up his smile. "How about now? Now works better…"

Hester pats his cheek like he's a good little kid. "Thanks for cheering me up. I'll see you tomorrow. Goodnight, gentlemen!"

Chapter 10

Monday, April 28th

WHEN MY FOUR o'clock client departs at half-past five, exhaustion sets in. It's been a long day; two new clients in addition to three hours of on-set coaching with an actress famous for her temperamental nature. If she were not inherently talented with accents, she wouldn't be worth the trouble.

I haven't had any time to oversee Enzo's training today, so I can only hope he's staying on track with the DVD program. As I approach the door to the kitchen, I'm in full fret about having slacked off in his training last week. Goodness knows if we'll have enough time for him to master the British accent. Just as I am making a mental note to build in mirror time for Enzo with his British consonants and vowels, the sound of his music registers in my brain.

I push through the yellow door quietly, pausing at the sight of my energetic student. Though his back is to me I can see he's nearly elbow deep in lasagna noodles. He's wearing his red muscle shirt and black shorts.

Enzo's lower half is moving in rhythm to Latin beats from his little radio as he carefully layers the wide noodles over a tomato sauce, meat, and cheese mixture. I'm hungry enough that the rich smell makes me want to grab a fork and take a bite even before it's been fully assembled and baked.

His head turns when he hears the door close behind me.

"Hey!" Enzo's grin is too full of energy for my mood. I wonder what's happened to the Nazi-esque trainer who made me perform six sets of squats with a seventy-five pound barbell slung across my shoulders this morning.

I swipe a dot of splattered sauce off the side of the pan and taste. "Mmmmm... you'll get no complaints from me, but what's with the fancy meal?"

He rinses his hands and wipes them on a tea towel. "I wanted to make something good to celebrate...got a call from Topaz' case worker, and she told me I've been appointed a lawyer for the hearing..."

"Enzo, that's fantastic!"

"Wait, I'm not done. I called the lawyer, and he says we can get a court date set..."

"How exciting!"

"And those blondes hired me as their personal trainer..."

I wrinkle my nose at him. "Fabulous..."

"Oh." He makes an 'ouch' face. "And Nigel called to cancel his sessions... sorry, I guess that's not good news for either of us."

I wave my hand. "No, it doesn't bother me. Honestly, I never even got attached to him. But how wonderful about the court date! Did the lawyer give you any idea when it might be?"

"He didn't want to get my hopes up I think, but he said anywhere between four and ten weeks from now."

"Oh, Enzo...how exciting. You must be over the moon at the prospect of getting Topaz back."

"Sure, but it means I have to figure out where I can live after I'm done here. I need a place with enough space for her to have her own room. A one bedroom apartment would be big enough 'cause I can sleep in the living room and give her the bedroom, you know? And now that she's in school full-time, I'll be able to do my personal training work during the day and still be with her when she's home."

I poke his shoulder below the skull tattoo. "And you have an excellent new client in Brent Logan. Not only is he a walking advertisement for whoever trains him, he knows a ton of other actors. If he's happy with your methods, he might refer friends to train with you, also."

A look of wonder plays across his face. "I know...I can't even believe it, Hester. I mean, who'd have thought? And it's all because of you..." He does a few dance steps in happiness and holds out a hand inviting me to join him.

I pause, knowing I can't dance properly to this music.

But his look says, 'c'mon, don't spoil the fun.' "We're celebrating, remember?" He goes to the radio and turns it up. The beat is really pumping. "How can you not dance to this?"

I can't help but laugh at the way he's started dancing and spinning around me. He's playing it up to entice me to join him. But I shake my head. "I don't know how!"

"It's all in the hips." He demonstrates, moving back and forth with an imaginary partner.

I watch, trying to discern the basic pattern of movement. When I think I see it I give it a try, small movements of the pelvis with steps and pivot turns. "Like this?"

He nods. "Bigger!" Enzo dances over and takes hold of my hips. He rocks them side to side and then around in a circle, then does the same move himself. "Like that..."

I try again, and though it feels entirely odd and wildly out of my comfort zone, the energizing beat of the music and the fact that no one but Enzo is watching allows me the freedom to experiment with the movement. My hips try the circular swivel he showed me again and then again. I practice until the song ends and another one comes on.

"Okay, this one is slower, but still a kickin' beat. So add arms, like this..." Enzo holds out a hand to me, and I take it. He spins me and shows me what to do with my free arm, elbow out, hand relaxed and moving to the music.

I practice like this for a few minutes before he pulls me in and starts leading me in a proper two-person dance. Because he's leading, it's easy to let my hips move in unison with his, following the pattern he establishes. One of my hands is on his shoulder and the other he holds with a relaxed grip. Every so often he sends me out for a twirl, pulling me close in after.

The song ends, and another begins. I understand now why Goldie wanted to take salsa lessons and why she looked so wildly happy when she was dancing with Enzo at the wedding. This is the most fun I've had in...possibly years. It's a world apart from the dry waltz we learned at school, dutifully paired up with another girl, marching the steps out in time to the music master's tapping baton.

Unlike many of my friends, I've never truly mastered party dancing. When the predictable clumps of people glom together on the dance floor and shake it, showing off their moves, I just imitate as best I can. I never even attempt it without a few glasses of wine in my system.

But this is different. With Enzo leading, I'm not worried about what to do next. The sureness of his deft touch sends me in the right direction, the timing of his movements keeps me with the rhythm. It feels as though it's second nature to him, and I wonder who taught him how to dance like this. Thoughts of my arduous day have vanished, and I'm in the moment, enjoying letting Enzo call the shots, losing myself in the music.

This song ends, and a Spanish ballad of some kind begins. It's all acoustic guitars and maracas and reminds me of mariachi singing I heard once in a Mexican restaurant, only less folksy. Enzo is still holding me, and I look up at him to see what's next. Do we keep dancing?

He's looking down at me with the same question in his eyes. I don't know how long we stand pressed together like that before a loud noise from the back of the house causes our heads to snap toward the glass slider.

The door slides open. "Oh, don't stop! It was simply marvelous...I confess I've been a bit of a peeping Tom out here for some minutes."

Oh my God...Mum!

ENZO

I let go of Hester, and she can't get away from me quick enough. Her Mom comes right on in and drops her purse on the table. She exchanges her kissy-kissy hug with Hester and then does the same to me.

"Hey, Mrs. Hastings, how's it going?"

"Fabulous, my dear, fabulous...but I want you to teach me, too." She starts up some hip action and spins, her floaty shirt twirling outward. "Christopher would love it..."

I play along, taking the hand she offers and leading her in a slow version of samba. When I look over at Hester she's watching us, her mouth pinched in as if her mother has trailed mud all over the white floor tiles and she ain't happy about it.

It's a short song so I have time to lead Mrs. Hastings around the kitchen island a couple times and then drop her off with her daughter as it ends. "Thanks for the dance, Mrs. H, but I gotta get back to that lasagna. If I don't get it in the oven, we'll never eat."

She claps her hands in delight. "Oh, are we having lasagna?"

"Mum, how is it that you assume you're staying for dinner? You know I dislike when you stop in without calling first..."

"But darling, you invited me! It's been on my calendar for weeks... Christopher should be here shortly as well. Remember?"

I can see Mrs. H is right when the pink comes all up into Hester's cheeks. "Oh my God, Mum. I completely forgot. I'm so sorry..."

"No worries, darling. If it's a bad time, Chris and I can go find a nice restaurant..."

I'm ladling a bunch of meat sauce onto the noodle layer so I hold it up for her to see. "It's a huge lasagna, Mrs. H. We can't eat it all on our own, so it's a good thing you guys will be here to help us, right Hester?"

"Of course, Mum. Please forgive me...it's lovely to see you. Enzo's making a special dinner to celebrate progress toward regaining custody of his daughter."

Mrs. H clasps her hands together. "Oh, how marvelous...congratulations, Enzo."

I can't help smiling. "Thanks. I feel like everything's dropping into place, you know?"

Mrs. Hastings nods like she knows exactly what I'm saying. "That is truly a wonderful feeling, my dear." She goes into the drawer next to the fridge and digs out a spoon. "I've felt that way myself, lately...now if we could only get Hester on the same path." She dips her spoon into the pot of sauce and tastes. The way she kisses her fingers like she's in some kind of commercial makes me laugh.

Hester don't think it's funny. "What exactly is wrong with the path I'm on, Mum?"

"Oh, don't get all upset, Hester. Nigel told Christopher that you two won't be seeing each other anymore, that's all."

Homegirl's hands are all on her hips now. "What else did he tell Christopher?"

"I don't know what you mean, darling…that's all he told me. And I am sorry it hasn't worked out with Nigel. He seemed like such a lovely chap."

"He *is* a lovely chap, Mum. He's just not the chap for me."

"What happened? Did you have an argument? Did you not have anything in common?"

"Nothing, Mum. Nothing *happened*. If you must know why it didn't work, I'll tell you…there was no attraction on my part. I liked him well enough, we had enjoyable conversation, but I didn't fancy him. Plain and simple."

Mrs. H puts an arm around her daughter. She lowers her voice, but I can still hear it. "Do you think there's something wrong with your libido, dear?"

"Mum!" Them cheeks turn pink again. "No, I'm perfectly fine."

"Are you certain, my dear? When was the last time you were attracted to a man…has it been a long time?"

Hester takes a deep breath like she's trying to keep from punching something. "Trust me, my 'libido' is just fine. You need to stop worrying about me. You can also stop trying to play matchmaker. I can meet men on my own just fine…in fact, Brent Logan was throwing himself at me just the other night." She turns to me. "Isn't that right, Enzo?"

Tryin' to throw himself into her bed, more like. But I nod to make her happy.

Mrs. H puts a hand to her chest. "Heavens…that man is such a hottie! Why don't you fancy him, Hester? He's so successful and sexy and also rich, I would imagine."

"Mum! First of all, he's a client. Secondly, he's a playboy. A reputation like his does not inspire a yearning for his attentions. I don't want to be with a movie star, Mum. I've had plenty of opportunities for that. Oh my God! Why am I even having this conversation? I don't have to explain my love life or lack of one to you. I'm sorry, Mum. You just have to trust me that there's nothing to worry about. Just because a woman isn't in a relationship with a man doesn't mean something's wrong."

Whoa. Chiquita's layin' it all out there. Mrs. H looks kinda shocked.

"Hester, my darling…I'm sorry, but I just have one teensy tiny little last question for you on the subject. Promise you won't get upset with me?"

Hester rolls her eyes…Girlfriend is so done with this conversation. "What, Mum? What is the question?"

Mrs. H waits a second before launching it. "Are you absolutely sure you like…men?"

Hester presses her hands to her ears like she can't believe what she heard. "Oh my God!"

Mrs. H is already scrambling for traction. "Well, it's just that Nigel is so nice looking, and Brent Logan is basically sex on legs, so perhaps if you don't have any attraction…"

"Mum, I am not a lesbian. And even if I was, there would be nothing *wrong* with it. But I'm not, okay? I can't believe you would think that!"

"Well, I don't think it's such a crazy thought. We did send you to that all-girls boarding school, and you're not attracted to *Brent Logan* for God's sake…" She turns to me. "Brent Logan!"

I don't say nothing, in part because the idea of Hester as a lesbo is just plain funny. I ain't got nothing against girl-on-girl, but even though Hester's all up-tight and can't find a man she likes, there ain't no way that girl is gay.

But Mrs. H puts me right on the spot. "Enzo, what do you think? Why isn't Hester attracted to Nigel or Brent Logan?"

Hester crosses her arms over her chest, and she's giving me a look that says, 'please, please end this conversation.' And Mrs. H moves in closer waiting for my answer, so I'm in a full-court press.

"I think your daughter is kind of like a fiddler crab." Both sets of eyebrows go up. "I saw a thing on T.V. about it once. Nature channel. A female fiddler crab is real choosy. She might check out a hundred suitors before she finds one she likes. It's pretty interesting."

Why are they both staring at me like that? I shrug. "Well, either that or she's a raging lesbo."

Hester grabs a damp dishtowel and throws it at me. Mrs. H is too busy laughing her ass off to even notice that her man's just showed up. Christopher is standing at the open glass slider, holding flowers and a bottle of wine.

He looks from Hester, to Mrs. H, to me. "Have I missed something good?"

HESTER

Christopher opens the bottle of wine and pours a glass for each of us. Once Enzo has placed the lasagna in the oven, we sit down in the living room to relax. Mum and Christopher claim the sofa, his arm comfortably around her shoulders. She looks so happy, radiant in fact. I should be delighted for her, and I am. For a long time, I've been hoping she'd find someone who makes her happy. But I confess that my delight is tempered ever so slightly by just a tiny bit of envy. For the umpteenth time since Nigel called it off, I wonder why it was that I didn't feel any physical attraction to him.

Mum chooses the moment Enzo is refilling her wine glass to ask about his progress with Standard British English. "Is it time to plan the party? How's it coming along?"

Enzo looks at me like, 'sorry I'm not doing better with it.' Then he says, "It's not quite coming natural, Mrs. H…"

"*Naturally*," I correct. "But it's coming along. It really takes so much practice, and we only just started working on it a week ago."

Christopher pats my mother's knee and shoots her a questioning look. She nods ever so slightly. He clears his throat. "Well, you're outnumbered three to one by Brits tonight, Enzo. Why not have an impromptu coaching session?"

Aha. Mum wants to play at dialect coaching and has goaded her boyfriend into setting the stage. Very clever.

"What a lovely idea, Christopher!" Mum's tone is all innocence. "Enzo, dear, why don't you let us hear you have a go at it, and we can offer some native-speaker suggestions for improvement?"

Though he's been put on the spot with no warning and his first reflex is to look my way for help, he doesn't appear to be panicked. If placed in the same position, I'm not sure I would remain quite as relaxed. When I don't jump in to save him, he shrugs. "What the hell, why not? It sure isn't going to hurt…"

Mum is beside herself with delight. She practically leaps up off the sofa and hugs my student. "Don't worry, Enzo. There's no judgment here." She turns to me. "How do you usually go about this?"

I consider our options. What would be least painful for Enzo? "Well, we've mainly been working on consonants and vowels so far. Let me think...why don't we concentrate on the long 'a' sound; words like 'half', 'cast', and 'task'." I glance at Enzo, but he seems game to try. "Go ahead and throw some simple phrases at him to repeat back."

Mum looks at Christopher excitedly, then turns to the task of inventing a sentence for Enzo to repeat. "How about...'half the task of casting the raft is quite a laugh'?"

We all look at Enzo. "Um, okay. Here goes...'half the task of casting the raft is quite a laugh.'"

We three Brits exchange a look that says, 'a bit off the mark, but not hideously awful.'

Mum has him try again, enunciating the phrase slowly before prompting him to repeat.

Still a bit off. Enzo looks a touch glum, but Mum is undeterred.

"Try this one: 'after the giraffe took a bath he sailed off in a raft.'"

It's like a new party game. Mum and Christopher think up silly phrases for Enzo to try, and he dutifully repeats. By the time we polish off a second bottle of wine, he's actually making a bit of progress. He begins to sound more South African than Australian, which is a step in the right direction.

Christopher comes up with another one. "Let's try a different vowel sound... how about: 'I've been to the green scene, and I'm keen to be mean'."

Enzo nails it on the second try. "Hurrah!" Mum raises her wine glass, and we all take a sip to celebrate.

"I know, I know..." Mum looks at me. "This was one of your father's favorites: 'around the rocks the rugged rascal ran'."

I remember this one from Dad as well. Enzo gives it a try but the different vowel sounds are problematic for him. He knows it's not come off well and makes an 'ew' face.

"Try again, Enzo. Listen: 'around the rocks the rugged rascal ran'."

"Around the rocks the rugged rascal ran."

Mum, Christopher, and I exchange a 'wow' look. Christopher sums it up. "That was pretty damn good."

I throw out another one. "'I talk when I walk plucking petals from the stalk'. Remember to pronounce the 't' on 'petals'."

Enzo makes a show of limbering up like he's about to go into the boxing ring. "I talk when I walk plucking petals from the stalk."

Mum and Christopher nod approval.

"He's got it now...he has the long 'a'!" Mum is so excited she sloshes a little wine onto the floor without noticing.

Christopher points to Mum. "Have him do the first one again...what was it?"

Mum racks her brain. "'Half the task of casting the raft is quite a laugh'."

This time it rolls off Enzo's tongue like he was born to the manor.

We all cheer, and Enzo smiles self-consciously. "Don't get too excited... it's just one sound."

But Mum is jubilant. "I'm going to send invitations next week. Hester, name a date, and I'll organize everything."

Christopher jumps in hastily. "But make it after June 10th...we're not back from England until then."

I look at Mum. "You're going away...together?"

Mum is flushed with excitement. "Yes, Chris and I are going to London... but only for a few weeks. I promise we'll be back in time to throw a fabulous party. So, let's set the date, shall we?"

I fetch my calendar from the kitchen. "Let me see...I don't want to rush Enzo." I flip the page from the last week of May into June. "How about the 14th?" I turn to Enzo. "That would be precisely three months from the day we first met..."

He nods a little uncertainly. "Sure, why not?"

"Mum?"

Christopher has fished out his iPhone and they are consulting his calendar together. He points at the screen, and she nods. "Yes...June 14th – a Saturday. Ooooh, I've got goosebumps thinking about it!"

I look over at Enzo, but he's gotten up from his chair and is heading into the kitchen. I watch him pull on an oven mitt and check the lasagna.

When he calls to us, I get the feeling his level of excitement about the party is exactly the opposite of my mother's. "It's done. You all ready to eat?"

Chapter 11

ENZO

Wednesday, April 30th

I'M ALL STRETCHED out on the sofa with *Robinson Crusoe* when the phone rings. Hester is in the studio with a client, so I pick it up.

"Hester Hastings' residence." This is how she told me to answer.

"Am I speaking with Enzo Diaz?"

"Yep...who's this?"

"Larry Thomas, your lawyer?"

"Yeah, man. You got some good news for me?"

"The first date I could get for the review hearing is June 23rd. It's a Monday. Eleven a.m. Can you make it?"

My heart sinks. I was hoping it would be sooner. "Of course, yeah, I can make it."

"You're still seeing your daughter on a regular basis?"

"Yep. Just took her out last Sunday. You sure you can't get a date any sooner than June?"

"I'll try and keep an eye on the calendar in case anything opens up, but that's the best I can do for now."

"Okay...anything else I gotta do?"

"Just document your visits with your daughter, collect any proof of employment...are you working?"

"Yeah, but I don't get, like, a regular paycheck. I'm a personal trainer, so I have clients who pay by the session. Is that a problem?"

"Shouldn't be. Just keep track of everything you earn…maybe set up an invoice system so you have proof that you're receiving payment for legitimate services."

I don't know how to do that, but I'll figure it out. "Okay."

"Do you have a permanent address?"

It ain't permanent, but with any kind of luck I can use it until after the hearing. "Permanent enough for now."

"Well, sounds like you've got your bases covered. Make sure you keep bills that have been mailed to you or accounts with your current address listed so you have proof you live there."

I nod even though he can't see me. "Will do, man."

"Call me if you move or your phone number changes. You have my details?"

"Yes. I got 'em."

"Okay then, hang in there. It won't be long now before you've got her back."

"Thanks, man. I appreciate it."

"You got it."

I hang up and think about invoices and opening a bank account to make a record of my address. Then I think about the next time I get to see Topaz. I'm gonna stop by tomorrow afternoon and take her for a swim at that pool they got there at the apartments.

It's hard to make myself get back to Robinson Crusoe, but I know Hester's gonna be quizzin' me all about it at dinner, so I open the book up and start back at it. I already finished the one about Gulliver and the Yahoos. Once you get goin', this classic shit ain't too bad.

HESTER

Friday, May 9th

Shockingly, Enzo claims to be more than halfway through the stack of novels I've given him. It's true that I tried to choose the more entertaining classic titles by British authors, but it's almost as though the man is making up for lost reading time now that he can see.

While we work at preparing a classic English chicken and mushroom pie for our dinner, he is extolling the virtues of Mary Shelley's *Frankenstein*. "She makes you feel sorry for the monster, because he's so self-aware of his predicament." The reading is doing wonders for his vocabulary. He found the dictionary on my bookshelf in the living room and has been putting it to good use.

I nod as I slice carrots into round orange coins. "Yes, it's hard to believe Shelley wrote it almost two hundred years ago. She was only twenty-one when she penned *Frankenstein*; it was considered a 'horror story' at the time."

"That woman was ahead of her time, yo."

"Yes, and she was quite a racy character. Ran away with a married poet, Percy Shelley, when she was still a teenager. They married when his wife committed suicide. The Shelleys had four children, but only one survived, and then the husband, Percy, drowned. Mary had experienced a lifetime's worth of tragedy by the time she became a widow at twenty-four."

Enzo is silent, and I imagine he might feel a kind of kinship with Mary Shelley. The tragedies in his own life have not been few in number.

I turn to a happier topic. "Did you have a fun visit with Topaz yesterday?"

He smiles. "Yes. We only had a couple of hours, but it never matters how much time we have. She's my sunshine."

I feel as though I'll never get a real handle on this man's character. He's devoted to his daughter, committed to staying in touch with a brother who may or may not even remember his visits, surprisingly adept as a personal trainer, yet he was willing to risk jail time and the loss of his daughter on a dubious scheme to try and 'get ahead.' Is that something I'd have been willing to do in his position given all that I'd stand to lose? I suppose it's best to hope I'll never find out.

Enzo has finished cleaning and slicing the mushrooms and onion; I've done the carrots and shelled the peas. When I made our Caesar salads with chicken for lunch I grilled up and diced some extra chicken breasts for the pie. We're cheating by using a store-bought crust, so we just need to prepare the sauce and get everything in the oven.

I place a saucepan on top of the stove. "Meat pies were one of my favorite dinners when I was at boarding school. Sometimes we'd have fish pie, or maybe steak and kidney pie."

"Kidneys like kidney beans, or like real kidneys from some kind of animal?"

"I think traditionally ox or pork kidneys are used."

Enzo makes a face. "I'm glad we're goin' with chicken and mushroom, girl."

"Well, the whole point is to acquaint you with traditional English fare. I acquired some good brown ale for the occasion as well."

He tries out his new accent. "Pray tell, my fair lady…what is 'brown ale'?"

His impersonation of a stuck-up Englishman isn't bad. Have I been making him watch too much *Downton Abbey*? "It's a rich type of beer, served at room temperature. A beverage widely consumed in Britain."

"Sounds pretty good."

"Shall I pour us some?"

"Sure. I'll give it a shot. I've never had brown ale before, but there's a first time for everything." Then he momentarily drops his polished manner and shoots me a look of distaste. "Just don't feed me no ox kidneys yet, chica."

Smiling, I locate my bottle opener and pop the cap off a tall bottle of Newcastle Brown, releasing its yeasty smell. It pours like creamy, rich liquid toffee into the pint glasses I purchased for the occasion.

I hand one topped with a half inch of white foam to Enzo. "This is the type of glass you'd be served beer in at just about any pub in all of Great Britain. Very traditional."

"Cheers, then." He raises his glass, and I meet him halfway with a clink from my own.

"Here's to all you've accomplished thus far, Enzo Diaz."

We drink, then wipe foam moustaches from our upper lips.

⇥⊙ ⊙⇤

By the time the chicken pie comes out of the oven we've polished off two bottles of Newkie Brown. Seeing as we had such a light lunch, it's gone straight to our heads. Enzo has donned both oven mitts, and after setting the cooked pie on a wooden board to cool, he does a spontaneous little dance wearing them. It's part robot-man and part Pillsbury Dough Boy, and so completely absurd that I can't stop laughing.

Perched on the island countertop, I'm literally gasping for air when he finally takes mercy on me and stops.

"Don't fall off the counter, girl!" He puts out a hand to steady me, and I take it. It's covered with an oven mitt, which starts me off laughing again.

Enzo regards me with amused disapproval. "Okay, I'm cutting you off from that ale."

He removes the mitts and lifts me down off the counter. I'm not drunk, but I do have a decent buzz on. It reminds me how he got drunk at Jimmy's wedding and tried to kiss me.

This makes me stop laughing. I also recall the morning after when he was so profusely horrified by the memory of it. The buzz has dulled my verbal censors. "The morning after you tried to kiss me you acted so horrified about it. Is the idea that distasteful to you?"

"What?" His expression is all confusion. "I never tried to kiss you."

"Yes, you did! The night of Jimmy's wedding, when you were so drunk."

He looks at the ceiling, calling up memories. "Nooo…"

Despite myself I'm a little insulted. "How can you not remember? We talked about it the morning after. You said you were so sorry and would never get drunk again…"

"I'm not drunk now," he points out.

"I know, I know. I'm not calling you out on anything. I just…it was a little off-putting that you were oh-so-horrified by the idea of having tried to kiss me."

"I'm still not following you. That morning I was all freaked out you'd hate me and throw me out because of what me and Goldie did."

"It's 'Goldie and I'…wait, what did you and Goldie get up to?"

He looks away. "Come on, I know how best girlfriends are; you chicas tell each other everything. You don't gotta play dumb for my sake."

"I'm not playing dumb! Seriously, what are you talking about? If I remember correctly, and I was just about the only one *not* drunk at Jimmy's wedding, I had a visual on Goldie the whole night. She even slept in my room..." A thought occurs to me. "Oh, are you talking about the sexy dancing?"

He looks at me like I've sprouted a unicorn horn. "Goldie slept in your room? All night?"

"Well, of course. I put you in her room because you were so drunk. Our suite had a bigger bed, and she needed to talk. She was absolutely distraught about Andrew just leaving like a, like a motherfucker..."

He laughs. "Whoa now, you're gettin' a bit loose with that word, Chiquita. It don't sound right on you."

"Anyway, yes, she was in my room all night."

He looks at me hard. "You sure?"

"Of course! What, do you think she snuck out and went and found you and had her wicked way with you?"

His reply comes a nanosecond later than it should. "Nah. You were right a minute ago. It was the dancing thing." The forced nonchalance in his expression tells me he's totally lying.

"Wait; did you really think...? Did you think you and Goldie slept together in her room?"

I can practically see the war being waged within him. Admit or deny? But it's too late for him to pull off a denial.

"You did! Oh my God!! You thought you'd slept with Goldie, and then... when we talked the next morning, you thought we were both somehow totally fine about it?"

He hides his face in his hands.

And what I feel is relief. He wasn't so horrified about the idea that he'd tried to kiss me, he thought he'd had a drunken fling with my best friend and that I'd never forgive him.

"You silly man! What would make you think Goldie had slept with you?"

He sighs the deepest sigh imaginable, relief almost visibly pouring off him. "Okay, it made sense in my hung-over mind at the time. I woke up that morning, and I wasn't...my clothes were all over the place. I was in Goldie's room, the covers were all rumpled like, well you know. Also, I had red lipstick on my face, and there was lacy underwear lying on the chair like it had been thrown off real quick…I couldn't remember anything about what had happened, except that someone massaged my back…"

Indignation rises in me at the memory of it. "That cougar, Liz."

"And that I'd been on the bed with somebody, foolin' around."

My hand flies to my chest. "That was me!"

"You?" The look on his face tells me he really doesn't remember.

"Well, except we didn't fool around. You tried to kiss me, and I stopped you because you were drunk."

He's quiet a long time, his gaze on the floor. Then his eyes rise to meet mine. "Is that the only reason you stopped me?"

Even in my buzzed condition, I recognize the significance of this question. The fact that I say the words that form in my head out loud is due purely to my less inhibited state. "Perhaps…if we try a re-enactment we can find out."

It's only once the words have left my mouth that I realize the invitation I've extended. My words hang in the air as he wrestles with interpreting what I've just thrown his way.

Emboldened by the alcohol, I take a step toward him. If he backs away, I know where he stands and can chalk my boldness up to the brown ale. If he doesn't…

With one step Enzo closes the remaining distance between us. He looks down at me, taking in my whole face with his eyes, and I wonder what's going through his mind. My heart is racing, and my body is already tingling with anticipation of what I realize I've wanted since that night when I stopped him from doing it.

When he speaks his voice is nearly a whisper. "Are you sure you wanna go there?"

I tip my face up to him, the answer in my eyes. When his face dips toward mine, I rise up on my toes to meet him halfway, placing a hand on his chest to steady myself. There's a delectable moment right before our lips meet when our eyes lock and time seems to slow and I want it to last forever, but I also want to hurry up and kiss him already. When our lips touch I feel it; the electricity, the fire…it's what was missing with Nigel and the thing about Enzo that I've been pushing to the back of my consciousness since I went with him to see Topaz that first time.

Now, there's nothing in my mind but the sensation of his warm lips on my own. At the beginning there's a tentativeness, as though he's giving me the chance to pull away. Then it deepens into a full-on, committed conversation without words. Slow and sensual, an exploration of possibility. My hands creep upward, work their way into his thick, black hair. His hands start at my shoulders, then slide around to my lower back, pressing me against him. This man knows what the hell he's doing...Enzo kisses with confidence, varying his technique as he discovers what pleases me. His skill makes it easy to let go, to lose myself in sensations that send the fire sparked by our connection deep into my body.

I'm happy for it to go on and on, have lost track of time completely. But when he pulls back and offers a sexy smile, I realize we need to stop. My head is still faintly buzzing from the ale, and I fear that if we go on I'll let this kiss take us straight to a place first kisses shouldn't go. But when he strokes my cheek and gently disengages, I realize he's not planning to lead me there.

"Maybe it's time to eat?" His voice is quiet, intimate.

I nod because I'm not ready to talk yet. A feeling of shyness is creeping upon me. What happens now? With the lines of our arrangement blurred by this kiss, I'm in uncharted territory.

Enzo puts the oven mitts back on and brings the pie to the table. We sit down, and I slice into it, steam escaping through the crust chasm I've created. The savory smell of chicken and tender pastry rises to my nose as I scoop servings onto two plates. Then I pass him his dinner and still have no words to say.

He must realize I'm starting to freak out a little, because his manner reverts to how it normally is at dinnertime, only more chatty. He starts to tell me all about his last visit with Topaz: what funny things she said, how enjoyable it is to spend time together without the constraints of everyday difficulties and chores to make it ordinary.

I'm already wondering if I'll tell Goldie about the kiss and ask her advice, or if I'm going to keep it to myself and ride this wave wherever it may take me.

ENZO

Saturday, May 10th

I ain't sure if things are gonna be all freaky this morning after what happened last night. Half of me is all psyched and wanting to see her again, and the other half is afraid it was a mistake. What if the kiss ruined everything? She was a little drunk, and maybe she's gonna wake up this morning like, 'hell's bells, why did I let that happen?' What if her whole self thinks it was a mistake? And here I am hopin' we can do it again.

The gym is all set up for her workout, but she's late. There's every chance she's gonna come on out here and have 'a talk' about how what happened can't happen again. I'll get smacked verbally, and then what? Is she gonna say I gotta go? Is she going to treat me like some kid who doesn't know how to keep his hands outta the cookie jar?

Best thing to do is lie down on the bench and start my presses. It's the fastest way to get calm. But eleven reps in, I hear that sliding glass door open and close. I stay where I am and keep going. If she's gonna smack me down, I might as well be liftin' when she does it.

The sound of weights being picked up tells me she's not gonna say anything right away. From where I'm lying I can see the back of her if I crane my neck up. She's gone straight into the triceps routine I showed her. Damn. If the shit's gonna hit the fan I'd rather it happen right away than wait and wait and then get splattered.

I keep pressin'. Up for three counts, down for four. I do so many my arms are shaking when I hook the bar back up on the catch. Okay, what now? Normally, I'd get up and check her form, make sure she's using heavy enough weights.

Man up, Enzo Diaz. Go check her form. Only, I don't think I can ever check her form again without thinking about what else I'd like to do with it. Not that I ain't had them thoughts about her before, but thoughts like that get real after a woman gives a guy a preview.

Sit up and breathe. Take a sip of water. Then I got nothing else to do but what I'm supposed to. When I go over there, I see she's started with too much weight.

"Why are you starting with your max weight? I thought you knew to start light and work up."

She turns and nearly drops the weight she's using for over the head triceps pulls. "Whoa!"

I reach out and take it from her. From the look on her face, I figure now's when I'm gonna get an earful.

"Thanks. You're right, I need to start lighter. I…"

I pick up twenty-five pounds and hand it to her.

"Thanks again. I, um…"

Before now I've never known this woman to have no words. I'm not sure why she can't find 'em until I look close at her face and see she's too scared to talk. What reason does she have to be scared? I'm the one with everything to lose.

I move a little closer. "You okay?"

"Um…perhaps not." She won't look at me. Oh shit. Here it comes. "I'm sort of freaking out about that kiss…you didn't…were you, um, just doing it because I wanted you to?"

What? A kiss like that, and she thinks I was doing favors? "Hell, no. You opened a door I've wished I could open a hundred times. I didn't know if it would ever happen again so I had to step in quick. If you're sorry about it and want to shut that door back up and lock it, I can handle it."

I look right at her, and she just stands there holding the weight I gave her. "So you're not wishing it had never happened?"

I shake my head, 'no way.' "How 'bout you?"

That gets a little shy smile. "No." She hoists the weight up over her head and starts another set of tricep pulls.

"So we're good?"

She nods.

Phew. I don't know if I'm sweatin' more from the lifting or from waiting for her to tell me to step off.

Thing is, now that I know it's all good, I'm thinking hard about when I'm gonna get to kiss her again.

HESTER

Sunday, May 11th

I feel his warm breath on my ear again, his lips on the side of my neck. Giving in for a moment is irresistible, but when his kisses find their way to my lips I disengage with a laugh.

"Concentrate!" I push him away gently. "We have to make some progress… there can only be kissing when you've said every word perfectly. So start from the beginning."

"Okay, okay." He straightens up in his chair, and I reach out to place a finger on his chin.

"My finger is there to remind you that the lower jaw needs to pull forward just incrementally more than you normally would for a 't' sound. I know it feels odd, but your mouth needs to make slight modifications to achieve the correct sound. Remember to say each word three times."

Enzo holds up the list of words with 't' in them and begins reading from the top. "Water, water, water…"

"Remember intonation as well…in British English the emphasis is on the first syllable, and the 't' is hard as ice; *wa*ter. In American English the emphasis is equally distributed between both syllables, and the 't' sounds like a 'd'; wuder. Try again."

Enzo glances sideways at me. "Water, water, water."

I nod, that was excellent.

"Party, party, party."

I smile, knowing he's trying extra hard so we can get to the fooling around bit.

"Tomato, tomato, tomato. Brighten, brighten, brighten. Fantastic, fantastic, fantastic. Bitten, bitten, bitten…"

So far, so good. I remove my finger from his chin to see if he can maintain it without the reminder.

"Barter, barter, barter. Tighten, tighten, tighten, Martin, Martin, Martin…"

He carries on down the long list, diligently assessing each word to determine syllable emphasis before attempting it. When he gets to the last few, he slows down to make sure he gets them right.

"Carton, carton, carton, mighty, mighty, mighty." He turns to look at me. "Beautiful, beautiful, beautiful."

"What?" I lean over to check his list. "'Beautiful' is a good one, but I don't remember putting that word on there."

He shows me the list. Beautiful *isn't* on there, but he's smiling his delicious smile at me, and I blush at the compliment he's built into the exercise.

"So how'd I do?" He's already leaning toward me, expecting the payoff for a perfect score.

"Not bad."

His expression turns from yearning to indignant. "Not bad!" He's using Standard British English. "I'd say it was bloody well almost perfect." He narrows his eyes. "Are you trying to avoid kissing me, woman?"

I laugh. Only a Brit paying attention would catch that his accent is slightly American. He could pass quite easily for an English native who's spent time living in the States. And thanks to the BBC America channel, he's picked up quite a few idioms specific to Great Britain.

Enzo's eyes go wide with surprise when I slide a leg over his lap, straddling his thighs. Taking his face in my hands, I lean in and kiss him full-on, no monkey business. His response is immediate and heated; strong hands slide up into my hair, and he pulls me forward so I'm practically lying on top of him.

We stay like that for longer than we should, given we have a lot of work still to do and I have to meet with a client in half an hour.

Finally, I force myself to sit up and straighten my shirt. "If we keep going we'll end up having to work through lunch."

"Hester, having lunch with you is always work for me."

Now it's my turn to be indignant. My hands are on my hips as he chuckles at my reaction.

"Don't get your nose out of joint…I just mean we always have to do all that talking. Conversation."

"Don't you enjoy our conversations?"

"Sure, but sometimes it's like work for me 'cause I have to remember to keep my language how you like it and to sit up straight, and not to talk with food in my mouth, and to wait until you're sitting down to start eating, and to put my fork in the right position on the plate when I'm not using it, and to wipe my mouth all tidy like you showed me and..."

"Alright, I get it."

"No, you probably don't. I enjoy it 'cause it's time with you, but there's all this stuff to remember the whole time. All those rules aren't second nature for me yet. I don't know if they ever will be."

"I suppose I didn't realize it took so much effort."

ENZO

"Well then, how about I educate you for a little bit, Miz Hastings?"

She slides off my lap, and I'm sorry to see her go. "How do you propose to educate me, Mr. Diaz?"

"Well, for starters you're standing way too tight. You got to relax your body and just let it all hang." I stand up and demonstrate how to stand all loose and chillin'.

She gives me a funny look and tries to copy. But she ends up just lookin' like some kind of mannequin that's been posed funny.

"Nah, nah. You got to really *relax*. Like, shake your shoulders and body loose, and then try again."

She looks at me like I'm crazy. So I take her wrists and shake her arms to loosen them up. Then I get an idea and tickle her sides.

Girlfriend lets out a shriek of laughter and, like, totally loses control of her body. I have to catch her to keep her from falling.

"That was totally unfair!" She gives me a wounded look, then reaches up and tries to pull my face close to start kissing again.

I back up and hold out a finger, imitatin' her. "Uh, uh. None a' that 'till you can repeat everything I say all perfect. Do like me...say, 'Homeboy you is lookin' fly today, yo.'"

She raises her eyebrows at me. "Home boy, you is looking fly today, yo."

"Nah. You ain't got it. It's not just the words. I know you're all talented with dialects and stuff, but with Ghetto talk you gotta breathe some life into them words. You gotta get your body standing right and get your street attitude on. Come on, follow me."

I start walkin' around the room, puttin' on the swagger she broke me of first thing when I got here. "Come on! Let me see you pull it off. Girls don't be walkin' like this, but it'll get you in the mood."

Hester wrinkles her nose at me all saucy, but I just give her a look back that means 'keep walkin' sista.' So she laughs at me and tries to copy. First, she looks kinda like she's trying to fake a limp or somethin'. But then she gets her shoulders into it. I see her face change; she gets all feisty with a look I ain't never seen her do before.

I keep strollin', giving her time to practice. "You got to channel your inner gangsta."

She's workin' it, which I give her credit for. After a couple minutes, I throw out another phrase for her to try. "Say, 'Yo brotha', that shit is off the chain.'"

"Yo, brotha', that shit is off the chain."

I grab my crotch. "Say, 'Homeboy, you ain't half-steppin.'"

She grabs her crotch, which 'bout makes me bust out laughin'. "Homeboy, you ain't half-steppin.'"

I nod. "Thass right, chica. Keep that Ghetto attitude comin'. Say, 'You a hard-ass mothafucka, yo.'"

"You a hard-ass motherfucker, yo."

"Uh uh. You ain't got it. It's 'mothafucka.' Got to roll off your tongue."

"Motha fucka?"

"You're putting the emphasis on the first syllable, but the emphasis is equally distributed through the whole word – and it's not two words, it's one. Like this, 'mothafucka'"

Her face gets all fierce. "Mothafucka."

"Yeah, man. That's what I'm talkin' about. But Hester?"

"What?"

"Don't ever say it again, okay? Even when you say it right, it just looks weird."

She play-slaps my chest, and I grab her up, give her a kiss she'll still be thinkin' about when her next client's practicin' vowels.

Chapter 12

HESTER

Tuesday, May 13th

BRENT STARES INTO the distance wistfully, then turns fiery eyes on me. "I've never wanted anythin' more than I want you…from the moment I set eyes on ya. You make me want ta be strong, woman. But I need ya ta give me yer pledge that you'll wait as long as it takes fer me ta make my way in the new world…wait until I can send for ya. Can ya do that? Can ya give me yer pledge?"

"Right…I see the problem. When you put the emotion into it your vocal technique goes right out the window." I fetch a small paperclip from my desk. "Here's what I want you to do…place this paperclip in the space between your lower front teeth and your lip." I hand him the clip.

He hands me a look of incredulity. "In my mouth??"

"Yes. Below the teeth, where the gum line starts there's a little ledge, and below that a little space in which to nestle a small object. If you have the paperclip in there it will be a physical reminder to pay attention to maintaining the accent even when you're really in the moment with the emotion."

"In my mouth??" He's still staring at me like I've asked him to eat monkey brains.

I roll my eyes. "It doesn't have to be a paperclip…but it has to be something small enough that it stays nicely in place."

Brent eyes the paperclip warily and brings it toward his mouth. "Wait…has this been in anyone else's mouth? Because if it has then that's just too gross."

"Of course not! I don't reuse mouth paperclips, cross my heart." I draw an imaginary X in the center of my chest for good measure.

He gingerly drops it between his lower front teeth and his lip. Then he shudders like he's been made to drink castor oil. After he's worked it into place and stretched his neck and shoulders, he's ready to try again. He summons up his emotion, and the fiery eyes are back.

"I've never wanted anythin' more than I want you…from the moment I set eyes on ya. You make me want ta be strong, woman. But I need ya ta give me yer pledge that you'll wait as long as it takes fer me ta make my way in the new world…wait until I can send for ya. Can ya do that? Can ya give me yer pledge?"

I applaud. "You see? Much better. And very moving, by the way."

He spits the paperclip into his palm. "Yeah, gross but effective. Thanks, coach." He plops down in an armchair as though now it's visiting time. "How come you don't use that wooden torture stick on me anymore? Did I graduate or something?"

"No, I just decided it was time to hang up the stick. I don't actually use it on anyone anymore."

"Legions of actors who will one day seek your dialect coaching thank you."

I laugh. "Was it that awful?"

"Just degrading, humiliating, annoying, and a little dangerous."

"Oh, is that all? I thought it was quite effective." I check the clock…he's got five minutes left and doesn't seem inclined to fit in a few last efforts at his speech.

He cocks his head, regarding me with the air of a psychoanalyst. "It's not only that you don't use the stick anymore. You seem kinda allover….different. More chilled out. Less 'frosty bitch' and more 'sexy professor,' you know?"

I shoot him a disapproving look. "No, I do not know, but…"

"Is it me? Have I inspired this change in you? Because I think it's sort of uncanny how it's happened while I've been your star client and everything." He slings himself sideways on the chair, looping his legs over the upholstered arm and linking his hands behind his head. "They say that repressed love, or even lust, can be completely transformational."

"No one says that, Brent."

"So, if it's not me, then who is it? 'Cause I can smell infatuation on a woman from twenty paces. Come on," he slaps his thighs in an invitation to perch on his lap, "come tell Uncle Brent all about it."

"You're being ridiculous…"

He suddenly points at me as though a hummingbird has just landed on my shoulder. "I saw that!"

"Saw what?"

"That little smile you did when you said 'you're being ridiculous.' You totally smiled, which means I'm totally right on the money."

"I'm not…infatuated with anyone."

His eyebrows rise. "Oh, so it's true love?"

"No!"

"Bingo." He sits up and points again. "You're blushing!"

My hands reflexively go to my cheeks. "I refuse to discuss this with you."

He shrugs. "No biggie. I'll dig up the dirt from our mutual personal trainer…In the meantime, I have a little proposition for you. I'm going on location to Southern Ireland this Friday, and I want you to come with me."

Seriously? "I've been perfectly clear with you that I do not fraternize…"

"Fraternize with clients. Yes, you have been *very* clear on that point. And besides, we've just established you're in love with someone else. What I'm talking about is a business proposition. I'm worried I'll get there, and the cameras will be rolling, and I'll choke with the accent. If you're there you can keep me on point… you'll be like the boxing coach in the corner of the ring at halftime, slapping me and squirting water on my face."

"Much though I would love to squirt water at your face, Brent, I don't often go on location with clients."

"I don't know how long I'll be there, but all I'm asking you for is the first three days. Please? I'll pay you a bonus on top of working hours and travel expenses." Suddenly, he looks weary. "I need you."

I narrow my eyes, trying to ascertain whether he's acting or he really feels that insecure about the accent.

"The critics will rip me to shreds if the accent is off, and you know it… Please?" He slides from the chair onto his knees and literally begs.

"Oh, get up. I suppose I can clear my schedule. But it's just three days, right?"

Brent draws an X on his chest with his index finger. "Cross my heart."

ENZO

Sunday, May 18th

While Hester's gone I train the Barbies, do all the homework she left for me, start in on *Great Expectations*, and see Topaz as much as possible. And I think.

What we've been up to isn't gonna last. A woman like her with a man like me? Nah. Soon as she finds out I've been lying to her it's all over. I know a man like Antwon would make the most of her ignorance, be in her bed every time he got the chance without worrying about nothing.

But it's gotten so that every time she smiles at me I think about how she'll look at me when she knows the truth. I can't get anywhere near her bed unless she wants it after I've told her. And I'm gonna tell her, damn it.

I don't know how long it's going to take Antwon to hunt me down, but I know that if he can he will. That's not something I can wait to let happen. But being brave enough to go ahead and say what I need to ain't quite happening either. Especially now that I can hold and kiss her like I've got a chance in hell at keeping her.

Guess I should count my blessings at being here at all. I've had two months and more of a life better than I thought I had a right to. Starting up my own business, learning all kinds of cultured stuff nobody can take from me. And I've had the woman of my dreams in my arms.

Shit. I ain't ever gonna be ready to give all that up.

I've got to make a promise to myself. When Hester comes home, I have to tell her. That first day. Making this promise makes me feel like every hour left in her house, every hour I have before she knows the truth is precious. I never in my whole life thought I'd wish so hard that what I'd gotten locked up for was drugs.

On the way home from my visit with Topaz, I stop by Albertson's and buy what I need to make salmon and sausage 'surf and turf.' It was the first thing I cooked for her, and I want to make it as her 'welcome home' dinner tomorrow night. Seeing as how it might be our last dinner together, I want it to be nice.

When I get back to Hester's place the sky's starting to turn dark and the gate to the yard is open. I could have sworn I closed it when I left. There's no car in the driveway, but Mrs. H might have stopped by when I was gone. She's always making Hester crazy with dropping by.

But when I come through the gate and see who's using my outdoor gym it stops me right where I am. Real slow, I put the grocery bags down on a lounge chair.

He's got the barbell loaded with weight, and he's watching me. Big smile. Knows he's got my full attention. The door to the cabana is wide open, so I know he's helped himself to anything he wanted from in there. Son-of-a-bitch! I should have known not to leave my training money in there. Livin' up here in Los Feliz has softened me up.

Which is about exactly what Antwon's thinking if I'm reading him right.

I think about making a break for it, running back to the store and calling the police. But he's seen me think it 'cause he puts down the barbell and pulls out that damn Glock he loves so much.

Then he nods at me all friendly like he ain't just stole from me. "You are one lucky son-of-a-bitch that your sugar-momma's not here. Otherwise, maybe I'd already be in there enlighten' her ass about a few things." Antwon starts comin' closer real slow like he don't wanna scare me off.

"I tole you I'd be comin'. But there wasn't nothin' much in your little hide-out that makes it worth keeping your secret to myself, yo. And tell me this; how come you don't get to sleep in the big house, huh?"

I stare at him hard. "You and me got kids who are cousins, man. Don't be like this."

"Yeah, we was practic'ly brothas once upon a time. But things change, man." He looks around at the house and the pool like he likes what he sees. "You up in here livin' the big life, and my ass is still down in Watts, hustlin'. I don't know how you scored all this, what you gotta do for her to earn your keep, but this here between us now ain't about nothin' but business. I want my piece of what you got."

I point to the cabana. "You already took whatever I got that's worth anything. Nothing else here belongs to me. Not even the gym stuff."

"I ain't talkin' 'bout what belongs to you, man. I'm talkin' 'bout what we can *take*. You let me in there," he points to Hester's house, "I'll make it look like a robbery, yo. Even give you a cut once I liquidate the merchandize an' all. Just need you to shut off that alarm, man."

I shake my head. "I ain't helpin' you rip off Hester. Take what you already got from me and get out of here."

He pretends like he's considering my idea. Then shakes his head. "Nah. I don't think so. I think if you don't help me rip your little girlfriend off, I'm gonna tell her all about what you usta do for a livin'. I bet a million real greenbacks you still ain't tole her."

"She's not here for you to tell."

A slow smile spreads across his face. "I'm a patient man. I might just hang here wit'cha till she come back from wherever she is." He points at my grocery bags beside me on the lounger. "You can cook me up somethin' Mexican like the old days."

"That's not gonna work for me, man."

Antwon raises the Glock higher. It's not exactly pointed at me, but the threat is there. "You know what man? *Fuck* what works for you. Just 'cause you so pretty you can come up in here and get all this for free don't make you any betta than me. You can talk all diff'rent, walk all diff'rent, and act like your shit don't stink…but that don't make you diff'rent than you eva was. You think playin' up in Los Feliz with some rich white bitch changes who you is?"

It don't seem worth saying anything back, so I just look at him.

The Glock drops a little lower. "Me and you grew up togetha, man. You s'posed to hang tight with me, bro."

"You didn't hang tight with me when you turned my ass in."

That shuts him up.

"Look, you already got my money and whatever else belongs to me in your pockets. I can call the police or you can give me back my money and get outta here."

Now he points the Glock right at me. "Not gonna happen. You gotta open up that house for me, man."

So I can see there's only one way this is going to end. I'm still standing next to the grocery bags. Looking down into the one closest to me I can see the red onion I bought. I start to reach real slow into the bag. "I do have something else I can give you…"

I whip the onion at him, and at the same time it bounces off his shoulder, I run at him and dive for his legs. When the Glock fires I'm pretty sure it's not pointed at me.

HESTER

Monday, May 19th

"Ladies and Gentlemen, you may now switch on your electronic devices. The current temperature in Los Angeles is seventy-eight degrees Fahrenheit. The local time is six thirty-two a.m. On behalf of the cabin crew, it has been a pleasure serving you. Thank you for flying Air Lingus."

I power up my phone as I wait to disembark. Having flown the red-eye gives me a chance at making it home in time for my morning workout with Enzo.

I check the display; two voicemail messages. One is from Goldie.

"Okay, Hess? You must be on the plane. Anyway, don't freak out…but Enzo's in the hospital. It's not bad, really, but he'll be here for a while so you might want to head straight over when you land. Okay? Los Angeles Memorial Hospital. Right now, we're on the fourth floor, but ask when you get here because he'll be out of surgery by then. Don't. Freak. Out. Okay, bye…"

I sit there, stunned, as people in the rows behind me get up and pass me. Enzo in the hospital? Surgery? What the devil is going on?

When I gather my wits I listen to the second message. It's from a number I don't recognize. "Miss Hastings, this is Lieutenant Sanchez from the Los Angeles Police Department. Two hours ago we responded to a call about a disturbance on your property. I'm calling to let you know that both a robbery and a shooting have occurred. The perpetrator is in custody, and the gunshot victim has been rushed to Los Angeles Memorial Hospital. Please call me at your earliest convenience to discuss the charges you want to bring against…" I don't even hear the rest. Lieutenant Sanchez will get a call from me later, after I've seen Enzo.

GOLDIE

Enzo is in recovery, but I haven't been allowed back to see him yet when Hester arrives.

Her face is white like tofu, and her eyes are practically bugging. "Goldie! I got here as fast as I could…what's happened? How is he?"

She's so flustered I have to grab her by the shoulders and make her breathe before I tell her anything. "Jeez, Hess…calm down. I told you not to freak out. The surgery is over, and he's in recovery. The nurse promised to come get me, us, as soon as he's conscious."

"Why can't we be there when he wakes up?" She's looking past me, presumably for the nurse. "Oh my God, Goldie – he's been shot?"

"Yes, but…" Hester pushes past me to get to the nurse who's just come out to summon an older couple back to recovery.

I just wait for her to come back, which she does when the nurse firmly resists her efforts to get into recovery sooner.

"Hess…it's okay. He got lucky, and the bullet went right through the thigh without breaking anything or hitting major arteries. The surgery was to repair torn muscle and close a nasty exit wound. Apparently, it was the best kind of bullet to get shot with."

"His thigh? What the bloody hell happened?"

"I didn't get called until Enzo was already here. I guess it was around…a little after nine maybe?"

"Do you know what happened before, back at the house?"

I shake my head. "Not everything. I only saw Enzo for a little bit between when they stabilized him and then took him in for surgery, and he wasn't very chatty. Said an old friend of his had shown up uninvited and wanted to rob your house."

Hester's looking tense enough to break a brick with her ass. "I think I know who shot him. Was it a fellow called Antwon?"

"Enzo didn't say, but I'm sure the police know. You should call them for the full report."

She shakes her head. "Not until after I see Enzo."

I need to distract her so she can get calm. "Okay…why don't we sit down, and you can tell me about Ireland until the nurse calls us. Was it fun?"

I have to practically push her into a chair. But then she lets out a huge sigh.

"'Fun' would not be the word I'd use to describe it. Ireland was wet and cold most of the time, but thankfully, the script called for wet conditions or I could have been there for God knows how long waiting for good weather."

"Did Brent behave himself?"

That gets a short laugh. "In his own way, yes."

"Are you ever tempted to just give in and have a fling with him so you can say you've been with Brent Logan?"

"Definitely not…Brent's funny and sort of charming, but no." She looks at the door to the recovery room again. "What exactly did the doctor say, Goldie?"

"They said he was freakin' lucky as shit and that they wanted to do the surgery right away before it started to heal wrong."

"How is he…was he upset? Scared?"

Is she serious? "Hess, we're talking about Enzo. He was fine. But you kinda owe him for not letting that guy rob your house…though, of course, the guy would never have been there if Enzo wasn't living in your cabana…"

"Can we be quiet for a minute?" Hester's face has gone from tofu to chalk. Her blue eyes are bright spots of color in her face.

"Sure, Hess."

I check my phone for texts, but a few seconds later the nurse comes out and calls us back.

Hester lunges out of her seat and flies like a shot past the nurse. Man, her crazy act has got me kinda worried. I wonder what's crawled up her butt? Jetlag?

Enzo is awake, but loopy as hell. He still looks good, though. Even in the hospital's pale blue gown, which technically should not play too well on his skin tone. Hester sits down on the narrow bed right next to him, and...

Holy crap! Hester's kissing on Enzo like he's Prince Harry at a charity ball. I never in a million years would have thought she'd ever consider…what the hell is she thinking?

Well, at least now I know exactly what's gotten into her.

ENZO

When it's night and the hospital finally releases me and they get to take me home, Hester and Goldie fuss over me like little girls with a new doll. They help me into the house and tuck me all into the bed in the guest room with an ice pack, hot water bottle, two smoothies and some crackers in case I get hungry, extra pillows, remote for the flat screen on the wall. I ain't never been in this room before. Hester never showed me the upstairs. The walls are yellow, the sheets and blankets white – which is a bad color for a dude who just got shot. Now I gotta worry about my bandage leakin'. But I got my own bathroom right here, and I'm guessing the room across the hall is hers.

If I wasn't so tired I'd watch some TV, but these women aren't about to leave me alone anyway. Now that they got me all set up with snacks, drinks, and pillows, I can see from how they're lookin' at me they wanna hear the whole story about how it went down with Antwon.

Hester sits at the end of the bed, and Goldie pulls up a blue chair from the corner of the room and gets comfortable. Hester lays a hand on my foot. "So, are you alright? Have you got everything you need?"

I nod. "Yeah, thanks. It's real comfy up here."

Goldie's too impatient to wait. "Enzo, tell us what the hell happened…why was that guy here trying to rob the house? Why did he shoot you?"

I remember my promise to tell Hester about the lie first day she came home. And for a second I think I'm gonna be able to make myself start at the very beginning and tell everything. Just let the words fall out. But then the way she's looking at me, all soft and concerned and trusting, makes me stop. When I promised myself I would tell her today, I didn't know I'd be shot and stuck here until I heal up some. So I give myself five more days. Surgeon said I'll be up and around no problem by then, and it seems fair to at least be able to walk away if – when – that's what she wants when she knows the truth.

So I stick to the facts. "Antwon must have gotten your name off the sign-in sheet from Tonya at the Day Center. He was here last night when I got back from Albertson's, waiting. The son-of-a-bitch already had the money I'd left in the cabana and wanted me to let him in here to take all your nice stuff. He had his stupid Glock, so when he saw I wasn't gonna go for it and I saw he wasn't gonna leave without a fight, I gave him one."

Hester's eyes look big as ping pong balls. "What do you mean? How? When did he shoot you?"

"I threw an onion to try and distract him." I shrug, remembering. "Then I ran at him."

Now Goldie wants more. "So that's when he shot you?"

I nod. "Probably by accident. He waves that Glock around a lot, but I don't think he's ever shot anybody before." I laugh. "Lucky me, right?"

Hester's not smiling. "Who called the police?"

"Your neighbor." I point to the east. "The one on that side. I had to grab the gun and hold onto Antwon until they got here, but the police showed up with the guy from next door in like, six minutes."

"So you're shot already at this point, right?" Hester asks.

I nod.

Goldie jumps in. "And you grabbed the gun and held the robber down?"

I nod again.

They're looking at me like I got a red cape and a giant S on my chest.

Hester looks all concerned. "Weren't you in pain?"

"A little, but you know, adrenaline and all."

They look at each other all amazed, like I'm so brave. But they don't know I did it out of selfishness.

I have to explain the obvious. "If he'd got away he just would have come back…"

Hester sees the sense of that. "Alright, so what happened next?"

"Police wanted to arrest us both, but I told them about the document you had made up to show I'm renting the cabana, and they went and got it. Looked at that passport you made me get to make sure I was me, too. Then they wrote down my statement about what happened and let the ambulance take me."

The girls wait for a minute before they see that's the end. Then Hester rubs my foot. "Well, obviously I owe you a huge 'thank you,' Enzo. Though I'd rather you'd allowed Antwon to just take everything than get shot." She looks at me all serious. "He could have killed you."

I shrug. "He wasn't even aiming."

Goldie's frowning at me. "Hester's right...think about where that bullet would have ended up if it had gone in about eight inches higher." I'm glad I've got my loose shorts on 'cause she's staring right at my dick.

I shrug again. That thought crossed my mind right before they put me under for the surgery. I started thinking about Ricky and all the places I could have been hit that would really change me.

Hester's pretending like Goldie didn't just say what she said. "I'm just grateful you're in one piece and that Antwon is in jail where he belongs. When I talk to Lieutenant Sanchez I'm going to make certain that...hoodlum is charged to the full extent of the law."

I'm not gonna argue about that. With Antwon safe in jail there's no way he can hurt Hester or spill the beans before I get the chance to tell her everything.

We're all quiet for a while, and even though Hester's told me it's rude to do in front of people, I can't stop the yawn that slips out.

Hester gets her worried look. "I'm sorry, Enzo. We've been rude keeping you up when you must be exhausted." She shoots Goldie a look that means, 'get the hell out 'cause we need a minute.' Goldie leaves with her eyebrows all up, staring at us like 'uh huh, I know what's goin' on.'

Hester moves up so she's right next to me on the bed. "I'm so, so sorry this happened. But at the same time it...it's made me realize how I really can't imagine you not being part of my life anymore." She wipes away a tear that slips out and smiles at me. "You've become...special to me, Enzo. I know your plan is to move out and find a place for you and Topaz when you're done here. And I wouldn't want to stop you from moving on with your life...but I want you to know that just because our 'educational arrangement' will end soon and you won't live here anymore..."

She sounds all unsure, like she's afraid I'll want to skip out of here soon as I can and never look back. But she's just said what I've been wishing for. I want to say back, 'I'm yours till you don't want me no more.' But I got that stupid lie standing between us. So I put the words into my smile and try to memorize her whole face, how she's looking at me in this moment.

Then I play it off like none of this is too serious. "Hey, girl. I'm your personal trainer...until you fire me, I'm in charge of your ass."

She laughs, but her eyes are still watery. "You know that's not what I mean..."

I stroke her cheek, guide her face closer so I can kiss her lips. Since I know only five days stands between that look she's giving me now and adios, I can't think of any more words to say.

HESTER

When I get to the kitchen Goldie's lying in wait for me like a lioness ready to hook her claws into dinner. She counts the questions off on her fingers as though she's been waiting to ask them all day. Which in all likelihood she has.

"How long have you been sleeping with our experiment? Why did you not tell me, your *best friend*? And what the hell do you think you're doing!?"

I will not let her ruffle my feathers. "I have not slept with him; I didn't tell you about us because I needed time to figure out what was really happening and also because I thought you might freak out." I shoot her a pointed look. "And I have absolutely no idea what I'm doing. But I think...I think I might really love him."

Goldie's face is unreadable. "How long have you two been playing kissy face?"

"I don't know...does it matter?"

"Absolutely yes. How long?"

I think back to the night we drank the brown ale. "Tomorrow will be two weeks."

She lets out a breath. "It's okay then."

"What do you mean?"

"You can't 'really love him' after two weeks. You're still in the infatuation phase. Plus, if you haven't slept with him, it's all still shiny and new and you can't know anything for sure yet."

"Goldie, how can you say that? People have been falling in love and getting *married* without having sex first since…since forever! Your theory doesn't hold water."

"But I'm telling you that as a modern woman, now, right here in today's world, you need to sleep with him…and I mean give it a week or two of just really full-out bonking like crazy…and then tell me two things: First, all about it, 'cause he looks like he'd totally rock a girl's world; and Second, if, after all the fun sex you still think you 'really love him'."

"I don't get it…wouldn't I just be more enamored of him if we became intimate? Plus, I've already been spending tons of time with him every day; I feel as though I know him extremely well. We've been eating almost every meal together for over a month…"

"With you as the teacher and him as the student! Oh come on, Hess. It's classic fantasy material. He's hot, you're teaching him, he's becoming more polished, and you like that. You're intellectually stimulated by his transformation as he soaks up your knowledge. You're attracted to the fact that he's different from the men you meet socially. He's attracted to you because you're different from anyone he's ever met, and as his 'teacher', you're kind of out of reach. He's hot… you're hot…it's the perfect storm!"

Damn her. I have to own that if the situation were reversed she might hear a version of the same thing from me. "Alright…I will allow that some of this might be accurate to a small degree. I understand how you see it, but I assure you we are not play-acting at some fantasy. There's a lot more to Enzo than meets the eye; it's not just his role as my student and his hot body that make me interested in him romantically."

Goldie scoffs at me. "Hess…I'm afraid it's mostly lust. Believe me, I understand. In your shoes, I might feel the same way. He has a charisma, a sexual appeal that's very alluring. So bonk away! Get it out of your system. When this is all over and he moves on, it will come to a natural end. He'll be grateful, you'll have some hot memories, and life will go on." She wrinkles her nose like she's breaking bad news. "He's not long-term partner material, Hess."

I regard my best friend carefully. She is kind, funny, smart, generous, and caring. I never realized before what a snob she is. "Do you mean to say that because Enzo is from Watts and hasn't benefitted from the same privileged education and upbringing we have he's simply disposable? Use him for my fun, and then move on?"

"This isn't specific to Enzo, Hester. I'd give you the same advice about Brent Logan if you told me you were hot for him. And I think you'll agree that he's not long-term partner material...yes?"

"Well, of course not...but he's different. He's a shallow, spoiled rotten, womanizing movie star..."

"And you haven't known Enzo long enough to know anything about him other than what he's let you see. Believe me, Hess, I never would have suggested taking him on as a project if I'd thought there was even the most remote possibility you'd fall for him. It's such a far-fetched idea that the notion never even crossed my mind! Aside from physical attraction, what can the two of you possibly have in common?"

Now I know I was right not to mention this to her in the first place. She hasn't seen him working tirelessly at everything I've asked him to do. Hasn't observed him with his daughter or seen him get excited about building his own business. She wasn't there when we went to visit Ricky. In fact, she's done nothing but take him shopping and dance with him at Jimmy's wedding. She sees him as an object to be dressed and enjoyed. And to be fair, in the beginning, I saw him as merely a shabby subject to be improved, smartened up. I knew nothing of his ambitions, what motivates him, his capacity for kindness and affection.

"Goldie, I don't expect you to understand. Frankly, when I view it from your perspective, I have a hard time believing it myself. I thank you for your words of advice...they've been thought-provoking. But I'm going to handle this my way. Whatever it is that Enzo and I are building between us is exactly that: between *us*. So let's change the subject and find something we can eat...I'm absolutely ravenous."

Goldie holds up her hands in surrender. "Whatever you say, boss. But, um, I have one more question for you before we start on food...would it be weird or piss you off if I went out with Nigel?"

It takes me a moment to conjure an understanding of what she can possibly mean. "Nigel Hemsworth? The Englishman who recently dumped me for not being attracted to him? You want to go out with that Nigel?"

"Well, I had a pretty terrific conversation with him at that pool barbeque thing you made me come to...and then he called me two days ago to ask if I would feel comfortable taking him on as a client. But I'm pretty sure that means he's going to ask me out. Usually when men try that, I make it clear I'm not available for more than business, but...I kinda like him...a little." She's looking at the floor like this is embarrassing to admit.

"Goldie, you have my complete and unreserved blessing to date Nigel. He's a lovely man, very interesting. In fact, my advice is to jump straight into bed with him and start bonking like crazy..."

Her howl of outraged laughter is so loud I'm worried it might wake Enzo.

Chapter 13

ENZO

Thursday, May 22nd

It's quiet and dark, and this bed is way better than the purple sofa-chair I've gotten used to, but I can't sleep. I'm thinking 'bout Hester and the fact that she's right across the hall from me. In her bed.

We didn't get to eating dinner until late. All day she had me either watching British TV shows or on that machine that gives me a score to show how well I'm doing. She was so happy I kept getting above ninety percent that she made me speak Standard British English all through dinner. It seems like she's happy with the accent, and now she wants to get me up to speed with what she calls 'British-isms', like how they say 'rubbish' instead of 'trash', and how when they hear the word 'pants' they think you talkin' about tighty-whities instead of jeans.

It's all kinda fun, but if I had to do it in front of other people I'd feel like the biggest phony-ass jerk. She keeps saying to pretend like I'm an actor preparing for a role that requires an accent, but I ain't no actor. Feels like I'm just playing some kind of game because Goldie and Hester want me to.

They say it's 'improving' for me. And Hester keeps talking about how fun it'll be to make the DVDs she wants me to be in. Seeing as how my days are numbered here, I just do what she wants me to. I focus on being with her, making her laugh, seeing her happy.

My leg is good enough that I don't take the painkillers any more. I only had to cancel one session with the Barbies, but then I got a new client referred by them and another from Brent. I told 'em all I can fit 'em in week after next in case I need to figure out where else to set up shop. I haven't done a workout session with Hester since she left for Ireland, but I know she'd rather have me studying TV shows, reading classic literature, or doing mirror time anyway since my gunshot wound's still healing.

She's been real sweet about my leg. Driving me to the hospital to get checked, asking every day if I've changed my bandage like the surgeon said to. Even though my leg's better she ain't said anything about me moving back to the cabana.

I'm thinking about how I should probably just go ahead and move back there anyway when I hear the soft swish of Hester's door opening. Even though my door isn't all the way closed, she knocks real gentle on it, checking to see if I'm awake.

I prop up on my elbow. "What's goin' on?"

Her head appears round the edge of the door. "You're awake?"

"Can't sleep."

"Neither can I." It's dark, but I can still see the shyness on her face. "Mind if I come in?"

I move over and make room for her up next to me. She creeps in, wearin' what she calls 'shortie pajamas'. Matching lacy top and short shorts. Since I been sleeping in the guest room I've had the privilege of seeing Miz Hastings in her shorties, and with no make-up on, and once in nothing but a towel. Ain't no hardship.

Now she snuggles up to me, and I wrap my arms around her wishin' hard for more. I know from how she's been careful about giving out kisses since I've been sleeping in the house that the guestroom bed don't give me a free ticket to the goodies. What she don't know is that even though it's about driving me crazy holding her in my bed right now, there's no way I'm taking them lacy shorts offa her. I ain't never had to work hard to try and *not* get in a woman's pants before. The way she's holding tight to me now means she's just about giving me the green light, too.

"Enzo?"

"Mmmm…"

"What do you want for yourself, you know, for the future?"

First thing I think is: You. Then I get it together. "Grow my business, open a gym if I can. I've been thinking about maybe, once I get my act together, starting up some kind of program where kids struggling like I was can come work out and learn all about fitness careers and stuff. You know? Learn what to study so they can have jobs like physical therapist, athletic trainer, gym teacher, things they can earn money doing. Keep 'em off the streets and help them make a career plan."

"That's a wonderful idea…I know you could raise money to help pay for a program like that."

"Yeah, well."

"Well what?"

"I got to finish what I started here first."

She's quiet for a whole minute. "I have a confession to make."

"Oh yeah?"

"Every day for the first two weeks you were here I expected you might quit."

I sit up so I can check out if her face is serious. "What?"

"I didn't know you weren't the quitting type, and I figured you'd get bored and tired of doing every silly thing I made you try."

"No way, man. I mean, you did make me do what seemed like stupid stuff. But you threw down a challenge, and I saw it might do me some good. That and I had no place else to go but the skanky shelter…"

She gives me her outraged look and tweaks my ear. I go to kiss her but she ducks me. She pushes at my shoulders hard, and I let her pin me. Then she slides her leg across my hips real careful so she don't hurt my thigh. And shifts her weight so she's sitting square on top of me. I know she can feel how much I want her, and she's looking at me all hungry and scared both.

I let the moment hang there for a bit 'cause it feels so good to know she's ready to take it further. But then I force myself to deploy the secret weapon I discovered to break the spell. The shrieks of unchained laughter that come from her mouth when I start tickling make me stop before some neighbor calls the police again.

But the job is done. She smacks me on the chest all playful as punishment for the tickle attack and then snuggles up against my good side again. I hold onto her until she falls asleep, and then I let myself relax and do the same.

HESTER

Saturday, May 24th

For the second morning in a row, I wake up in Enzo's arms. He must have woken earlier because as soon as I roll over his eyes open and he smiles at me. The slow, sexy smile that commanded my attention the first time I saw it. It amazes me that this is the same man who barely smiled at all in that first month of study. Yesterday, when I woke under his gaze, I felt shy, but this morning I feel exhilarated by his proximity. I allow myself to enjoy gazing straight into his warm eyes, the sensation of moving my hands across his smooth tan chest.

"Good morning, Enzo Diaz."

"Good morning, Miz Hastings."

"It's Saturday…we have the whole morning before I have to go meet Jessica and Philip."

"I was thinking…" He kisses my shoulder. "How about I make you chocolate chip pancakes for breakfast?"

"Mmm…you know my weakness."

"But then after that I think it's time to get back to hitting the weights."

"What about your leg?"

"I'll stick to bench presses and telling you what to do."

This sounds worrying. "Try not to hurt me too much…it's been over a week since I did any exercise."

By the time I locate my workout clothes, get dressed, and come down to the kitchen, he's made me a cup of tea and started on the pancakes. When he opens the bag of chocolate chips he dumps some into a little bowl for me. I eat a few, then start tossing them for him to catch in his mouth.

"Ready?"

"Hold on." He cracks an egg into the bowl and beats it into the milk with a whisk. "Okay, ready."

I toss a chip high into the air, and he has to lean forward to catch it. He does a little bow when I applaud, then goes back to mixing ingredients into the batter.

"I wish we could get Jessica and Topaz together again for a play date. They had so much fun in the pool last time."

"Good luck with that. Philip must have had a sixth sense we'd get together; he hates me."

"Well, at least he's letting me have time with her today, even if he is tagging along for the whole thing. I haven't figured out how to get back to the way things used to be. But you know what's funny?"

"What?"

"Jessica doesn't call me as much anymore. I used to get a few calls a week, but now it's been probably a week and a half – because I had to cancel on her last weekend – since we've had any contact at all. It's like she's outgrowing me or something."

"You think Philip's not letting her call?"

I hadn't thought of that. "I don't think he'd be that mean…ready for another chip?"

He stops mixing and puts on his game face. "Bring it on, girl."

I toss this one too flat, and it hits him on the chin, rebounding into the pancake batter.

⊶ ⊷

I am so full of pancakes I'm grateful we're going to work out this morning. He has me warm up with some light weights and then starts me kickboxing on the punching bag. My kicks have come a long way from the feeble first attempts I made weeks ago. Now they land with a solid thud, and I follow up each kick with a one-two punch Enzo taught me. It is immensely satisfying.

Perhaps because he's not as distracted by a workout of his own, Enzo really puts me through my paces. Lunges, squats, pectorals, deltoids, triceps, and the dreaded planks. I'm hot and slick with sweat when he's finished with me.

Enzo tosses me a towel, and I dry off best I can. "Ugh. I'm so hot."

He spreads a yoga mat out on the wooden slats of the porch floor. "Time to cool down."

I stretch and bring my heart-rate down to normal with some slow breathing. He's watching me the whole time. I think I like it better when he has his own exercises to do. Just when I'm starting to feel really self-conscious, he comes over and shows me a new move. Only this maneuver involves two people and a lot of kissing.

By the time he releases me my heart rate has shot back up. "Now I need another cool down."

He nods sagely. "I know just the thing."

Enzo scoops me up like I weigh nothing and treats me to his slow, delicious smile. I admire the curve of his lips, enjoy knowing what it feels like to have those lips kiss my own. Though I have no idea where he's taking me, I give myself over to being held. My hands go around his neck, and I focus on the feeling of his strong arms supporting my back and knees, cradling me like something precious.

Eyes closed, I sense the motion of his steps as he carries me. Then he bends, and I feel his muscles come to life as he throws me, launches me from his arms. For a brief moment, I am flying through the air, my eyes wide open now, my mouth forming a small 'o'.

When I break the surface and go under I am enveloped by the warmth and wetness of the water. As I come up I catch a glimpse of Enzo diving in sideways off his good leg. There's only a second to catch my breath because the angle of his dive has put him on a straight trajectory toward me. He slices through the water, gliding on the momentum of the dive until he grabs my legs and pulls me under.

The silence is total. We are deaf to the world above the surface. He lets go of my legs, and we face each other, treading water, eyes wide open. My hair floats around my face, and I feel the freedom of near weightlessness. Enzo's eyes move from my eyes to my lips, his gaze sliding down my body in a way that makes me yearn to feel his hands on every part of me.

With a smile, I spin and swim off to the shallow end, a glance back over my shoulder inviting him to chase. It doesn't take long for him to catch up and slide an arm around my waist, pull me up against him.

When we break the surface I have only just taken a breath when his lips are on mine. Playful nips at first, and then deep, sensual kisses that make my body respond with an insistent longing for more. He stands, and I place my feet on his, encircle his chest with my arms. One of Enzo's hands cradles the nape of my neck, the other is firmly on my back, pressing me closer. My hands slide up to the wet hair on the back of his head, telling him 'more, I want more.'

My physical response to his touch is almost painful, a passionate ache to feel his body even closer. I'm not a stranger to physical intimacy, but I've never been touched, kissed, held in a way that satisfied me more. Enzo is all I can think: his lips, arms, body are all I want. The throbbing ache within me grows until I'm moaning my desire for more of him.

My hands slide down his back and take hold of the hem of his sleeveless shirt. I yank it upward, peeling it off and tossing it as far from me as I can. It lands with a wet splat on the poolside pavement.

I can't stop my hands from exploring every inch of his chest, arms, shoulders. His skin is warm and smooth, his muscles hard under my palms and fingertips. After enjoying his body as eye candy for so long, it's supremely satisfying to revel in having full access to it.

I am fiercely aware of his obvious desire; the grind of his pelvis against my abdomen allows me to feel the rigid length of him despite the clothing between us. My breath has shortened, and I'm panting like an animal. Blood is rushing through my veins and making me feel alive in every part of my being as I lose myself in the pure pleasure of sexual passion.

I have no idea how much time passes before I tow him to the pool steps. "After all this exercise and swimming, I think we need a shower."

Forehead pressed to mine, Enzo grins. "I've never heard a better idea."

He lifts me out of the water and carries me up the steps. It is such a Harlequin Romance moment that I laugh out loud, throwing my head back and imagining what my Mum would think of my sexual preferences if she could see us now. I suspect she would be alarmed by the depth of my lust for this man.

Enzo carries me into the cabana and puts me gently on my feet in what I've come to think of as his lair. I head straight to the shower room and turn on the faucet. While we wait for the spray of water to warm I turn to the task of freeing us from our wet clothing. He helps me peel off my shirt-bra combo and then his hands are all over my newly exposed skin. Together we move under the shower, kissing hungrily and exploring each other. Blindly, he feels for the liquid soap dispenser on the wall and pumps some into his hand. As he works the lather into my breasts I'm nearly wild with ecstasy. I'm making noises that have never escaped my lips before. By the time he rinses the soap off and goes to work with his mouth I feel I might lose control completely.

The man has a talented tongue, and as he lets it rove across my chest I reach for the waistband of his shorts. I pop the snap above the fly and work at trying to shift a stiff zipper. But he reaches down to stop my hands. I fight to keep at my task, but he pushes my hands away.

"No...we can't go there. Not today."

"What?" I gasp as his tongue finds my nipple again. "Why not?"

He straightens up, caresses my cheek with his fingertips. "Because it can't be now."

My anger rises...why is he trying to deny me what we both want? "Why the hell not?"

"I'm not ready...there are things...things you don't know about me."

"So tell me."

An expression I can't place gives the impression he's aged ten years in the space of a second. "I can't right now."

"Enzo, we're standing half naked together in the shower. When is a better time? Shall I go fetch my calendar so we can pencil it in?"

He looks away, and I can't read his expression. "I'm sorry. It's just not the right moment. Can't we enjoy this and save the rest for later?"

"Now that you've driven me nearly mad with desire?" I kiss him again, trying to express the depth of my need for him right now. "Don't you want to?

He lets out a short laugh. "Damn straight I want to...want to rip those little spandex booty shorts off you and.... Hell, yes." He closes his eyes for a moment, and I feel him pull away ever so slightly.

"Then what? You know I want you to...I'm practically begging you to..."

"I can't."

The man who couldn't get enough of me two minutes ago moves away, and I'm left standing alone in the shower, shirtless, rejected.

"Enzo!"

He rubs his face with his hands. Shakes his head.

"No."

ENZO

God-*damn*! It's so hard to make myself stop. *Son-of-a-bitch*.

Here she is right in front of me: the woman I want, so beautiful and more than willing. It takes everything I got and a little more to stop. Tell her no.

But I have to. Why, oh why didn't I tell her at the very beginning when she wasn't into me? Then maybe she'd have had a chance to get over it by now, and we could still have this…whatever this is we have. I'd like to think she could forgive me for what I've done in the past…but my timing sucks.

I want more than anything right now to say, 'hell with it,' and do what she wants, what we both want. Let the chips fall all the fuck over the place.

But I can't. She'll hate me even more if we do. I can already see the look of disgust she'll have on her face when I finally find the courage to say the words out loud. Tell her the truth about why my ass was sent to jail. And that's why I haven't been able to tell her, and why I can't let us finish what we started here.

These last two months have been the best of my entire life. One dream coming true after another. Now I've got the total package: a woman this fine here with me, wanting me.

I reach over and turn off the faucet. Grab a towel from the shelf and hand it to her.

"I'm so sorry, Hester. More than you know, I'm sorry. But I think it's better if you go back to your house now."

HESTER

I clutch the towel to my chest. It's clear he's not joking. A bitter feeling rises up in my throat. I watch him bend and pick up my wet workout top. He hands it to me, and I take it, disbelief still flooding the core of me that was so recently drenched with desire.

Looking at the beauty of him, underwear-ad sexy, deeply tan, still wet from the shower, I feel like a teenager tricked into a cruel locker-room trap. I half expect his buddies to appear from nowhere and laugh at me.

There's nothing I can say that I won't regret later, so I wrap the clean, white towel around my body and leave Enzo's lair.

Back at the house I finish undressing and get into my own shower. I can't stop my mind from replaying the passion that almost ran its course and the moment it was brought up short. I feel short-changed, incomplete, and worst of all, rejected.

I'd like to be a big girl about it, after all I've never slept with a man on the first date, have always demanded the utmost respect from my sexual partners. I would absolutely expect a man to stop halfway through if I told him I'd had enough. And it's not as though I'm accustomed to wild sexual encounters. But while I haven't had many partners, I've had enough to know that a man who makes me feel like Enzo just did – before he rejected me – is a rare thing. One I've never had the pleasure of knowing until now.

It's not as though we haven't had time to get to know each other. Enzo and I have been on a journey together, a highly personal one in some respects. He's not the same man who came knocking at my door eight weeks ago, nor am I the same woman who chose to take on the task of teaching him.

He's helped me become more grounded, centered. Taught me things about myself and the world that have changed my perspective, shaded my expectations and understanding of people, relationships, possibilities. I smile despite myself; he's made me feel more alive and less chained by my own self-imposed constrictions.

What could he possibly tell me now that would change how I feel about him? I know the worst: the man is an ex-con. He's done illegal things that landed him in jail. Does he not remember that I met him the day he was released?

I suddenly realize that I have no idea what time it is. How long were we fooling around in the pool?

I peer through the fogged glass shower door at the clock next to the sink. Hell's bells...I'm ten minutes late for meeting up with Jessica!

Though what I really want to do is crawl into my bed and sulk, I quickly get dried, dressed, and ready to leave the house. Faced with the prospect of spending time with Philip, who has insisted on coming with us to the aptly titled Awesome Playground in Pasadena, I am overcome by a feeling of foreboding so strong it almost stops me in my tracks.

What am I worried about? I've spent plenty of time in the past with Philip. Used to enjoy it, in fact. I think that for the sake of having quality time with Jessica, I can manage this even without having Goldie along as a buffer. But I really must put more effort into thinking of a way to get my home sleepover visits with Jessica back.

ENZO

Tonight. I'm gonna tell her tonight. I'll make a dinner I know she likes and have it all ready by the time she gets home from her day with Jessica. What's her favorite dish? I never did get to cook up the food I'd bought for when she came home from Ireland. But I know there's some salmon in the freezer. She really liked the mashed potatoes I made way back that first time I cooked for her. And she loves green stuff, too. I'll get out that salmon, grill it up, then put it on a bed of sautéed spinach with the potatoes on the side.

I clean up in the cabana, get all my stuff together, and stack it up on the purple sofa. If she makes me leave after I tell her I can just stuff it all in the suitcase Goldie bought me and get outta here.

I ain't said a prayer probably since my Abuela died. But I say one now: please let me finish what I started here. Let Hester understand and forgive my lie.

By the time I get to the house she's gone out already. I have a smoothie and get down to work. I've got to practice the list of words she gave me in the mirror, watch a DVD about tongue positioning for proper enunciation, read two chapters in *Great Expectations* out loud into the tape recorder she left on the kitchen table, call Topaz to tell her when I'm gonna pick her up tomorrow, and get dinner rolling.

While I'm doing the mirror work I try not to think about what I'll do if she wants me to leave. I've got enough money for a few nights in a motel while I look for a cheap apartment. I could call Goldie, but she'll probably side with Hester and be all disgusted by me, too. Plus, if I have to leave here, I'm not gonna rely on anyone else to help me. When I go, it's time to start doing for myself again.

I got my clients. I know my man Brent won't mind if I start coming to his place to train him. He's probably got better equipment than I have anyway. And the blondes, well, I can meet 'em at the park and run 'em through circuit training until I get my own equipment. Girls don't care as much about workin' out with weights as guys do.

As for my best client, my favorite one, I'm not sure how long it will take me to recover from losing her.

But maybe a miracle will happen. Maybe I'll tell her, and she'll look at me and say, 'Enzo, I know you were only doing what you thought gave you the best chance for making a better life for Topaz.' Maybe she'll understand.

But then I remember about the world she comes from and who she's used to hangin' out with and how high and mighty her expectations are, and I know, there's no way in hell she's gonna understand.

HESTER

Jessica is so excited to have me and her Daddy both with her at the same time it breaks my heart a little. In a perfect world, Philip would have been a man I could trust, a man who showed me his love and loyalty, a man like Enzo. But life isn't about perfection; it's about making the best of whatever situation presents itself. Making decisions you can live with. Staying with Philip despite his transgression is not a decision I could ever live with.

Philip insists on driving, so I buckle up in his Camaro, as I've done many times before, and we head out to Jessica's choice of lunch venue, the establishment known as Peanut Butter and Everything.

"Hester." Jessica's front teeth are halfway grown in already, and I miss her little lisp. "Why can't I come to your house for sleepovers anymore?"

I look at Philip. What has he told her?

He saves me the trouble of coming up with the right answer. "Jessica, sweetie. We've talked about this...you know the answer."

She sniffs, disappointed. "I wanted to see if Hester had the same answer. I don't think she'd be friends with Mr. Enzo if he wasn't safe."

I turn to Philip. "Did you tell her Enzo's dangerous?"

"No." His voice is measured, careful. "I told her that strange men she doesn't know can be dangerous, and we don't know Mr. Enzo."

"I do know him...he went swimming with us!" Jessica's little face looks conflicted despite her decisive tone.

"Jessica, your Daddy is right about being careful of strangers. But as long as a person you know you can trust, like me or your Dad, is with you when you meet someone new, it's a pretty safe situation." I look pointedly at Philip. "I would never leave you alone with anyone I didn't absolutely know is a safe person."

A little sigh of frustration sounds in the back seat. "I just wish you and Daddy were married so we could all be together all the time."

Now it's my turn to sigh. "I know, sweetheart. I'm so sorry it can't be that way."

"Daddy says it's your fault it can't."

"What?" I turn to her father. "Did you tell her that, Philip?"

"Not in so many words..."

I twist in my seat to look at Jessica. "The important thing is that your Dad and I both love you and that you and I still have our special time together, right?"

Jessica looks at her Dad, who can see her in the rear-view mirror. "Dad says you have bad judgment. But I told him I don't think you even know any judges. Do you?"

"Philip, have you been denigrating me in front of Jessica?"

He pretends he's too busy watching out for other cars to look at me. "Can we talk about this later?"

I turn to Jessica. "What else does your Daddy say?"

"He says you like bulging mussels. Is that like clams? 'Cause I tried a clam once, and it was yucky."

"No, sweetie. But your Dad and I need to discuss the word 'respect'. Do you know what that means?"

"Yeah! Like treating people nice and how you want to be treated, right?"

I nod. "Exactly."

Philip hazards a glance at me. "Hard to respect someone who's showing so little respect for herself..."

I can't believe he's launched this smear campaign against me. "What's that supposed to mean?"

He shrugs like it doesn't matter. "Just that you no longer seem like the person I thought you were."

With Jessica's little ears behind me I choose to remain silent, knowing my words could be used against me.

-->==● ●==<--

After a somewhat sticky lunch we drive to the Awesome Playground. If there had been one of these in my neighborhood when I was Jessica's age, I would have spent all my waking hours there. Zip lines, mechanical digging buckets you can sit on to excavate the enormous sand pit, tire swings, structures three stories high with slides, tunnels, and hidey holes, trampolines built into the ground with foam-core edges to avoid nasty falls. It's a child's paradise. Nearly the instant we arrived, Jessica spotted two friends from school and ran off to join them. Leaving Philip and myself to find a bench and keep watch from afar.

I suddenly regret my choice of venue for our visit. We haven't been sitting for more than a minute before Philip clears his throat and begins to speak.

"Hester, I know this isn't the right time or place..."

I hold out a hand to stop his words. "Philip, I must insist we not go there. We had our time together, and it's over. There's no going back to the way things were."

He laughs at me. "Your ego is too much...now I feel a lot less sorry about what I'm about to tell you. But before we get to that, you need to know that I've asked my girlfriend to move in with me. Jessica's been spending a lot of time with her, really likes her. I think it's best that we keep your visits with Jessica like they have been lately, few and far between. It's not fair to Veronica to let Jessica stay so attached to you."

"Veronica? Your new girlfriend?" I feel a stab of jealousy, but it has nothing to do with Philip. She can have him. I'm jealous that Philip is undermining my relationship with Jessica, installing Veronica in the 'surrogate mommy' spot that belongs to me. "You want Veronica to replace me in Jessica's life...'

He doesn't look at me. "I wanted it to be you. You know I wanted you to marry me, damn it. And I don't want to rehash the past. The point is, you didn't marry me. You turned me down and expected me to keep on going the way we had been as though you hadn't rejected me as your partner in life. That was tough to take, Hester. But now I have someone new, someone who does want to marry me. Jessica needs the chance to bond with her without you in the way. And even though you might think that telling you what I'm about to tell you is some kind of revenge for you dumping me, I assure you I take no pleasure in it."

Suddenly I feel weary. "What? What is it aside from firing me as Jessica's mother-figure that you have to tell me?"

He still won't look at me. "That guy you have living with you? I know all about him. I hired a PI..."

"PI? Private Investigator?" This is too much. "Philip, I can't believe you! This is just beyond the realm of reason. I can't believe you paid someone to spy on us! And for your information, I know what you're going to tell me. He's an ex-con...he spent a year behind bars. I know already, so you've wasted your money on that PI."

"So you knew, and you still think he's safe to have hanging around Jessica?" Philip's face is so filled with outrage I shrink from him despite my confidence that he's wrong about Enzo. "Frankly, Hester, I'm shocked that your personal standards have fallen so low that you'd allow that beast anywhere near yourself."

"Beast? You're talking about a man who's working hard to improve himself so he can provide a better life for his daughter. Shall I call you a beast for cheating on me and lying to me about it?"

"That was a single mistake, Hester. A mistake I bitterly regret." His voice gets low. "You were the best thing that ever happened to me. I guess that's why I detest the idea of that cretin taking advantage of your gentle nature."

"What are you talking about? No one's taking advantage of me..."

"Well, I didn't know that you knew what kind of man you were dealing with until just now."

"So he got involved with drugs somehow," I shrug. "Lots of people do. Lots of rich, respectable people. People you and I probably know…"

"Is that what he told you? Drugs?" Philip lets out a bitter laugh. Then he looks me in the eyes. "The man was a prostitute, Hester."

ENZO

At the store I buy a bottle of white wine I can't really afford. When I get home I pinch three hot pink camellias off the bush by the gate and bring 'em inside. I get a little dish down from the cupboard, fill it with water, and float the blossoms in it. It makes a nice centerpiece on the table. She likes shit like that.

I set the table with two wineglasses, her favorite flowery cloth napkins, a salad fork and an entrée fork, knife and spoon on the right of the plate. Then I rinse the salmon and give it a little olive oil and lemon juice on top. Cover it with plastic wrap and slide it into the fridge until it's time for grilling.

Though I want to keep puttin' off telling her, since this morning the thought of not doing it has become worse than just ripping off the stupid band aid, hairs and all. After I peel a load of potatoes I go to the cabana and practice what I'm going to say. Do I tell her during dinner or wait until she's eaten?

"Hester, there's something I've been wanting to say…" No.

"I'm real sorry about this morning, but I can't have sex with you until you know…" Double no.

"Hester, I wasn't really in jail for drug possession." I might as well say, 'Hester, I told you a bald-faced, honkin' lie.'

I bury my face in my hands. Why can't I have normal problems like back hair or athlete's foot?

HESTER

I feel like I've been slapped. "A what?"

"A sex offender. Took money for sex. Prostituted himself." He sighs and reaches into his back pocket. "I wish I didn't have to show you this." He unfolds what looks like a glossy pamphlet. It's a bi-fold, like a theater program or a menu. "I should have realized you didn't know the truth." He opens the pamphlet to reveal pictures of men in various stages of undress. Their poses are suggestive, and they've all got props, like riding whips, or top hats, or cowboy chaps, and not much else in the way of clothing. Most of the men's faces have cheesy, seductive expressions, and they are all, without exception, extremely well-built.

Each picture has a heading: Sexy Stockbroker, Hot Jock, Gorgeous Gunslinger, Motorcycle Mayhem. I feel sick to my stomach as my eyes follow Philip's finger to the second page. There, in the middle, sandwiched between Roman Gladiator and Southern Stud is a picture of Enzo. He looks so different I have to check twice to be sure it's him. His head is shaved, and I can see the scalp tattoos on the side that's angled toward the camera. He's sporting an aggressive moustache-beard combo that I've heard Goldie refer to as a 'van dyke'. There's a menacing look in his eyes, like he's about to hurt someone. The skull tattoo on his shoulder is the clincher. There's no way the man in the photo isn't Enzo.

But I can't believe what Philip has said is true. "You could have had this Photoshopped…"

Philip sighs. "Hester, you know this isn't trickery. The PI got it from Enzo's defense attorney. He gave it to me yesterday."

I can't tear my eyes from the photo. Enzo's caption reads 'Homeboy Gangsta'. His muscled arms are crossed over his chest, and his prop is a ridiculously large gun tucked into the very low-slung jeans he's wearing. In the bottom right hand corner of the photo are two black letters in caps: S. O.

What the devil does S.O. mean? "I don't understand…this isn't…he said it was drug possession."

"Hester, would you have taken him into your home if you had known he was a sex offender?"

I look at Philip. Of course the answer is no. Even though Enzo is not a rapist, or a child molester, if I had known he was a prostitute, it would have been a deal-breaker. The defiant piece of me, the one who so enjoyed Enzo's affection in the pool this morning, she wonders why it would have made a difference. Selling drugs, selling sex. But the rest of me understands. Understands in such a visceral way that I'm already feeling shame about having been ready to give myself to a man who has sold himself to others. Sex is personal, it's invasive. I'd always viewed prostitution as the lowest depth to which a person could sink. Something you did when you were drug addicted to the point of not caring what you had to do to score your next hit.

When you were so abused, poor, and desperate you thought no better of yourself than to go on the streets and exchange sex for money.

Philip puts a hand on my shoulder. "I'm really sorry, Hester. If it's any consolation, this was a very high-end sex racket. When the police ran their sting operation it was front page news because the two women who organized it were married to well-known producers…"

"What does S. O. mean?"

"Straight Only."

Oh. I'm so naïve. I hadn't even considered the possibility there might be anything un-straight about it.

Philip tries to slide a comforting arm around my shoulders, but I shrug him off. I stand and walk to a raised platform from which I can see Jessica better. I don't ask Philip if I can keep the 'man-menu.' I tuck it into my purse, next to my wallet.

When Jessica looks over to find me, I smile and wave. She locates me and smiles back. For a moment, I wish we could switch places and I could be the happy, innocent little girl enjoying the Awesome Playground.

GOLDIE

I'm helping Nigel pick out new sportswear when my phone starts playing "Sledgehammer," which means it's Hester. I send my new client into the changing room and answer.

"What's up, Hess?"

"Remember back when we first met Enzo and you promised to do research on him to make sure he was safe?"

It's ancient history, but still makes me feel guilty. "Yes…I remember… the guard we asked said he was cool. What about it?"

"You never did the research, did you?"

Uh oh. "Okay, here's the thing…I really meant to do it, call people or go to the courthouse or whatever. But I was working with David Hasselhoff, you know how he's trying to reinvent himself again and everything, and…"

"Give it a rest, Goldie. I just wish…I wish you had. I wish you'd just done what you said you were going to do. If you had…"

But I never find out what's got her panties in a bunch because she hangs up on me. It's timely, because Nigel has just come out in a Puma tracksuit he picked out – ew – but all the same I make a mental note to call her later. It's not like Hester Hastings to leave a conversation unfinished.

ENZO

The mashed potatoes and spinach are ready, and as soon as her car pulls into the driveway, I lay the salmon to sizzle on the hot oven grill. But then she just sits in her BMW for a long time. I start to worry, and then the salmon gets done, and it's time to plate up.

Why doesn't she come in? I go outside to see if she's on the phone or something. When she looks at me, I wave, tell her 'dinner's ready' even though the windows are rolled up tight and she can't hear me.

When she finally gets out, I start wishin' she'd stayed in. I didn't know she'd still be mad at me about this morning, but looks like she is 'cause her face is all stormy. And kinda red around her eyes like she's been crying.

Oh shit.

Hester walks right past me like I ain't even there and goes into the house. She doesn't stop and put her keys and purse down in the kitchen or look at the plates of food right there on the table. Just heads straight through the yellow kitchen door, I guess going to her office.

I wanna think maybe there's a dialect emergency happening to one of her clients or something else she's got to take care of right away. But a sinking feeling says this is about me. I fucked up somehow.

When I knock on the office door, she doesn't answer. "Hester?"

She doesn't say, 'come on in.' She just opens the door and stares up at me. I ain't never seen a more disappointed look on a human face in all my life. Even when Dad got arrested for the last time and we had to go tell my Abuela he wasn't probably ever coming home.

I don't know who did it, or how it went down, but somebody just told the woman I love that I lied to her about what I did to get thrown in jail. I lost my chance to break it to her myself, and now I know for sure I'm leaving.

HESTER

Enzo reaches for my shoulder, but I jump back out of reach. "Hester…"

"No, you don't get to 'Hester' me anymore. Did you think I was so stupid you could lie to me forever?"

He shakes his head. "No…no. In fact, I was planning to tell you myself when you got back from Ireland, but then I got shot. And then it was supposed to be tonight…but who told you?"

"It was extra special to hear it from Philip. Oh, and yes, I totally believe you were going to tell me tonight. How convenient."

"I said so this morning when we…remember?"

"How could I forget?" I shudder. "Obviously, I'm thrilled now that you rejected me so kindly this morning. It saves me the trouble of worrying what disease I might have caught from you."

He takes a step back into the hallway as though I've pushed him. "I don't…I would never…" His face registers shock at my cruel words and a desire to protect me at the same time. "I don't have any diseases, Hester. But I was hoping maybe you'd understand why I chose to…"

"To sell yourself? Tell me, what was your price?"

Now I've inflicted a hurt that shows in his eyes. I'd feel sorry for him if I wasn't hurting so badly myself.

Standing on the other side of the open door, he looks smaller. When he speaks his voice is low and soft. "You know I never tried to do anything you didn't want me to. Please don't be like this."

But I can't stop. My anger and hurt feelings have spilled over, and I can't contain them. "Enzo, you lied to me! I made a decision about being with you based on believing you were honest. When I think of you selling yourself to whomever selected you from that…man menu…it makes me feel sick."

ENZO

I close my eyes at the thought of her seeing my picture, the way I had to pose for that ad. It was the most humiliating moment of my life, and she's seen it.

When I can breathe again, I open my eyes and she's staring at me. "I never pictured you like that, Enzo. I never pictured you servicing random women for a living."

"Would it make it any different if I hadn't gotten paid? If I'd just had over a hundred different girlfriends and had sex with all of them?"

Hester gasps, and I wish I could take back my words. "Were there more than a hundred?" She lets her breath out slow. "I can't believe you kept count...but then again, how else would you know your paycheck was correct?"

I try to backtrack, even though I know the damage has been done. "No, there weren't that many different women...most were repeaters."

"Oh, well, that makes it all okay then, doesn't it?" She looks me up and down like she told me not to do the first day I came here. "You must be worth the money to get repeat customers."

I can't think of anything to say that will fix this. It's even worse than I ever imagined it would be. The look in her eyes, the disgust.

But I have to try. "Look, haven't you ever done something you wished you could undo? Something you knew was probably a mistake but you did it anyway?"

She levels her X-ray death glare at me. "Yes, you. This whole experiment. I wish that when you first knocked on my door I'd pretended I wasn't home or called the police or anything but let you into my home." I can see she's trying not to cry, and I wish I could put my arms around her and make it better. But it's because of me. Those tears are my fault.

"This...hurts." She thumps her chest. "In here. I can't...trust you anymore. The thought of you being a plaything for...'repeaters,' of what they wanted you to do, what they paid you to do."

"There wasn't nothing crazy kinky..."

"'Wasn't *anything*,' Enzo. If you're going to say it, say it right. And I can't believe what you say anymore, so save your breath." She looks up at me, and I see the tears start again. Her voice becomes a whisper. "In fact, you should really just go."

I take a step forward. "Hester..."

She shakes her head, tears coming down her cheeks. Then she shuts the office door in my face.

HESTER

The tears won't stop, and I'm shaking. I sit down in the chair Enzo first sat in when I did his evaluation ten weeks ago. He's made a fool of me. If Philip chose to, he could destroy my reputation by spreading word of Enzo's past. How I got involved with a prostitute. He could insinuate all kinds of ugly, nasty things that would seem, from an outsider's perspective, like the truth. Maybe Nigel was right all along. Enzo might have been playing me for a fool the whole time. Though my heart rejects the thought, my pride hammers it like a weapon against my own stupid ego. He was a stray dog who started with a bowl of food and ended up sleeping in my bed. Or very nearly. Just this morning, I was begging him for sex. Why didn't he do it? When he's already been with so many women, what's one more?

But beyond feeling the fool, I'm absolutely gutted emotionally. I feel like a raw nerve that's been exposed and beaten bloody. I adored him, that much is clear. He seemed like everything I wanted: rough around the edges with a heart of gold. It's what I wished for, right? Ha. I should call Goldie and give her a laugh. Tell her the whole damn truth. Why in God's name did she not find out why he was behind bars before all this started? Why didn't I?

I was so trusting. It must have been easy for him to navigate the stepping stones of my loneliness, my insecurities, all the way to my heart. He was so believable, played all his cards just right. But then, he's had a lot of practice. Playing the role of whatever fantasy was purchased.

Homeboy Gangsta. I didn't pay for a fantasy, but I got one anyway.

I don't suppose there's any chance for a refund.

MRS. HASTINGS

London calling! I can scarcely believe that by this time tomorrow, Christopher and I will be winging our way over the North American continent and the wide Atlantic to the little island nation where we both were born. Years apart, of course. I play the demure maiden to his role as wizened seafarer. It's been said of me that if I'd not married so early I would have been bound for the silver screen. I suppose that's why I feel such an affinity for movie stars.

Though I've lived in Los Angeles for nineteen years, England is still very much my home. I find that most of the British ex-pats I know in America feel much the same way. My daughter might be a different story, which is odd considering how much of her English identity she's chosen to retain despite her ability to mimic a perfect American accent. One day, I shall have to ask her about that... but today, I'm on a mission to brief her about the party I'm throwing for Enzo and assure her that the wheels will be in motion even though I'm thousands of miles away. I've hired a fabulous and wildly popular party planner who should have most everything ready by the time I return. Oh, and of course, I need to say 'goodbye' to my only child before we leave.

I am so intent on getting to Hester's charming domicile that if Enzo Diaz hadn't just looked directly at my car, I wouldn't even have noticed him there on the sidewalk. Carrying a suitcase. When he sees who's in the car and I wave, he looks away as though he's been caught doing something he shouldn't. Oh dear. Perhaps the poo has hit the fan.

I pull over and roll down the window. "Yoo-hoo! Enzo, where are you going with that suitcase, my dear? Are you running away from home?"

Enzo looks like a man who's just lost a match with the heavyweight champion, only there are no visible bruises.

He waves half-heartedly. "Hey, Mrs. H. I think you probably shouldn't be talking with me. Hester threw me out for a pretty good reason, so I got to move on." He looks down at his suitcase. "It was good to know you...I'm sorry I screwed up."

Then he's off again, headed away from Hester's. Hmmm. It was my intention to go say my goodbyes to my daughter before flying to England with Christopher tomorrow. But this is an emergency.

I hastily back into a parking spot on the side of the road and exit the car. "Enzo!"

He turns around, perplexed. "Wait for me!" I trot down the tree-lined street, treading carefully to avoid a miss-step.

When I reach him, he backs away defensively. "Seriously, Hester won't be happy if she knows you've been talking to me. Your daughter hates me...and it's time for me to figure out what to do next."

"Oh Enzo…surely it's not as bad as you think it is. People say all kinds of things in the heat of the moment."

His emphatic headshake tells me the poo didn't just hit the fan; it must have detonated. "You don't understand, Mrs. H. She thinks I'm the most disgusting man on the planet. I've done things…before I met her, that she can't forgive."

I give him my most compassionate, motherly smile. "I know, Enzo."

He shakes his head again. "No, you don't."

Now I nod insistently. "Yes, I do. You think I'd come across a man such as yourself living in my daughter's back yard and not research a thing or two about him?"

He stares at me.

"You see? I do know. And I also know that you haven't finished what you set out to accomplish with this dialect project you've been working so hard on."

Enzo is still all astonishment. "You knew? This whole time you knew I'd been in jail and all about what put me there, and you didn't tell Hester?"

"Enzo, when a person gets to be my age, life, love, pain, and romance look a bit different from where you stand now. I wasn't even sure at the beginning what Hester herself knew about your whole story. And I admit that the business about the sex for money did put me off at first. But when I saw you two dancing together that night…remember?" He nods, and I see a tiny glimmer of a smile. "I knew enough to keep my mouth shut."

"You don't mind your daughter getting involved with someone like me?"

"I've met a great many people, Enzo. Rich, poor, famous, obscure, and everything in between. And it's clear as day to me that you're one of the good guys." I change pace and shoot him a stern glare. "Not that you don't have quite a bit to learn, mind you. But there's something about you that suits Hester in a particular way, manages to make her happy…and that's not something I was going to mess with. I'm only sorry she's such a snob she can't see beyond the nature of your crime to your motivation for committing it."

His expression flickers quickly from hopeful to dejected. "She's never going to forgive me. Not in a million years."

"If you walk away now, you'll never find out. But if you do something, make the grand gesture to show the door is still open…prove you're not giving up on her…"

He cuts me off with a vehement shake of the head. "Mrs. H, I appreciate how you want to be all helpful, but I don't think there's anything I can do to change how much that woman hates me now."

"That depends…" I step closer, and he doesn't move away this time. "Tell me this: are you still prepared to see your studies through to the end?"

He regards me as though he's just discovered I have a hearing problem. "I can't! She wants me out. It's done. Terminado."

I lift a finger. "Hester may say it's finished, but I say it's just beginning…"

"No offense, Mrs. H, but you're not making any sense. I got to go find a place to stay, figure out what to do next."

"No, my dear. What you need to do is finish what you started." I throw caution to the wind. "And perhaps a little holiday from reality…Christopher and I are leaving for London tomorrow, and I've just had the most marvelous idea…I think you should come along."

I watch surprise, confusion, and 'lady, you must be crazy' play across his face.

Using the momentum of my surprise attack, I push further. "There's no substitute for total immersion within a foreign culture. Hester's done her best, but what you really need in order to complete your dialect studies is two weeks in-country. Studying the locals, going native…"

He shakes his head in confusion. "I can't go to England. I promised to see Topaz tomorrow…I've got to find someplace we can live after I get her back."

"Enzo Diaz, you listen to me right now. I know you're in love with my daughter. I know you've spent two and a half months learning what she has to teach you about the Standard American and English dialects. Don't give up, not now when you're so close. Come with us to England, finish your training, and show Hester what you're made of. Show her that Enzo Diaz doesn't quit what he's begun."

"You don't understand, Mrs. H. What you're suggesting is totally crazy. Me performing some accent correctly isn't going to erase how much Hester hates me now."

"I think you'll find that I understand more than you suspect." I give him a little wink. "This is your one chance, Enzo. Soon you'll have little Topaz back with you full-time, and life will be too busy. It will swallow you, and then you'll never get another chance for a re-do on this one. Take my advice and come with us. England is lovely this time of year, and there's so much I want to show you!"

For a moment, I think I can see him wavering. Then his pain and frustration win out. "But there's no point to any of it...the accents and the constant studying, it's all just a bunch of stupid pretending."

"Aha...there's where you're wrong. It just feels like stupid pretending. In reality, it's character building." I poke his muscly chest. "It's proving something to yourself. It's an exercise in learning to reinvent your life. No one is suggesting you walk around pretending to be Lord of the Manor all the time. But exploring the idea of being someone else, something other than what you were before... that's evolving."

Enzo lets out a big sigh, and I can see from how he's standing, ready to take off again, that there's more work to be done.

I look at my watch. "Gracious me, it's dinnertime already! Enzo, let me at least take you out to dinner. Please?"

He looks down the road in the direction he was headed, then back at me. When I see him shrug and tighten his one-handed grip on his suitcase, I hold out my arm in an invitation to link elbows.

As we stroll together toward my car I fervently hope, 1) that I can win him over, and 2) that my daughter forgives me for it if I do.

Chapter 14

GOLDIE

Sunday, May 25th

IT'S PRETTY EARLY, but I know Hester's one of those 'gets the worm' kind of people. Sure enough, when I pull into the driveway, I see her on the cabana porch, curled up in one of the upholstered chairs. I helped her pick out the fabric for those, and after four years of constant exposure to the weather, it's wearing well. Maybe I should think about expanding into home décor...

Once I'm out of the car and through the gate, I can see she's hardly after the worm. She's dead-to-the-world asleep. I wonder if she's spent all night out here. After the attempted robbery and shooting, that would hardly be wise.

Not wanting to frighten her, I creep up as quietly as I can. She looks peaceful, but pretty rough otherwise. Her wavy hair is a mess of tangles. She hasn't washed off yesterday's makeup, and her eyeliner and mascara is smeared all to hell. The cabana door is open, and one peek inside tells me why she looks like crap. There's no trace of Enzo in there.

I perch on the teak coffee table in front of her chair. "Hester?"

She turns her head but doesn't wake.

"Hester, honey. Wake up, Hess." I pat her leg gently. Then push at it a little harder.

She wakes up cranky, opens one bleary eye. "What do you want, Goldie?"

"What did you do to Enzo?"

The other eye opens. "Shouldn't you be asking, 'What did that man-whore do to you, my dearest friend'?"

"He's gone, and you're here. So I stand by my first question: what did you do to make our man leave?"

She rubs her eyes irritably, smearing the eye make-up around even more. "He's not 'ours,' and I told him to go."

"What did you say to him? What else did you do?"

"Goldie! What do you want? You wake me at the crack of dawn with the inquisition...and by the way, your failure to follow through on researching 'our man' is the whole reason I'm stuck out here half hoping he'll come back. If we'd known about his past, I would never, ever have gotten involved with him."

"Listen, Hess. I'm really sorry I didn't check out his record back when I said I would. But after your last call, which was totally vague, panicked, and unhelpful, I finally did it, and you know what? Yes, it totally sucks that Enzo was a sex offender. But it's not like he raped or killed anybody...he's even more harmless than we thought – no drug dealing after all." I take another look at the depth of her dishevelment. "And it's a damn good thing I'm here because you are in need of serious repair, my friend. Even if he did come back now, he'd probably run away again when he saw the she-wolf nesting outside his door."

She aims a withering glare at me. "I'm sorry my appearance doesn't meet with your approval. I'm going through a bit of a crisis here. You say Enzo's harmless?" She points both index fingers at herself. "*Look* at me. I both wish desperately he'd come back and hate him and never want to see him again. I can't even trust my own judgment...was he conning me this whole time or was he really the person I thought he was?"

Wow, she's torn up about this more than I imagined she would be. "Hess, I'm so sorry. So very sorry. If we had known from the beginning, we might have handled him differently...but then again, I truly believe he is exactly the same person he was before we knew..."

She gives a huffy sort of snort. "The same person we never really knew properly."

Her prickly pain makes me feel protective of Enzo. "Hess, give him a break. The guy was only doing what he could to try and maximize earnings to support his daughter. He's a single dad without a high school diploma."

"I know, I know! Don't you think I've already thought of that? I've replayed what I said to him over and over in my mind. But while half of me wants to go find him and beg him to come back, the other half is still shuddering at the thought of him as Homeboy Gangsta."

"What's a Homeboy Gangsta?"

Hester searches around the cushions on her chair and finally finds what she's looking for under her butt. She hands some sort of pamphlet to me.

When my eyes find his picture on the second page, I cringe. I detest van dyke beards. What was he thinking? I also understand why she's upset. This brochure has put the image of him as sex fantasy for hire into her imagination where it has no doubt grown into a hideous miniseries of his sexual escapades with women who, for whatever reason, chose to pay to get exactly what they wanted. Poor Hester.

"I don't want your pity, Goldie."

Jeez, am I that transparent? "I just feel awful for you." I look at the picture of Enzo again, fascinated by the tattoos on his scalp. "Except for the van dyke, this is actually a pretty hot photo…"

Hester snatches the brochure from my hands. "Don't you see? A man like that, with lots of practice giving women what they want…perhaps he was just giving me what I wanted."

"Hess, that's a bit unfair."

"Is it? He lived here, had time to watch me and suss out that I'm single and…have financial resources. Don't you think it's possible he was playing me all along?"

"Okay, so you think he could see into the inner workings of your brain and figure out exactly what kind of role to play to be your ideal man in order to capitalize on your generosity?"

Her eyes look a little possessed. "He could have, right? I mean, he cooked for me, danced with me, and it was so endearing that he wanted his daughter back so badly. I tried to keep things professional, all business…but he crept into my everyday thoughts, became an enjoyable part of my life. Isn't it possible he's a better actor than we gave him credit for?"

In her desperate state I have to tread carefully. "Hess…I don't think…what you're suggesting is a huge stretch."

"But possible, right?"

"The man would have to be a mind-reader. A virtuoso at manipulation and a conniving strategist. Do you really see Enzo as that kind of man?"

Hester lets out a tired sigh. "Goldie, I don't know how to see him anymore. I thought I knew him completely…but he's clearly not the person I thought he was, and he was pretty damn good at being the man I wanted him to be. Wouldn't it be the height of irony if we've put in all this effort teaching him how to pretend to be someone else while the whole time he was *already* pretending to be someone else?"

"Oh, Hess. You're torturing yourself…"

She looks me square in the face. "Can you tell me for sure he wasn't playing me?"

"Yes. I think…I'm almost one hundred percent certain he wasn't."

My best friend's mouth twists into a bitter sneer. "He must have thought we were idiots…laughed behind our backs."

"Have you considered the fact that what you do for a living and what he did are not so dissimilar?"

This wins me a righteous look of outrage. "I'm not even going to dignify that comment with a proper reply."

"No, think about it. You get paid for providing a service, something you're good at. Who's to say that Enzo charging for something he's good at is so bad?"

"The fatal flaw in this line of reasoning is that what he did is illegal…and sort of soul-less."

"But if he was going to do it, he did it the classiest way possible, right? Does he get any points for that? It wasn't like he was doing tricks in the handicapped stall of some sleazy bar bathroom. This was high-end prostitution. Swanky hotel rooms, rich and famous clientele…did you follow the story when it broke?"

"Not really, but I spent hours reading everything I could find on the internet about it last night after he left. You know how much those women who set it up were charging to provide 'escorts'? $1,000 to $2,500 per hour. I know it was high-end, but does that change the fact that he was shagging tons of total strangers for money? That any woman with enough cash could select Enzo from that menu and experience him in the most intimate way? I think not. And that stink-rat Philip was so smarmy about breaking it to me. So self-satisfied."

Ah, I was wondering how she found out. I bet Philip just loved being the bearer of heart-break to the woman who broke his heart. Enzo should have played his cards better and just flat-out told her himself.

With no warning, Hester's bitchy paranoia turns to full-on grief. Tears come heavy and hard, her words punctuated by uncontrollable inhales of breathlessness. "Goldie, Philip really does have a new girlfriend...and he wants me to wean Jessica...from her attachment to me...so this new woman can...bond and become the mother-figure. I'm losing her!"

Oooooh. Double whammy: Jessica, Enzo. Man, that A-hole Philip has a lot to answer for.

I squeeze in beside my best friend on her chair, pull her into a hug, and let her cry all over my silk Donna Karan tank. Though I know all this drama will eventually blow over and she'll survive, the pain she's feeling in this moment is so intense I can feel the ache in my own chest. If I could, I would absorb some of it from her like a sponge to ease the intensity.

When she's cried as much as she can for now and her mascara has traveled all the way down her face and off her chin onto me, we sit for a few minutes in silence.

Her voice is a hoarse whisper. "Goldie, I'm never going to see him again, am I?"

I look at my friend with deep compassion, stroke her tangled hair. Then I grab the man menu she showed me earlier and hold it in front of her face. "Look at him. This is part of who he was before he met you. That fact is never going away. Can you live with it?"

Silence. I guess it might take her a while to make up her mind.

A sigh escapes me; this will be a long day. "Come on, get up." I have to pull her to her feet. "We're going to get you showered and changed into something fresh and stylin'. Then we're going to see if we can find Enzo Diaz."

HESTER

After driving around Los Feliz and over to Watts to stop in at Ricky's Day Center, the closest we get to finding Enzo is Topaz' foster mother, Martha. We drive to Villa La Pueblo in Bellflower after lunch, and Martha says he was there for a quick visit with Topaz this morning and told her he'd be unavailable for a few weeks. We missed him by a mere two hours.

I don't expect to find him at the shelter he'd mentioned staying in before he came to my place, but we stop there anyway. When Goldie comes out and gives me the 'no luck' shake of the head, I wonder where else we can look. And if I really want to find him.

We sit in the car outside the shelter, brainstorming. "Okay," Goldie says, "think about all the places he might go. What would he be thinking at this point?"

"He would have had to find some place to stay last night. And today, if I were in his shoes, I'd buy a phone so I could keep in contact with Topaz, her case worker, and the lawyer."

"Okay, well, Martha didn't have a number for him, so tomorrow you can call the case worker and the lawyer and see if they have new digits to reach him. What else?"

I'm trying to think of people he mentioned knowing or favorite places he might go. Aside from Ricky, he never talked about anyone. He seemed to want to put his past behind him; now I know why. "Perhaps the Barbies – clients of his – it's possible he might stay in contact with them."

"Alright, so you can call the Barbies…"

"I don't have their number." Damn it. There must be someone who knows where he is.

Goldie rubs my shoulder. "How ya doing?"

I sigh, wishing the achy feeling in my chest would subside. "Honestly? I'm not even sure why I want to find him. I'm still scared he was playing me for a love-struck idiot…"

The way Goldie looks through me tells me she's problem-solving. When she comes up with an idea she pokes my arm. "So we need to find proof that he wasn't lying to you about anything other than the sex-for-money thing. Will that help?"

Suddenly, the horrible scene with Philip at the Awesome Playground pops into my head.

It makes me shudder, but it is almost certainly the easiest way. "I think I know where we can get a full report about Enzo's past."

"Where?"

I make a 'yuck' face. "Philip Brewer."

--›══◉ ◉══‹--

I certainly do not intend to grovel at Philip's feet to get the information his PI collected. My best chance at success is to catch him spontaneously, so he has no time to plan humiliating demands in return for the favor.

Since it's Sunday, we take a chance and stop by his house. When we pull up in front of Philip's angular, modern two-story in Silver Lake I take a deep breath. I intend to behave as the mature, reasonable woman I am. But if he starts in with the 'oh poor Hester I'm so sorry you fell for a prostitute' act, I might spear his foot with the heel of the power-stilettos Goldie talked me into wearing. Though, of course, I can't actually wound him because I need something from him and I'm not leaving without it.

I can't send Goldie into battle for me this time so I pull together my most devastatingly frosty expression and click up the long flight of stairs to his front door.

My frosty expression abandons me when a woman who must be Veronica opens the door. "May I help you?" She is a pretty brunette with a pixie cut, and she's wearing a look that says, 'who the hell are you?'

"Oh, hello. I'm Hester Hastings…a friend of Jessica's…"

"I know who you are. Jessica's with her grandmother this afternoon. I'll let her know you came by."

She's already closing the door, so I reach out and stop it mid-swing. "Actually, I'm looking for Philip. I just need a moment of his time."

Veronica looks behind her, then leans toward me. "What do you want from him?"

Taken aback by her confrontational tone, I smile to diffuse the tension. "Just some information…and to come to an understanding about my role in Jessica's life." I didn't intend for the words about Jessica to come out, but now that they have, I realize this is actually more important to me than getting details about Enzo. "I've been kind of a surrogate mother to her for a number of years now, and I understand that Philip wants that to change, but I'm quite attached to her and would like to know how often I can see her from now on."

The edge has come off her sharp expression, and she nods. "Hang on a sec…"

Veronica leaves the door open while she goes to find Philip for me. A few minutes pass before he comes to the door, Veronica by his side. When it doesn't appear as though she's going to politely retreat, I resign myself to having her listen in. I'm certainly not about to request a private audience with her boyfriend.

They don't invite me in, so I begin. "Hello, Philip. I have two matters to discuss, briefly, of course. One, I'd like to settle on how often I can see Jessica in future." As thoughts coalesce in my mind, the words form on my tongue. "I propose that I take on a role not unlike that of Godmother; having her for a day once every month, with the option of seasonal outings to celebrate birthdays and special occasions – not interfering with family celebrations naturally. Does this work for you both?"

I can see the cogs rotating in Philip's mind, and I suddenly realize that Veronica's presence will work in my favor. He's not about to act like a demanding toddler in front of her.

Pushing this advantage, I forge onward. "Every third Sunday each month? It will give you both a little break, and I'd like to stay a constant, if more remote, presence in her life."

Philip looks at Veronica, and she shrugs. "Sounds reasonable to me, hon."

"Okay, Hester. We can begin a trial period of six months with that arrangement and see how it goes. But I expect her time with you will not involve anyone else, as we've discussed before."

I nod; understood. Alright, now on to more sensitive matters. "I wonder…
seeing as how you were so kind to share information with me yesterday, I wonder if I might ask to see all of the documentation you had compiled about my
student, Enzo Diaz?"

A stifled snigger erupts from Veronica. I suppose Philip has told her all
about how his silly ex got involved with a male prostitute. Though I can't stop
the blush that rises to my cheeks, I maintain my confident posture and await his
response in silence.

Attempting to hide a snarky smile of his own, Philip assumes a generous air.
"Certainly, Hester. In fact, you can keep it." He motions for me to wait, and they
disappear back into the house.

This gives me a moment to fully regain my composure and assure myself I
don't give a rat's ass what these two think of me. When Philip reappears, he is
alone. He hands me a brown, legal-size accordion file held shut with an elastic
band. "I have no more use for this, so enjoy. It's all yours." His smile drips with
condescension, and my gaze drops to his foot, which is bare and would make a
fine target for my sharp stiletto heel.

But instead of wounding him, I flash a brilliant, gracious smile that stops
his belittling attitude dead in its tracks. "Thank you, Philip. I wish you every
happiness with Veronica, and I will send you an email with an outline of what
we agreed about Jessica."

Before he can speak, I've turned and descended his many stairs with, I dare
say, as much panache as the Duchess of Cambridge.

Monday, May 26th

By the time my first appointment arrives at ten I've read the file through three
times. Topaz' birth certificate, Monique L. West listed as mother and Enzo
Victor Diaz on the 'father' line, his mother's death certificate, jail records including blood test results on the medical form declaring him healthy. I'm totally exhausted, but confident that the only thing Enzo lied to me about was the reason

for his conviction. On paper, his life is even more heartbreaking than he made it out to be. In fact, it's rather a miracle he only got involved with something as relatively harmless as prostitution. I'm sure there are many men with similar backgrounds serving life sentences in prison. Enzo's own father has spent the majority of his adult life incarcerated.

I spend the time between clients making calls. When I track them down, Topaz' case worker and Enzo's lawyer say the same thing. Enzo called and left messages saying he would be out of touch for a while but would call in regularly. He left no phone number, and neither of them can give me the number he called from.

It appears as though Enzo Diaz, ex-convict, dialect student, personal trainer, and the man with whom I've inconveniently fallen in love, does not want to be found.

GOLDIE

Wednesday, May 28th

I'm in Menswear at Neiman Marcus picking out some ties for Nigel while simultaneously continuing my role in crisis management with Hester on the phone. It's taken me two days to drag it all out of her, but my dear friend has just now finally told me every detail of her last encounter with Enzo, and I have to say I don't really blame him for disappearing.

"Goldie? Are you still there?"

"Yes, I'm here. I'm thinking."

"What? What are you thinking? Was I too harsh? Of course I was…I was a beast. I accused him of being diseased and said I wished I'd never met him."

"Well, one thing's for sure…"

"What?!"

"Well, it's kind of irrelevant at this point because you've already fixed things with Philip, but you definitely lost our bet big time."

"Fuck the stupid bet!" Damn. I've never heard the F-bomb from Hester before. Then she gets quiet. "I'm worried about him, Goldie."

"Hester, he's a big boy. He hasn't limped off into the woods never to return..."

"Perhaps not, but he's out there probably thinking terrible things about me, feeling like he can never show his face here again."

"Do you want him back?"

A pause. "He wasn't finished with his studies...we had more work to do."

"No, Hess. Not as a student. Do you want him back as a man? Your man, your boyfriend, your home skillet...can you imagine being with someone who has that kind of history? Because if you don't, you should probably find a good therapist and start working on getting over it. There's no point trying to find him or wishing he'd come back if you're just going to send him away again. You don't bring someone back so you can say 'sorry' and feel better about yourself." I hear a soft sniffle. "A few weeks ago you told me you 'might really love him.' Is that still true?"

"I don't...I mean, yes, I was in love with him. Yes, being with him made me happy...but I don't know about the home skillet thing. It was kind of perfect the way it was before I found out..."

She can't say it so I help her out. "That your dream boy has a past you find beyond disgusting?"

"If I'm being honest, yes. I hadn't really thought about what would happen with him long-term. I just imagined how nice it would be to go on having him as a fixture in my life."

"But he's not your cabana boy. You can't just keep him on staff because he's sexy and makes you happy. There's either a commitment, or it was a fling and it's over. Which one is it?"

Silence. I thought so.

Chapter 15

HESTER

Friday, June 6th

I'M SURPRISINGLY PLEASED to see Brent when he shows up for his one o' clock. He flops into the same armchair Enzo favors and grins at me.

"Long time no see, little lady." His John Wayne impression is appalling.

"Hello, Brent. How was the Ireland shoot? Did you get on alright with the accent after I left?"

He waves a casual hand. "Oh yeah. That paperclip idea? Solid gold. But it was my natural accent that scored some acclaim among the local lassies."

"Lassies are in Scotland, Brent."

"Whatever...you catch my drift. Anyway, don't take this the wrong way, but you're not looking quite as gorgeous and perky as usual."

I incline my head in acknowledgement of the truth of his observation. "Lack of sleep will do that to a girl."

His eyebrows knit together in pity. "Insomnia, huh? You know, I happen to be an excellent remedy for that condition..."

"You can stop there, Brent. I am totally not in the mood for your flirtation, and we have a lot of work to do. By the end of the film your character has been living in America for over twenty years, and his accent should reflect that." A thought pops unbidden into my brain, and though it's decidedly unprofessional I can't resist asking. "Though I do have a quick question before we get started…have you, um, seen or heard from Enzo lately?"

"Yeah, he left a message a while back to say he couldn't train me for a couple weeks. I was in Ireland anyway, but it was decent of him to let me know. What's up? Is he in some kind of trouble?"

I shake my head. "No trouble. I just need to talk to him and can't find him anywhere. Did he, uh, leave a number or anything?"

"No, but he called my cell. Hang on."

My pulse speeds up as Brent digs his flashy phone out of his pocket and flips through the settings to find the number.

"Here…" He holds out his phone, and I look at the screen.

I check the sequence of numbers twice in disbelief and shake my head. "No, that can't be right. And what is she doing calling you anyway? Wait…are you sure that's the number?"

"Yeah, man. I saved it to his profile 'cause it wasn't your number. He always called from here before…" His eyes widen, and he looks at me with an 'aha!' as though he's just discovered a cure for AIDS. "Damn! You saucy vixen…humping the personal trainer! I didn't think you had it in you." He looks at me appreciatively, like a proud uncle.

I sigh. "I was not 'humping' him. But there was a bit of a budding romance."

"I knew it! I knew you were getting frisky with someone…what happened? Did your frosty bitch act scare him off?"

I can't think of a better explanation that I want to divulge. "Sort of…"

"No offense, Miss Hastings – do I still have to call you that even though I know what a skank you are now?"

I shrug.

His expression shifts from shock at my unprofessional attitude to delight in a nanosecond. "No offense, *Hester*, but you shouldn't have kicked him to the curb. Enzo is good people."

"I know! That's why I want his number. But that number you have can't be from him…it's my mother's number."

"Your mother? Holy shit, this is getting better and better…if she's as hot as you, maybe they ran off together."

"Don't be ridiculous, Brent. Are you absolutely positive that's the number he called you from?"

"How the hell else would I have your mother's digits?"

Hmmm. Come to think of it, she never stopped by before she left for London. In fact, I've heard nothing from her since before she left. I've been so preoccupied with my own crisis I hadn't even noticed. She said she'd be gone for two weeks; Enzo told Brent he'd be gone for a couple of weeks. And it was my bloody idea to get Enzo a passport…

Motherfucker!

MRS. HASTINGS

Eventually, I'll have to answer. But I leave the phone silenced and let the messages flood my inbox.

Right now there are more important things to attend to.

Enzo is looking at me uncertainly. "You think I should?"

I nod emphatically. "It's an offer you can't pass up, my dear." I wish Christopher was with us now. Enzo always gives his opinion more weight than my own. It must be a man thing. "After the last one, you need to keep going. And consider this: what were the chances we'd run into our mutual friend? In my opinion, this is destiny at work and you should absolutely follow the path opening at your feet. If you don't do it you may never get another opportunity of this caliber, and on the other hand, if you go ahead and do it, what on earth could there be to regret?"

Enzo's extraordinary eyes are thoughtful as he ponders his options. I've come to know him as a fellow who considers all angles before committing to action, a trait I respect. The extent to which this trip has been a success may not be solely due to his efforts, but no one can fault the man for his effort once he's made a commitment.

HESTER

Monday, June 9th

When the FedEx driver hands me the orange and purple cardboard envelope, my eyes eagerly examine the return address.

London.

Oh, thank God! Mum may not be answering her phone, but at least she's communicating. I tear open the envelope greedily as I push through the yellow door to the kitchen and dump the contents on the tile countertop.

What the devil is this? Mum has sent me a copy of *HELLO!* magazine. I hardly think she's eager to catch me up on all the celebrity news and royal gossip from London...so what on earth?

I flip through it and run across one dog-eared page. Hell's bells! A picture of Enzo laughing with a group of socialites...and the caption: Scrumptious up-and-coming model Enzo Diaz finds favor at Club Zero.

What is she playing at? Staging a pretend career for Enzo and pulling strings with her cronies to get him a photo op?

Oh Mum. Why?

I can't help examining the picture of Enzo. He looks, well, scrumptious. Freshly shorn of his beard, his face is both familiar and foreign. I see a shallow dimple in the center of his chin that I never knew was there. His delicious smile is even more sexy sans the facial hair.

I start computing...if this magazine has been sent overnight from London, and it's already in circulation, when was the picture taken? I know the celebrity mags have to get their issues out fast before the news is too old to print, so maybe a week ago?

A wad of jealousy settles in the pit of my stomach as I force myself to take another look at the admiring group of people surrounding him. Mostly women – of course – and they are all gorgeous, trendy, and younger than myself. Letting my eyes hop from face to face, I peer closer and think I recognize...oh bloody hell, it couldn't be...could it? Toward the back of the pack of admirers is a face that looks unpleasantly familiar. No.

Oh no, no, no!

GOLDIE

Hester's call catches me in the middle of a lunch date.

I scrunch up my face in apology. "I'm sorry, but I have to take this…it's Hester."

Nigel nods in understanding and takes out his own phone to check for messages while I'm busy.

"What's up, Hess?"

"What on earth is that woman thinking?"

"Sorry, no comprendo. Which woman?"

"My mother! She's throwing Enzo to the wolves and…and cougars!"

Say what? "Okay, I need a recap, like 'previously, on Hester's Crazy Life'…"

"You know how my mother kidnapped Enzo and they're in London…"

"Yep."

"Well, she's gotten him into a celebrity gossip magazine, and guess who's with him in the picture?"

"Um…Prince Harry?"

"No!"

"Nigella Lawson?"

"No, no. Liz the cougar!!"

"Who?"

"That woman who cornered him at Jimmy's wedding…the blonde with all the jewelry?"

"Oh! Shit. You're right, that's probably not good."

"No, it is not good. And Mum won't answer my calls or texts. Do you think I should fly over there?"

I consider the idea for less than a second. "Depends. Have you decided that you want Enzo as a keeper boyfriend?"

She sighs audibly. "I'm still thinking."

"Then absolutely not, Hester. Unless you're prepared to go over there and proclaim your everlasting love for him, you're not part of the picture."

"But…"

"No. This is his life, and he gets to make his own decisions. Besides, I hardly think your mom is going to let him run off the rails…"

"Goldie…you have met my mother, haven't you?"

HESTER

Wednesday, June 11th

Just after lunch the FedEx guy is back. I rip open the envelope right there on my doorstep before he's finished making notes on his little tablet.

Another magazine: *Men's Health*, UK Edition – a mock-up of the as-yet-to-be-published August issue. I'm absolutely gobsmacked.

Enzo. Shirtless. Pumped up. Cover model.

How in the devil did Mum pull this one off?

Oh shit...Liz!

After ogling the unbelievably ripped muscles and sexy half-smile on the cover model who happens to be the man who used to live in my cabana house, I flip through the rest of the magazine. Sure enough, another dog-eared page.

The heading reads 'Seven Strategies for Securing a Sexy Six-pack.' A series of photos featuring Enzo in various exercise poses meant to illustrate how easy it can be to end up with six-pack abs if you simply work out every waking moment. In the pictures, his muscles are dazzling. I knew the man had a body, but for heaven's sake! I can imagine men all over the UK reading the article whilst envying Enzo his sculpted abs. Girlfriends of subscribers will flip through and enjoy the eye candy much as I used to when he sat across from me shirtless at breakfast.

Forget Goldie's question about whether I want Enzo as my boyfriend. After all this media exposure and the doors it will open for him, the real question is: would he ever again want me as his girlfriend?

Liz the cougar has been prowling through my thoughts since seeing the *HELLO!* photo on Friday. I know she's part of this modeling equation, and I should trust that Mum is keeping tabs on Enzo. But he's hardly a child, and I can't help wondering if Liz has managed to put another notch in her lipstick case.

Grrrrr.

No, don't think about it. Goldie's right; I have no claim on him unless I'm prepared to forgive and forget. But when I close my eyes, I can see Enzo as Homeboy Gangsta romping with every conceivable kind of woman, a stack of hundred dollar bills left on the bedside table over and over. How will I ever get this out of my relentless brain?

Get a grip, Hester. Move on. Take another peek in the FedEx envelope and throw it in the recycling bin.

And it's a good thing I check, because there's something wedged in there at the bottom.

Quality cardstock, cream colored with black, stylized writing.

An invitation.

GOLDIE

I finish outfitting Hasselhoff for a Knight Rider convention and send him on his merry way before heading over to Hester's. When I get there she's on the cabana porch, bench-pressing a barbell stacked with some impressive weight.

She makes me stand there until she's finished all her reps. "Feeling frustrated?"

Hester gives me a withering look, sits up, and hands me a card, face down. Before even turning it over, I know what it is.

I feel a little hot under the collar knowing I received mine two weeks ago. It's seriously tempting to keep quiet about it, but guilty thoughts about how I neglected to check Enzo's rap sheet three months ago make me 'fess up. "Hey, you know...it's kinda funny. I actually already got one of these." I make my voice breezy as though it's no big deal.

The look she gives me could melt kryptonite. "When."

It's a demand, not a question. "Um...a few days ago."

"And you didn't mention it to me because...?" She waits, eyebrows raised menacingly.

"Oh, Hess. I didn't want to upset you more. I figured you'd tell me if you knew, and when you never said anything I figured it was probably better if you didn't have too much time to stew about it, you know?"

"No. I do not know. And I wish someone would tell me what the devil that woman is trying to accomplish..."

Seems pretty obvious to me. "I think she's trying to finish what you started?"

Hester slaps the padded bench she's still straddling. "Yes, but why would Enzo let her do that? What's in it for him?" She wipes sweat off her face with a hand towel and wraps it around her neck. I have to admit, she's looking pretty buff after all that training Enzo gave her.

"If I had to guess, I'd say he's trying to get your attention."

"Well, it's stupid. Mum has gone too far."

It's really best to stay quiet, so that's what I do.

"I mean, the whole idea was stupid from the very beginning! What were we thinking making a wager over changing the course of someone's life?"

I can't resist a quick comment. "Technically, that bet is still valid."

Ooooh. This earns me Medusa's gaze of stony death. "The bet is stupid, this party is stupid, and my mother is stupid."

Though I know her fury will pass, I feel helpless standing in the epicenter of its hurricane-force winds. There must be something I can say, something I can do that will make her feel better.

When I finally speak my voice is so hushed that even I can barely hear it. "You feel like ordering pizza?"

Chapter 16

ENZO

Saturday, June 14th

I'M SHOWERED, SHAVED, cologned, dressed in the Armani suit Mrs. H had tailored for me, and my goddamn feet have never been so cold. I was more relaxed when Topaz was born, and that scared the shit out of me. I feel like the fool of the century sittin' here in Mrs. H's ritzy guest room trying to call up the courage to play British Guest of Honor at this big Hollywood party.

Even though we've been back in L.A. two days now, I'm still kinda in shock from how much happened in London. It was like a year squished into fourteen days. And now we're here, and I'm even more in shock about this party and being in this huge house, and I keep asking myself why the hell I ever thought I could pull this off. Mrs. H's house is, like, so enormous and fancy I feel like I shouldn't walk or sit on any surface. She's got sweet-smelling flowers put out everywhere and two huge bars – inside, and out in the garden – and about a million servers in tuxedoes with silver trays they're gonna fill with puff pastry and fried snails and fancy shit like that. When I first got outta jail three months back, I would have been feeling like the luckiest man on earth to score a job waiting on people at a swanky party like this. It's the kind of job I thought Hester's training might help me get when Goldie first explained they wanted to teach me polished manners. Having a rich lady throw a huge party for me is for sure the craziest-ass thing that's ever happened to me. I really need to lift something, but I'm too scared I'm gonna break her fancy furniture if I try.

Shoot, what if Hester doesn't even show up? What if she thinks I'm just plain stupid trying to go through with all this after she already told me she doesn't want anything to do with me? But Mrs. H says she'll come, says Hester's 'too curious a cat' not to show up.

Shit, I don't even know if I hope she's right or if I want her to be dead wrong.

HESTER

By the time Goldie and Nigel come to collect me I've decided not to go.

"Hester," Goldie's talking to me like I'm a toddler refusing to eat my peas. "You know you'll be sorry if you don't. Enzo will be looking for you…"

"You yourself said I shouldn't go looking for him if I don't want him for keeps, right?"

This gives her pause. "Well, yes. I did say that…are you totally sure you want to give up on him?"

My silence tells her I'm not sure of anything.

"Hess?" Her voice is tentative, like she's about to say something I don't want to hear. "Remember how I told you Enzo's not long-term boyfriend potential?"

I practically snort my answer. "How could I forget?"

"Okay, so I'm taking it back now. These past two weeks you've been absolutely miserable and tortured. You can't bring yourself to let go of Enzo, but you won't allow yourself to forgive him either. So I'm giving you permission to forgive him, to love him, to want him as your long-term sexy dude. And if you can't do that, then at least come to the party and get closure. See him, apologize, and celebrate the culmination of all the work you two did to get him this far. Celebrate the man he's become since that day he walked out of jail and into our clutches. The things you taught him, your confidence in his potential; he's not the only one who gets to take credit for his transformation, you know."

I feel tears begin to well up, but taking a deep breath holds them at bay. Listening to my friend, I hear the truth in her words. But can I do this? Can I face him again and not want him the way I did before? Or can I do what Goldie says and just forgive him and fall into his arms? And what if he no longer wants me? What if he's decided a posh life as Liz's toy-boy model is preferable to mucking about with the likes of me?

Well, if he wants Liz, he's definitely not the man I thought he was anyway.

Nigel clears his throat to pull me from my inner thought-storm. "Hester, may I say that you look lovely in your glittering party frock?"

I glance down at my deep purple beaded Valentino to remind myself what I'm wearing. Then I give him a smile of gratitude. "Thank you, Nigel. As my friend Brent would say, you're good people."

Goldie gives me a questioning look. "So you're coming, right?"

MRS. HASTINGS

Standing next to me in the foyer Enzo looks perfect, flawless, stunning; could be mistaken for a prince from some lesser-known tropical island nation. The house is bedecked with baubles and ornaments worthy of a royal ball, and the large arrangements of bright freesias, green bells of Ireland, and fragrant tea roses are making the air itself smell divine.

Though I know he thinks this is all a bit frivolous, Christopher has been wonderful. He's in the breakfast room giving the bar staff their orders now. The kitchen is filled with servers and trays loaded with the most delectable morsels for my lovely guests.

As the first car arrives and the lead valet charges out to greet the guest and whisk their vehicle to the grassy side lot, I clap my hands.

"Oh, Enzo...you've worked so hard to get to this moment. How do you feel, my dear?"

He shuffles his feet, belches, and thumps his chest with a fist. "Kinda like I'm gonna throw up."

I waggle a finger at him. "No, no. There's not an ounce of namby-pamby in you, young man. Push out your chest and put on that posh British accent."

"Mrs. H, I'm not sure..." He does look a little green around the gills.

"Nonsense. You are Enzo Diaz, and the world is your oyster." I raise both fists in a gesture of strength. "You are Atlas holding the sky aloft, Hercules vanquishing the Hydra, and you are Enzo showing Hester the lengths you will go to in order to prove your love for her."

"Ease up on the drama, my darling, you're scaring the poor chap." Christopher has strolled into the foyer looking debonair in his dinner jacket and crisp white collar. "Though you do look ever so lovely when you're giving motivational speeches." He kisses me on the cheek and takes my hand. Then he thumps Enzo companionably on the back. "Just like we practiced in London, mate. Righto?"

The man of the hour nods nervously, managing to look pale despite a deep skin tone made yet darker by the sun. "Righto."

HESTER

We are fashionably late and enter on the heels of James Cameron, Penny Marshall, and Ewan McGregor. My mother is holding court in the marble-lined foyer, greeting guests and generally behaving like a much younger and more attractive Queen of England. Her dress is an amber sequin sheath layered over a teal silk tunic. Classic and yet daring at the same time. Typical Mum.

A flicker of anxiety crosses her face when she spies us. But it is gone in an instant, replaced by her 'world's most gracious hostess' expression. "Darling Hester!" She crosses the floor to meet me in the middle of the room, arms held wide.

"Mother." I allow her to peck both my cheeks. I'm still angry enough with her to throw a royal hissy-fit, but she knows firsthand that I'm entirely too well-brought-up to make a scene here at the party.

She greets Goldie and Nigel, surprised and delighted to learn they've come together. I have to say, they do make a surprisingly appropriate couple. And Goldie has assembled a fresh wardrobe for her new man that quashes his damp Englishman persona and makes him look quite dashing.

Before we move on to the next room, Mum sneaks up beside me and whispers, "Be nice, darling. Enzo's only doing this for you."

I want to demand a complete report of everything that happened in London, but she's already spun back into position to receive the next guest with air kisses.

Nigel leads us into the parlor and grabs flutes of champagne from a passing tray. I down the entire contents of mine within seconds.

Scanning the room I recognize, among other celebrities, Orlando Bloom, Kate Beckinsale, Sean Bean, and Pierce Brosnan. I've worked with them all, but I'm not in the mood to mingle. Casually, I stroll into the sunny atrium and pretend to admire the potted flower arrangements. When a server glides by with more champagne, I help myself to another glass. This one I intend to nurse until I either decide to talk to Enzo or flee the scene.

The atrium begins to empty, so I follow Kate and her husband into the garden and discover that this seems to be where the action is. Jude Law, Kate Winslet, and Bernardo Bertolucci are chatting under the shade of a large palm tree while Isabella Rosselini and Ian McKellan laugh in response to an anecdote related by Donald Sutherland.

I hear Enzo's voice before I spot him. A conveniently placed potted fig tree provides me with semi-effective cover. I need to hear him talk, but I'm not ready to be seen. Forcing myself to close my eyes and just listen to his words instead of searching for him is more difficult than I would have thought. But I have to hear what two weeks in London has accomplished. I'm not sure who he's speaking with, but the accent of the man asking Enzo about his stay in California is definitely German.

"It's been lovely so far, thank you. Miriam has been kind enough to invite me to stay here until I find my feet." Enzo's voice sounds deeper, but he's not 'putting on the ritz.' "So you can see I'm hardly roughing it."

After the German chuckles, he continues. "The past few weeks have been quite a whirlwind, but I feel lucky to have found a gracious hostess to help me get settled. Tell me, how do you know Miriam?"

Polite, just enough about himself, and then an inquiry about the other person's status. Not bad. And the accent is spot on; not posh and stuck up, but rather more 'I may have attended Cambridge but I'm a down-to-earth sort of bloke.' I'm both impressed and annoyed that Mum's instinct to take him to the source of the accent was the best way to put a sheen on it. Enzo sounds educated yet approachable, formal yet friendly. He sounds like someone I'd like to get to know.

Opening my eyes, I focus on shifting myself as quickly as possible to a better hiding spot without attracting attention. I want to observe Enzo's performance but I'm not ready to talk to him. Concealing myself behind a French lilac bush I can see that the German is standing directly in my line of vision, blocking Enzo from view. Peering through the branches I wait for him to move. When he shifts to the right to take a king prawn hors d'oeuvre from a server, I get a full shot of Enzo.

Any thoughts I had of staying calm and reserved are blown. My pulse is racing, and I blush at the visceral memories my mind is replaying of what it feels like to let my hands explore his body, to feel his sensual touch on my skin. And after the initial rush of hormones, I realize how much I've missed his companionship. Missed making dinner together and talking over meals, missed our workout sessions, missed his masculine presence around the house. He may be far from the most educated man I've been with, but he is certainly the most enjoyable and surprising.

Sudden pressure on the small of my back makes me jump nearly straight out of my strapless Valentino. The urgent need to avoid attracting attention is all that keeps me from shrieking, whirling, and whacking my assailant with my silk clutch. A slow turn of my head brings a familiar smirking face into view.

"Hi, gorgeous. Feeling a bit on edge?" His hand remains on my back, now keeping me steady on my feet.

"Oh my God, Brent. You nearly gave me a stroke."

"Missed me that much, huh?" I roll my eyes, but he is undeterred. "Pray tell, my love, why are we hidin' behind shrubbery?" I must admit, his Irish accent turned out pretty damn good.

I shush him and lower my voice. "Who invited you? You don't even know my Mum."

His look of dejection is quite convincing. "I'm crushed. I thought you couldn't live without me. Plus, do you know how hard it is to find a girl who's hiding behind a bush? You should totally be psyched to see me." Then his grin is back. "I had your mom's number on my cell, remember? Curiosity got the better of me and now we're practically Siamese twins. She invited me by text."

"This century we're calling them 'conjoined twins', and you need to go mingle or something." I shoo him with my fingertips.

Brent shakes his head. "If Miss Goody-Two-Shoes is up to something, I want in."

I take a deep breath to keep from killing him. "Brent, please go. I don't want to be noticed, and you're about as subtle as a fire-breathing dragon."

"I'm an actor. I can do subtle." He presses in close to me and peeks around the lilac bush. "Who are we watching?"

"No one, just…"

"Ooooh. Just spotted your main squeeze. He's looking pretty snazzy…no beard, nice suit. What's up? Why aren't you on his arm? Wait, are you two secretly assassins and you've been pitted against each other? I think I saw that movie…"

"Brent! *Please* just go."

He pretends to consider obeying. "I could, but this is more fun. Why don't you tell Uncle Brent why you're spying on your personal trainer-slash-lover and who knows? Maybe I can help."

I've gone beyond deep breathing to desperation. "Okay. If I tell you will you go?"

He nods.

"And will you please, please, please not tell anyone who Enzo really is? Just pretend like you don't know him?"

That earns me a significant raise of his supple eyebrows. "I can barely contain my curiosity. Why all the secrecy? What are you two up to?" He lowers his voice. "Is it dirty?"

Preparing to explain it to Brent makes me feel ridiculous. Worse, I feel manipulative, sneaky, and less than honest. Why did I let Goldie talk me into the Enzo project? No, I can't blame Goldie. I have to take responsibility for my actions. "Enzo is pretending to be an English actor."

Brent's face goes from blank to perplexed. "Why?"

Suddenly, I break. "Because my best friend challenged me to a bet, okay? I was supposed to take an ex-con from the street and pass him off as a British actor. Because I was in a rut, and my ego got all out of control. And then because it was satisfying, and then even fun, and then I fell in love with him. But then I realized what a self-indulgent, meddling thing it was to do and he turned out to have a past I couldn't handle and it broke my heart. Okay? Now you know the most ridiculous, thoughtless, stupid, embarrassing thing I've ever done. Are you happy?"

The shock on Brent's face is oddly satisfying. "Whoa." He slides an arm around my bare shoulders, but not in a creepy way. "That is totally whack…are you okay?"

Must not cry. "No. I am not okay. Until this moment I thought *he'd* hurt *me*. But right now, I can see that I'm the one who did the damage. I had no right to play with his future or his feelings. I took him in and thought I could make a better life for him…how arrogant was that? I mean, he would have been fine. Happier, maybe, if I had never met him."

"Hey, I don't know all that went down, honey, but I'm sure you didn't hold a gun to Enzo's head to make him do anything. Your motives were generous, if a little twisted." He shakes his head. "I can't believe that *you*, my frosty little sweetheart, made a bet with your bestie about making him over. Damn. Even I've never done anything like that. Poor dude."

"Yes, alright, I'm a terrible person. Can you please go now?"

Brent withdraws his arm from my shoulders and salutes. "Yes, sergeant. And I promise not to screw up your little game." He winks and is gone, quietly returning to the house.

Hester, get a grip! I close my eyes, deploy all the Zen-like inner peace I can muster and take a few cleansing breaths. I'm not proud of how I've messed with Enzo's life, caused him pain. But what's done is done. I can only watch this situation I got him into play out to its conclusion. When I open my eyes they immediate lock onto Enzo. It is only once I manage to still my mind and focus on watching him that I notice his confident, open posture, his genuine smile and attentive listening. I shake my head in wonder, remembering his old defensive swagger, stony tough-man expression, and near inability to converse with ease. The thing is, he seems more natural, much more himself now even though he's actually putting on an accent he's worked hard to learn. And he looks damn fine in that tailored suit.

I watch Enzo shake hands with the German and excuse himself gracefully, moving into the atrium in search of something. Someone. Me?

ENZO

Seems like nearly everybody here is somebody big. I nearly pissed my pants when Mrs. H brought me over to meet the chica from *Titanic*. Kate. If Mama hadn't been cremated, she'd have been doin' backflips in her grave knowing I was meeting 'Rose.'

Kate and I were introduced and even said a few words to each other before moving on. Meeting her reminds me of how I thought Hester looked a little like Kate when I first saw her. But Kate's older now than she was in that movie. Still slammin', though, and pretty nice from what I can tell.

Now I go on back into that huge sunroom and look around. It's a bitch to try and keep my focus and still be on the lookout for Hester. My jumpy nerves are making me hungry, too. Right when I'm popping a puff pastry something or other into my mouth someone grabs me from behind.

"Hey!" I turn around, trying to figure out the etiquette for greeting somebody with a mouth full of puff pastry when they surprise the hell out of you with a sneak attack. But then, I see it's just Goldie. I wipe my mouth with the tiny napkin that came with the pastry. "Hey, chiquita…I mean hello, Goldie, it's a pleasure to see you again."

She looks me up and down, smiling and shaking her head. "You look fabulous, Enzo. I'm seriously bummed I wasn't there when you shaved your beard off, but wow, does it make a difference. You are, to borrow a word from your old vocabulary, totally 'slammin'.'"

It still feels weird to take a compliment, but I do it anyway. "It's kind of you to say so. Do you like this suit? Mrs. Hastings chose it."

"Yes, Enzo. She chose well. Though it's your hot bod that takes it to a higher level. Miriam might have picked it out, but you fill it out." She squeezes my bicep and adjusts my collar. "Have you seen Hester yet?"

I look around without meaning to. "No, do you know where she is?"

"I saw her in the parlor about fifteen minutes ago…want me to look for her?"

This plays up my already insane nerves, so I shake my head. "Thank you, no. I'm sure if she wants to see me she'll find me."

"Oh, Enzo. You know she was frantic when you disappeared…"

"She told me to leave!" Shoot. I messed up the accent there. But I pull it together. "I believe she'd gotten quite a shock, so it's not surprising she would have been out of sorts."

Goldie frowns. "Your accent may be perfect, but it takes away your Enzo-ness. Have you seen Topaz since you got back?"

I look around and lean in closer, dropping the accent on purpose this time. "We just flew back two days ago…stopped in to see her on the way here. Mrs. H gave her so many presents my baby girl thought the woman was a real-life fairy godmother. Then when we came to this house and Mrs. H showed me how everything was all ready for the party, I was so freaked out, man. That lady had like, a staff of people working on it while we were in London." I can't help shaking my head because this all still seems like some kind of crazy dream. "I can't even believe how insanely dope this place is, yo. Did you see that chandelier in the front hallway? I bet it weighs over a thousand pounds."

Goldie smiles. "Yes, I've been here before. It's pretty swish, but then so is Hester's mom."

"You ain't kidding…"

Her face gets all worried. "Listen, I'd better leave you alone before I screw up your act." She peeks over my shoulder and her eyes get wide. "Oh shit, here comes Miriam!"

I get myself all back into character while Goldie runs away. By the time Mrs. H puts her hand on my elbow I'm ready.

"Enzo, dear…I want to introduce you to Jude and his lovely companion."

She tows me back outside, and I feel like maybe Hester's nearby, but I don't see her anywhere.

HESTER

I'm just thinking about abandoning my lilac bush in order to get a fresh glass of bubbly when Mum leads Enzo back outside and over to the fish pond pagoda, where I watch as she introduces him to Jude Law – lovely fellow, but has great difficulty with Standard American English – and the petite blonde who appears to be with the actor.

Enzo and Jude seem to hit it off immediately, which I might have expected. But if anyone's going to suss Enzo out as inauthentic, my money's on Jude. I can only watch their lips move as they engage in quite a long conversation. Jude is charming, interested in hearing about whatever Mum is making Enzo talk about – perhaps the modeling thing – and then they appear to get off topic, and Mum's face goes all anxious. Despite myself I hold my breath. If Jude has asked Enzo where he went to university or anything about his background, my student's cover could be blown in a heartbeat. I watch Enzo's lips moving and can't for the life of me make out more than two words. But then Jude bursts out in a loud guffaw and they are all laughing and Enzo is still an Englishman.

It's a long wait until Mum drags Enzo away from Jude to go meet some older women I don't know. Probably her ritzy friends from the Hollywood Garden Conservation Society. They don't actually garden so much as throw money at Mexican landscapers to keep public gardens beautiful.

While Enzo's back is to me I sneak out from my hiding spot and pinch another glass of champagne, plus a handful of hors d'oeuvres on a cocktail napkin to keep me going and soak up some of the alcohol I'm going through more rapidly than I intended. Thus armed, I take up my spot behind the shrub again and watch the action.

I nearly drop a pastry puff when Liz the cougar saunters into view from the stone patio and places a hand proprietorially on Enzo's shoulder. A handful too many precious gems adorn her fingers, and her hair is at least two shades lighter than the last time I saw her. A memory of the red lipstick she left on Enzo's cheek at Jimmy's wedding rises unbidden into my consciousness.

Liz apologizes to the Garden ladies, probably something along the lines of, 'so sorry ladies, but I have to steal him away' and drags Enzo off. I can only watch as she pulls Enzo to the relative privacy of the cedar gazebo. Hanging baskets of lush ferns shield half of Enzo's face from my view, but when he leans forward to hear what she's whispering into his ear I can see his mouth. He smiles and says something back. I can tell he's using his American accent by the way his jaw moves. I wonder what she's told him?

Then the cougar takes advantage of their proximity to plant a kiss on his cheek.

That's definitely enough for me. Time to go. I leave the safety of my lilac bush to slink back indoors. If Goldie and Nigel want to stay I'll get a taxi home.

ENZO

After Liz goes off to find her next target I use the white napkin from my drink to wipe her kiss off my face. I appreciate what she's been doing to hook me up with fitness modeling gigs and all, but that lady needs to quit crushing on me.

It's shady and quiet in this little hut, though. I'm alone in here, so I've got a second to breathe and think. Seems like everything's going okay so far. Mrs. H invited just about every Brit she knows to this shindig. I've been deflecting personal questions like crazy, just like she taught me, but there's been a few close calls. Good thing its only water and ice in my glass 'cause one real drink, and I know it's all over. Takes all the concentration I got to keep this accent on.

I see Mrs. H hustle on out of the house lookin' for me. That woman has introduced me to just about everybody but the one person I wanna see. Though I ain't asked her to find Hester 'cause there's every chance that girl won't want to talk to me anyway. Shoot. I wish I knew where her mind was at. Whole time I was in London I was thinking about how nice it would be if she saw me do this, what she wanted me to do from when she started teaching me. Thinking about how maybe she'd be so happy about the accent she'd forgive me and look at me like she did that morning in the pool before she found out how bad I'd screwed up.

Aw, no. Mrs. H has me in her sights. My chill break is over.

"Enzo!" She calls at me from the patio. "Please come and let me introduce you to Timothy Dalton…you might recognize him as one of the actors who played 'James Bond.' I think he made two of those films. Anyway, he's simply brilliant, and you must come have a chat."

Here we go. Though this one I'm kinda lookin' forward to. It ain't every day I get to meet 007.

HESTER

I make my way through the house in search of Goldie. And now that I'm out of hiding I have to stop and talk to everyone I know along the way. Kelly Preston is here with her agent; she says John had another commitment. Sir Richard Branson considerately asks about Philip, whom he met at one of Mum's parties a few years back, but I don't have the heart to explain we split up ages ago. I execute a quick double kiss greeting with Jude as I breeze through the parlor, grateful he's already busy chatting with a couple I'm not acquainted with. By the time I reach the foyer, my cheeks are tired from summoning a fake smile for people whom normally I would be genuinely delighted to see. I'm considering a quick cut and run out the front door when Goldie catches me by the elbow.

"Where have you been?" She hisses.

"Hiding behind a lilac bush like a total idiot."

"Spying on Enzo?"

I nod guiltily.

"Hess, you need to just go up and introduce yourself to him as though you've never met before and start over."

"I saw him with Liz…and she kissed him."

"What?" She looks shocked, but then her eyes narrow. "Kissed like, 'I'm your sexy sugar- momma' or like 'you're a fabulous client, let's do lunch'?"

I feel deflated. "Oh Goldie. Does it matter? I really just want to leave."

"Wait a second…" She skitters off around the corner, disappears into the dining room, and then gallops back all excited. "Enzo is talking with Timothy Dalton and Nigel, and I found this great hiding place where we can totally spy on them!"

I know I should just leave, but her energy overwhelms me, and I end up plastered against the crimson wall behind the enormous dining room door with Goldie. We can peek through the crack without being seen, and I can hear every word of the conversation taking place in the wide hall.

Mum: "Timothy, Enzo is a fitness model who's thinking about trying his hand at acting. He's just arrived from London…have you any words of advice to offer?"

Timothy: *Makes a face* "Develop a thick skin, my friend. Be bloody well sure it's what you want before you start slogging away at auditions."

Enzo: *Laughs* "I appreciate your candor. Show business does seem a bit more daunting now that I'm actually having a go at it."

Nigel: "At least you've got the modeling to fall back on…"

Enzo: "Too true. I've been lucky."

Mum: "Yes, I believe you have been very fortunate, Enzo. It's not every day a man like yourself gets a shot at something really special."

Enzo: *Rubs his chin* "I had a pretty good shot at something special not too long ago, but I'm afraid it didn't play out quite the way I had hoped."

Timothy: *Chuckles* "That's show business for you. It'll knock you down more than lift you up in the beginning. Keep at it, and if it's really what you want; don't give up. Now if you'll excuse me, I told my friend I'd meet her out by the pond… it was lovely to meet you both."

When Timothy departs, Mum flaps off after him, no doubt wanting to speak to the 'friend' as well. She's incorrigibly social. Enzo leans toward Nigel and drops the accent. "How am I doing?"

Nigel claps him on the shoulder and smiles. "A damn sight better than I ever thought you would."

"Have you seen Goldie? Or…Hester?"

"I last saw Goldie in the atrium, and I haven't laid eyes on Hester since we arrived. She's wearing a purple sparkly something, hard to miss."

"If you come across her, can you please tell her I'm…I'd like to see her?"

Nigel smiles kindly and nods. "Absolutely, mate. I'm going to fetch another drink…can I get you anything?"

"No thanks, bro. See you later."

Nigel disappears into the breakfast room where the indoor bar is set up. Once Enzo is alone, he exhales loudly, shakes his head as though he's taken too many punches in a boxing match.

Goldie grabs my hand and squeezes hard, tries to push me out from behind the door. I shake my head and push back. She's strong, but before she can oust me Enzo moves off down the hall and exits the house through the conservatory.

"What's wrong with you?" Goldie flicks my shoulder hard.

"Ow!" Her glare is scathing. "I don't know...I just can't see him now. It's a really big party, and he's doing such a lovely job with the accent...I don't want to jinx him."

"Bullshit." She points a scarlet-tipped finger at me. "You're scared, Hester."

"Why do you even care?"

"Because I can see you're never going to get past this unless you face him again."

I'm staring down the hall at the glass doors he just walked through. "He makes a lovely Englishman, doesn't he?"

"Yes he does...it's actually pretty fucking incredible that he's pulling this off, Hester." I can feel her looking at me. "In fact, it would be entirely appropriate for you, his dialect coach, to go congratulate him. I think he's earned at least that much, don't you?"

I am spared the necessity of a reply by a sudden popping sound and the faint buzz of the intercom switching on. A bell rings to get everyone's attention, and then Mum's voice is being broadcast through every room in the house, ringing through the garden speakers to reach everyone at the party.

"My dear guests, please join me in the garden to toast my guest of honor before dinner is laid out on the buffet."

Oh no! Poor Enzo...I never knew my mother was such a heartless soul.

ENZO

Mrs. H didn't warn me about this part. Every last someone comes on outta that enormous house, and champagne is served all around. Holy shit, yo. This is really happening.

I pray and pray that she won't make me say nothing. That wedding where I said the stuff Hester told me was wrong to say is right up in my brain.

Everybody's lookin' at me and Mrs. H as she hands me a glass of champagne. She's holding a mini microphone so nobody can miss what she's about to say, and she smiles at me like I just rescued her poodle from drowning or something.

"Enzo, on behalf of the greater Los Angeles community, I welcome you! Please accept my every wish for your success and prosperity here in the City of Angels. Hollywood has been kind to many of our fellow countrymen, and it is my hope that you will also find success in this den of wolves."

Even though I'm sending her big-ass messages with my eyes not to do it, Mrs. H holds out the mic to me.

HESTER

Goldie has dragged me down the hall and through the conservatory. We fall in behind a group of latecomers and hastily accept the champagne flutes that are pressed into our hands by servers who seem to be following a 'no guest left behind' mandate. I spot Brent Logan across the crowd, watching me with a knowing gaze. Oh my God, please do not let him do anything crazy!

Mum is grinning like a maniac, making me wonder how much she's had to drink. Enzo looks stone cold sober and somewhat panicked when she practically forces the mic onto him. From the expression on his face, I know this is an unwelcome surprise.

He takes a drink from his glass and clears his throat. Forces a smile. "Um... thank you all for welcoming me so warmly. When Miriam invited me to come and stay, I was overwhelmed by her hospitality. In the past...people have not always been so kind. Thank you." He can't hand the mic back to her fast enough.

Then there's a long moment of silence in which everything seems to slow down. As though there's a giant magnet glued to my forehead and his eyes are made of steel, Enzo's gaze finds me in the crowd and locks on.

I hear his unamplified voice say, "Hold on a minute." Still looking at me, he takes the mic back from Mum. "I also want to say that I feel blessed in every way to have had the pleasure of meeting Miriam's daughter." At this, all eyes follow the trajectory of his intense gaze to me.

Oh heavens! Breathe, Hester...

"She is a woman unlike any other I've met. Generous, smart like a whip, funny, caring, and...I'd like to take this opportunity to thank her also. I owe her my gratitude for trusting me when no one else would have. For spending all that time on me, pushing me to do better. And thank you, Hester Hastings, for letting me get to know you even though I probably never should have gotten the chance to." He pauses to look around, and everyone's eyes swivel back to him. "I want everyone here to know what an amazing dialect coach Hester Hastings is…"

I realize what he's decided to do only when the next words tumble out of his mouth in his native rhythmic cadence.

"What I gotta say is, I'm not exac'ly what you all been seein' tonight. And it ain't like I started out with the idea of pretendin' to be somethin' I'm not. But you all should know that I ain't new to this city. I was born and came up right ova in Watts." Gasps of surprise circle round the garden. Not only has Enzo dropped his British accent, he's shed the polished posture as well. His street attitude instantly refigures his stance as though it's been hovering in a cloud above his head all along.

He nods. "Yeah. True story, yo. And when she met me I was straight outta L.A. Men's Jail…didn't have no money or no place to go, neither. Hester and her friend Goldie…" He pauses to point at her as if to say, 'you knew I wasn't gonna forget you.' Goldie smiles, happy to have the spotlight for a second.

Enzo has the entire crowd transfixed. They await his next words like penniless drunkards, faces pressed up against the liquor store window.

"Hester and Goldie decided to help me out, take me on as a student and all. It was Hester that took this here ghetto accent and changed it all 'round." His accent slowly morphs into Standard American English. "Maybe she was a tough teacher, but she never gave up on me. That woman got me reading classic literature, learning about history, manners, upscale conversation, confident posture. Shoot, she was downright relentless, man."

Laughter ripples through the crowd, and they look at me again.

"But I realized what a gift she was giving me the day I stood in front of a police officer using my new accent and he didn't treat me like a piece of dirt because of how I talked. I learned what real respect from a stranger feels like.

"So then she wanted me to learn this English accent, the one you've been hearing from me all evening. And I did it because I wanted to stay near her as long as possible. I was afraid once she'd finished teaching me I'd never see her face again. And more than the things she taught me, more than her belief in my ability, I wanted to keep seeing her face every day."

Oh for goodness sake, he's got me all teary. And from the look of the crowd, I'm not the only one. Mum's pulled out her hankie. More than one person is filming Enzo's performance with a cell phone.

He turns to look at Mum. "Miriam Hastings organized this party so I'd have the chance to test the final outcome of all the work we did to get me sounding this way. I hope you will forgive us for deceiving you." Enzo's eyes turn back to me. "And I'd like to ask everyone to please join me in raising a glass to Hester Hastings, dialect coach extraordinaire, and downright classy lady."

He raises his champagne flute to me, and everyone else follows suit, including a very amused Brent Logan. And then all hell breaks loose.

ENZO

Seems like after that speech everybody's coming at me at once. They're all asking questions about why I really did it, want to know am I telling the truth and why Hester chose me to help out of every other ex-con she could have picked. That last one I don't have the answer to. It only just now occurs to me that I never thought to ask.

Through the crowd, I can see her watching me. I don't want to be rude to all these people, but what I'd like to do is push 'em all out of the way so I can go be with her, find out if she's forgiven me, if I have a chance.

I hand the mic back to Mrs. H, and she grabs me up in a hug like she's my Mama. "I don't know who couldn't forgive you after a speech like that, Enzo. Go find Hester."

"Thanks, Mrs. H. Thanks for all you've done for me."

She nods and smiles. "It's been an absolute pleasure, my dear. Now get going!"

I start picking my way through the crowd but a young-looking dude with white hair stops me.

"Enzo, I didn't get to meet you yet…but I'm Anderson Cooper, from *60 Minutes*? And boy would I love to do a story about you and Hester. Can we talk?"

"Um, that would be real nice, but we gotta do it later, man."

Mrs. H must be watching because she raises the mic to her mouth and says, "Please excuse our guest of honor from taking more questions at this time. I will be happy to field all inquiries…"

The white-haired guy hands me his card and heads over to the hostess like she said to. People I met earlier shake my hand and pat me on the back as I pass through the crowd easily now. Everybody is smiling and looking at me like I'm something special.

My man, Brent, catches me and it ain't like him not to say anything. But I guess he knows I'm in a hurry 'cause he just shakes my hand like he's proud of me.

Jude Law is the last one who's name I remember that I run into. He stops me with a handshake and says, "That American English is a real bitch, isn't it? I can't even imagine how difficult the British accent must have been for you. Well done, Enzo…you had me completely fooled."

"Thanks, bro."

I can't see Hester anywhere, so I keep on moving toward the house, getting stopped two more times by people I don't know. One hands me his card, and the next asks me do I want to be interviewed for an article in *People* magazine.

"Thanks for the offer, but no thanks, man."

I'm almost home free when somebody grabs me from behind. From all the rings on her fingers, I know it's Liz.

"Enzo, that was totally freakin' amazing! How come you didn't tell me all that earlier? I knew you had the two accents, but I wasn't sure if you were American doing an English accent, or the other way around." She lays a hand on my chest. "You are going to be so in-demand it's not even funny. Since I consider myself your agent, can I work with Miriam to schedule some interviews and photo shoots?"

"What, about me faking accents and pretending to be British at this party?"

"Well, about the journey from being in jail to being a guest of honor here tonight. The whole thing…"

I shake my head. "No. I'll do more fitness modeling stuff if you want me to, but I'm not gonna do interviews and all." Now I'm worried somebody's gonna dig up my past, the reason I was in jail, and tell the whole world. That's not going to help my chances with Hester. "I gotta go, Liz."

I break away and hear Liz yell after me. "Bye! I'll call you tomorrow!!"

A tuxedoed server dodges me as I run through the atrium, the huge fancy living room Mrs. H calls the parlor, and into the front hallway that has the big-ass chandelier.

Where the hell is that woman?

HESTER

At home I take a long shower. The image of Enzo standing in front of everyone with the microphone, the words he spoke. I can't get it out of my mind.

Goldie has already left messages on my phone, but I turned the thing off and put it in a drawer. I have to get my head straight and I can't do it with Goldie's voice harping in my ear. Or Enzo's speech replaying endlessly in my brain.

It touched me to hear Enzo singing my praises, but I feel guilty also. I've been so preoccupied with figuring out how to forgive him, that I've only now realized what I really owe him is an apology. I couldn't do it at that party, but I know I'm going to make myself go to Mum's tomorrow and see him even if I'm still not ready.

Once I finally towel off and get into my pajamas the sky has gone dark. With my hair still wet, I go downstairs to find the book I've been reading. All I want to do is curl up in bed and zone out so my brain can process everything without my annoying thoughts getting in the way.

After I search the living room, I pad into the kitchen. When I see him lurking on the path outside the glass slider I startle from both fright and excitement. My heart rate shoots up. Enzo has shed his suit jacket, and his white dress shirt nearly glows in the darkness. He gives a little uncertain wave.

Of course I unlock the door and slide it open. "Don't you still have a key?"

"Yeah, but I didn't want to scare you...I thought I shouldn't be just letting myself in anymore. You know, 'cause you've been making it real clear you don't want me anywhere near you."

"Then why did you come?" I don't mean to sound so harsh, but I can't think of a way to soften it.

Enzo holds out his hand, and I see a small jade figurine lying in his palm...a tiger. "I left this here when I cleared out of the cabana. It's kind of special so I wanted to come back and get it. Oh," he fishes in his pocket for something and then holds my key out for me to take. "I should give this back."

Even though he's trying to be discreet about it, I can see that his eyes are taking in my body, noticing that I'm not wearing anything underneath my shortie pajamas. My pulse is already running on staccato, but it bumps up a notch.

I hold out my hand, and he drops the key into it. His fingers don't touch my palm.

He puts his hands in his pockets and looks at the ground. "You left the party so quick I didn't even get the chance to say hello."

"I'm sorry...I know it was wrong to leave. But after what you said I felt so bad about...everything."

He's eyes rise to meet mine in consternation. "I didn't say it to make you feel bad...did I fuck up again?"

I can't help but smile. "No, Enzo. I'm the one who fucked up this time."

The confusion on his face is so endearing I want to reach out and smooth away the creases on his forehead. "You want me to go?"

"No...come in." I stand to the side to let him pass, resisting the impulse to wrap my arms around him. "I owe you an apology on two counts, and it's time to make myself confess."

ENZO

I don't know what she's talking about but I get in that house fast before she changes her mind. Standing in the kitchen where we ate so many meals together I wait to find out what she wants me to do.

When she goes into the living room, I follow and sit on the sofa when she motions for me to take a seat. She chooses the armchair, curling her bare legs underneath her butt and hugging the little pillow she once told me is there for decoration. It's good she's holding it against her chest, 'cause it's pretty distracting that she's in them lacy shortie pajamas.

"You were a near to perfect student, Enzo. When I saw you tonight at the party I was more proud of you than I've ever been of anyone."

Okay, then why'd you run off after? Get to the good stuff, girl. I stay quiet so she'll keep going.

"When I saw that Liz woman kiss you..."

"Ugh. She's always doing that! But I promise all she's been doing is helping me...she recognized me at a club in London, and it turns out your mom knows her also. She helped me get a few jobs modeling for fitness magazines."

"I know...Mum sent me the mock-up of you on the cover of *Men's Health*."

"She did? I thought it wasn't coming out till August?"

"They do mock-ups in advance to make sure everything looks right. Like a practice copy."

"Okay." I look down at my hands, feeling like I don't want to see her look all disgusted with me again. "Did you think it was okay?"

"Honestly? It made me want to jump on a plane and go find you in London."

Hearing that makes me smile so big. "That woulda been fine with me!"

When she doesn't smile back its easy to get serious again. She takes a breath and I know some real stuff is coming. "So here's what I need to say: I'm sorry for what I said, how I reacted to you when Philip told me about your past. I was cruel and unfair. I can't make any excuses for myself, I handled it poorly, and I'm truly sorry for that."

Is that all? "No problem, Hester. I'm sorry too, so sorry I didn't tell you earlier. I wish so much I could do it over. When you met me I was...what I'd done was a pretty embarrassing thing to admit. I wanted to put it behind me, you know? I should have been honest that first day outside the jail, but I didn't know what all was going to happen with the coaching, and then you and me..."

She's nodding at me. "I know. You never thought it would become an issue. And speaking of that first day outside the jail...I have a confession to make. Goldie and I never planned a research project about helping underprivileged individuals rehabilitate themselves. We were lying to you. The truth is, Goldie saw you come out of the jail and bet me I couldn't transform you so that you could pass as a British actor. It was a stupid and infantile thing to do, and I'm sorry we lied to you and roped you into an experiment based on nothing but a silly wager."

HESTER

There, I've said it. Enzo is silent for a moment, then stands up and walks into the kitchen. He slowly circles the island and comes back to the living room.

Then he's standing larger-than-life in front of me, hands on hips. "You mean to tell me that from the moment Goldie told me I could come here and get dialect coaching...all that started because of a *bet* between you two?"

I nod, coaching myself not to make excuses.

His expression is still incredulous. "So...you just picked me 'cause I happened to be there when you made the bet?"

I nod again. "It was stupid, snobby, and careless of us to intentionally toy with your life. I'm sorry, Enzo."

He kind of squints at me and then goes for another lap around the island, then walks over to the glass slider and looks into the darkness outside. I can't see his face, but when his shoulders begin to shake I'm really worried. Is he angry? Crying?

But then his rumbling chuckle becomes audible, and I breathe again. I watch as he throws back his head and howls with laughter.

When he finally calms down he turns back to me. "You just decided, like on the spur of the moment, to offer a newly released criminal all that intensive coaching...what, kind of for fun?"

"Well, it was Goldie's idea. And of course, I thought you'd never go for it so I wouldn't have to go through with it. But then you showed up, and..."

"Aw girl, you musta been so freaked out when I knocked on that door!" He starts laughing again and doesn't stop. The deep rumble in his chest works its way into peals of uncontrollable hilarity.

I didn't think it was funny, but at least he's not yelling at me.

Enzo is wiping tears from his face by the time he finally calms himself and plonks down onto the sofa. "Oh my God, you and Goldie are so damn stupid I can't stand it. Do you have any idea how lucky you were it was me coming out of that jail when you made that bet? All this time I thought you'd planned it out and considered the risks, maybe asked somebody at the jail to recommend a good candidate for your 'study.' Though I should have realized you woulda known all about me and what I did to get arrested if you'd done your homework. Damn. I knew guys in there who woulda ripped you off soon as look at you." He shakes his head, then looks at me all serious. "You ever done something like this before?"

"No, of course not."

One of his eyebrows goes up. "You planning to ever do it again?"

"No!"

Enzo leans back and regards me silently for a minute. A look of calculation creeps into his serious expression. "So is there any chance we're even now? I lied to you, you lied to me…I know what I lied about is worse, but have you…can you forgive me?"

I nod. "I forgive you for lying…"

He waits for me to finish my sentence, and when I don't he asks the question I'm not sure I can answer yet. "Can you forgive what I lied about?"

"I've been trying, Enzo. I look at you now, and I want to jump off this chair into your lap. And then I think about all those woman…how they bought you. I…"

"S'okay. You don't need to say more." He stands up. "Can I tell you something before I go?"

I nod. I don't want him to leave yet.

He fishes in his pocket and brings out the jade tiger. "I've been carrying this little guy around since about six months after Monique died. I'll never forget the day I bought it. Topaz and I were walking through Chinatown on our way somewhere, I can't remember now where we were headed. This was when I was trying to decide about whether to do the escort thing, and I only had, like five dollars in my pocket. That's it. No home. No job. I was sleeping on the floor at Topaz' Grandmama's place and taking care of my baby girl all the time. She was three and a half years old." His eyes get lost in the memory. "Baby girl was riding on my shoulders, and she spotted this little guy in a window. Begged me to go in the store and buy it for her. Monique's favorite animal was a tiger, and when I told Topaz 'no,' she started to cry like her Mama had just died all over again. So we went into the store and I paid three dollars for this. Then I sat Topaz down on a bench on the sidewalk, and we looked at it together. I knew she wouldn't understand all of what I was telling her, but I said it anyway. I told her, 'This here little tiger is our special symbol. It means I'm always gonna take care of you no matter what happens. I'm gonna always be honest with you and do what I need to do to be a good Daddy for you.' I guess that was when I decided to go ahead and take the escort job even though I knew what it meant I'd be doing." A bitter laugh escapes him. "Turns out trying to be a good dad got me taken away from her. So I let her down pretty bad."

I want to hug him, kiss away his regret. Instead I use words. "I know you did it so you could take better care of Topaz. And I think she's damn lucky to have you for her father even though you made a mistake that got you locked away from her. After you disappeared, I went to see Martha, looking for you. She told me how you wrote letters to Topaz from jail, drew pictures for her. You're a wonderful father, Enzo."

He looks down at the floor for a moment, and when his eyes lift up to meet mine I see hope in them. "I know I let you down pretty bad too. And after you did so much for me. Thanks to what you taught me, I feel better in my own skin, you know? And it's not just about how I speak. You opened my eyes to a bigger world, Hester. You gave me confidence and the tools I needed to start my own business, the chance to provide for my daughter in a way no one ever did for me. No one believed in me like that before you did. I don't think there's any way you can know how deep…" Enzo stops, but I can tell he's not finished.

"So I need to tell you what I told Topaz when we got the tiger. If you can forgive me, I'll always be there for you. I'll be honest with you and do whatever needs doing to be a good friend…a true partner to you.

"I'm always gonna be who I am, Hester. No matter how many accents I learn, or how 'posh' I behave, this is me. I was raised up in Watts, and went to jail for something I regret, and I've got a daughter. And then I met a beautiful woman who believed in me, who made me want to be a better version of myself. I gotta accept it if you don't want to be with me. But that won't ever change what's in my heart for you. If you ever need me, my man Brent will have my digits."

Before I can reply, Enzo heads toward the slider to let himself out. He's closed the door behind him, nearly disappeared into the night before I hurl myself from my chair and dash to open the slider.

"Wait a second!" I can't let him leave before I try something. Something that might help reprogram my thoughts. Help me let go of the monster in the closet that is Homeboy Gangsta.

Perhaps Goldie was onto something earlier when she told me to just go up to him and start over. I wonder...

Enzo has turned and is peering at me in the darkness. Waiting.

"Can you do me a favor and go around to the front door and knock?"

He looks at me quizzically as if to ask, 'what game is this?'

I flap my hand to wave away his question. "I know it's weird, but can you please do it?"

He points to the front of the house with eyebrows raised.

Offering him a grateful smile, I nod. "Yes, just a simple knock."

He shrugs and heads around the house. I don't have time to put on make-up or get changed, but I fluff my still-damp hair out a bit and check my reflection in the window above the kitchen table. For heaven's sake, I think I've gone just about totally crazy.

By the time I hear him knocking I've wedged the yellow kitchen door all the way open, until it sticks that way. Though I've never before in my life considered opening the front door of my home to a visitor while wearing pajamas, I unlock it and pull it open.

Framed in the doorway is Enzo, half-smiling and looking completely baffled. Hair short and jaw shaved smooth, he looks like a completely different person from the man who came knocking three months ago. This Enzo is more than I ever imagined he could be. And not much because of anything I taught him. Yes, I may have polished him up; but he was already a gem.

Alright, here we go. "Hello, I'm Hester Hastings. Please come in." I step aside to let him through. I extend my right hand, inviting him to shake it.

"Um, okay." His handshake is warm and genuine. "I'm Enzo Diaz. It's a pleasure to meet you, Hester."

"Likewise..." What now? Oh, I know. "I'm a dialect coach, what's your line of work?"

He squares his shoulders, getting the hang of this. "I guess I'm a personal trainer and fitness model."

I close the front door and lock it. "Have you had dinner yet?"

He smiles. "Actually, it's a funny thing. I was supposed to have dinner at this party I was invited to, but I had to leave before it was served."

"I have some leftover meatloaf in the fridge…"

His eyebrows rise. "Miss Lettuce-Leaf made meatloaf?"

I shrug. "I got a little tired of salad. Anyhow, I hear you make fantastic mashed potatoes, and I have an apron that would just about fit you…" My words give out as his proximity overwhelms me.

Enzo steps closer, and I don't move away. The intensity of our attraction is eclipsing any unwanted thoughts I might otherwise be having about his past. He slides his hands down my bare arms and takes my hands in his own. Nearly transfixed by his golden-green hazel eyes, I realize he is waiting for a sign to continue. This is the moment I have to decide…if I can't forget, can I at least forgive his past actions and accept all of who he is?

I tilt my head, taken in by those dreamy eyes. It comes to me that I've seen him look at someone like this before. Topaz. His eyes are showing me love, trust, tenderness. I reach up and caress his cheek, smooth in one direction, like sandpaper in the other. My index finger travels to the shallow dimple in his chin. "I had no idea this was here." On impulse I rise up on tiptoe and kiss it.

He's received his invitation and doesn't hesitate. Enzo's hands slide up into my hair to cradle the back of my head as his lips meet mine. Pressing into him I lose myself in the sensation of his body aligned with my own. His kisses start out deeply sensual and slowly transition to a hungrier rhythm. I feel his desire to reclaim my affection and in response I release my fear, giving him the heat his lips are seeking. He wants a promise from me, a commitment to love and be loved. My hands slip from his hair and travel down his shoulders and around his torso, pressing into his broad back to pull him closer.

In the deepest part of me I know my intuition about him was correct from the start; he is genuine, determined, capable. I can trust this man to care for me.

ENZO

Sunday, June 15th

I have to find a place to live. It's cool of Mrs. H to let me stay here, but after Hester opened the door to us being something for real last night, I have to step up. She's giving me the chance to start over, and I've got to make it solid this time around. That means I'm not gonna stay at her place any more, and I'm not gonna let her put out any more money for me. And though Mrs. H's place is totally dope and a man could get used to this kind of luxury, I can't stay here either.

Last night was crazy! The party, all those people wanting to know about me after my stupid speech that freaked Hester out. I don't even know what's going to happen next. Mrs. H said this morning that a whole bunch of people already called her about trying to talk with me about my 'story.'

Then there was after the party with Hester. She was lookin' so fine in those shortie pajamas, and after all that foolin' around we did, it was near to impossible to leave and go back to sleep at Mrs. H's. But I'm making a clean break from being Hester's student project, and there's no way I'm sleeping there again unless she invites me to stay over in her room. No way do I want to mess up this good thing we've just started.

So today, for me, for Hester, and mostly for my baby girl Topaz, I'm going apartment hunting. I know I can't afford much in Los Feliz, but I gotta be near my woman, and they have good schools for my baby girl up in there. Plus I got a little foothold already with the personal training. If I can get some more clients, especially ones like Brent, I'll be able to pay my rent with extra left over to spoil my girls.

Mrs. H says I can 'write my own ticket' professionally from now on, and I damn sure hope she's right. Once I get Topaz back and I'm working more, I've got to trust that things are going to keep getting better for me. Work hard, keep out of trouble, and love this amazing woman I got so lucky to find. If I get Topaz and I have Hester, that's everything I need.

HESTER

Saturday, June 21ˢᵗ

Enzo's new apartment is microscopic. The entire footprint would fit in my kitchen. And it's very possible some kind of bugs are already in residence. But he is so proud of the place he can't stop smiling. I smile back and make a mental note to locate an exterminator service.

After showing me the combined living-room-kitchenette, he proudly leads me down the short hallway to the first bedroom and turns on the lights. "I'm giving Topaz the biggest bedroom 'cause she can fit a bed and dresser and desk in here, and for me I don't need anything more than a mattress anyway. I want her to have some space to play and have friends over, you know?"

The small room is empty, but in my mind I'm already decorating it. Goldie's going to want in on this, too. "Oh Enzo, you have to let me buy something adorable to go in here. A princess bed? Or perhaps the desk?"

He shakes his head, dead serious. "Not a chance. I already told you that now I've got an income, I don't want you paying anything more for me."

"It wouldn't be for you! It would be for *Topaz*." I poke him in the chest.

He takes my hand, threads his fingers through my own. "No way, girl. You can't get around it like that."

But I already know how to get around his new rule. Goldie and I will get Topaz a dress-up box and fill it with all kinds of girlie princess costumes. It will be a gift for his daughter, and he will accept it.

Enzo squeezes my hand gently to bring me back to the conversation. "And I got a surprise for you. It's not big or anything, so don't get too excited, but come on and see my room."

He tows me along past an eeny-weeny bathroom and pushes open another door. Because it is night, all I see is a patch of wood floor illuminated by the living room light. I follow him in, and as my eyes adjust, I see one window and a mattress on the floor. When he flips the light switch and I see that the room is almost entirely filled by the queen-size mattress, I'm a little shocked. It's hard to imagine sleeping in here, on the floor, with insects possibly doing whatever they do during the night around me. I give an involuntary shudder.

Enzo's smile drops. "It's that bad?"

"Not exactly…" *Yes. Yes it is!* "It's just that…I'm sorry, I guess I'm pretty spoiled." I try to imagine the bed he slept on in jail. To him this set-up is more than adequate.

He shrugs, accepting my negative judgment of the room he is proud to call his own. "Never mind. Let's go on out to dinner. But next time you come, I'll be all moved in and I'm gonna cook us some…"

I stop him with a kiss. He is surprised, but doesn't object. I need to kiss this man because just now when he was talking I noticed something about the mattress beyond that it is on the floor and takes up the whole room. His 'surprise' for me is that the mattress is made up beautifully. He's only just signed the lease this morning, and already he has somehow gotten this mattress here. Probably carried it on his back up a hill or something. He has also purchased sheets the same peachy-pink color as the ones I have on my bed at home – a color choice he would never have made for himself – and a beautiful white quilt similar to the one in my guest room. Two plush pillows I know he tested for softness have been carefully placed at the head of the bed. I feel his continued surprise as I reach up and slide my hands into his hair, settling into this kiss like it's not going to end any time soon.

Enzo may still be a little rough around the edges, and this apartment that I find objectionable might feel like a palace to him, but he has clearly made his bed up to try and please me. The same way he wants Topaz to have the bigger room and furniture she loves, he has made this bed up for me in the hope that I might be happy sleeping here. With him.

I've been scared to go there. To any bed with him. He's been sleeping at Mum's since the party, and it's awkward that after months of sharing the same space, it now feels odd to think of him sleeping in the cabana or guest room of my house. Yet I haven't felt ready to bring him to my bedroom.

Yes, we've forgiven each other and started over. But hitting that reset button didn't completely erase knowing all that I know about Enzo. We've been like teenagers, aching for each other while settling for kisses and cuddles. Stopping before we get anywhere near a commitment that might end in a bedroom.

Tonight, I am with a man in his apartment, and he is kissing me with a heated passion I invited, and I know I want more. I need more from him.

I let my lips explore his jawline and drop lower to the tender skin below his ear. His hands move to my waist and slide under my shirt, caressing my back. Enzo kisses my forehead and his lips move to my ear. "You don't wanna go eat?" He is kindly giving me a way out.

I shake my head, look into his eyes. His pupils visibly dilate as he takes in what I want, and he gives me the tiniest smile. Then he kisses me with a sensual intensity I haven't felt from him before. He's always held himself in check, knowing he wasn't going to push me before I was ready. Giving him the green light has unleashed his need for me, and the fire in his response flames my desire.

As I return his kisses, my hands find their way under his tee shirt, exploring his abdomen and chest. They travel around to stroke his solid back. His muscles move under my touch as his hands slide to my hips and pull me closer. I feel him hard between us, and a surge of carnal lust kicks my already racing pulse up to full-tilt.

I lean into him, pushing him back a step. He resists my next push for a moment, then realizes I want him in his room, moving to the bed he carefully made up for us. Enzo breaks away from my kiss momentarily and brings a hand up to smooth my hair back from my face. Seeing his stunning smile that caught my breath from the first time I saw it makes me laugh aloud in wonder at how, against all odds, we came to be here together at this moment.

"I love you, Enzo Diaz."

His smile broadens. "You don't even know how long I've wanted to hear that from you." He strokes my cheek, kisses me gently. "You're the most beautiful person I've ever known, Hester. I've loved you since that day you tried to whack me with your stick and I grabbed it from you, and you didn't even throw me out. You just knew what was going on in my head about getting my little girl back, and you were tough, but all sweet with me at the same time. I didn't know I was falling for you back then. But from where we are now, I see it."

I make a contrite face. "I'm sorry you hated that correction stick. I never use it on anyone anymore, you know."

He grins. "And that's a good damn thing, woman."

I take his hand and lead him to the bed. "Come on, I want you to show me these lovely, silky sheets."

"Five hundred thread count Egyptian cotton, baby. Bet you didn't think I'd know what 'thread count' means…"

I slap his chest. "Give it up, Enzo. You learned that from the saleswoman, didn't you?" I play-push him onto the mattress, and he pretends to fall hard.

"You got me! But you better come here…" He reaches up and pulls me down onto the surprisingly comfortable mattress.

Then he rolls on top of me, and he's not smiling anymore. His face dips to mine for a deep kiss and I close my eyes, trying to burn these moments into my memory as I start to lose control. His lips are on my throat, my chest. He pulls my shirt off, and then I roll myself back on top and lean into him hard with my pelvis.

He moans, and I run my hands under his shirt, up his chest, and when he lifts his head and shoulders I pull the shirt off and toss it behind me. His torso is a thing of beauty. Solid muscles, smooth tan skin with a trace of chest hair forming a treasure trail down past his navel and under the waistband of his jeans.

The last time we were shirtless together was in the cabana shower when I wanted all of him so badly and he turned me away. Before I knew about his past. I push those memories from my mind and start to unbuckle his belt.

"Hold on, baby." His voice is soft.

Enzo reaches up to slip the bra straps from my shoulders. He sits up, cradling me on his lap, which puts his mouth level with my own. His kisses are soft now, tender. They travel down my neck and onto my chest. He undoes my bra clasp so gently I don't notice until the lacy garment falls between us and his mouth is exploring my breasts, teasing, stroking, then pulling at my nipples with more force. I can't help moaning, loving every second of his attention. I feel his strong hands supporting me, holding me steady as I writhe with pleasure at the increasing diligence of his tongue.

I feel like my head might explode from the intensity of sensation. Surges of sheer pleasure run through my body, making me grind my pelvis against his. When he has me crying out, he smoothly maneuvers me underneath him and his lips travel to my abdomen. His soft kisses are an exquisite juxtaposition to his beard stubble rubbing roughly against my skin.

Then he is popping the button on my white capri jeans, unzipping the fly, and kissing downward as my flesh is exposed. He pulls the jeans down past my knees and off, pushing them to the floor as his lips travel over my thighs. His strong hands part my legs, and he kisses the insides of my thighs, using his tongue to make a trail of teasing sensation that runs straight upward. When he slides off my lacy panties, I am breathing so deep and so fast I feel slightly drunk. My hands are on his head, fingers taking hold of his thick hair. My back arched, with all his attention on giving me full-on pleasure, I can barely keep still as the waves of bliss wash over me relentlessly.

Once I climax, I need him. Immediately. I roll Enzo onto his back with a force he didn't see coming. My lips are on his chest, kissing lower as I unbuckle his belt and remove his jeans. I run my hands over his muscular legs, loving the feel of his skin under my fingers. His gunshot scar is an angry red, but flat and healing nicely. It is the work of a moment to strip the boxers from his body. I gaze at Enzo, exposed and vulnerable, yet looking more powerful than I've ever seen him. Though I want to straddle him right away, I take a few minutes to tease him gently with my tongue. My mouth explores this new territory, his hot skin, until his breathing becomes ragged and he touches my shoulders, inviting me to indulge us both.

I hate to slow us down, but even intoxicated with arousal I am aware we need protection. My voice is a husky whisper. "Please tell me you have a condom."

It's the first time I've seen him blush. "I didn't want to assume this would happen, but..." Enzo leans over the edge of the mattress and pulls a small square packet from underneath.

When I finally sink down on top of him, the shock of pleasure makes me reach for his hands to steady myself, interlacing my fingers with his. I can't stop smiling as I enjoy all of him. This man I once hoped would never knock on my door is now fully inside me, has stolen my heart, won my trust, earned my respect. I close my eyes, feeling safe to lose myself in the rhythm of our synchronicity.

After I cry out at the ecstasy of further surrender, Enzo rolls me over without breaking our embrace. When he looks at me, I feel warm tears roll from the corners of my eyes. But we are both smiling, and his gentle motions gradually become stronger as his momentum builds. My hips rise to meet his at every thrust until he loses himself in his own climax, a throaty moan escaping his lips as a new surge of pulsating pleasure runs through me.

I hold him for what feels like a blissfully long time, until he kisses me tenderly on my lips, then my cheek, and buries his face in my hair. When his lips find my ear, his whisper is low and soft. "I never said it to anyone but my little girl since I've been grown, but I hope you know how much I love you."

I nod and hug him to me, another warm tear escaping the corner of my eye. Gently, slowly, he rolls to my side, raising his arm in invitation for me to lay my head on his shoulder. When I slide my hand across his chest he places his hand on top of it, warm and strong. I enjoy the sensation of his chest rising and falling as he breathes, and I know that my choice to love this man is right.

ENZO

Monday, June 23rd

The only mirror in my new place is in the bathroom and about two feet square. The whole apartment is small, but the bathroom's downright cramped. I have to stand on the edge of the tub to see if my suit looks okay. I'm still not used to wearing 'em. But it's a gray one Goldie picked out, so it must be presentable enough.

Topaz' jade tiger is sitting on a little white dresser in her room. I don't have much furniture in the apartment yet, but her bedroom has a pink bed, purple curtains, and a polka-dot rug. Hester and Goldie helped me pick everything out, but the only thing I let them pay for was the dress-up box filled with princess outfits. Tiana, Ariel, Belle, Jasmine, and that one with the freeze ray fingers whose name I can't remember; they're all in there.

I get down on the floor and do some quick push-ups to calm myself and then go check out the window again to see if Hester's here yet. It's not time, but I was hoping she'd be early. Hard to believe after all this waiting that today's the day.

Shoot. I go back to the mattress on the floor of my room. Makes me smile to remember how Hester helped me feel at home in my new bedroom the other night. But looking at the row of ties I laid out on the bed earlier makes me nervous. Why did Goldie buy me so many? Now I can't decide on the best one to wear at the court. I wish I knew the judge's favorite color. My lawyer told me all the paperwork looks good and he's sure there'll be no problems, but I'm still so jumpy I can't even pick out a stupid tie.

When the bell rings I really do jump. Hester! I run to the door, sliding the last few feet in my socks on the hardwood floor. She's smiling when I open it and hugs me tight right away.

"Today's the day! Are you ready?"

Then she sees I'm not wearing a tie and don't have shoes on yet.

She does that squinching thing with her lips. "Well, good thing I'm early." She pulls a box out of her purse and hands it to me. "I got you something for luck."

"You're not supposed to be buying me things anymore!"

"I know, but this is different. Open it."

I give her a 'you've been a bad girl' look and open the box.

A red tie.

"Aw, baby. You really shouldn't have…but thanks. It's just what I need for good luck…but I'm so damn nervous. Help me put it on?"

HESTER

I'm securing the knot when he kisses me. Not a hot and sexy kiss that would make us late for the hearing, but a gentle and warm one. A kiss that speaks of shared experience and appreciation.

When I step back to examine my handiwork, Enzo's face is serious.

My eyebrows furrow. "What?"

He rubs his dimpled chin. "You know when I have Topaz back it's gonna be full-time. There's no one to take her on weekends, and there ain't no way I'm sending her to spend the night at her drunk grandma's place. I'll be Daddy all the time."

"She'll be in school all day, and I hear you have a pretty flexible work schedule…" I take hold of his tie and pull him in for one of the hot and sexy kisses.

When I push him away a few minutes later so we won't be late his face still registers concern. "Seriously Hester, things are going to change."

"Seriously Enzo, I know." I place my hands on his shoulders. "We're different people now from who we were just three months ago. And we'll be different people again in a year's time. Change is constant. I know we won't have the same amount of time together anymore. And I know your first priority will be Topaz. But that 'good Daddy' thing is part of what I love about you…" His expression is still anxious, and I look straight into his worried eyes. "We'll communicate, talk through our challenges and make it work. Coordinate our schedules to be sure we have time together. Have sleepovers and make Topaz chocolate chip pancakes for breakfast…change is good, Enzo. Haven't we weathered a fair bit of it already?"

I reach up and hold his handsome face in my hands. "Let's go get your daughter back."

Acknowledgements

I give my heartfelt thanks to:

My hubby, Jon Bealer, for listening to all my outlandish ideas about what these characters might get up to and helping me keep my feet on the ground. And for reading the first draft and not laughing.

My mom, Kathryn Averett, for reading and laughing/crying in the right places. And for her undying encouragement always.

Jay Ghingher for getting me writing in the first place. Thanks, Dad!

My big bro, John Ghingher, for critique, drawing the first version of the book cover, and his font expertise.

Pat Ghingher for reading an early draft and offering suggestions.

Chris Eary for reading both my novels and being honest yet kind.

My dear friend Allison Joyce for reading, being the 'comma Nazi', her enthusiasm, and notes.

My kids for being my best cheerleaders!

Longtime friends Areti Georgopoulos & Vanessa Harnik for input and cheering me on.

Martha Vollmer for her copy editing skills, great critique, and editing 'the scene' for me.

Lisa Guarrera for putting the cover together.

Rafael Alvarez for being my mentor, hon.

Carol Cooper for her legal advice. You must have thought I was crazy!

Jennifer Ghingher Snouffer for reading my other book and liking it.

Tim and Belinda Gardner for telling me I can do this.

And my readers: I am so grateful for you! Please check out my Facebook Author Page, or my blog, aimeebealer.wordpress.com. **And if you liked** *Pronouncing Enzo*, **please leave me a review on Amazon.com!**

About the Author

Aimee Bealer had a hard time staying in one place after she traveled to France as an exchange student at seventeen. She has lived in Baltimore, Hartford, Cincinnati, East Anglia, Seoul, and London. In London she clubbed a hot Brit over the head and dragged him home to America. Now the mother of two dual citizens, Aimee lives with her husband and children in Maryland. Find out more at *aimeebealer.wordpress.com* or visit her Facebook Author Page.

If you liked this book, please leave me a review on Amazon.com!

Made in the USA
Charleston, SC
13 February 2016